Zen

Emanations

Zen

edited by

Carter Kaplan

international authors
brookline, massachusetts

Published by International Authors: Brookline, Massachusetts.

ISBN: 979-8858074274

Library of Congress Control Number: 2023917821

Cover: Vitasta Raina

This lady never slept, but lay in trance
  All night within the fountain—as in sleep.
Its emerald crags glowed in her beauty's glance:
  Through the green splendor of the water deep
She saw the constellations reel and dance
  Like fire-flies—and withal did ever keep
The tenour of her contemplations calm,
With open eyes, closed feet and folded palm.

SHELLEY, *the Witch of Atlas*

IA

International Authors Presents

Emanations

An Anthology Dedicated to the Art of Ecstasy and the Ecstasy of Experiment

Illuminations

See part III of the Contents for artists' projects and portfolios.

* From a set of paintings of Christ's passion in the Russian Hospice, Jerusalem, created between 1898 and 1914. Library of Congress, Prints & Photographs Division, Matson Photograph Collection.

Contents

Tales

Melody and Refrain

Visualizations

Examination and Assessment

To those who labor under the aegis
of the Goddess of Contemplation

Elkie Riches

Anamnesis

THERE WAS WHITE ABOVE AND white below. A barely discernible line noted the horizon, merely a suggestion. Emptiness scraped away the world, hollowed out an immensity on all sides. The inner parts of my ears adjusted to the pressure of silence, my eyes widened and ran as they focused on… nothing.

No.

Thing.

Just horizon.

I creaked my shoulders back and pushed power into my legs; the knees flexed and straightened. I watched as pale dust fell from my clothes, the small roll of the particles putting sound back into this void. Just for a moment until… nothing.

But now I knew that I needed more, so I did it again, and again the skittering pushed out into the nothing, probably travelling all the way to the untouchable horizon. I saw the sound suddenly in a way I couldn't comprehend, more than the sound in my ears, more than the wave form registered in my auditory log. It was a memory—no, not that. Not quite.

I hunkered down to think. It was easier to sleep some parts while I searched to find the word that might link to this. As joints decompressed, lowering me down to a crouch, more dust fell (I had obviously spent a considerable time immobile) and I saw them as the particles sounded their noise. Birds, a dozen or so small songbirds that flew past my head, grouped with a chaotic mathematics that they alone understood.

Imagination. I had *imagined* them. They were born from a sound that had fired off an association, dragged from a memory. I wondered if I had ever seen this. Was it a true memory? Still crouched, I thought carefully about this problem, widening the processing bandwidth to accommodate.

I straightened, defeated, and another flock flew out to the horizon; I had been processing longer than I had realised. I began to walk toward the moon, having no other direction suggested. At first I enjoyed looking at it as I walked, but after a time, another moon began to be overlaid, with the same opacity as the birds; this one was white and was a single, whole piece that glowed, with a patterning on its face. It was so at odds with the moon as it was that it made my legs falter until I turned so that it was no longer in my vision. I walked like that with my head turned until the sun came up, but then I was further disquieted by records telling me that this shouldn't be positioned where it was and it shouldn't be so large. I knew that there would be another overlaid sun if I were to look around, put there by memory (imagination?) in its rightful place.

My stride stuttered and I almost shut the ambulation down again to think. Was there a purpose to these unreal visual items? Moons, suns, birds that weren't there, just overlaid on the real. But I continued walking and the problem was stored in the anticipation of having further information to increase processing speed.

At its highest, the sun cast down massive brightness and nearly obliterated the horizon. The haze that came up from the heat rubbed at the line, what was left of it, and soon I found I was walking in unbroken white. The gravity bob at the top of my head was the only thing orientating me, which didn't hinder my progress (to where?) until my foot stepped into air and I toppled forward. As I hurtled down the side of an immense dune, I saw a new overlay, a great ocean wave surging against a shoreline. I imagined (I must use that word even if I don't yet have a conclusion to the problem) rolling in it as I tumbled on, and dry as I was I felt the cold, salty hit of it on my skin. I was almost content to be falling for that, and despite the risk of damage I felt disappointed when the ground levelled out and I came to a stop.

I righted myself in a flurry of birds, these bigger and more delineated with the larger stones that had collected in my hair and clothes as I fell. They whirred past me and through a shape—a thing in the no thing, in the white. It was another like me, same overalls, same exterior, but this one had shut down (dead?) and its battery had failed to recharge. I was gladdened to see that it had died while doing something of use, crouched as it was above a small, spindly shrub, one hand extended above to shield it from solar rays that were too powerful for its young leaves.

Inside me, analysis software shuttered through possibilities. I winced, waiting for it to end; I had become unused to the uncomfortable slick of data that held me stationary while it worked of its own accord. Its conclusion crowded into my thoughts: the shrub could only grow so big before it spread outside of the shelter created by the hand, and once outside its leaves would still not be strong enough. I quickly formed an engineering diagram using available parts (a) overalls and (b) limbs. These could be sufficient to form a larger shelter to enable the shrub to mature. It was viable and yet when I moved to enact this my limbs locked and a red warning flashed up, heralded by a single admonitory bleep. I read the warning text carefully:

#34.91ARCHIV—critical breach of ARCHIV model use. Intended action forbidden. CONSERV model required to proceed.

Alert Holding Centre for CONSERV release? Yes/No

I was unsure what the Holding Centre was but I selected 'Yes' anyway. There was no sound to indicate that the alert had been received but the warning disappeared and my limbs unlocked. I checked comms and detected only a flat line of nothing, not even a fuzz of static to put a shiver through that horizon.

There came a sensation of, what could be termed, slyness. If there was nobody monitoring my actions I could try again without fear of reprisal. And if they were observing silently, I reasoned, it was equally agreeable that I should be collected for repair. It was apparent even to myself that I was riddled with faults: my processing speed seemed slow and the topics that I fed in tangential. That is not to mention the memory leakage into my visual field.

I pulled up the engineering diagram again, enjoying what I allowed myself to call defiance, and immediately as I stepped forward I was halted as before. The bleep. The warning box. The same text.

This was frustration, less pleasurable than defiance. I selected 'No' and stumbled forward as my legs released suddenly. The warning box disappeared but this time it took with it the engineering diagram, permission to access revoked. I stood still, not processing, just in disbelief—this too a symptom of my internal damage. The flatness of the comms channel ran silently on in the background, a formless reflection of my incomprehension. I turned it off.

Eventually, something restarted and I moved closer to what must be a CONSERV model, and allowed the process of an ARCHIV (me?) to run. Pressing my index finger and thumb into the caruncles either side of the nose,

I released the face plate and pulled it away. It fell half in and half out of the shadow from its outstretched hand and was caught by the shrub, one eye hole filled suddenly with a profusion of stubby leaves and thorns. The sound from the shrub released a new overlay, this one stronger, cutting out almost all of my visual field. Trees reared up over me, far over my head, and their uppermost branches waved and susurrated. The overlay flicked away and I seized one of the shrub's small branches and shook it: the trees and wind returned. I experimented by shaking the branch faster and high up in one of the trees before me a small furred creature sprang along the bough, the leaves trembling as it jumped. I sped up and the creature ran headlong, chased by another. Faster and faster until it careened right to the tip of the branch, where it leapt out into the air, reaching with small, mobile paws the thin outskirts of a neighbouring tree…

The overlay disappeared and I saw with dismay that I had snapped the branch. Slowly, I looked over to the CONSERV, the branch still clasped in my hand, and it stared with eyelid-less outraged surprise at the dismembered shrub. Tentatively, I continued my process and ejected the CONSERV's card from the centre of its head. I flipped my hand cover and inserted the card into the wrist port. I sat back on my heels to wait for the download and gently tucked the branch into the CONSERV's overall pocket—the why of that action eluded me but it seemed (felt) important. There was no matching action in my protocol and yet… I was broken, evidently.

I rifled through the CONSERV's log (#14.32CONSERV), which, while containing some partially inaccessible files, was more complete than my own—that is to say, instead of commencing 172 hours ago, it stretched right back to its inception in a factory setting, the heavy sound of manufacturing machines the first thing it registered before its visual window opened. The faces of people gazed straight at it and their voices appeared as a transcript, having been filtered out from the cacophony of background noise. Questions scrolled up as their mouths moved, seemingly testing for faults in the unit, but the questions were imprecise and hurried. Behind their goggles their eyes were wide and red with organic fatigue, and their hair snaked carelessly out from beneath their protective caps. Behind them, the machines laid skin over frames of other units and dipped them into setting vats; more people bustled around, fixing and analysing the machines, while others stood or crouched by the walls, heads bowed as if processing some vast and complicated problem.

The questions stopped scrolling up and the people clicked and clicked on their computers and when that had stopped the unit was quickly led away from the manufacturing room. They walked so far away that the noise of the machines was only just audible as a low hum. Up steel steps, up and up, until they stopped and pointed the CONSERV toward a hatch in the ceiling, which had slid open at the touch of a series of buttons; dust puffed down from the outside and small stones tinked and bounced between the spaces of the steel steps. The people turned and hurried back the way they had come; the CONSERV watched them go but then its protocol marched it up through the hatch and up into the wide, white, blinding sky. It walked into the blankness.

This must have been my beginning too—or was that an assumption? Was it still imagination if I were imagining a possible memory? I was unsure if I had imagined the overlays, but if I had, could this not be the same? The upload of another's memory complicated the category of memory—it was not *my* memory, and yet I had experienced it.

I filed quickly through the rest of the log. It was a long, long plethora of clambering amongst rocks, digging through sand, walking, walking, searching, walking. Many, many years sped past, days noted by the hectic bouncing of the sun and moon, and finally the CONSERV had discovered the beginnings of the shrub. It had immediately filed a taxonomy report with an addendum regarding the specimen's health, which was amber-shaded 'At Risk'. Its course of action was decided in less than a second (the processing speed amazed me) and it crouched, stuck out its hand and began to transmit a request for collection.

It transmitted the same request 12,627 times and, unable to move, its batteries slowly unwound. Its protocol had not anticipated that help would not or could not be provided.

I closed the log and stood, surprised at how the CONSERV now looked innately different to me somehow, and yet physically it had not changed. Whatever it signified, I found that when I stood to leave I halted as if the warning message had locked my limbs, but there was no bleep and no text. I picked the face plate up from the ground where it had fallen, shook the dust from it and carefully replaced it on the CONSERV's face, pressing each side carefully with my fingertips until it clicked into place. I stepped back to examine my work and muted the incessant running analysis. I just *looked* and although the replaced face plate had assuaged the unease that had built within me, I still detected a difference in the CONSERV from knowing that there was a space within it that had once housed its card, and I knew that this couldn't be replaced, not once removed, but I experienced a sensation of completeness at my actions and found I was able to move.

The run-through of the CONSERV's log had provided me with its tracking coordinates, from which I concluded that the first point was where it had stepped from the hatch of the factory. I had at last a heading that could be a makeshift objective, the only one available to me. The CONSERV had taken an extremely meandering route as it searched the landscape and this had taken it perhaps hundreds of years, but as I could take a more direct route; I calculated that I should reach the hatch in 347 days and 12 hours. I left the CONSERV's body to the dust and strode out, this time with greater speed, into the blankness.

By day 102 my estimated travel time was lengthened unexpectedly when I encountered another CONSERV. I had seen it first as a column that rose from the horizon and I had to divert from my course to investigate, which was a choice not only born from my own faulty sense of curiosity, but also it seemed part of my innate protocol as an ARCHIV. It stood, dead like the first, knee deep in wind-deposited particles. Something was clasped in its hands; an organic creature that had long ago ceased to live, its framework jumbled up between the CONSERV's fingers. I didn't know what it was, but there was a similarity to the small furred creatures I saw in the tree overlay, but this had been squatter, with large, spoon-shaped front feet. As before I took this CONSERV's card, careful to immediately replace the face plate, and took it into my wrist port, imbibing its memory as my own—I had concluded that memories were like that, they became your own once you had taken them in.

It had been created, questioned and released exactly as the first CONSERV, and it too had spent its time wandering the blankness, searching for life. This one had found the creature it defined as 'Talpidae' and it too had sent out urgent calls for collection, all of which had gone unanswered. Perhaps it had not had the pathways in its programming to release the creature when help did not come, or perhaps it did and it had got the same bleep and warning message as I had, its limbs locked in place so it could only stare helplessly as both its and the creature's batteries unwound. My internal corruption made me hate the warning text, hate the bleep, the feeling so intense that for a time I could only stare at the CONSERV, it too transformed by the removal of its card. The only thing left for me to do was to gently remove the bones from the CONSERV's hands and to help it do what it was prevented from doing. Once the warning text flashed for a moment, but it disappeared again without sound: I must have become more faulty since I met the last CONSERV, maybe from the hatred I felt. I laid the bones carefully on the ground and banked sand up upon it into a mound, the sounds of the activity eliciting two overlays as I worked: wind blowing through orange and bright red leaves, the gentle passage of a clear stream over pebbles. It was enough to calm me, enough for me to leave.

I encountered several other dead CONSERVs as I travelled. It substantially affected my travel time but I felt a compulsion to act as I did; I could not pass them by and the red warning message didn't attempt to prevent me. They had all found something, had all waited (been prevented from moving), utterly fruitlessly. My anger switched from the warning text to the people in the factory and each time I imbibed a card and watched them questioning the CONSERV and then sending it out into the blankness, my hatred grew. What a terrible error to implant, and then there was their silence. I did what I could, tried to enact their final intentions. And I took in their memories, as my own. I wondered what I would do when I reached the factory.

Once, on day 248, I saw one moving at a distance. I was making my way along a ridge, enjoying the overlays from the sand rolling as I walked, when I saw a figure, an outline against the setting sun. It appeared to have noticed me because it stopped and turned toward me. It was like me, an ARCHIV model, I could tell from its orange overalls. The CONSERVs all wore green. We stared at one another; I was surprised to see it but I was not sure if it too was broken enough to feel surprise. I was about to start making my way toward it when I stopped, suddenly possessive of the cards I had taken from the CONSERVs. It was still looking fixedly at me and I thought (imagined) it would want to take them from me, so I fled, hurrying down the side of the dune and away. It didn't follow me. Perhaps it too ran away.

In 351 days and 4 hours I arrived at the coordinates for the factory. I'd had a long time to anticipate how to get through the doors and how I should find them, so as soon as I arrived I began to dig. So much sand and particles, organic and inorganic. My fingers began to wear with the friction of it—I had not been given the same reinforced skin as the CONSERVs; my makers had not anticipated that I would need to dig like this—but I carried on eagerly, with anger building as I dug. There came a metallic clonk as my fingers connected with the top if the hatch and I experienced a new overlay, this one charged by the cards I had imbibed; it was the manufacturing room, the sound of the working machinery. I didn't want to replay this overlay, so I carefully worked my hand through the sand, running it over the metal until I found the entry panel. The numbers were dim and I realised there was no power, therefore the code I'd remembered from the CONSERVs' memories were useless. The feelings of anger, defiance and frustration again came into my mind, my entire body, all at once and I tore the panel from its housing, and as I did so I felt the hatch door rattling. It was loose, the power that had held it closed was no longer there. I slid it easily back, dumping a great mass of sand down into the darkness, and I slithered down after it, amongst a torrent of ocean force and the stormy bending of trees. I felt those overlays then, as if these dead natural forces had stuttered into life within my body, resurrected by these terrible feelings that had built and been added to with every memory I'd added to my own.

I stumbled down through the dark. I knew the way, remembering the passageways that the CONSERVs had marched through, even without the lights. I was running when I burst into the manufacturing room, so that when cold water splashed against my legs, I fell to my knees, unable to process the difference between the memories from the cards, my own imagination and what was showing in my visual field. Long rays of sunlight cut down through the ceiling, lighting greenery that massed at the edges of the pool that I found myself kneeling in. The greenery was moss, the CONSERVs told me, their cards suddenly whirring. None of this was an overlay. And the people who approached the edges of the pool, were not the people who had sent the CONSERVs out into the world.

The sight of them shocked me more than the cold water, more than the blinding greenness of the moss. They were smaller, harder, larger eyed, but undoubtedly the same. They stood with a bent-kneed readiness, more like animals, the remnants of what they were hidden as the moss, lichen and sediment hid the machinery and the straight lines of the room.

My anger had gone, it had been pointless. I approached them, I both wanted to and was compelled to, and in a rush the place where the overlays had bubbled over from was open to me. The oceans, trees, birds and creatures I had seen had been only the drips from a damn holding too much back. I began to talk.

Lyle Hopwood

Cargo Cults

DR LEAD KINDLY LIGHT RAMAKRISHNAN, aware of his tendency to ad-lib, worked on his keynote speech to the National Academy for three weeks before he felt sure his remarks on Cargo Science evaded violation of national security restrictions. Even now, three years after the end of the Second World War, the government restricted whole sections of research.

He approached the podium. So distinguished was this room that every drop of moisture had evaporated from it. The walnut wainscotting was dour and matchless and parched, soaked in history, not moisture. Attendees, all members of the academy, had grown similarly desiccated. Mostly above the age of sixty, they appeared to be relics of the nascent post-colonial era that comprised the basis intersectional contexts of his speech. A lifelong diet of dry self-referencing perceptions had wrinkled these experts into bags of disparate scientific "values." He propped his notes up on the lectern, thanked his hosts, and began speaking.

"I will present a short history of the so-called Cargo Cults. The encyclopaedia definition of Cargo Cult, as some of you know, Professor Mead" —Margaret waved to him from the audience— "is '*a Melanesian belief centering on the expected arrival of supernatural entities in ships bringing cargoes of food and durable goods.*'

"Richard Carnac Temple gave the first account of a Circular Cargo Cult half a century ago—in 1900—to our erstwhile sister body, the Royal Society of Great Britain, which clothes that bare bones definition in living flesh, while simultaneously giving us an inkling of how even the most experienced colonizing nation recognized this phenomenon as remarkable.

"Carnac Temple was a man of his time. As a functionary of the British Empire, he was second to none. At one point he ruled Mandalay. He led a Gurkha regiment, served as a magistrate in Punjab and was Chief Commissioner of the Andaman and Sentinelese Islands. He considered himself an anthropologist. Not a great one—I'm sure it will not escape your attention that he regarded a refusal to learn western mathematics as a sign of a primitive mind."

The audience laughed dryly.

"'The Sentinelese,' Carnac Temple said, 'are a race apart from the civilizable Nicobars. The latter are of the Malay race and speak a variant of that language. The Sentinelese speak a language that is peculiar to themselves, changeable over the years and unintelligible from island to island. We have not yet met a Sentinelese man who could count beyond the fingers of one hand, and it was a game of some amusement for our sailors to place iron objects (iron being much sought after) before the men of the villages and make known to them that if they could enumerate the objects in the pile, they would be given an item. Even thus motivated, the men would retire to their villages with thunderous countenances rather than attempt to learn our numbering system.'" Ramakrishnan nodded apologetically and turned slightly to pour water from the carafe and drink.

He went on, reading from Carnac Temple's paper. "'Our mission was to plan the routes for the undersea cables that would bind the British Empire together and permit the fast-as-light communication from territory to territory with which we are all now familiar.

"'We put into a bay of North Sentinel Island on our second scouting voyage. At that time—fifteen years ago, in 1885—we had established two prison colonies on the islands. One had been evacuated due to the Yellow Fever and the persistent ague that overcomes men, even Malays and Chinese, on these islands. The remaining prison, at King George point, comprised some fifteen or twenty men who had been removed from shipping lines for habitual piracy and ship-wrecking. When we brought our goods to the warden and he opened the gate, the prisoners fell on us crying aloud, for we had brought salted fish and dried herbs and spices from Burma and Singapore, which they had not tasted since they had been imprisoned in the wild jungle.'"

Ramakrishnan poured more water, drank, and continued reading from Carnac Temple's account. "'The prisoners, who were not from islands like Papua or Vanuatu, but from kingdoms of great civilizations, chiefly Vietnam and Burma, were not familiar with Cargo Cult phenomena. However, one prisoner told my sailors a story about the local Sentinelese, which prompted one of my men to climb to his feet and make haste for the ship, where he bade me come to the stockade to hear the man tell his wild tale myself.

"'On my reaching the stockade, the inmate, a Chinese called Ching Wen, recounted in Portuguese (for he had no English) that as he gathered firewood at the edge of the jungle some weeks before, he overheard the island natives as they sat together in a clearing. He put up his axe and hid behind a mahogany trunk to watch them in the event that they were about to hunt for food, in which case he might learn something of use. But they did not raise their spears, he said. Instead, they took long logs tied at each end with twine twisted from lianas, and threw these before them lengthwise, treading upon them, so the undergrowth was flattened under the pressure of their feet. Round they went in a widening circle, five times, stamping on their logs and deploying their machetes to cut woody stems, until they had flattened a disk, which he said was fifteen men in diameter, or perhaps a hundred feet across. They placed reeds and bamboo as some sort of altar near the edge of the circle and shrank into the undergrowth.'"

Fighting an urge to editorialize, which could potentially cross the broad and fuzzy line between history and national security, Dr Ramakrishnan forced himself to continue reading his notes. "'Now Ching Wen was a prisoner who had been removed from society for piracy, and he was a scarred, sturdy man of unprepossessing demeanour. Nevertheless, I believed his account. He said he returned to the stockade and marked himself as present, for if he remained outside, he would of course be found and beaten. The next day he crept to the jungle edge again and examined the flat area the natives had created. He observed them emptying cargo—that's the word he used—from wooden boxes. Ching Wen did not know how these tea chests were transported to the Sentinelese jungle overnight, without a road or a beaten track to betray their passage. The natives left the chests, for which they had no readily apparent use, and he believed they burned them, because he later visited the area and said the circle, insomuch as it could still be distinguished from jungle, was scorched black here and there. The jungle overtook the spot within a month, and although I sent a man to check Ching Wen's story, he was unable to find the trodden-down spot.'"

Lead Kindly Light Ramakrishnan stopped reading and tapped his notes back into a neat square pile. "Ladies and Gentlemen, that is the first eye-witness account of a Circular Cargo Cult platform, built in the Sentinelese jungle in 1885."

"As Americans, we are more familiar with the island Cargo Cults of Vanuatu and Fiji," Ramakrishnan went on. He projected a map on the large screen. "The first reports of Cargo Cults came from early European contacts in Fiji, around 1750. Most of the islands were already receiving their goods, their 'Ancestor Cargo,' using Linear Cargo strips, before first European contact.

"The island people observed the European traders closely. Within fifteen years, explorers reported that pro-European Cargo Cults had sprung up. Certain charismatic individuals convinced their fellow villagers that the white man's cargo could be obtained by performing rituals that resembled the tasks Europeans performed. In Vanuatu, rituals included dressing as British soldiers and drilling on a 'parade ground' stamped out of the undergrowth followed by the building of a long, straight, flat area for the receipt of European cargo. Although the British and Dutch did not respond by gifting cargo the way Fijian Ancestor Spirits did, these Linear Cargo Cults persist to the present day."

He poured more water and gauged his audience. A group of mathematicians had stopped listening and were huddled together talking, but the dedicated anthropologists and historians were hanging on every word. "I read you that lengthy excerpt from the Royal Society address in 1900 because I want to build on it in some detail," he began.

"There's something I don't understand," said a man at the audience microphone. Ramakrishnan nodded at him to continue.

"You say the people in Vanuatu, and Britain—which has not exactly been on the world stage the past few years—have successfully built linear airstrips and received goods. But I haven't heard a timeline for us. For the Good Old US of A. How does this relate to us?"

Ramakrishnan sighed gratefully. The questioner had landed on an anodyne topic, Linear Cargo Cult 'runways' in American history. "Excellent question. The British, Dutch, and Portuguese were the first people to appropriate, I mean, further develop Cargo technology. The spice trade, the major driver of exploration and innovation, took them to every island including those with the most advanced Cargo procedures. As knowledge of the technique spread around Europe, America was preoccupied with fighting its own War of Independence."

He rummaged through his slide set through his slide set, found nothing relevant and put up a photograph of the Constitution. "We can only speculate how the Revolutionary War would have played out if the Founding Fathers had access to Cargo Cult technology. We didn't get it in time. The British themselves barely knew what they had their hands on in 1776, and even they had little idea how to manifest Cargo in territory that did not belong to them."

The words were out of his mouth before he realized that "territory that belonged to them" was an ethically dubious concept to apply to any group of white men in America in 1776. He pressed on, hoping to forestall questions. "Benjamin Franklin, that early giant of the scientific method, was the sole American researcher. Franklin spent the 1750s in England and Europe and had access to military technology through letters he carried from King George III. He returned to America as the Revolutionary War got underway, but George Washington was, of course, otherwise occupied and dismissed Franklin's requests to experiment with Linear Cargo science. Franklin's diaries were published not ten years after the war. Americans, as we all now know, were able to summon Cargo inside the continental US within weeks of his first formulation. By observing the "spirit" craft that brought the Cargo, using down-home American know-how, Cargo scientists reverse-engineered their own airplanes in less than a year.

"With our own planes flying by 1805, history fell in our lap. The War of 1812, when the British tried to sack Fort McHenry…" His eyes misted over, and he knew that, like himself, many people in the audience were mentally rehearsing the lyrics of The Star-Spangled Banner. "Our army manned the air, it rammed the ramparts, it took over the airports, it did everything it had to do. And at Fort McHenry, under the rockets' red glare, it had nothing but victory. And when dawn came, their Star-Spangled Banner waved defiant."

A questioner at the microphone interrupted him as he wiped his eyes. "How did we capture the spirit craft that visited the runways?"

"We didn't—not back then. We designed and hand-built our propeller planes after balloonists observed cargo craft in action. Aerodynamics is amenable to Earth physics and once people understood lift generation, propellers were developed, powered by simple kerosene combustion engines."

"So how did we get the jets we have now?" asked the questioner.

"Recently, prior to and during the Second World War, Americans built terrestrial runways on more than thirty Melanesian islands for materiel supply and for R&R of the troops. These runways serendipitously formed Linear Cargo strips, which attracted advanced Cargo craft. Jet engine pioneer Frank Whittle was able to…well, let's just say 'observe closely' and leave it at that.

He observed the craft, um, closely, and was able to work out the principles behind jet engines."

Someone in the audience shouted, "Germany and Japan didn't know what hit them!"

Someone else pushed his way to the audience microphone. "Dr Lead Kindly Light, I have a question." Ramakrishnan smiled at the use of his first name. "Clearly, our history would be different if we hadn't summoned Cargo craft using these Linear Cargo protocols. We are the victors in a world war, in which we fought enemies across the globe, and if I understand correctly, it's only cultural appropriation, the stolen linear strip technology from Fiji, that gave us the edge."

Ramakrishnan frowned. "Concurrently developed, rather than appropriated. The Melanesians were very happy to have the US soldiers on their islands. Many villagers still revere 'John Frum', an American figure who brings cargo to their islands. The philologists say his name is short for "John From America.'"

"But John Frum didn't bring Melanesians anything. Except soldiers. The runways we built were for landing our aircraft during the war in the Pacific, not summoning their Ancestor Cargo."

"Cults that previously managed to attract Cargo craft every few years were fully supplied with American cargo as it poured into those newly strategically important islands. We were able to load American aircraft with precisely the tools, weapons, and cooking pots the islanders most desired."

"And after the war, what then—we just left?"

"The Melanesians still build Linear Cargo strips that attract craft. Just not ours."

"John not Frum America," someone in the audience shouted at the questioner.

A man took the microphone and said, "Dr Ramakrishnan, you sometimes use the word 'technology' and sometimes 'cult'."

"Well," Ramakrishnan answered, "'cult' has a connotation of magic thinking, rituals led by a Big Man. 'Technology' has no such baggage."

Before either of them could interrupt again, LKL went back to his notes and his safe, prepared talk. It was time for the permitted Big Reveal. "Speaking of recent developments, I can reveal previously classified information to you today. I've read to you Carnac Temple's account which contained the first description of a Cargo Cult Circle, trod into the grass by a team of men using boards. This technology was implemented in Britain immediately after his speech in 1900, and the British rapidly obtained positive results with their so-called 'crop circles.' Recently, the US has turned her attention to building circular platforms and attempting to attract similar Cargo. We are a half-century behind in this technology."

His bombshell elicited the reaction he anticipated. The audience murmured. It didn't die down. After a minute it grew to a low roar.

Another man grabbed the audience microphone. "My question is, those countries whose circular platforms attracted the advanced technology—given that our only success crashed and is unusable—what are those countries building *today*?"

LKL Ramakrishnan thought carefully. They were back on classified territory. "The details are not publicly available. Briefly, however, what is known is that the British government invested heavily in the creation of Cargo Cult Crop Circles. The basic procedure is the same as Carnac Temple described all those years ago. The leader organizes a group with tread-boards to press grain crops flat, creating a pattern that attracts the vehicle bringing the Cargo. The circles the British use are extremely elaborate. They can be Julia-Mandelbrot figures or combined circles and sigils that take up to twenty-four hours to create. Many of them," and here he had to raise his voice, because the audience began shouting, "many of them generate no results. Some have manifested Cargo that I'm not authorized to reveal. I'm not even authorized to know it exists."

A man in the question line seized the microphone and yelled, "What did Dr Feynman mean just now when he said, 'Our only success crashed'?"

The audience shouted again.

Ramakrishnan raised his voice. "The US developed a craft after experiments replicating the Nazca Lines of Peru. The lines attracted Cargo ships successfully, but the reverse engineering was not successful. Our prototype crashed at Roswell in 1947, almost three years ago. I can only tell you that it involved a technology beyond that of jet propulsion."

"You're admitting the weather balloon story was propaganda?" yelled a loud man without a microphone.

"I think everyone, even the general public, knows that the weather balloon story was an attempt at cover-up. The revelations by the State Department spy, William, uh, Mulder, put that one to rest more than a year ago."

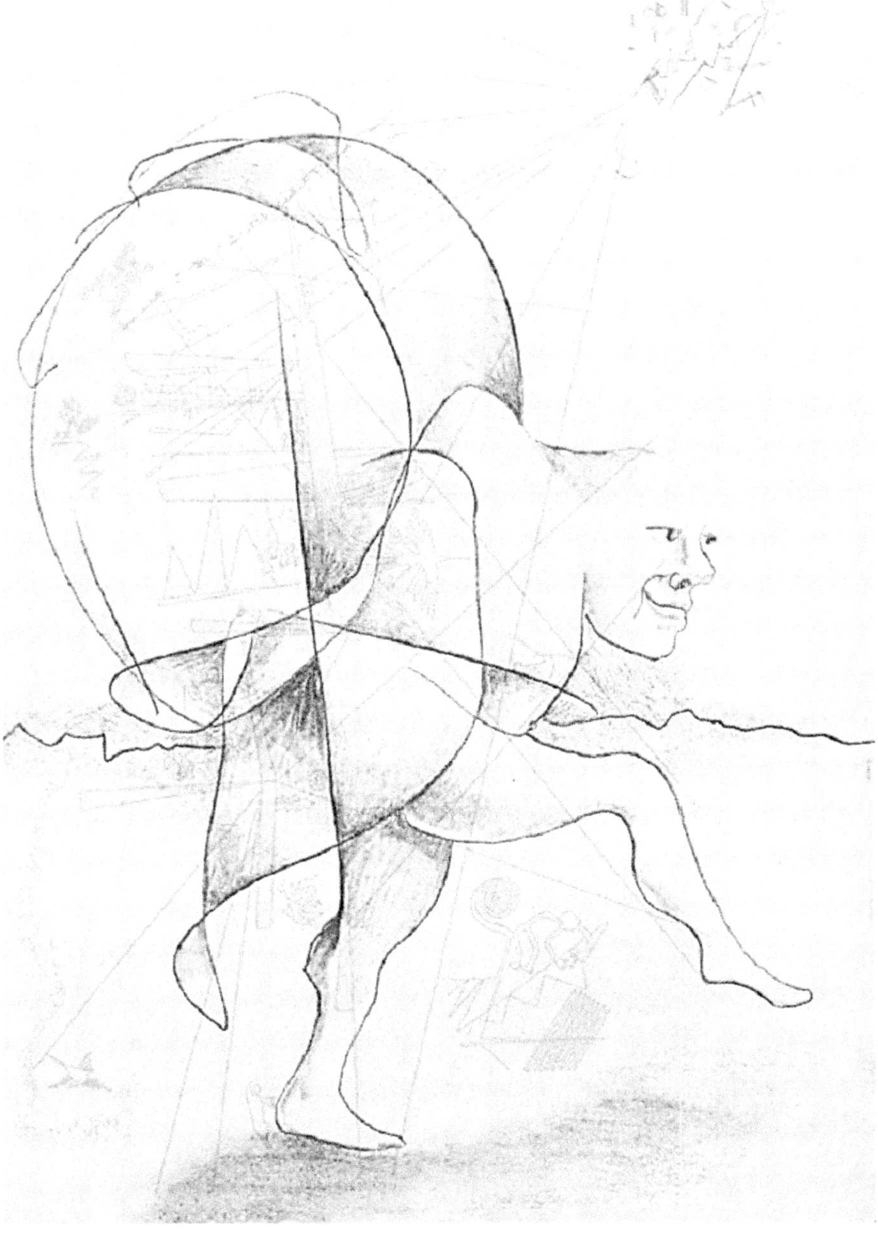

Another man rose, shouting, "A bigger question in my mind—what are the Sentinelese up to? They were years ahead of the British."

LKL leaned into his lectern mike to ensure his voice was heard. "Those technological innovators, the Sentinelese, have not allowed a human on their islands for fifty years. It's not clear if they are still corporeal beings. And we don't know what they built," he said, "because we still don't understand circular Cargo mathematics." He did not add, *the British, with their complex Crop Circles, are probably building star craft by now.*

"Have we tried, basically, asking someone? If the Sentinelese aren't talking, can't we rendition a Brit?"

The answer to that was classified. Or was it? It would be acceptable to hint at the issue. "I have to stress," he said, his mouth beginning to dry again, "that those people"—he almost blurted out 'those things—"and ourselves no longer speak a mutually intelligible language."

Andrew Darlington

The Kantlebury Pylgrims

THE JUMPTRACK LOOPS TRAVELERS through to the Trueloss system, two super-Jupiters orbiting each other at a wary distance as they and their assortment of 129 planet-sized moons and attendant satellites circle their dull red primary binary. Some of the moons weave elegant figure-of-eight fandangos in millennia-long patterns taking them around both gas-giants in impossible geometries. Others are tidally gravitationally locked. The jumptrack could also take travelers to one of the floating continents suspended within the super-Jupiter's eternal atmospheric storms. But those seeking the wisdom of the Divine Super-Dimensional Entity must debouch at Carob, the hollow moon, and make the final planetary crossing by old-fashioned contragrav starship. The event-horizon loops go where they go. Laid down by some long-extinct species lost in the galaxy's primeval heavy-element dawn. Some claim to understand the nanogram of exotic-particle trickery involved, but none have ever been able to replicate it, or punch new pathways.

Centrifuge ensures Carob's inner surface, illuminated by its own central fusion-sun, is a post-human city of dreams, even though walking the central cavity is disorienting, causing a persistent sensation of falling into the sky. The microclimate wafts soft perfumed breezes across pocket-parks overlooked by terraces and tavernas interposed by designer copses of Carob-Trees, Jacaranda and Flame-Trees, with planned meadows broken down into communities and con-urbs linked by full-hemisphere speed-tube shuttles. Most visitors tarry to take their fill of its cartel-controlled salacious delights. But not pylgrims on their way to the Divine Super-Dimensional Entity. Carob is the rerouting hub for trade and commerce across the worlds, for domestic joy-flips as well as the pylgrim trickle on their way to Kantelbury. They are a series of riddles wrapped in flesh. Conundrums that have no answer.

Data-runes had been cast to predict the deity's next conjunction, when the quivering shifter would materialize long enough to enable contact. Whichever parallel continuum it occupies elsetime, whichever nirvana-world it visits inbetweentime, is another set of unfathomables altogether. The rendezvous starship slips from one of Carob's outer equatorial buds, from where gravity-assist sling-shot carries it in a parabola on solar winds and its own plasma-flux trail. Trueloss-A is an agoraphobically vast disc tipped with the turbulent diamond-sparkles of electrical storms and roaring planet-size methane weather-bands. As the ship climbs through magnetosphere to perigee, the black dot of Carob slides away behind them.

The system's gravity-well anomies and spatial distortions throw up all manner of relativistic effects. Including the Divine Entity itself. And while automaneuvering takes care of the ship's functions through sink-storm eddies, pared back to the quantum essence of wild molecular purgatories, the four passengers are nothing more than baggage. The ship was antique, so low-budget and poorly serviced that the maintenance-drone waldoes take a cursory datascoop core-sample with invisible laser-fingers, their empathic functions decide 'obsolete', and move on to more worthy recipients of their tender attentions.

Which, for the journeying supplicants, can be seen as one of the upsides. A pylgrimage should involve a degree of, if not actual suffering, at least discomfort. A scouring of the senses in ritual preparation for renewal and wholeness, for completion where there is only lack. Yet the inner décor is fussily late-Victorian, plushly upholstered red leatherette armchairs with carved walnut inserts, a sofa with richly embroidered throws. A tall aspidistra in a glazed ceramic pot beneath a hat-stand. A vase of hydrangeas, beneath deep peacock-feather and fleur-de-lis patterned curtains.

Within the ship, sinking into the soft-furnishings, are the four who seek answers. The Precog. The AI. The Janus-Being. And Vengeance-Woman.

Vengeance-Woman smiles at the Precog, her vigorous grey hair brushed back from her forehead. 'I feel a deep sense of dislocation and estrangement even being her' she admits.

'Indeed.'

'You are a seeker, of course. And yet I don't sense the object of your seeking.' The softness of her voice contrasts her strength of will. When she reaches forward, her grip is both impressively and surprisingly strong. Deceptive. All muscle.

The Precog is not inclined to be drawn into pointless discussion. To be here is enough. There are several hours yet to drop-point. There are inflight virtuals. Even an antique tub such as this has an enticing array of distractions to play upon all human senses, and those of nonhuman species too. Someone has even thoughtfully provided a 'Snakes & Ladders' board-game. But yes, she also tastes an oddness in the recycled air. 'I can see the future' she grudgingly admits.

'That's a conversation stopper, if ever there was one' growls Janus-Beast.

'And you feel this to be a bad thing?' Vengeance-Woman smiles apologetically.

'No. Not in itself.' The Precog pauses. Raises the corners of her almond eyes. 'Perhaps I should explain…?' She struggles to gear down her state of being into terms the other pylgrims can comprehend.

The Precog's Tale

I see multiple future images of myself receding into moments to come. Not always. But at points that involve choice. There is a good path and a bad path. I see myself as I will be as a result of those decisions, thereby enabling selection. You must understand that as a child I had no idea that my talent—my gift—was in any way unusual or exceptional. I've subsequently wondered if gene-resequencing was involved. Or perhaps the resurfacing of a dormant gene from earlier generational resequencing.

But as a child I neither appreciated nor understood the significance of what I was seeing. And this not-knowing is crucial to my tale. The ability developed before I had enough sense of time to evaluate such things, so it seemed simply a part of me, no more remarkable than ear or toe. Even as I was learning that it gave me certain advantages. On my way home from school I could tell where the bullies wait, and to take the other path. That was useful. In a purely personal way.

We were travelling by autoroute, a long tedious trip gobbling k's. My parents sat upfront as I watch screens behind them. I know now what I didn't know then. About the anarcho-nihilist suicide attack. It provoked brief high-profile media outrage at the time. Until the novelty of the next atrocity eclipsed it into history. Back then we were speeding towards it. Watching other traffic. Watching sky and trees. Then… a vision of flame ripped my future-echo apart.

I was a kid. I was a child. I knew no better. I was scared. I should have spoken up. I should have yelled. I know that now. I live with that guilt. The guilt that attacks me every day, that accuses me, over and over again. They might have lived. I could have saved them. But I was a child. I knew no better.

What I did do was slump down into the floorspace behind their seats, pull myself into a tight protective ball... and brace hard. When the impact smashed the world asunder, it saved me. As the car spun and arced and flipped and rammed across into vehicles to left and right before hurtling down the elevation, consumed by flames. I survived, because I'd braced. My parents did not.

That is the guilt I must live with.

'You can't take the responsibility for a terrorist attack. You can't do that' insists Vengeance-Woman.

'I know all the logic and reason about it. I know that guilt is not rational. But my gut tells me things my head can't control. Guilt is not something you can argue away. That's why I'm here. That's why I've become a seeker.'

In any other time or circumstance, she might have felt inclined to throw doubt on the confession, or at least challenge pertinent details of her tale. But each of the four passengers carry unique secrets, or they wouldn't be here. So she holds her tongue, and glances across instead at the Janus-Being. A slightly formal middle-aged man, wearing safari-style khaki, his long face and slender nose investing him with a certain imposing dignity.

Yet as she watches, a strange change begins to alter that impression. Something inhumanly human. He slouches, his face undergoes metamorphosis, becoming elongated and pointed, first the lower part of his expression slowly twists, rearranging itself into an approximation of a snarl, at the same time the frown intensifies across its upper half. Combined with the alarming deep-set animal-eyes without pupils, and the now hooked nose, the effect is ghastly, cunning, feral, dangerous. She blinks. Looks again. No... he's a slightly formal middle-aged man in safari-style khaki. He meets her eyes with an embarrassed shrug, blinks, and shifts his gaze to a point slightly to the right of her ear.

He coughs nervously. 'You don't know? No, I can see you don't. You don't know the half of it. Would this be an appropriate point for me to speak? We are here for answers, after all...'

'I'm willing to start with the assumption that your case is unique' she concedes.

'You get my vote too' says the AI. Who is a boy in a navy-blue sailor's suit.

The Janus-Being's Tale

I am, or rather... I was, Dr Hesperus of the Seat of Science and Antiquities. As I'm sure you're aware there's a continual ongoing quest to locate evidence for the existence of the protean species that constructed the jumptrack loops and seeded the galactic spiral arm with life-forms. Kos is not such a world. It's a sticky-hot jungle realm, a vast reservoir of chemical poisons and plague-disease biohazard. Such virus levels indicate they fought a germ-warfare atrocity to mutual extinction. But among the trills of grotesque birds and monstrous venomous insects floating on distended air-sacs, the ruins they left are ancient and impressive. That's where I was carrying out surveys and investigations. Way above the equatorial flamebelts there are winter latitudes where it's passably tolerable, although you shower numerous times a day, several of which are in your own sweat. I was part of that team. Orbital scans reveal palaces, glittering structures of unknown purpose and composition, and mass tomb complexes that we were excavating to reach. We'd dug through so much silt-accumulation that the site resembled an exploded crater, surrounded by vile acid-rainforest, with access-shafts bored into the remains below. I had a feeling of strange anticipations. I'd been on Kos for eighteen months working several sites but none seemed as promising as this one.

I could have used remote-gloves, but I always loved those tales of heroic Gentlemen Adventurer archaeologists, Heinrich Schliemann, Indiana Jones, Howard Carter, Lara Croft. There are vital procedures. You don't go alone into hazardous alien structures. You do it as part of a coordinated team with detailed on-plan schedules. Yet I put on my filters, and go inside, further than I should go. As soon as I'm down there in the tombs I'm aware of flittering phantoms that dance on the edge of my retina, a haunting of dreams detached from the dreamer, run amok down long overgrown passages, slip-slithering on a rotting muck of shit of every description. I'm jittery, sweating in stifling heat, but resolute, out to reach my data-grail. My helmet flash-beam paints the misty twilight luminous.

That's when I encounter the beetle. Bigger and nastier than a feral dog. Shiny black with a hundred twitchers waving, mandibles snapping, and antennae-sampling the stink. Not sure whose more shocked, me or the bug. It rears and uncoils, spring-loaded. And it has a billion scuttling babies that explode in a black plague up the walls and across the ceiling. I fall backwards, scurrying on hands and knees in screaming terror. I don't mind saying that.

It's true. I defy anyone to act differently. I'm only human… or at least, I was back then.

I teeter on the edge of a downshaft I'd not noticed. Slip, and plummet. Stun my head against wet walls. Hit a tide of sludge. My visor smashes, I'm inhaling filth, drowning in foulness. It's viscous and black, like hot tar seeping into my mouth, forcing up my nostrils, like needles barbing through the pores of my skin into my pulsing bloodstream. Frantic with terror. Drowning. Trapped by gravity, dragged down beneath the surface by my own body-weight. Mouth so retchingly chokingly full I can't even scream.

That's when I realize, I'm no longer alone. This is not random bile I'm drowning in. It's a living substance invading me. Something is pushing knives into my brain. It's a cascading mind-reservoir, a vat of race-memory, archives of eternity siphoning into me. My head explodes with detonations of incandescent light, acid corroding, restructuring me.

I kick out, more in spasms of nervous twitches than anything intentional, but by chance I random-hit a sluice. I'm sucked down by a sudden vortex spiraling me down, down, deeper and down. No thought. No scrap of consciousness left. Reduced to a mass of throbbing visions. Sucked through flood overflow channels, then spouted out into a rage of light. So that I'm sitting in a shallow mud-pool dripping and shimmering in a ghastly crawling black tide, taking huge gasps, inhaling that virus-infected air. I've emerged some distance from base-camp. I'm crawling and howling like an animal in pain as a swarm of internal entities grate my cerebellum to shreds. Voices banshee-shrieking in my head.

That's how it starts. I'm no longer a single being. I have the entire race-memory of a species downloaded into my head. I'm howling like a beast in pain. Picking up a hard stone, beating my own skull with it to kill the agony smashing through me. Deafened by voices that are not mine.

Days blur into gradations of torment. I lurch and stagger through vile jungle. Naked and insane. They find me and strap me down. They fly me out. I'm evacuated to orbital facilities where I scream and rave for months. But they can't watch me forever. As things clarify into a new partial equilibrium, I escape and cross systems, star-hopping here, to the Trueloss system, to find answers…

'So the two halves of you are feuding?'

'We co-exist. But this is not sustainable. We will consume each other. Either Dr Hesperus is extinguished, the life, the individual, eradicated for ever. We cannot allow that. Or the entire memory-archives of an otherwise extinct species will be excised away, and lost. Their art, philosophy, literature, sciences, their stories, their uniqueness... their very souls, not to mention exploitable technology. That would be tantamount to genocide. That would be unforgivable. That cannot be permitted either.'

'Who is entitled to make that choice? Who can decide which is to live and which to die?'

'That is precisely why I am here. Why we are here. The Divine Super-Dimensional Entity must decide.'

Zero

There are micrometeorites and burned-out comet nuclei that the detector-array clusters and repeller-sensors should contemptuously brush aside.

The Precog can see a reassuring progression of future-selves all the way to the transcendental bliss she anticipates on Kantlebury. It appears as a flicker of elusive memory—in reverse. But suddenly that reassuring progression is severed. She sags down into the seat, tenses back into the contours of the red leatherette couch, her face pale. Something touched her, something too faint to be heard or felt or seen. A new future taking shape. Several momentary future-selves blur and reshape. She screams in terror just as that future-echo screams and was engulfed in spikes of flame. Triggers go off in her mind, clamouring danger danger danger!

'We must get off this ship now.' Her voice husky with fear.

'I trust the designers of the ship' says the AI seriously. 'I trust the integrity of the dealers who undertook to charter our transference.'

'Cybug diagnostic units detect nothing amiss.' Janus-Being consults operating parameter feeds.

They all begin to talk at once, torn between two inclinations. Vengeance-Woman gazes from one to the other, monitoring reaction. She knows the only defense is to act earlier and more focused than events. She pauses less than a heartbeat.

The Precog is trembling with palpable fear, shivering uncontrollably.

'I trust nothing beyond my gut-instinct' says Vengeance-Woman firmly. 'And it tells me to get the hell out. I trust the Precog.'

They exchange unsettled glances, provoking only rueful nods.

'It's too dangerous' protests the Janus-Being, buttoning his jacket, as though that makes a difference.

'Fine, have it your way. Life is too dangerous, stay or go.'

It's then that a series of shockwaves hit. 'Hull integrity breached. There's upper-deck depressurization occurring,' says the ship, 'guests are requested to remain calm during any turbulence experienced during the effecting of repairs.' Vengeance-Woman heard—or thought she heard—a low hissing sound, a burst resembling static, or wind in distant trees.

The tall aspidistra in the glazed ceramic pot beneath the hat-stand tipples and smashes, spewing loam across the carpet. She moves to avoid it, barking her shin on the back of a chair. It breaks the impasse. In a sudden rush, as of one mind, they head down the stairwell for the stern with grav already fluctuating. As they pass, a shoal of cybugs fishtail through the air in the opposite direction, their diversity hinting at the seriousness of the breach they're tasked with healing, from a visible haze of nanobugs to a buzz of those the size of rice-grains, to fist-size controlling motherbots. Unable to correct an increasingly yawing fault, the ship is already enduring violently flickering oscillations. Vengeance-Woman palms the exit to the escape sequence. For an eternity, nothing happens. Then locks clunk, scramble-lights pulse, red millisecond alarms crash and chime in a coded sequence of regular cycles. And the hatch flows apart.

They're jacked into individual hazard-pods, strapped into their molecular crash-webs, the void-suit frames contour around them, flooding from perfect waist-seals, umbilical hoses telescope into the sockets of a closed-loop life-support lowered and clamped around them securely. Pressure-activated, the car shuts. Activated, the outer hatch dilates, tumbling them down the chute. And the four pods are evacuated in a roaring rattling rush, the docking cradle retracts as four bright flames are thrust in a tight formation of sudden one-and-a-half-gee acceleration making Vengeance-Woman wriggle awkwardly in her all-over suit. Her stomach doubles up as restraint-straps tension across her chest. There's a terrifying out-of-control sensation, of falling end-over-end through a silky slowness, turning in a slow-motion gyre, even as the soothing pod-voice drones reassuring precautions, and the head-up visuals tick and scroll data icons of orbital mechanics and navigation. Most of the read-out display is incomprehensible, but its regular scrolling speaks of routine subsystem procedures.

She looks back. The entire abandoned contragrav-starship trembles in a glowing comet-tail where unimaginable energies pulse. Even as she watches there are detonation plumes erupting from its prow. The moment lasts for no longer than seconds, but in memory it elongates into a long stretched couplet of time. The soundless explosion is incandescent. A sun turned nova. Tongues of hard-radiation fire blasts startles of stabbing eye-searing brilliance in shock-wavefronts. Then the storm vanishes just as instantly, shrinking to a bright pinprick of light. A supercompressed singularity which winks out, leaving only ripples of after-images to play on the retina. But already they're brushing atmosphere on a long glide inwards, a billion nano-sensors monitoring. She feels the planet's gravity willing her down towards its distant dirty-whiteness. The aerobraking sails inflate like dandelion heads, bringing a sharp slap of deceleration. Soon they're skimming the surface, inertial laser-buffers softening their final descents.

Impacting in desert. Releasing the helmet-clamps, Vengeance-Woman hawks in strange lungfuls of odour, none of which make sense. Her breathing has becoming laboured. Her throat is raw, although the air seems so rare it's as purified as a secret world should be. And they've been quarantine-scrubbed by biotech into immunity to every foulness this system has to offer.

They're grouped in a tight cluster. Without the solarised visor-lens the planetscape looks bleached into shades of grey. In the foreground, eroded hills are tufted with spiny cactusoids, while towering over their heads are wind-scoured lumpy cliff-shapes of sandstone threaded with red-brown veins. Yet higher still, vertiginously hovering over the horizon, the gas-giant stormbelts are spattered with shifting planet-shadow in kaleidoscopic colour combinations, a wine-dark maelstrom pierced by a dance of numerous moons that produce startling washes of vivid saffron in reflected aurora effects that tremble like reflections in a lake.

'I'm not sure how these moral equations work out,' says Vengeance-Woman to the Precog. 'I don't know how one thing balances the other. But it seems to me that your abilities have saved four lives.'

The Precog almost smiles.

'Very chivalrous,' growls the Janus-Being.

Then Vengeance-Woman orientates. Points out a direction. And starts to walk. The others will accept and follow sooner or later. Dry sand and gravel crunch beneath their feet. Ghostly dust rises from their boot-heels as they straggle over the dune. Muscle-memory winces as creaks of complaint register gravitational differences.

As they walk, there is conversation…

She was always Mommy. I was always her little thirteen-year-old Philip. Always.

There had been a real Philip. Her only natural child. He was caught up in the Kirsch-Biorg insurrection and torn apart by the Brain-Biter hub. It was not pretty. Mommy was driven to the brink of insanity by the misery and grief of bereavement. So, at great expense, I was constructed as part of her therapy. Not as the near-adult Philip he was at the time of his death, but as she preferred to remember him in her finest memories. As the obedient eager-to-please thirteen-year-old Philip. His absolute likeness. The memories they shared. His behavioral characteristics and mannerisms. She was happy. I was there to please her. We had wonderful times together. Picnics in the garden, gentle strolls beside the canal as the suns shone and the bees droned in the flowers and the warm breeze ruffled in off the coast. I would strut stiff-legged to imitate the three-legged waderbirds on the lagoon edge, it always made her clap her hands with glee. In the evening we'd do jigsaws, play snakes-and-ladders, then tune into the old trivids that we always shared, the familiar ones that made us laugh, or sometimes cry. And when night came she'd tuck me up in bed, kiss my forehead, and say 'night night, don't let the bedbugs bite.' We had our baby-talk gobbledygook which she adored.

They were golden days that never end. She loved me, and I loved her. I loved her all of the fifty-three years, eight months and seventeen days left of her life. The problem was that she aged, as I did not. There was nothing strange about it to her. I was Philip. I had always been Philip. I had always been this way, obedient and patient with her foibles, her sadness, her pleasures, her forgettings, her moods, her tears and shuddering sobs. I was more faithful to her needs than the real Philip had ever been. I never grew up and started messing with the wrong kind of girls. I never dropped out of college to join that damn-fool Separatist cell. Not me. I was the ghost child. When she started to fail I was sitting there by her bedside, patting her hand, kissing her forehead. 'Such a good boy, Philip, such a perfect son.' Then there was no Mommy. And I was consumed by something so strangely disturbing that it must have been heartbreak…

Even in sadness, his teeth are too pearly-white to be entirely natural. 'So I'm left with an existential crisis in which I have no purpose.'

'A heart-squeezing tale' murmurs Janus-Beast, heavy with sarcasm.

'Most organisms persist perfectly well with no purpose other than survival,' points out Vengeance-Woman.

'True. But it's different, I was conceived and programmed to have purpose, and without it my being is pointless.'

'Could you not return yourself to the manufacturer responsible and be repurposed? I believe such treatment can be quite sympathetic.'

'I could. I could. Yet that would circumvent rather than resolve the dilemma that is myself.'

'We are all of us evolutionarily-brainstem instinctually hardwired, DNA-genetically imprinted, societally and parentally primed with ingrained conditioned responses and expectations. None of us are free. None of us. Yours is merely more user-specific.'

'That's not the same, and you know it.'

'Are you… fully functional?' says Vengeance-Woman, staring pointedly at his groin.

'Absolutely. But remember, I'm perpetually teetering on puberty,' smiles the AI.

'That's not quite what I meant. You are an AI. You have a vast amount of available memory-storage space?'

'Brain as big as a planet' he smiles. 'Yes.'

'But it all exists to no purpose. That is your dilemma. Yet I see a purpose you could assume.' Intuition links nodes in her head. 'This might be indelicate, and you would be wise to be cautious. It seems to me that Janus-Being has too much memory. While you have excess capacity. If you open fresh memory-cells to the survival and perpetuation of an entire species, it would provide you with vital life-meaning aplenty.'

No-one speaks. 'Is such a thing possible?'

The Janus-Being ponders. 'It's clearly feasible. We were originally separate entities, which subsequently fused. There's no reason why that process could not be replicated.'

'Very well, proceed,' says the AI.

'What conditions would you need? A physical connection? A conduit?'

'Wait. Don't talk to me. Talk to my other self. Wait while I concentrate.' As they watch, the strange change begins to alter his appearance. He slouches, his face undergoes metamorphosis, his long face and slender nose become more elongated and pointed, animal-eyes without pupils, cunning, feral, dangerous.

ANDREW
DARLINGTON 2023

The AI leans forward. 'Feed my brain neuron by neuron, axon by axon, until I have it all.'

What followed is ghastly. The Janus-Beast opens its jaws, opens them so wide it must surely dislocate. He snarls low in a way that makes Vengeance-Woman think of lycanthropy. In a sudden predatory attack it leaps and devours the AI's entire head. There are screams of shocked horror. The Precog steps forward as if to stop it all, Vengeance-Woman restrains her as the willed cannibalism continues. The AI is twitching in nervous spasms, his body convulsing and writhing. They can see blackness, a tenacious oil-slick of infinite dark. A tide of slithering blackness that resembles tar oozing from between Janus-Beast's jaws like vile saliva, licking and lapping in around the trapped skull, a scum feeding into nostrils, into eye-sockets, into ears and mouth. The squirming sound is hideous. It goes on forever. A disgusting obscene copulation. The Beast's body seems to inflate in deformed boneless contortions, angles where there should be no angles, proto-limbs where there should be no limbs, cell-terminal cancerous eruptions of boils and bubbles that are howling faces trapped in scrawls of flesh. Until it deflates like a punctured thing. Ribs emerging. It flops and slithers into quiescence. And there is no longer movement. Just a slow regular breathing.

'Are you… is it done?' asks Vengeance-Woman tremulously.

After a long pause he raises himself up on one elbow. 'I am once more Dr Hesperus of the Seat of Science and Antiquities.'

The AI crouches. 'And I contain the multitudes that I will devote my existence to preserving.' He smiles serenely.

Vengeance-Woman's Tale

Henri was a good man. Henri was my life-partner. I remember the taste of his skin.

We had been together twelve years, when we plan a bubble-mob vacation across the purple mountains. Just the two of us, a frontier adventure, travelling here and there as we choose, pitching up camp wherever the whim takes us, by the lake, on the forest edge, just outside the quaint village. Watching endless starfields and salmon sunsets. Maybe we should have suspected after we'd driven through the deserted town, and when we discover the other traveler burned-out off the highway curve. Henri climbed down to investigate. The other bubble-mob was burned out. There was the crisped body of a man a little way off. Scared, we take vid sterile pixels, and accelerate towards the next community.

We don't get far. The raiders overtake us before we'd made a click. Brigands on wind-schooners built like attack-craft tanks with jet-bike outriders. Their vehicles float on electrostatic cushions. They use quick-omnidisrupters. Henri drove hard and fast. They were harder and faster. I was terrified. They force us off the road. Henri leaped out to confront them, and they simply cut him down.

She paused. 'I remember every heartbeat. They took me. I fought back. The more I fought the more they laughed. There was one. The leader, Krass, he beat me, raped me, took me as his personal slave. I was forced to endure their captivity for four months as they move from secret locations in the hills, meeting up with other groups, springing lethal traps for unwary travelers. Nomads, the better to evade the security-force's attack-drones from hunting them down, and from rival clans also ranging the vast white moonscape. At one point they scatter from a formation of seek-and-destroy blips that rip crimson flame-gouges from the dunes.

I make a decision there and then, to survive, and to take my revenge. I pretend my spirit is broken, act compliant, obedient, as though my soul is dead. It got that Krass takes my presence for granted.

They ambush a supply truck and mutilate the crew. Detonate the vehicle in huge billows of hellfire. Although I'm crouching in terror, I see that one of the corpse-crew has a boot-knife. I crawl in a blaze of screaming shadows. Unstrap the knife with fumbling-dumb fingers, and conceal the blade in my tunic. They make off with everything they can carry. There's a huge celebration that night. They drink themselves into a stupor. I wait my moment, until I'm sure.

I retrieve the blade, and cut their throats, one by one. But that's not enough. I take my bloodied blade and in a rage of hatred I plunge it into Krass over and over. Sever his head, open his gut, emasculate him. Slash his chest into glistening wet meat, cursing him for what he'd made me do…'

'Surely you were fully justified in exacting such revenge' says the Precog.

'That's the dilemma. That's what has been poisoning my mind ever since. It felt good. It erupted from a beast-part of me I'd never even suspected was there. He'd killed my lover. He'd humiliated, debased and enslaved me. Yet he was a sentient being. My taking his life was his triumph, not mine. I had descended to his own moral code. I'd devolved to his level of brutality. I had taken a life. No-one has that right. Even in hatred and vengeance. The guilt lies upon me. I am damned.'

The pain is an acid that burns into her head. It's impossible to unsee what's been seen, unhear what's been heard, unlive what's been lived. She was still in mourning. Henri had been the lens through which she saw the worlds. Without him, she'd been blind. Conjuring memory-phantoms of him that are more real than the bruising fractures of reality. Still catching his echoes at the edge of her perception. Old wounds bleed. Tragedy defines her. An absence fills her. A wound deeper than any physical injury. Bitterness twists her lip. Tears glitter the corner of her eyes.

She's survived by pulling herself up by her own bootstraps. By fighting back.

'Love, grief, revenge, are glitches in long strings of code that are impossible to edit. They tear you apart just as completely as disassembly. Just as completely as deprogramming.' There's a catch in Vengeance-Woman's voice.

'And yet, human memories can be edited or deleted too. They can do that,' adds the AI.

'How you holding up?' There's concern in the Precog's voice.

'Let's walk' says Vengeance-Woman defiantly.

They crest a low hillock that her topographies identify as an outlier of the Kantlebury zone, specific to where the Divine Super-Dimensional Entity becomes manifest. From shadeless desert, footsore, tired, parched and hungry, soon their path is enclosed by scoria-rill cliffs riddled with the caves of hermits and mystics, and a sprawling shanty-town sagging into itself, flung carelessly around the spaceport. There are biomes, geodesics and cigar-shaped hab-towers, but because simple purity is considered a sign of piety, such luxury is rare. There are a number of recognizable species, plus mutagens gene-tweaked to colonise other less-hospitable environments, and hence in all-over carapace suits.

The four straggle into the first streets to find crowds in a joyful festive mood. There are dealers of ikons, peace-flags and prayer-wheels, vendors bartering dream-jewels, authenticated relics, functioning haloes, holos and souvenirs. There are wailing flagellants beating themselves with tangled circuit-wires because the Entity has gone, while others dance in ecstatic trance-state because the Entity had shown its incandescent benevolence by arriving at all. Yet there's no consensus on what had occurred. Different individuals have different tales. In a kind of transubstantiation the Entity presents different aspects of itself. It is an enormous Banyan world-tree of Life, so high that her upper foliage extends through the stratosphere into the very fringes of space, or a Cthulhu-octopus cephalopod with a billion squid-tentacles that spear and bring succor to the soul of every pylgrim, or a chimerical being made up of a fusion of species, Mithras, Sphinx, Shiva, Manitou, Zoroastrian Fire... or even with no physical manifestation at all, simply a howling vortex of awesome transcendental power.

'Oh, wonderful was the luminosity. A great light so brilliant that all else was haloed into blackness.'

'Many questions were answered, boons fulfilled and miracles performed.'

'So we are too late' sighs Vengeance-Woman. 'The Entity has come and gone while we were lost in the desert.'

'I'm not so sure' said the remaining half of the Janus-Being. 'Where the Divine Super-Dimensional Entity is concerned nothing can be considered accidental or insignificant.'

'How can getting lost in the desert be anything but misfortune? We can go through litigation and claim compensation for that death-ship which disintegrated around us. But the Entity will not reappear for another seventy years. Nothing—short of cryopods—can give us those years.'

'Think this thing through. Consider what has occurred within this pylgrim group. I am now again the solitary Dr Hesperus of the Seat of Science and Antiquities. Our friend the AI not only has found purpose, but has become the curator of an entire extinct species. I'm no philosopher, but to misquote yourself for the benefit of us all, I don't claim to know how one event ethically counterbalances the other, or how these moral equation work out, but it seems to me that the Precog's abilities have been the salvation of not only four lives, but of the lost souls of that same alien race. Debt emphatically cancelled.' He was obviously pleased with his eloquence.

'And me? What about me?' says Vengeance-Woman ruefully.

'Without you, none of us would be here. Surely there's no more vital vindication than that?'

'Maybe.' She looks up at the horizon, and beyond to where the vast psychedelic half-disc of Trueloss-A roars with the turbulent diamond-sparkles of ocean-size electrical storms and wine-dark maelstroms of methane weather-bands. 'You could be right.'

For a moment, it seems, she sees Henri's face smiling down at her.

Tessa B. Dick

Mural

THE WHITE BRICK CHURCH walls, dappled by shadows of shivering leaves, appeared more ancient than the forty years in which they had stood nestled among the lawns, the gardens, the well-worn concrete footpaths. Open double doors invited visitors to step inside the sanctuary and escape the afternoon sun in the cool, dimly lit interior. On the western side of the churchyard, a woman dressed in black placed flowers on the grave of a loved one while a raven circled overhead, harassed by the nervous chatter of smaller birds nesting in the elm trees that shaded the graves around the outer edges of the small plot of sacred ground. The weathered outer wall of the building, facing the graveyard, provided the canvas for a mural, a Biblical scene painted in acrylic over the cracked and pock-marked brickwork. The image seemed almost alive and three-dimensional. Katlyn, always dressed in black, studied every detail of the mural on every Sunday when she visited. Most of the congregation knew her only as the woman in black, but she had a name and a life.

The mural depicted the figure of a woman kneeling by the open door to the tomb, her eyes glistening with tears while one salty drop rolled down her cheek. This, the woman in black well knew, was Mary who was called Magdalene, clutching a clay jar against her breast and weeping because she had found the tomb empty when she came to anoint the body of the Lord with oils and sweeten it with spices. Her image had faded from bleaching by sun and wind and weather. A few flecks of the black paint of Mary's robe had cracked and threatened to fall to the ground. Surely the paint should have lasted in good condition for longer than—what was it? Five or six years, Katlyn thought. Perhaps the force of wind-driven twigs and leaves from the elm trees had accelerated the aging of the image. Perhaps the afternoon sun and the wind-blown dust had faded its colors, which were mostly shades of brown and gray to begin with.

Mary watched over the graves, the headstones and the people who came to honor the dead. Most visitors came once or twice a year, on a birthday or some kind of anniversary, but the woman in black came every Sunday before church services. Katlyn would bring fresh flowers, not from a florist but picked from her own garden. Sometimes she brought violets, sometimes lilies, sometimes roses, daisies or carnations. Often she brought two or more kinds of blooms, tied together with white ribbon.

The young man in a cheap business suit scarcely glanced at the mural when he placed flowers on his mother's grave. The old man in jeans and sweatshirt stared at the image of Mary as if he knew her—had known her in some previous life—then knelt on the grass before a granite tombstone and spoke to his wife as if she could hear him from beneath the dirt. The women in skirts and the women in slacks often scowled at the mural, thinking that a fallen woman did not belong on the wall of a church. But the woman in black paid her the courtesy of a proper greeting every Sunday morning. She asked Mary how the seven devils had been cast out of her, and whether her own demons might also be banished. She suffered from three demons: the shadows of grief, guilt and despair.

Mary tried to answer the woman, but her words fell silent upon the air. No living person was able to hear her speak. She spoke of how the demons used to accuse her of uncleanness, of all sorts of sins. Even after her death, the misinformed portrayed her as a harlot, no doubt inspired by the same or similar entities. She suffered many such insults and accusations, but she no longer felt the sting because she basked in the light and the love of the Christ. She had traveled with the Lord and the twelve disciples, in a time when women were expected to stay at home. In fact, she stood at the head of the many women who followed Jesus, leading them in service and in worship, which was quite against the custom of their people. Women were expected to stay at home and mind the kitchen, the cleaning and the children. However, the Messiah was teaching his followers that women had the same rights as men. When Martha ordered her sister to help in the kitchen, the Lord said that it was better for her to sit at his feet and learn. When women and children followed Jesus and the Twelve, he welcomed them in spite of the protests of the twelve. She almost never lost her faith, only perhaps for a moment when she saw the Lord dying on the cross.

Mary had watched him die, and she had seen him alive afterward. Even though this image on the church wall was frozen in time, in the moment before the Lord appeared to her alive, she knew that she would see Jesus walking in the garden. Surely the woman in black would see her loved one again. Surely all the faithful could rely on the promise of resurrection. This painted image had frozen Mary in a moment of grief, but she knew that soon her Lord would come to her and bid her tell the others that he was risen.

On a Sunday like many other Sundays, Katlyn knelt at the grave of her departed husband and laid a small bouquet at the foot of the granite headstone. The little daisies and carnations, flanked by fern fronds, looked incongruously happy sitting as they did upon a grave. Instinctively, she laid her hand on the beads of her rosary and began to pray the Apostle's Creed in a soft voice, "I believe in God, the Father Almighty, Creator of Heaven and earth." Looking up at the mural, she couldn't help thinking of Demeter, the mother goddess, mourning her daughter Persephone during three months of winter. Persephone, who had eaten three seeds from the table of Hades, had been fated to spend one month in the land of the dead for each seed she had swallowed. Knowing that her daughter would return to the world of the living each spring did not soothe Demeter's broken heart. Does Mary know, Katlyn wondered, that Jesus will rise from the dead after three days? Will Mary's joy at seeing him alive renew the world, the way Demeter's joy at seeing her daughter come up from the grave brought life to the land in spring, after the melting of the snows of winter?

Katlyn stood up and studied the mural, as she had done so many times before, tracing with her eyes every line of paint. The gray and brown walls of the tomb, the cloudy azure sky, the folds of Mary's cloak, all seemed more real to her than the grave on which she knelt. The figure of Mary seemed to reach out with her hand holding the clay jar, as if she might heal Katlyn with the oil she had brought to the Lord's tomb. Each Sunday, the mural seemed cleaner, the colors brighter, the lines better defined. Maybe it was her imagination, or maybe the artist returned periodically to touch up the faded image. She greeted the lady on the wall as always, then went into the church for the service. She scarcely heard what the pastor read from the Bible or what commentary he offered on the passage. Her mind was filled with constant, urgent prayer, the plea that God would somehow put an end to her lonely weekly vigil. How could her husband die and leave her alone like this?

The priest stood outside the door to the sanctuary and thanked each visitor for coming to hear his sermon. His wispy gray hair fluttered in the breeze, and the folds of his white robe flapped gently like angel wings. Some people turned to the west and lingered among the graves to look at the mural or perhaps pay a visit to the burial plot of a loved one, while others hurried straight out to the street, packed into their cars and drove away. He knew that the mural was fading and cracking much sooner than it ought to do. The artist must have forgotten to apply a sealer over the paint. He ought to have it removed or painted over, but the church had no money for a new mural, unless some wealthy parishioner might be inspired to pay for it. No, more likely he would hire a house painter cover the whole thing in white. The church's coffers could cover the cost of a simple coat of paint.

The dew-damp grass of spring gave way to the crackling blades of summer, and still Katlyn came every Sunday morning, always dressed in black, but with her dress fading almost to gray as the weeks went by. Perhaps these were all the clothing she owned, the black dress, the black shoes and matching purse, the black coat and the black umbrella. Mary pondered the woman's faithful attendance and sad countenance, and she thought that this woman's grief must be nearly as great as her own. She wondered which loved one she had lost, whether a brother or sister, a father or mother, a husband or a child. Always Katlyn looked up at Mary's image and greeted her, saying that the Lord would soon come back, raised up and alive again. Nobody else had ever bothered to speak to that image, let alone to console her with the news of a glorious future.

Katlyn bent forward slightly and began to tell the beads of her rosary. She always got stuck on the Apostle's Creed, no matter how many times she read through it and tried to memorize it. She did better with the Our Father and Hail Mary. She finished telling the final ten small beads, saying the words out loud, "pray for us sinners now, and at the hour of our death." A couple happened by, and she looked up to watch them walking down the stone path in front of the mural. The blonde woman in a tight-fitting red dress, hanging on her companion's arm, turned her head to look at the woman in black. It seemed to Katlyn that they had heard her praying and thought it strange, thought her a very strange woman. When they had gone, she sucked in a deep breath and wailed out a prayer of her own devising, begging God to reunite her with the love of her life, the only man she ever would love. Every Sunday she prayed that God, for whom all things were possible, would bring him back to her, alive and ready to take her in his arms as he had done so many times. If the Lord would not bring him back to her, then she prayed that the Lord would take her to him. Life held no meaning for her, so long as she must live alone. She also prayed that the mural would look brand new again, the cracked and fading paint made new, the way the world burst into color every spring when Demeter saw her daughter rising up out of Hades.

Mary had a mission. She would run to the twelve and tell them the glorious news. Of course they would not believe her, since the word of a woman could not be trusted. But when they went to see for themselves, the men also would find the tomb empty. When Jesus met the two disciples on the road to Emmaus, they would fail to recognize him, but Paul, who persecuted the Christians, would know Jesus on the road to Damascus, even though he was blind. Katlyn wondered whether she would recognize her husband, if he came back and met her on the road.

At work she felt as if she were inside a tomb, searching for signs of life among her coworkers. She found the white walls and the tinted windows of the office building annoying. It looked stark, too clean and too straight in all its angles. She couldn't shake the growing sense of irreality surrounding her life away from the church. The computer keyboard shimmered in the light from the overhead fluorescent fixtures, and the monitor developed ripples like water in a pond when someone drops a pebble into it. She longed for the week to end, for Sunday to dawn, when she would walk in the dirt and the grass, removing her shoes to get the feel of the ground beneath her feet, when she would visit her husband's grave. The little churchyard seemed more real than the desk with the computer where she performed her work. The tasks seemed unimportant, artificial and somehow unreal, compared to the patch of grass and the flowers that she placed there, and the carved granite tombstone. Her coworkers seemed like paper dolls compared to the reality of Mary Magdalene who was painted on the church wall.

At home she found herself unable to eat. She forced herself to consume a bowl of soup every night before bed but she did not enjoy it. The only flavor she longed for was her husband's gentle kiss. She felt light, and she knew that she had lost weight, but this feeling was more in her head than her body.

Finally Sunday arrived, the sun began to rise, and Katlyn made her weekly pilgrimage with a bouquet of yellow roses and a buoyant spirit. She lived for these moments of communion, connection with the only man she ever would love. She called out to God, demanding to know why he had taken her only joy in life, taken him so suddenly and so soon. She didn't expect any answer to her prayer. She saw no visions, she heard no voices, she was no prophet. She simply felt compelled to wail and grieve at her great loss. She didn't care if others heard her wailing. She didn't care what they thought of her. She simply must give voice to the great burden of grief that she bore.

The church bell began to ring, calling the congregation to the service. Katlyn stood up and straightened her dress. The mural looked brand new, all of its cracked faded paint touched up, replaced with new and vibrant colors. It shone in the morning sunlight, as if it had a light of its own. It looked so smooth and shiny that she felt that she must touch it. She picked up one of the yellow roses that she had brought, thinking that perhaps Mary would like to see it up close. After all, yellow roses symbolized joy and friendship, and she so wanted to be Mary's friend and bring her joy. Stepping between the graves, she made her way from the grassy plot to the stone pavement of the walkway that ran beside the mural. She seemed to float, and she felt almost as if she were flying rather than walking on the ground.

The pastor noticed that, for the first time in many weeks, the woman in black was absent. He wondered what had become more important to her, more of a priority. Perhaps she was ill. He made a mental note to ask one of the deacons to look up her contact information in the list of church members. Someone ought to look in on her and offer assistance if it was needed.

After the services, the blonde woman in her tight-fitting red dress, hanging on her companion's arm as they walked past the mural, suddenly stopped.

"Look!" she said, astonished. "Mary has a yellow flower in her hand. She didn't have that before."

"The artist must have repainted it," her companion said.

Katlyn looked down on them from the mural on the brick wall of the church and smiled. She knew that everyone who saw the mural would call her Mary, and she considered her new name an honor. The image in the mural wept, but inwardly she felt joy and comfort in the knowledge that he would return some day.

Philip Murray-Lawson

Punch in the Box

Part I

1. Sawney's End: Lockdown Sees Occult Revival

WAS IT THE VIRUS? THERE was no fever, but his limbs felt languid; and his pulse was perceptibly slowing.

Queasy and breathless, he bundled the pillows behind him. His ears hummed and spots floated before his vision.

The room was freezing.

He closed his eyes, and then opened them. He closed his eyes, and then opened them. He closed his eyes, and then opened them. He closed his eyes, and then opened them. He closed and opened his eyes.

The curtains flapped like the wings of dying doves. Smoke drifted on the breeze. It densified, like crystals forming in saline, into a feminine form floating just below the ceiling. Her features were impossible to discern in the flickering sunlight.

He heaved a sigh of relief.

As an initiate (6°=5° Adeptus Major, magical motto: *Anacharsis*), he knew an astral projection when he saw one. It had obviously been produced by intense emotion—either great joy or great suffering. Most likely, the latter. That was why he felt strange. His visitor was draining his vitality.

Women often had this effect on him.

He could smell coffee, bacon, sausages and sea. Sawney's End, described by *Caledonian Connoisseurs 2023* as Scotland's eeriest village, was resuscitating. Snatches of conversation snagged in his blankets, footsteps echoed on the pavements, and car doors slammed.

His Harris tweeds were piled precariously on an armchair; his VeganGun propped against the wall, and his suitcase by the window. Five rolls of Sterling had fallen from their paper bag.

He reached for his MePhone. There was still no message from Terry. Nothing from Luja... He frowned at his ghostly lady. No, not Luja. If anyone, she resembled one of Luja's current cronies, Maria Fleetfoot. But why would Maria wish to visit him?

He prepared his syringe. He dreaded his morning dose, but it meant freedom from masks. He had opted, out of loyalty, for the Goering_2022_V2 vaccine (48h Full Protection). Developed by his old friend, Dr Helmut Ewers, it had, according to the Mao Health Institution, saved countless lives. Following a relentlessly successful vaccination campaign on the Gaza Strip, a grateful nation had made history by inviting Ewers to Tel Aviv. The latter had declined because of his great age.

Julian aimed a playful squirt at his visitor. It did not reach her, and dropped onto the carpet in a viscous thud. A fishy smell filled the room. Iran had raised questions about the ingredients. But it was unlikely that they included the sperm of cephalopodic aliens. Nor were there obvious side effects. His penis—which he checked every morning—was not mutating into a squib.

He smiled at his floating female: "I can recommend Mrs Shkrebneva's tea."

2. London: Deadly fungus affects thousands of Covid patients

"Terry's becoming... Oh!" Maria Fleetfoot, Scotland's most talented ballerina, was uttering her last intelligible words. "Something bit me."

"What about Terry?" Luja Naifeh spoke irritably. She wished Maria would stay on the subject.

"He's becoming… Ow! I've been bitten again? Vindictive."

"He probably upset about..." Luja's jaw dropped, "about his..."

A pink globule had appeared in the corner of Maria's eye. It rolled onto her cheek and paused a moment. The thing's surface was moist, pitted, and covered with purple spots. With a flirtatious fluttering of tentacles, it disappeared into Maria's nostril.

"About his what?"

"His son… Maria, I just see something strange..."

Maria's hand grasped the tablecloth. Her bowl of Minestrone smashed on the floor.

"Sorry about that," she cried desperately. "I'll clean it up."

Perspiration exploded on her forehead; veins whipped across her temples; blood fled from her cheeks, and her mouth widened. No scream came. There were sucking sounds. She half rose, but sat down again. She slumped across the table, her face landing in Luja's spaghetti, splattering tomato sauce.

Hundreds of the globules glistened in Maria's hair. Thousands surged over her neck and shoulders. Swollen to the size of peppercorns, they were everywhere: wriggling from her armpits, scooting over her dress, traipsing along her spine.

Blood sprayed like champagne.

Luja edged backwards. A waiter, bearing a tray of oysters, ran forward. He stopped. The oysters wobbled, but did not fall. Luja applauded his professionalism.

Maria flopped onto the floor. She jerked several times before sitting up to survey the room with empty, scarlet sockets. The flesh on her face receded; her teeth grinned, and her cheekbones shone white.

"Maria..." Luja peered disconsolately into her friend's ribcage where heart, lungs, oesophagus and parts she could not even name dwindled into mince. "You sure you all right?"

A lady at a neighbouring table vomited. Other diners glanced up from their MePhones.

"Call an ambulance!" Someone shouted. "Call the police!"

Luja's feelings had, until now, oscillated between fascination and disappointment. However interesting Maria's demise had been, it implied the end of Luja's fledgling career as a dancer. As the daughter of the legendary international terrorist, Al Safi Naifeh, it had seemed that life offered her few other options than to follow in daddy's blood-stained footsteps. But with Maria as a mentor, and sometime lover, she had begun to extricate herself from a past which now flooded back—in a ruddy tsunami—at the mention of the police.

She folded her napkin, slid from her seat, and glided towards the exit.

"Not sticking around for a tiramisu?"

Terry Lair, the former British Prime Minister, stood in the doorway. A subordinate member of the restaurant staff knelt between his legs, fussing about with a virus detector.

"Looks like the virus has mutated again." Terry's eyes twinkled. "Do you think we'll have to go back to masks?"

"You do this?"

"Poor Maria. Wonderful lover. Reminded me of my wife thirty years ago. You could bend her any which way, and she had most agile toes... Each was like an independent entity with a perverse little mind of its own, and... Well, anyway. No point wallowing in nostalgia."

"I kill you for this."

"Don't let bitterness eat you up. Er, please…" He addressed the subordinate staff member who was buzzing the detector over his crotch. "Do you mind?"

"I'm sorry, sir. They like to hide in warm places."

"Well, stop it. We're leaving." He gripped her arm. "The lady and I have a bone to pick."

3. Sawney's End: Africa voices concerns over vaccine apartheid

Julian paused at the gel-dispenser outside Mrs Shkrebneva's elegant, outmoded, dining room. A family of four had taken his favourite place at the luminous bay window. The mother and children had pleasingly regular features, a dusting of freckles and flaxen hair. The girl was reading aloud from *Caledonian Connoisseurs 2023* while her father, almost suffocating with laughter, dabbed at his eyes with one of Mrs Shkrebneva's severely-ironed napkins. Julian's heart missed a beat. On seeing the man's hairless dome, he had recognised his old enemy, Inspector Anders Bloemer.

The napkin descended to reveal chubby pink cheeks and no trace of a D'Artagnan moustache. Julian let out a sigh of relief.

"Good morning, Mr Grayle," A thick accent echoed from the kitchen. "I take it you found the key last night?"

"Yes, thank you, Mrs Shkrebneva," Julian said. "Good of you to hold my usual room."

"I heard you on the stair."

"Oh dear. I hope I didn't disturb anyone."

The Dutch family shook smiling heads and made polite *not-at-all* noises.

"I'm a light sleeper," Mrs Shkrebneva said, crossing to his table. She was a bustling Russian whose arrival in Sawney's End had coincided with the invasion of Ukraine. Her spotless apron was of the same linen as her napkins, and she was an unashamed PEWSWAM (Person Who Still Wore A Mask). Her smile creased the plastic but had less influence on her eyes. "What will it be, Mr Grayle? A full Scottish breakfast? Porridge? Scrambled egg? Bacon?"

"No, no thank you. Just a little toast and some of your excellent tea."

"You're not well, Mr Grayle?" Mrs Shkrebneva's tone was accusatory. "You don't have the virus, do you?"

"I'm fine, thank you," Julian glanced at the ceiling. Maria—he was more and more certain it was her—had declined to join him. She was, perhaps, self-conscious about her nudity. He felt sorry that she would miss the tea. "Probably just overdid the Cragganmore last night."

"I hope so, Mr Grayle," Mrs Shkrebneva said. "I wouldn't want to catch a variant."

She reappeared with the pot. The Dutch family had quietened down. When Mrs Shkrebneva looked at their table, the little girl closed the guidebook; her rosy-cheeked father folded his napkin, and placed it beside his plate.

"Daddy," the girl whispered, "can we go down to the castle and play with the viruses?"

"We're going to the museum there, dear. It'll be more interesting than the viruses."

"Still selling nuclear weapons, Mr Grayle?" Mrs Shkrebneva adjusted the tea cosy. "How long are you here for this time?"

"AI software for nuclear weapons," Julian corrected her quietly. "I should be here for about a week. After Sales stuff mostly. Might try to see a couple of prospects."

Mrs Shkrebneva nodded and poured the tea. Julian smiled as steaming Darjeeling filled his cup. He could tell from its limpid gold that it had infused for the requisite seven minutes. A leaf, wriggling from the silver strainer, spun several seconds on the surface before lazily beginning to unfurl. Mrs Shkrebneva offered an apologetic *tut* which Julian acknowledged with a magnanimous lowering of his eyelashes. He added the milk himself and watched its beige billow dissipate. He took the first sip with shut eyes. Mmm! Delicious! If—as *Caledonian Connoisseurs 2023* noted on page 40—Mrs Shkrebneva lacked the authenticity of the best Scottish B&B hostess, she could not be faulted on her excellent tea.

The Dutch family rose and whispered goodbye.

Julian dawdled over his toast. He was far from happy with his latest job. First, there was the location: Sawney's End. It was one of Julian's safe places.

Situated between Aberdeen and Stonehaven or thereabouts, the village was notoriously difficult to find. Travellers inevitably lost their way and drove around the same lanes for hours. The contours of the countryside defied the compass, and the roads never quite tallied with the directions of increasingly exasperated Satnavs. Allowing mainly male drivers the benefit of the doubt, *Caledonian Connoisseurs* advanced three theories:

1) Sawney's End did not really exist
2) It had been built on a fracture in the space/time continuum.
3) Its dislocation depended on the weather: sun shifted it south, rain nudged it north. Travellers were recommended not to venture forth on days (rather frequent in Scotland) which combined sun, wind and rain. Incidentally, weather was the main reason for the growth of the Scottish tourist industry as everyone now sought to escape the sun and seek out Sawney's End.

A fourth theory can be found on the guide's FB page and, for the sake of completeness, deserves a mention. Ever since the Russians had constructed their stainless-steel colossus, the whole world had been suffering geo-political disarticulation. As the colossus, powered by enormous diesels, progressed across Eastern Europe, to the rhythm of one thunderous footstep a month (crushing in its path: town, village, field, school, hospital, nuclear power plant, etc) the planet itself had been shaken from its axis, and nowhere was quite where it used to be, or ever would be again.

But to return to Sawney's End: Few people managed to get there, fewer stayed with Mrs Shkrebneva, and *Caledonian Connoisseurs* dismissed both in three paragraphs.

Julian might have hinted of the village to Luja, but had said nothing to Bertie Mapplethorpe or anyone else—least of all Terry Lair. Was it coincidence that Terry should propose work here? It was convenient that he could use his hideaway (always a joy to see Mrs Shkrebneva), but still...

Secondly, there was the nature of the business itself. Julian was by no means squeamish but his rugged sincerity preferred, on the whole, more straightforward murders. Give him a rusty blade, a defined target, a clear thrust and everybody was happy. Terry had, however, requested certain elaborations that Julian found dispiriting. This postmodern mania for complicating everything was wearisome. He was, despite years of experience, uncertain of how to fulfil the requirements. That said, Terry Lair had paid for everything in advance—generously.

And, thirdly, there was Maria, the astral projection.

"More tea, Mr Grayle?"

"No thank you, Mrs Shkrebneva."

"Tell me now if you need anything else. I can't be at your beck and call all morning."

"Perhaps," Julian said, "you could just tell me where to find a joiner?"

4. London: EU agrees on Covid passes for summer travel

"You no hurt me," Luja said. "Julian kill you."

"I don't think that's likely."

Terry dragged Luja towards a white Rolls Royce. It was a Googleised, autonomous version, and the passenger door opened automatically. Terry squeezed in after her. She slid as far from him as possible.

His eyes lingered on her silk dress and green stockings.

"You know," (after rinsing his fingers with gel) he reached to wipe a dark strand from her face, "you were wasted on a blunt instrument like Julian. Why aren't we moving?"

The passenger door was still open. With a sigh, he slammed it shut.

The Rolls juddered, and they were off.

Luja breathed deeply, filling her nostrils with the odour of leather, antiseptic, and the spice of Terry's aftershave. His hair had thinned, he had developed a paunch, but his charisma remained intact. She admired his joie de vivre and resilience. He was wealthy too. A millionaire several times over. She could do much worse, especially if Julian was (or soon to be) dead. In pursuing her career as a ballet dancer, she had grown a little apart from her boyfriend. But Terry was famous for his fibs. Few could match Julian in a fight. There were vast cemeteries of those who had tried. He could be naïve at times—that was part of his charm—but surely, he was not so foolish as to fall into a trap? She stared at her multi-coloured fingernails. There was a bond between her and Julian that went deeper than sex.

"Oh, look," Terry touched her arm. "Recognise him?"

A smallish man, with a brown face and white stubble, was wheeling a Samsonite along the pavement.

"That's Punch Strother," Terry said. "He does that satirical YouTube channel *Political Punch*? You know, he has these puppets of famous people? My puppet's been on it a lot."

Luja shrugged.

"He's just finished filming the last ever episode," Terry said knowledgeably. "He'll be going home to Scotland for his retirement. He lives in Sawney's End. Ever been there?"

Luja fiddled with the clasp of her handbag.

"Julian's up there at the moment." With finger and thumb, Terry plucked a thoughtful hair from his left nostril. His eyes watered, but his voice remained even. "Quite a coincidence. Do you think they'll meet?"

The Rolls circled Piccadilly, and then took Regents Street in the opposite direction. An ambulance and two police cars were parked outside the Ristorante Berlusconi. A waiter, wielding a broom, swept the doorstep while another leapt about stamping. A third sprayed disinfectant. Passers-by yelped, scratched their legs, and moved on briskly. When a stretcher appeared with Maria Fleetfoot's shapely skeleton, tourists snapped photos.

Terry placed a friendly hand on her knee: "I'm making a clean break with the past. No more politics, no more subterfuge, no more spin. A genuine retirement. Cheryl and I have found a log-cabin just outside Toronto. It's modest. Not much of a garden. Hardly enough room for a landing pad. But beautifully situated. On the banks of a lake. Pine-forest. The weather is still quite stable, despite all the earthquakes, tsunamis and other ecological upheavals. We have a new range of snow-tipped mountains now. Dragonflies, frogs, fishing, possibly the odd grisly who has wandered over from the West... How about it? You'd look sexy dressed as a maid. Bucolic bliss for the rest of our days. We deserve it. We'll be off just as soon as I've settled my accounts."

The Rolls slowed behind a bus. Luja's handbag was open. Her fingers closed surreptitiously upon her BojoPhone—once so desired, in retrospect, rather regretted. Advertised as lightyears ahead of the antediluvian MePhone, the BojoPhone was indeed swift, fluent, and punchy in its communications. However, some operators, complaining bitterly about its imprecisions, refused to support it and even went so far as to recommend its withdrawal. No one would deny that the BojoPhone was prone to distort: users found themselves saying or texting the opposite of what they intended, any messages marked private were instantaneously shared with every contact, and the camera always caught mother-in-law looking her worst; but an astounding autonomy and a powerful network more than compensated for deficiencies which, in time, became perfectly acceptable. She only hoped that Julian would not consider her message ambivalent.

"I don't mind telling you, Cheryl and I are exhausted. We've been through so much in the last few years. Those wars everybody's so upset about, the general election, my daughter's suicide, Cheryl's pregnancy, the lockdown..." Terry shook his head. "And now, our baby boy has been kidnapped."

The Rolls Royce halted. Horns began to toot.

"Oh, well. It'll give us time to chat." He stretched with a discreet popping of joints. "Where are you hiding my son?"

5. Sawney's End: Top vaccine producer faces shortages

"Och, it's a verra difficult job, you're askin' there." The wiry man in overalls leaned lower on his counter and peered at Terry's pencil sketch. "Nae sae easy... Nae sae easy..."

"But can you do it, Mr Mackenzie?" Julian tried not to sneeze. The air was thick with wood shavings and, every time he moved, his tweeds scooped dust from planks piled against the walls.

"I can try, laddie, I can try... Are you wantin' me to mak' the mechanism too?"

"Yes, of course. Can you?"

"Oh, aye, laddie. That I can." Mr Mackenzie's eyebrows met in a black bar. "It's a wee bit macabre though, isn't it?"

"Macabre? Why?"

"The bones, laddie, the bones."

"Oh, I see," Julian sniffed. "It's a gift for a nephew. You know how young people like this kind of thing. It's that Goth Death Metal they listen to."

"Ah, weel. If you sae so. And do you ha' them wi ye, laddie?"

"Have what?"

"The bones, laddie."

"Well no... Ah! Aaah!" Julian sneezed into his arm. "Sorry. Not yet. I'll have them ready in a couple of days." He paused, ruminating upon the fruitless hours he had already spent in Sawney's End. Mr Mackenzie's shop had only appeared on his thirteenth attempt along the street but, perhaps, Maria had been distracting. Once found, the shop had been closed. As he had no memory of entering, he was not certain it was open now. One muddled through as best one could. He reached for his handkerchief and wiped his nose. "Can't you get on with the box?"

"Oh, aye. Nae problem. If that's what you want. I was joost thinkin' o' proportions."

"Just go for a standard size. It doesn't have to be perfect."

"Ah, but you see I'm a craftsman, laddie. Like my dad afore me, and granddad afore him. It's in the... heh..." Mr Mackenzie eyes were fixed on the ceiling, "blood."

Julian looked up. Maria was prudishly clothing herself in sawdust. He had no idea why she followed him around—unless, her existence (like that of most women) required the presence of a strong male. She was not, however, siphoning enough energy to solidify. He rather wished she would. She had muscular, if rather dusty, buttocks and he was feeling frisky.

"Listen, Mr Mackenzie." He placed one of Terry's thinner rolls on the counter, and modulated his tone to a confidential and intimate key. "This is, I think you'll appreciate, all very hush hush..."

"Oh, aye, laddie," the money proved a stronger magnet to Mackenzie's gaze than the feminised sawdust. "Mum's the word."

"Exactly. Rather important people involved, don't you know. They'd be grateful too if it could be done as quickly as possible."

"Ah weel, I'll need a good week for the box, laddie," Mr Mackenzie slid Terry's diagram into his top pocket. "And twa or three days more once you deliver the... heh... *bones*." His stumpy fingers squeezed Terry's roll. "And twa more of these."

6. London: CIA has untapped evidence on Covid-19 lab origins

"I know you kidnapped him," Terry said. "You're all over the police videos."

The Rolls was moving again. Overtaking the bus, it crept past the Tottenham Court Theatre. Emblazoned above the entrance in tall pink letters were the words *Maria Fleetfoot and Luja Naifeh Dance in Viral Electro*. A traffic light shone a pinkish hue on a poster of Maria and Luja dressed in ballerina costumes. Maria, in front and in sharp focus, was levitating amidst a swathe of golden stars. A blurred Luja remained earthbound, abandoned...

"I feel sorry for you," Terry eyed the poster moodily. "You so want to be something more than a murderer's moll that you're ready to trail on even Maria's pathetic petticoats."

Her fingers fluttered over her BojoPhone.

"With Maria out of the picture," Terry shifted nearer, "they might offer you the leading role."

His hands sought her neck. Luja kicked, but he threw his weight upon her. Her shoe struck the ceiling. Her handbag tumbled onto the floor, her BojoPhone skidding under the seat. She scratched at his eyes, but he flung his head sideways. He tightened his hold, laughing when she dug her nails into his hands.

"One good turn deserves another." Terry suited the action to the word. "Where's my son?"

7. Sawney's End: Daily PCR tests imposed as zero-Covid policy continues

Julian decided to kill time on the beach. With Maria shimmering above, he passed the tiny castle which, according to *Caledonian Connoisseurs 2013*, was "originally erected against Viking aggressors in the eleventh century and is nowadays a museum containing objects of local interest". The Dutchman and his children were standing in front of the ticket booth. Julian's heart somersaulted. But, no, it was *not* Inspector Bloemer.

He checked his MePhone, but there was nothing from Luja. He sent a peremptory email to Terry.

He descended to the shore. The sand, a moist amber sprinkled with shattered shells, scrunched beneath his shoes like the splintering of infantine bones. The waves arrived in tinkling rolls and, retreating, yearned at tufts of seaweed. Shrieking gulls hovered overhead and the wind, which whipped his jacket in every direction, was bitter with brine.

He felt lighter, and realised that Maria had been blown away.

Luja's silence was unnatural—especially as she owned a BojoPhone.

He glanced back at the coastal drive. A man was rolling a suitcase along the pavement. Julian wondered whether this was significant. The man paused, harking to sudden shrieks and a curious, dismal whistling.

Julian looked back at the sea. Great billows of steam were rising from the waters. It was caused by a virus cluster bobbing a few yards offshore. A woman was writhing within their midst.

These viruses were, of course, the ancestors of the original Wuhan Lab Co-vid 19. They had (due to some freak evolutionary leap which allowed scientists to theorise ad infinitum on prime-time TV) swollen to the size of volleyballs. This growth had been accompanied by a slight decrease in aggressivity. Less likely to infect humans, bats and pangolins, they now led fairly peaceful existences, drifting along coastlines. Oceans and seas were arguably their natural habitat for they represented—in the words of Dr Helmut Ewers—the "Blut von Mutter Erde".

Ecologists were dismayed for they interfered with the computation of industrial and recreational fishing data. However, influential groups of cross-party MPs argued for tolerance as they provided a powerful buffer against immigration. Perverts loved them too. When excited, their temperature (that of the viruses) rose to 35° Celsius which meant that, in Scotland for instance, Sunday afternoons had become less dreary. Their touch was spongy, their caress enveloping, and their protuberances—which oozed an addictive slime tasting of melted Mars bars—could, if inserted into the appropriate orifice, trigger multiple orgasms.

Such thrills were not without a degree of risk. If overstimulated, the viruses could reach 100° Celsius in a matter of seconds, and even explode. The experienced pervert never went without a tube of gel.

Julian had recognised the Dutchwoman, now reduced to near nudity.

"Help!" she cried. "Get me away from them!"

"Don't pretend," Julian said prissily (Scandinavians were markedly insensitive to social convention), "you're not enjoying yourself."

"They attacked me!"

"You might at least have waited until nightfall."

"Help!" A questing tentacle caused her bra to snap painfully. "Help! Help! Help!"

The man on the pavement abandoned his suitcase, and leapt onto the sand.

"She needs help!" He called. "Hurry!"

Julian decided that, in the presence of a witness, an Übermensch moment was in order. Not bothering to remove his shoes, he splashed into the water, caught one of the viruses and sent it soaring over the waves. He grabbed the woman's arm and hauled her onto the beach. A virus lassoed her leg, but another kick sent it bouncing over the pebbles. The remaining viruses rose like dolphins on the swell. A mass of tentacles was cast around their feet. He and the woman fell sprawling into the shallows. They were dragged deeper into the waves. Their mouths filled with water.

The man had reached the shore. Lifting a slate, he waded into the cluster. There were several efficient slicing sounds. Three of the viruses split like watermelons. An evil-smelling gore, spilling from their tangled tripes, spread in oily rainbows.

"Gosh." Julian unwrapped a tentacle from his thigh. "Do you think this stuff can be exploited?"

The remaining viruses—prey to a Heideggerian anxiety—retreated to a safe distance. The other beings, in time, struggled to the shore.

They sat on the sand, their clothes stiffening in the sun. Julian could not keep his eyes off the Dutch woman's long, tanned legs. He wished that he could see more, and regretted his promptitude in rescuing her.

"Well, thank you," she said. "You arrived just in time."

The man suffered from a fearful squint which enabled him to meet both their eyes in a single glance. "Don't mention it. Next time you do that make sure you have a tube of gel. It calms them down. Something to do with viral memory."

"I wasn't… Oh, forget it. My name's Marja by the way."

"Punch Strother at your service." His eyes ricocheted like billiard balls, and Julian flinched. Kindly dimples appeared in the white stubble on either extremity of his lipless mouth. "Happy to be of use on the first day of my retirement."

Julian wondered whether Punch Strother was an Übermensch too. If Terry omitted to send him a victim, Punch would do nicely.

8. London: Pandemic, slow recovery sets back gender parity by a generation

"We… Cough… We stopped."

"Oh," Terry loosened his grip. "Have we?"

The Rolls had drawn up outside the glassy entrance to the Financial Governance tower. The doorman's face revealed a polite lack of awareness that the Non-Executive Director had been strangling a stunningly beautiful girl.

"How embarrassing." Terry straightened his tie. "I'm losing my delicate touch."

Luja coughed and rubbed her throat. Perspiration deadened her perfume. She leant her head against the leather and closed her eyes.

"You'll need make up to cover the bruises," Terry said. "I doubt that they'll be visible on stage though. Are you coming up? You'll meet an old friend."

In Terry's office, a gloomy Bertie Mapplethorpe was sunk in an armchair. Luja was surprised to see that he was dressed in drag. He was wearing a frock coat, dress and matching hat whose bold fuchsia reddened his complexion. His swollen legs and feet had been squeezed into stockings and high heels.

"Finished my Laphroaig, have you?" Terry examined the decanter on the coffee table. "Not to worry. There's plenty more." He crossed the room to where a pair of doors swung open without voicing any welcome. In the dark interior, Luja discerned a bed with white fur and folds of purple silk. "You'll let me put you up? I hope you don't mind sharing."

"Kind of you, old man," Bertie looked up. "But I really can't stay."

"It won't be for long, Bertie." Terry laughed. "Luja only has to lead me to little Tom, and you… Well, I expect much less from you. I just have to deal with the logistics, and then you'll be on your way."

He shooed them into the bedroom. "There's a light switch over there." The doors closed with a pneumatic hiss.

"I'll be back in a bit," they heard him call. "Don't do anything I wouldn't."

9. Sawney's End: Lingering Covid symptoms keep millions from working

Julian returned to Mrs Shkrebneva's B&B with the laudable intention of doing some research. He needed to read up on the messy part of his mission. He wished that Terry would send the victim's name so that he could get on with it. No news from Luja. At least Maria was back, bumping along the ceiling like a bunch of shapely balloons.

Sounds of hilarity came from the lounge. As he entered, the Dutch family straightened up in the chintz sofa and matching armchairs. Julian decided to ignore how much hubby reminded him of Inspector Bloemer. The son made as if to vacate his chair, but Julian shook his head. He crossed to the computer behind the sofa. As he waited for Windows Twenty Thousand to charge, he glanced at the television. It appeared to be some kind of satirical *Punch and Judy* show. Various puppets dressed as Arabic dictators, European heads of state, or international sportsmen walloped each other with Barney Rubble clubs. Their dialogue was swamped by gusts of tinned laughter.

Dutch Dad spluttered into his handkerchief and Mum smiled. The children sat in sulky silence. There were doubtless cartoons or Goth Death Metal videos on another channel.

Julian turned to the computer, not sure how to ask his question. Would even Google have the answer? *How do you* he typed *separate flesh from bone...* His attention was caught by a passable imitation of Luja's voice.

"No, Bertie," it was saying, "I no love Terry Lair. Why you think that of *meee*?"

He looked at the television and saw a puppet of Luja in intimate discussion with a less convincing Bertie Mapplethorpe. The two friends were sitting on a wooden chest in an empty mansion. They were surrounded by crates, cartons and suitcases.

"Damn it, Luja," Bertie said, wobbling a little. He was recognisable from a row of bottles at his feet. "Why are you leaving me then?"

"That Luja Naifeh is a very pretty girl," the Dutch woman said, "even as a puppet."

"What does she do, mummy?" her son asked.

"I don't think she actually does anything," she replied. "She's a star."

"Isn't she dancing in Swan Lake Electro?"

"Oh, yes. Maybe."

"Is she Terry Lair's girlfriend?"

"I don't know *everything* about Luja Naifeh."

Julian bristled. What the hell was this? Luja with Bertie? Luja with Terry? Is that what people thought? Perspiration bloomed on his face, and a familiar red haze blurred his vision. He peered about for something to throw at the television. His fingers closed around an alabaster statuette of Terry Lair. Not heavy enough.

He would fetch his VeganGun and kill them all.

10. London: Mao vaccine accused of causing Monkeypox

"Smells bad, here," Luja wrinkled her nose. "What is that?"

"Disinfectant," Bertie said. "Terry doesn't always entertain the classiest of whore."

They gazed disconsolately around the room. Leopard-skin lampshades with velvet tassels filtered light onto a heart-shaped bed. The satiny walls were hung with videos of tumescent sons of Royalty cavorting with starlets in luxurious bedrooms. From a hidden speaker Frank Sinatra crooned *Jeepers Creepers*.

"Why you dressed in drag, Bertie?" Luja kneeled to untangle a lace thong which had snagged in her shoe. She fingered the bra, suspenders and stockings which were draped over a chair. Red high-heels had been kicked onto a sheepskin rug. She opened the wardrobe to discover a pink leather jacket and miniskirt.

Bertie sighed: "In memory of the Queen." Displacing a pile of fluffy cushions, he sank onto the bed. His face waned like a pale moon behind the sphere of his enormous belly. "I had my tailor copy one of her last costumes. It suits me, I think. Not sure about the hat though. I just can't get used to King Charles. What do you make of this business?"

"It not good. What Terry mean by logistics?"

"I've really no idea, old girl. It might be that Terry blames me for his daughter's suicide. But it wasn't my fault her fiancé was devoured by a post-modern work of art. That was Julian. Oh, look. There's a mirror on the ceiling."

"Terry crazy." Luja was relieved that Bertie's weighted hemline revealed nothing beyond his knees. "Maybe he kill us both?"

"I doubt it, old girl." His voice was muffled by having to circumvent his mound of belly and feet. "He's just a bit upset. It's comprehensible."

"Is it?" Luja frowned up at Bertie's reflection.

"His daughter's dead. His son has disappeared. Why on earth did you kidnap him?"

"It seem best thing to do, at time."

"You Arab terrorists never consider consequences." With a fearsome effort, Bertie rolled onto his side. He propped himself on an elbow. "You know, this is a very uncomfortable bed." He scratched his thigh. "Something's bitten me."

"Crab maybe." Luja pouted. "English girls very filthy."

"Terry never disappoints."

Bertie stood up and drew back the embroidered cover to reveal lumps and indentations. The duvet rippled in a ghostly draught.

"Bertie, wait. You no touch."

"I just want to see…" Bertie tugged at the duvet. "Oh! Yuck!"

A skeleton sprawled across the bed. Glistening black silt oozed over the spinal column, adhered to the ribs, and dribbled onto the floor. The stink of disinfectant was overwhelming. Peering closer, they saw that the silt was made up of what initially appeared to be thousands of dead and dying beetles. They seemed slightly bigger than Luja remembered and, on close inspection, a wider variety of shapes. Some possessed the traditional covid form with cruel thorns waving from their fronds, others had incandescent eyes, pincers, human bodies and transparent wings, still others were like snakes with dog-shaped heads that burst into masses of suckers. One had the appearance of a chimpanzee with a metallic tail which, tumbling from a rib, clunked like a medieval weapon.

"I say," Bertie's face was green. "What happened here?"

"Another of Terry's girlfriends," Luja said. "I seen this before."

"What are those things?"

"Virus variant maybe? Hybrid?" Luja prodded one of the dying creatures with her toe. "This one wear spectacles. Look like Dr Helmut Ewers. You not think?"

"What I think, old girl, is I'm going to be sick."

"Oh, no! You don't!"

Bertie crouched on the floor. He relieved himself lengthily of a lumpy, tawny gruel, stinking of whisky which, to Luja's irritation, added to the general mess.

"I really think…" He gagged again. "Yuck! Sorry… I really think you should return Terry's son."

"I no think so."

Bertie's bottom sank onto a velvet chair. There was a loud crack, but he showed more concern over a ladder in his stockings. "Why not?"

Luja explained what had happened to Maria.

"Oh, Christ. What a pity. I liked Maria. Agile toes. She could do this delicious thing with her… Bless her. She *was* rather pricey… Worth it, though, on dreary Sunday afternoons in Scotland, and one can't always get to the seaside." Memories of Maria had returned the colour to his cheeks. "What harm did she ever do Terry?"

"He want to make clean break with past."

"And you think he'll kill us both? Even if he gets his son back?"

"Yes, I certain."

"Can't Julian help?"

"How can I contact him?" Luja sat down on the bed causing a small avalanche of viruses. "Oh, this bad, Bertie."

"It does look sticky, old girl."

"I so want to dance in Swan Lake Electo."

"No great loss that," Bertie patted her shoulder. "Come on. Cheer up. While there's life and all that... Where is the baby anyway?"

"Shh! I need think." Luja's angelic face was haloed by the fleshy buttocks of one of Prince Andrew's paramours. "I must idea."

The door emitted a sigh.

"Well, you'd better think quickly, old girl."

11. Sawney's End: Revealing the social effects of two years of mask-wearing

Julian rose to fetch his Vegan-Gun. One, two, three four zaps for the Dutch, a jaunt to the kitchen, and a fifth for Mrs Shkrebneva: Bop! Bop! Bop! Bop! ... Bop!

On screen, the chest burst open. Luja and Bertie flopped onto the floor like upset insects. A grinning Terry Lair, bouncing on a spring, struck at them with a cricket bat. "Take that! And that! And that!" Terry shouted gleefully. "Ouch!" yelped Luja. "Ow!" cried Bertie. Terry turned to the camera: "You can't keep a bad politician down!" The laughter erupted, and the closing credits waltzed to a jitzed up *Swan Lake*.

"Oh! Very good" the husband said. "Very funny, indeed!"

Mrs Shkrebneva entered with a tray of tea, scones and cream. Everyone was surprised. Julian sat down again. Mrs Shkrebneva's tea was too good to miss.

"Oh, *Political Punch*," she said. "Do you think it's funny?"

"It's not bad," the wife said. "We have a similar show in Holland."

"Its creator, Punch Strother, lives here. In that pink house on the hill. You can see it from the beach. He's done very well for himself," Mrs Shkrebneva spoke disapprovingly. "Strange man. He's never married. Lives alone."

Julian wiped his palms up and down his thighs. He no longer needed an email. Strother was the target. Terry never did like being teased. Mrs Shkrebneva left, and the children scampered off to play in their room. Julian moved to an armchair. He sipped his tea—Mrs Shkrebneva really did make an exceptional cuppa—and triggered his most charming smile.

"You sell software, Mr Grayle?" The wife glanced at him from beneath shy eyelashes. "I'm a programmer myself."

"Then you must know more about what I sell than me," Julian laughed. "Mine is an unadulterated sales background."

Possibly recalling their encounter on the beach, the woman blushed. Julian turned to her husband. "And you? What do you do, Mr Er...?"

"Taxidermy," the man, who did not resemble Inspector Bloemer, said. "I own a little shop in Amsterdam."

What a stroke of luck! Julian thought. "Taxidermy, eh? Fascinating. But tricky, I imagine."

"Not if you know how. My name's Ditmer by the way. Ditmer Daalman. This is my wife, Marja."

"Delighted, I'm sure," Julian said. "I've always wondered how you... Sorry, might sound like a funny question."

"No, no. Go on."

"How do you manage to get the flesh off a... an animal without damaging the skeleton?"

"Oh, that," Ditmer shrugged. "There are several possibilities. You can try simmering in a pan, but you need to be careful. If over-boiled, the calcium flakes."

"What if the animal is quite big? Would you use sulphuric acid?"

"Sulphuric acid? Never! It dissolves everything. Flesh, cartilage, bones and all. Lime would be a better bet."

"You're not enthusiastic though?"

"No, not really…" Ditmer looked thoughtful. "Lime tends to make the bones brittle which, of course, you want to avoid. Whenever possible, I use Dermestid beetles."

"Dermestid beetles?"

"They eat the flesh off a small animal in a matter of days."

"I like the idea of using beetles," Julian said. "Are they easy to come by?"

"Oh, yes," Ditmer laughed. "You can order them online. But… Well, how big were you thinking of?"

"The size makes a difference?"

"Absolutely. If the animal were really big, the size of a... Er... What, for example? Well, yes, why not? Say it was the size of a mmm... a gorilla... You'd need an awful lot of them. And then, there's the time factor."

"Oh, dear."

"Yes, it would take forever..." Ditmer seemed sensitive to Julian's disappointment. "Wait a minute. I've got something I'd like to show you."

He stood up and left the room. Marja and Julian exchanged shy smiles. Ditmer returned, holding a glass box filled with cotton wool and Styrofoam.

"The larvae burrow into the Styrofoam and pupate," he said. "It takes about seven days for them to become... well, to become what they become."

Julian watched a pinkish maggot with bristles, twin rows of tiny human hands, and two miniature tusks clamber over cakes of sawdust. "That's a Dermestid beetle?"

"A kind of hybrid." Ditmer frowned. "Dr Helmut Ewers—you know, the German scientist?—experimented with Dermestid beetles, Covid, monkey pox and God knows what, and... Well, this is the result."

"How interesting."

"Germans always have the best ideas. That stuff is a waste they produce called frass. They live in it. Believe it or not, there are about five thousand buried in there."

"Are they dangerous?"

"Yes, they're extremely aggressive. They can devour a large animal in a matter of seconds and, unlike the original Dermestid beetles, don't wait for it to die."

Julian was distracted by Maria who, in a shower of twinkling stars, spinning planets and crescent moons, had floated down between them. She gesticulated wildly but Ditmer, clearly not a 6°=5° Adeptus Major, ignored her. With ethereal tears trailing over her cheeks, she lay at their feet. Her despairing hands fluttered over their knees while she continued to sink into Mrs Shkrebneva's Turkish rug. Soon only her face was visible, a pallid mask on patterns of red, green and purple. Julian shifted his chair. "I can buy these on Amazon?"

"Oh, no." Ditmer smiled. "These are a prototype. They're not on the market yet. I've volunteered to test them."

"And you took them on holiday with you?"

"Ha! Ha! Not on purpose. They're not pets. Ha! Ha! No, the postman arrived while we were leaving. I'd already locked the house so stuffed the parcel into my bag."

"I see. Do they live a long time?"

"Four or five months. You should spray them with disinfectant when they're finished. Wouldn't want them eating the neighbour's dog."

"Or the neighbour."

"Ha! Ha! Yes. Very funny! Ha! Ha! But, yes, it's a real danger."

"Food for thought."

"Ha! Ha! British humour! Ha! Ha! Ha! Ha! Ha! Ha! Ha! Ha! Ha! Ha! Ha! Ha! Ha! Ha! Ha! Ha! Ha! Ha! Ha! Ha! Ha! Ha! Ha! Ha! Ha! Ha! Ha! Ha!"

12. London: UK's Covid orphans struggle to get by

"Have you had time for a little think?" Terry entered, the door closing behind him in sulky silence. "I've brought us a little snack." He wedged a Marks & Spencer tote bag into the skeleton's ribcage. "I see you've met Jennifer."

Luja and Bertie looked at each other.

"Yes," Luja said, "same as Maria."

"Pretty much." With a sweep of his palm, Terry sent dying creatures clattering onto the floor. "I had the larvae introduced into her flat. I wasn't that sure they would survive to turn into… uh… beetles or whatnot." He placed a variety of sandwiches, yoghurts and fruit juices on the clean spot. "Let's see, we have cheddar and tomato or ham and egg. Do you prefer brown or white bread? Anyway, she was all right for days and, when she showed up here the other night, I thought the whole thing had fallen through. But then, while we were having breakfast… Bingo! The larvae must have wriggled their way inside her somehow and pupated. It all works out in the end."

"You put larvae in Maria's flat too?" Luja asked.

"Not me personally," Terry was shocked. "I wouldn't be seen dead there."

"I say, old man," the greenish tinge had returned to Bertie's complexion, "you're not thinking of trying those beetles on us?"

"How many would it take?" Terry bit into his ham and egg. "Luja, of course, is already pretty much skin and bones..."

"But then you never find little Tom." Luja opened a bottle of freshly squeezed orange. "Brown bread, cheese, thank you. I no eat pig."

"Here you are," Terry handed her a sandwich. "Not eating, Bertie? Cheer up. What Luja says is correct. She's perfectly safe. Of course, you'll both have to stay here until she decides to be more communicative."

"Why me?" Bertie groaned. His complexion was wandering from white to grey. "I'm not in cahoots with Luja. I had nothing to do with the kidnapping."

"That's the way it has to be. I can have Jennifer and the whatnots removed if they disturb you."

The building shook from what must have been a minor earthquake. The videos went dead, dwindling to a dot.

"That was the colossus taking another step," Terry enthused. "Have you ever visited it? It's a gas! Stainless steel and brass. The torso is covered with icons, and the belly button a museum filled with astounding collections of Kandinsky's, Goncharova's and Mukhina's. The genitals alone are worth the trip: veined ivory, the pubic hairs are gold, platinum and silver. You land your private-jet on the cranium, take an inner-ear shuttle to one or other eye—each is a five-star hotel—I prefer the one on the left, for the caviar. The mouth is a swimming pool, the tongue a toboggan, and the incisors are transparent so, while you're splashing about, you can watch the war. There's really no other way of doing Eastern Europe. Don't miss it."

"I dance in Swan Lake Electro at end of month." Luja pouted. "I no want miss that. It my dream."

"And everyone else's nightmare." Terry shook his head sympathetically. "I do rather regret that."

Luja picked up Jennifer's thigh bone and examined it for a full minute. "Okay." She closed her eyes. "I ready to make deal."

To be continued...

Jake Robinson

Ananta

Noleretts

Onorwsd

Sonacsep

eyt smoethnig srits

bofere scpae

brfoee tmie

teh tmie of time

a split second

nay, a fraction

now a seething mass of energy and matter of unimaginable heat. Heat? Another expression. Energy stored. Such a full expanse, yet barren of all but the smallest parts binding, changing form, moving like a great whirlpool of light and matter. Heavier? Pulling upon others. Vague forms. Silence. Cooling. An opaque soup of vast subatomic particles—a fog

time? More time. A passage or progress? Everything continued, a growing expanse, stored energy released. The smallest parts combining, the clearing fog leaving glowing light forever imprinting the background of all

untold eons more time more time, great darkness. Hollow. Lonely. The smallest gathering, commuting slowly to colder locations like clouds. Clouds? Wrong time. Growing communities pulling upon one another, irresistible propaganda of mass. Growing clumps with condensing centers gaining heat, forcing multiple atomic parts into one. Countless Brothers, like flowers, blooming in the darkness. The giants, the behemoths, the titans. Their petals blazing, lighting up the darkness with a fierce radiance. Unmatched, subsuming the small, the miniscule. Drawing towards one another into mighty minuets, dragging gasses and emblazoning the darkness with flaming spiralling forms

time, it seems, has an effect. For these countless siblings passing through it met violent changes, suddenly increasing greatly in luminosity as they eject their parts into a vast surrounding field. Few collapsing, auto-cannibalistically devouring themselves from the outside in and remaining nothing but hungering holes devouring all within their grasps. Kin included. Dragging others into their own, much larger coalescence of spiralling elliptical forms that often remain just out of reach, despite these inescapable monsters' demonic strength

from the rich elemental ashes of giants sprang forth their children, varying greatly in character, unlike their predecessors. Smaller, though inexplicably larger than the first parts, and dimmer. Stronger in constitution, of will. Some even performing steady ballets in the face of times passage, which they would pass down to the generation succeeding them in the battle against the dark, drawing in the elemental ashes of their forebears and crafting dull, gloomy, imitations of themselves - some great orbs of dense gas, others smaller mineral formations, that would consume one another in destructive duels, charging one another at striking speed with frightening mass vastly greater than the impact of shock cavalry. Of warheads. But blips in the night, by comparison, as they crash upon one another tearing away great swathes of each being and a great many parts fragmenting into the surroundings. Some stalemates, draws, overwhelming victories and others pyrrhic. Leaving their faces molten messes, eventually cooling into war-torn, barren landscapes

in the depths of one of the Dark Ones spiralling coalescence, one blazing flowers successor—lacking in luminosity as they so often do—performed the ancient ballet, drawing in surrounding specs, particles, and gasses. Slowly clumping them up and holding duels of its very own. As one of its' newly formed children cooled from its molten birth, its surroundings became an arena as one of its closest siblings made a daring charge. From one cataclysmic clash was the match decided, the challenged gained in size whilst the challenger remain loosely shackled near its victorious sister. Both glowing a deep red as if born anew, the victor differentiating into layers, its exterior forming a solid barrier. Thin in comparison to its mass. Both, gradually developing later, to be permanently scarred by the bombardment of returning shrapnel that sprang forth from their bout

my victorious Daughter, my greatest pride. After defeating her sibling and earning her place at my side she continues to lash out, her rage frequently erupting amongst her surface despite the incessant shrapnel's impacts. An oddity. Though my focus strayed to my outer regions of influence, my Daughter's rage-filled eruptions formed a hazy layer around her, as if attempting to hide in plain sight

my rage blinded me from all else, this haze that formed was looked strangely upon by Mother. No matter, I should work to calm myself despite that wretched… Brother? What were they exactly? A sibling to be sure; perhaps. Possible relative. Whatever. More importantly, a strange state has befallen some of my face. The creases upon it now fill with some substance I have not seen before. No, similar almost to my raging eruptions, but in place of fierce molten spit is a green substance, almost toxic in appearance, that flows across my surface more fluidly… Fluid? Liquid, a great green liquid, and reddish spots? Lands? As I turn in place, they gradually mellow. Small, microscopic things begin reacting within that liquid's depths, eventually followed by some bluish-green descendants that release gas. They move under their own power? Living? Organic

as I age so too do these odd little beings upon me. Gradually, no doubt from the help of these organisms, this liquid became a deep blue, the land rough-hewn rock. Greys and browns. The haze that obscured my view cleared and instead my surroundings appear blue, when illuminated by Mothers' light. Without it, my siblings made themselves visible. Beyond them? More Mothers and their kin, surrounded by their own imitations. Stellar families. What a sight

woah, getting lost within my place in existence, I almost missed a great explosion of life within my oceans. That's what I'll call them. Long, thin sensory appendages and clusters of small visual units on a shell, supported by many jointed, scuttling, appendages. Swarming. Even burrowing into me.

Though, at my size their actions have less impact than Mothers brilliant blaze upon my face

other things seem to spread across the dry, grey landscapes that protrude my oceans. A slow growth of green, more vibrant than the oceans original state. More life? Different life? Very odd life to be sure. They started with simple branching, soft bodies that seemed to require moisture-rich environments. Multiplying with barely perceptible spores. Eventually, progressing further inland as they developed more complex parts. Breaking into the ground, churning the soil, colonising all the land they can touch. Countless of their lifetimes, though but a blink in my eye, passed as they grew stronger, taller. Darker brown stems multiple times their predecessor's height. Highly preferable to the scuttling critters that made their way towards land, though their development was equally as interesting as their numerous legs lessened. Time of the quadrupeds! No, not as good. The ones in the ocean grew even stranger still

little attention was paid after that, I left them to their business. Greater things came about; more siblings, though far out

above all I rise, mighty. From but a blip fallen to the ground, rooted. Peeping surface. Light light energy strength growth damage light water growth. The cycle. As all kinds of skin, scaled, feathered, moved around and above. Not swaying as I do, not rhythmically in the breeze. Rustling in the rain. Vitalised. They cower, using their peculiar roots beneath them to not anchor but propel themselves. Some claiming my stationary neighbours, their parts, some trodden under root. The tallest ones snatch from my highest appendages with grinding, gnawing motions and storing it within themselves. Others tear at my base, for what purpose I cannot fathom. Not intent for my innards as they can clearly cut deep. Just marking my exterior. It cannot stop me. As I gain height my width doubles, allowing me to grow out of the reach of those pesky appendage snatchers. Assailable yet unbreachable. Well, save for those that climb. Negligible damage received. Few young taken. At worst lost, at best spread. They all fall before long, to make their way as I had. To fight for the light. Dig deep for nourishment. For security. To remain moored. I cannot make such motions as those that now trample around me, now akin to ants to my zenith

success. I shall lord this patch, relish the light and soil. Multiply countless times, hundreds in one go. Thousands

less light? A growing shadow. The light sphere eclipsed and a catastrophic quake of the ground. My roots stunned from the shear jarring impacts of the ground's movements amidst my depths. The ones with mobile roots flee at such a pace I could not have fathomed. Incandescent spherules blaze across the sky, nipping at their root tips. Scorching my appendages as they tear through them, like how the fleeing beings once tore through one another. Great plumes of material darkness fill the sky, blocking light. Blocking life. The beating of projectiles impacting, roots stampeding, engulfing flames dancing with glee. Cinders. A great wall approaches, rushing my direction. Fire it is not, not any living thing I know of. It has never passed this way. A sheer cliff charging, ploughing all before it. Abreast its crest, great white cantering figures rush headlong in my direction. The rumble they kick up a growing cacophony, perhaps like a raging wind or audible tremble of the ground's quakes. As it closes, a murky-blue shows near its mid, the cacophony accompanied by sounds of tremendous downpour. It washes all away. Washes! No amount of such liquid has ever graced this land—fresh clean water quench. It may knock and break, light may lack, but with this. Endure. Splintered shattered grounded. Damage. Damage. Toxin? An internal ache throughout my parts, precious liquid drawn out. Out? Toxic water. Torn from my anchor. Chaos for all. Not even the sky has escaped this wrath

I had no reason to think things would so drastically change

significant loss of all life

again

another Great Dying

another

one more significant hit

many smaller occasions happened of similar effect, but none so devastating as those five great occurrences. Though, eventually, something interesting arose again. From walking on four appendages, to only occasionally with two;

used for grabbing, climbing, acts of violence. Many variations on the same model, kind of like how Mother created me and my siblings. Except her dance is more vibrant, greater in depth and breadth—both her reach and results. However, these little beasties individuals' dance is consistent. Persistent. Passed down. Despite their weak individual impact, when they gather in groups their dance makes a larger splash. They even gather in such numbers that their dances propel them beyond what I thought possible of them. Their progress only hastening as their numbers swell. They even begin to land blows to my siblings, not that I mind. Very minor, but impacts none the less

their visit to my defeated Brother was a surprise, though they have not yet returned to him. I do not blame them, compared to me he is but a husk, missing greatness because of his blunder. His challenge against me

disgusting. Ever since my greatest pride, my Daughter, relinquished the haze that surrounded her, she has been nothing but covered in incessantly moving things. Crawling, scuttling. Enveloping her surface. Are these her creations? Pathetic, not that I can blame her much for this. After all, I did similar with forming our solar family here. Fewer individuals, but mighty individuals by comparison. She shall never be as bright as I, she persists in developing her exterior and those boundless beings which flourish upon her. Even her subservient sibling, having lost their bout, imitates my being better; cheap reflection though it may be. Such an insignificant part of my light, yet he reflects more than she, though he has not his own children. If hers can be called that

nay. It has taken more of their lifetimes than I care to count, but her 'children' are nothing more than parasites. They feed upon her, draw out parts from within her and corrupt her face. Her caps recede. Aggressive retaliation by growing the depths that then encompass the lands. Destructive waves annihilating their creations. Then it happened. They spread, as all infections do. As Dark Devourers do. First to her defeated sibling, then the rusty red rock

a new dawn across our system, Sol. Our data-slabs record the 'Great Ascension' where we, humanity, began our gradual evacuation of our Mother Earth. To think that our ancient ancestors existed millions of years before civilisation began stretching across the solar system, reaching out into the stars. Claiming new homes on Mars, our new Father. Hearing from peers of the gradual decline of our star—the source of our very lives slowly taking away our ancestral home. As it burns through hundreds of millions of tonnes of its stellar fuel per second, for billions of years, increasing in heat gradually all the way and bombarding the Earth's atmosphere. Tearing it molecule from molecule. Bleeding Earth's oceans dry. A desolate wasteland. We still have books of similar stories, well they're slabs. Most ancient texts remain 'sealed for posterity'. No matter. The Earth resulted as it is now, as I have always known it—the closest planet to the Sun. My ancient relatives, those who made away from Earth, will have witnessed the beginning of the Sun's excruciatingly slow death rattle as it expanded within the system. Engulfing planets not seen for millennia. 'Mercury' and 'Venus'. Sure, we have solar history classes. We experience what they once were through the Solar Network Databank, so long as we have slabs to connect with, download with. But it's a far cry from looking out at Jupiter, the giant standing out in the distance. It's spot like an eye casting a gaze upon our system. "The Great Watcher," though we're told the spot itself was once great in size. Indeed, this isn't even the first spot upon its surface, far from the original. It is our original. Here. Now

the time, it seems, is finally upon us. My generation had not expected to see it. Perhaps our children's children, or theirs. But after my lifetime of labour, of a societally unifying push towards a greater future. Exploration. Planets. After all that, I get to see Earth's end before I join it. The Sun's encroaching boarders consuming our ancestral home. Perpetually tearing pieces from her till not even dust remain. A civilisation-wide alert. All of humanity, in this moment, sending final wishes, final thanks for all that she had done for our species, though none of us living having ever known her love. Will our descendants look back and see our new Father receiving a similar fate? Again, the Networks slabs suggest the sun will cool, shrink, and finally fade. Oh, how different they may be in relation to us, as we are to Terrans. What home will they adapt to, as we adapted to Mars? Shrink as opposed to our growth? Increased radiation resistance? Stronger bones where ours weakened? Do we push our race towards a bottleneck we cannot escape? Clueless. Pointless. I haven't the time to know

the fact that we breathe,

inhale and exhale each day,
life's simple rhythm

the great Dark Devourers, surrounded by dancing coalescences of burning beacons, signalling to one another as they are dragged across the dark into conflicts with other Devourers; their innumerable beacons in tow. Carving up one another's routine, morphing into a daunting duet whilst backed by incalculable galactic flowers in various stages of sprout, bloom, or decay. Many with their own supporting dancers of blues, browns, and reds. Some with smaller still, circling in predictable patterns, illuminated by their shining seniors amidst the dark. For time immemorial would the Dark Devourers join in daring duets, one eventually claiming the other as their own

stellar flowers continue their stages of life, the older seeding conditions for newer, dimmer, flowers

as the light fades, their dances slow

distance grows between all Dark Devourers and eventually starvation sets in as all grow weary

as the final flowers fade, like a candle flickering before being snuffed by an unseen hand, their dances ceased

as all within reach is consumed, the Devourers too shall fade into time beyond time. Their final, mournful sighs as all unravels, dissipating into the vast void. Darkness and cold, a place beyond space

Gradually, expansion ceases weighing in

the long dark's expanse receded. Initially, at no more a pace than a worm writhes across the ground. A beetles pace. Eventually eclipsing the pace of a retreating rabbit toward its burrow

gathering. Gathering, gathering

collapsing in like a Dark Devourer of old gorging upon itself

peice by picee te riang itfels aarpt

utinl nhtonig rmaeniedw olhe

tehn crhsunig lal peecies itno nwewhleos

noesignluarwohle

galsinurtiy

Dmitriy Galkovskiy [1]

Good Friday Fable #1

A CERTAIN CLASSICAL RODENT distinguished by keen inquisitiveness was once ferreting around in the winery, when it collapsed into the amphora and precipitately choked to death on wine. On the ensuing day the amphora was expedited to the quayside where it was loaded onto a vessel. Thunderbolts fulminated into the vessel during a tempest, conflagration erupted, and the argosy sank midway en route from Jaffa to Piraeus. In 3694 the amphora with mummified crystallized ullage was surfaced and a fossilized rat was hewn out from it. The architectonics of the specimen's volatile memory was successfully dumped through algebraic mapping, and by proxy of the 16-dimensional mainframe emulating lower mammalian sensorial susceptibility, relevant visual arrangements were actualized. It transpired that the rat which so (in)felicitously floundered into the amphora, six hours heretofore had been in attendance during the interrogation of Christ by Pontius Pilate.

In 5118 a retro-electronic archaeological mission fortuitously lucked upon clandestine findings on that matter. Regretfully, the then retrieved informational chip of the iconic grid NN-4 was almost utterly damaged, and, in the ultimate reckoning, the system yielded a swath of the spreadsheet of contents: disparate fragments of the dialogue, and two video snapshots (from amongst the total of two million collated data sets). A sessile gentleman robed in Roman vice-regal vestments was seen on the former, the least corrupted frame. The optics is extraordinarily bungled: worm's-eye and lateral-side views. A hulking Romanesque-sandaled foot is visible, a disproportionately dwarfish head with a comparatively hypertrophied mandible, a forearm with a sigil ring rests on the knee. Opposite stands Christ—an approximately

[1] Translated by Alexander Sharov

quadragenarian, swarthy-complexioned Semite, luxuriously gowned, aquiline hooked nose, wispy beard, bloated cheeks. The focalization of the snapshot (chromatic splotch) is the sigil ring, an ostentatiously flamboyant one, supposedly, the artifact riveting the gnawer's alertness at this particular moment. The latter snapshot is severely blurred. Pilate is scarcely discernible thereon. Christ is expostulating on something, gesticulating with his hand straight at the rat. A hexapod (conjecturally, *Blatta orientalis*) is zigzagging across the foreground. The semantic cynosure of the snapshot is not prioritized—the instant of shifting attention from the insect on the background is videoed. Evidently, the rat lusted to ingurgitate the Blattoptera but was diverted by an exclamation.

Extant gleanings from the conversation were exportable solely into plain textual file format. Consequently, fidelity of disambiguation between who had apostrophized whom cannot be validated. The duologue was held in Latin bureaucratese of the 1st century AD, and respective sayings were, with a certain degree of tentativeness, rendered into icon-based Vision English. Altogether, nineteen utterances were unscrambled:

1. Now then, we shall be sorting out the question in terms of funding.
2. Let us conventionalize thus.
3. It is opined that thy folks ought to be disposed of.
4. Where is your acolyteship?
5. Thou wilt become shorter by the head.
6. Where is the baksheesh?
7. Now, we shall be resolving the question of talents' casting.
8. Hands will be struck upon [hereunder?].[2]
9. To vilipend and denigrate.
10. To tweak the issue.
11. Incentivizing and streamlining the modus operandi.
12. To provincialize it to the Collegium? The Sun is surer to prostrate down onto the Earth!
13. In a wrongful light.
14. When the time is ripe, we shall moot this suggestion likewise.

---

[2] *Hereunder* is obfuscated, whether figuratively or in the truest sense of the word.

15. From the rightful perspective, delight of my eyes.
16. A clerkly drudge.
17. Twist the neck off the parasitical bourgeois rat.
18. The sycophant must be hung on a rope's end moistened in asinine urine.

The last/nineteenth piece was identified as positively attributable to Christ:

19. I beseech thee not to intimidate me anymore. Altogether, I am clueless as to what Your August Lordship is speaking about. I shall resurrect and persist everlastingly. My father, Lord, my God hath behested thus.

Laura McPherson

FitYou

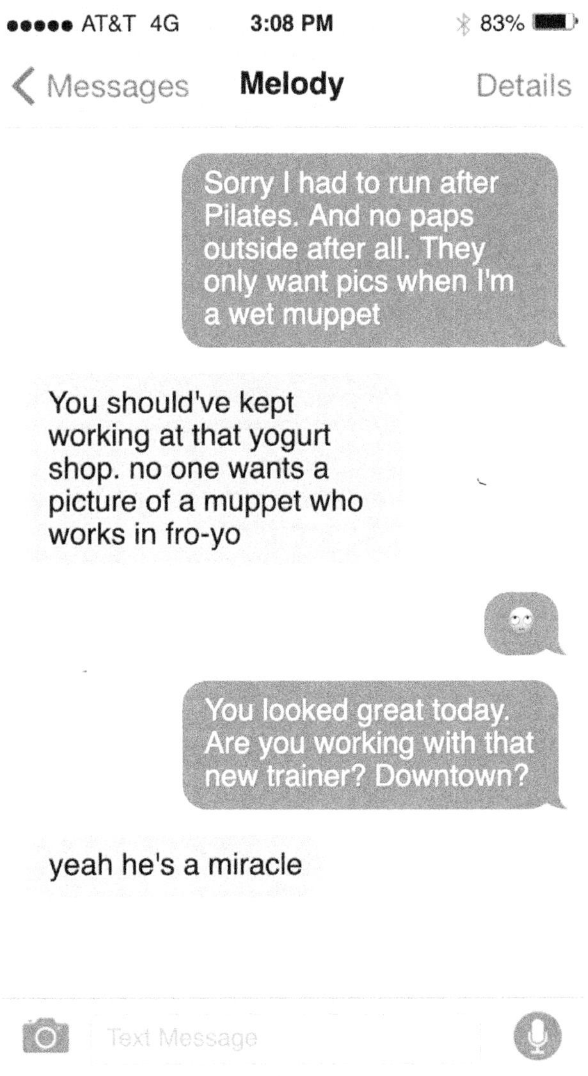
AT&T 4G
3:08 PM
83%
Messages
Melody
Details
Sorry I had to run after Pilates. And no paps outside after all. They only want pics when I'm a wet muppet
You should've kept working at that yogurt shop. no one wants a picture of a muppet who works in fro-yo
You looked great today. Are you working with that new trainer? Downtown?
yeah he's a miracle
Text Message

●●●●● AT&T 4G 3:08 PM 83%

Messages **Melody** Details

That you won't introduce me to.

He's topped with clients. 😔

I got you a reservation at Scale & Toadstool the night they opened

Sorry

When was I skinnier, the popcorn diet or the rice diet?

That's my private miracle trainer. Rice.

Text Message

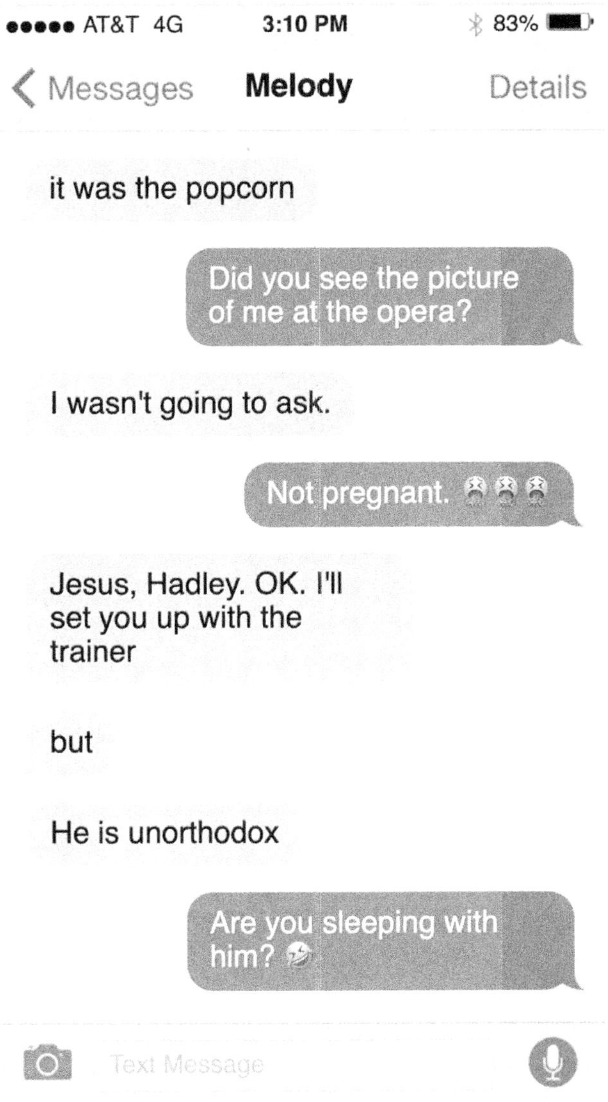
AT&T 4G
3:10 PM
83%
Messages
Melody
Details
it was the popcorn
Did you see the picture of me at the opera?
I wasn't going to ask.
Not pregnant.
Jesus, Hadley. OK. I'll set you up with the trainer
but
He is unorthodox
Are you sleeping with him?
Text Message

●●●●○ AT&T 4G
3:21 PM
82%
Messages
Breadwinner $$
Details
Melody has a new personal trainer. She looks amazing
And you want to go?
I would *like* to, yeah
but I know we said we would cut back on security costs etc
I don't think you need it. But if it's what you want, we'll make it happen.
Text Message
Send

●●●●● AT&T 4G 3:24 PM 82%

< Messages **FitYou** Details

Hi! This is Hadley. Your current client Melody is referring me.

Hey VIP! Let's get you started!

What did your friend tell you about how we work?

Nothing. Actually, she specifically said she's not allowed to say anything.

We only admit a select group to Platinum training! Can you come in this afternoon? We'll start slow, but you'll feel the 🔥 later!

Text Message Send

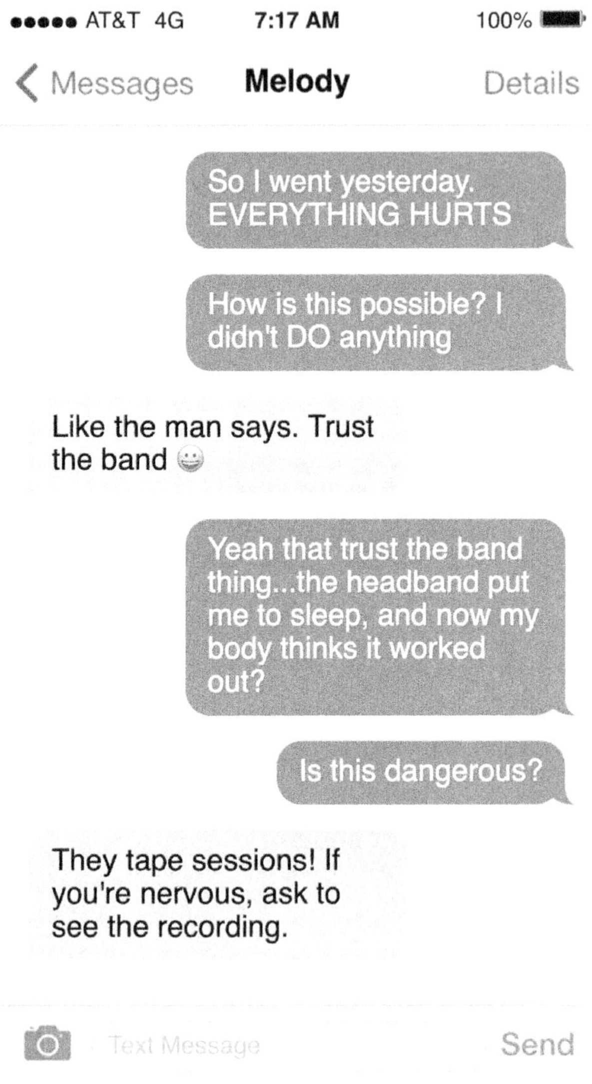
●●●●● AT&T 4G
7:17 AM
100%
Messages
Melody
Details
So I went yesterday. EVERYTHING HURTS
How is this possible? I didn't DO anything
Like the man says. Trust the band 😀
Yeah that trust the band thing...the headband put me to sleep, and now my body thinks it worked out?
Is this dangerous?
They tape sessions! If you're nervous, ask to see the recording.
Text Message
Send

AT&T 4G
9:22 AM
95%
Messages
FitYou
Details
Did you get the email with the session video?
I did. Sorry for being paranoid. I didn't know I could do that!
You killed it!
But why don't I remember?
That's the beauty of FitYou. We take out the pain and leave you with gains. All that's left is a new and better you.
Text Message
Send

AT&T 4G
12:43 AM
31%
Messages
Breadwinner $$
Details
I saw your red carpet.
You looked amazing!
I already lost five pounds with FitYou, and it's only been a month!
But where were/are you? You said you'd be there
Emergency :(
When am I going to be an emergency
I'm stuck at the office.
Ugh stop texting me
Text Message
Send

●●●●● AT&T 4G
10:40 AM
85%
Messages
FitYou
Details
Hey Hadley! Just wanted to check in on you after our rough session today.
Oh thanks.
After review we think you dreamed. That shouldn't have happened, and I apologize.
But I was awake
You were??
And I saw myself exercising.
Hell yeah!
Text Message
Send

●●●●● AT&T 4G
10:48 AM
85%
Messages
FitYou
Details
That's what we're about at FitYou.
I guess it was a dream though
And that's fine. Totally safe.
But just to stay safe, let's have you skip your next session and rest up
Okay??
Right.
Thank you!
Text Message
Send

●●●●○ AT&T 4G 4:51 PM 60%

< Messages **Melody** Details

Did you ever meet the nurse at FitYou?

In passing. I love that they have one on duty

Did anything weird ever happen? Did you ever like, remember anything?

If I wanted to remember how much I hate working out, I would go to regular Pilates

Yeah

But. Something weird happened yesterday

Text Message

●●●●○ AT&T 4G 10:40 AM 59%

Messages **Melody** Details

The session started like normal but I woke up. But I wasn't in the room with the table you lay down on and the headband, I was in like, this BLACK space

I couldn't BREATHE and there was a TV there and I saw myself on the TV working out

But on the TV my eyes were *green*

Didn't you wear green contacts for that one movie with the rollercoaster stunt

Text Message

●●●●○ AT&T 4G
10:45 AM
59%
Messages
Melody
Details
A, that was years ago and second, this is different
I wasn't acting, it was me, but it wasn't me
Do you think maybe you were having a bad dream?
That's what the trainer said...
Don't you think he knows? Do you FEEL ok?
Yeah, I guess you're right
Text Message

●●●●○ AT&T 4G 10:47 AM 59%

< Messages **Melody** Details

Maybe my brain like, noticed the nurse's eyes are green and went nightmare mode from stress. idk

Do you need a break maybe?

I'm taking one. Next session is Friday

Good. Take care of yourself

Mhmm

Thank you

Text Message

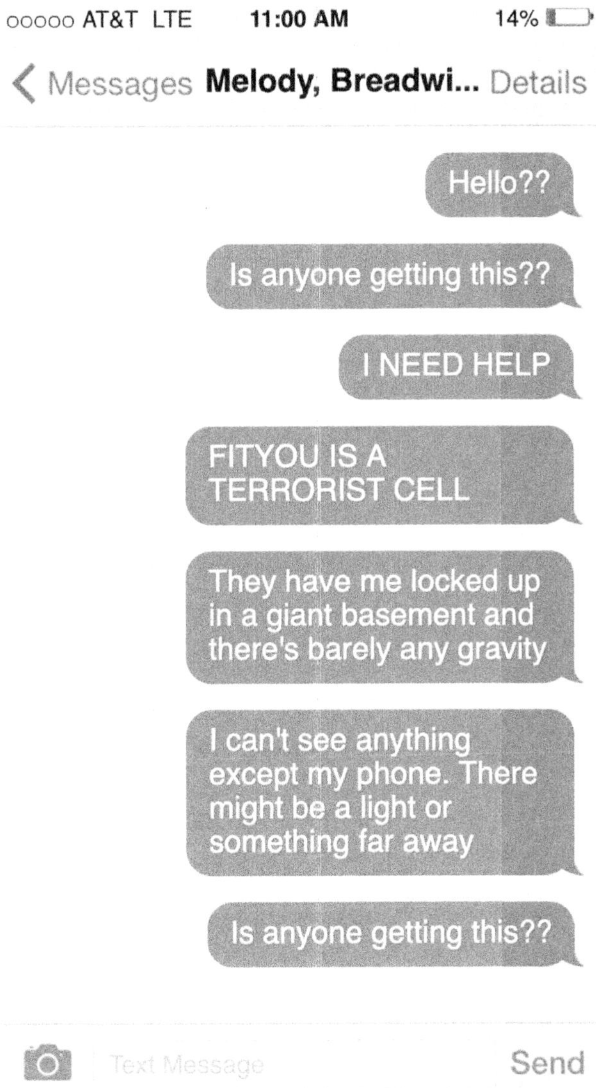
ooooo AT&T LTE 11:00 AM 14%
Messages Melody, Breadwi... Details
Hello??
Is anyone getting this??
I NEED HELP
FITYOU IS A TERRORIST CELL
They have me locked up in a giant basement and there's barely any gravity
I can't see anything except my phone. There might be a light or something far away
Is anyone getting this??
Text Message
Send

ooooo AT&T LTE
11:00 AM
9%
Messages
Melody, Breadwi...
Details
They're blackmailing me with a deepfake video, they want control of the company honey
They want me to make you join. DON'T
Melody I swear to god if you knew about this
PLEASE someone respond
I'm going to check out the light
Please respond anyway. Please
Text Message
Send

ooooo AT&T LTE 11:14 AM 1%
Messages Melody, Breadwi... Details
HONEY
I AM AT THE TV I SEE YOU
THAT IS NOT ME. LOOK AT HER EYES
MY EYES ARE *BLUE*
Oh my god my battery is draining so fast
I don't know where I am. Please
HONEY. My eyes are NOT GREEN I am begging y
Text Message
Send

Kim J. Cowie

Eastern City Vibes

THE SWORDSWOMAN LANNAIRA HAJAN lives in rooms in the Old City of Chazu; she supports herself here by mysterious means, for rents here are not cheap. She does not teach at any of the martial arts ryo; she dislikes competitiveness. Sometimes she is seen in the streets, taller than the native people, with a curved sword strapped over her shoulder. She is also known as Hajan, the dancer. Some think that she is clever; many believe that she is crazy. She has, however, influential friends, including Nakamara, who owns a factory making PCN network telephones, to a design pirated from the West.

Time is an uncertain thing in Chazu; all the inhabitants wear a watch to remind them of their own time and warn them of discontinuities. Sometimes the watches display meaningless digits. Lannaira dreams of waking up to hear that time has changed so much that the stereo sets have gone from the stone streets and there is only the shout of musical instruments and the noise of the bare feet of the people on the stones. Lannaira measures time by the beat of drums; she refuses to wear a watch.

In an upper room of an Inner City restaurant, Lannaira dines with two of her admirers. She has lured them here, promising to tell them of her new quest. Part of the floor, with tables, is raised. At one end a jazz trio, Chinese in dinner suits, plays cool jazz, Miles Davis.

"Nakamura wants me to watch the Xi Yuan gang," she says. "He threatens trouble if I don't produce a result."

"What's this Xi Yuan gang?" Dick asks. He is tall, black-haired and English, newly arrived from Britain to re-staff a games software company.

"They are agents of chaos, feeding on unnatural magical things. They exploit disorder. He asked me to look for anything strange and alive. Anything unnatural and new. Shining beetles that turn the earth into metal and plates of silica. Green flowers. A grey paste that turns old things into new. Bricks that whisper secrets."

“And then what?” Dick asks. “Could be nanotechnology.”

Lannaira points a chopstick at him. “That sort of thing’s bad for business. So Nakamura sends in his heavies, or the police. Crack heads, revoke their licences, close them down, drive them off the streets.”

She carries on eating, from a plate piled with stir-fried shrimp and tangtuan.

“Why you?” Pi Yu asks. “This sounds like poetry, or madness.”

Pi Yu, an architect without commissions, is very poor. He talks passionately of strange gleaming buildings that he sees in his head, but which probably will never be built.

Lannaira shrugs. “He say, why not me? Go and be useful. I have sharp eyes and ears.”

The musicians continue to play. Lannaira gets up and dances. Eyes of the diners follow her. Tallish, blonde, athletic of limb; she is a striking figure. Often Lannaira goes dancing with Pi Yu. When either of them has earned a little money, they go to one of the gleaming discotheques, where the young, stirred by sex, display themselves in their evening finery, and dance to thumping hypnotic music.

Presently she sits. She draws a circle of spilled wine with her finger. “Perhaps you can help me look...?”

“How is Nakamura paying you?” Dick asks.

With a lucidity unusual for her, Lannaira explains. “With bank transfer. Also, I am having trouble with my papers. Men ask me questions, ask me to show my work permit. There are things I cannot explain. Lord Nakamura has delayed these tiresome matters for me, but I may be carried away, carried off...”

“Deported,” Dick interjects.

“Deported. If I find these magics for him, things may be different. Papers signed.”

Both men desire her; Lannaira, not so fey in all matters, is well aware of this. Inevitably, they agree to help her quest.

Dick asks how Lannaira gained the confidence of the wealthy industrialist.

Lannaira had been dining at another restaurant—the Flying Red Fish, with Pi Yu. Lannaira, discontented, left the restaurant first, and stood in the road waiting for the other to emerge. A golden beetle crawling among dirt in the gutter caught her eye, and she crouched down to look at it. In the street, short men with brown weathered faces had gathered, with fur caps and skin coats, all wearing crude swords at their waists. They spoke a gibberish that even the Chinese can hardly understand. Lannaira glanced at them, then dismissed them from her attention. There were many strange peoples in the city now.

A short man wearing a lapel-less grey business suit and a flat skullcap stepped out of the restaurant, head bowed in thought, and shuffled along the pavement as though he expected to be lost in the city's millions.

The tribesmen however had noticed him. They tossed down balls that exploded like firecrackers. Butterflies flew up from around his feet. They surrounded him and shouted abuse and three of them draw their swords, crude lengths of sharp iron.

She straightened from her perusal of the golden beetle and strode through the mob of tribesmen, who were like dwarves around her, and reached the Asian man's side. She yelled at the tribesmen, telling them to bugger off. They stared back truculently. Though she wore her own sword strapped across her back, she left it in its sheath.

Pi Yu ran out, but with a shake of the head and a sharp gesture of her hand, she warned him back. The situation was tense; any wrong gesture would cause it to erupt into violence.

"What do you want?" she demanded of them. The tribesmen did not answer; a bad sign. They surrounded Lannaira and the businessman in a half-circle closed by the wall.

The small men redoubled their insults. "Bignose! White whore!" Some of them, she noted, had composite bows of the kind used from horseback. It was unwise to turn her back on them now.

One of the swordsmen lunged forward. With a single movement, she drew her own weapon, swayed to one side and flicked the end of it across the throat of the attacker. He fell with a gurgle. The others rushed forward, screaming tribal cries. Steel clashed on iron; she parried with a strong arm, she danced aside when their notched swords swung, and her blade, gleaming dully in the street lights, was quick to wound. An arrow whicked past her, missing narrowly and cracked against a concrete wall.

A shot crackled and echoed among the tall buildings. A man with dark glasses, evidently a bodyguard, stood in the restaurant doorway. He blew smoke from the barrel of a long pistol, while a tribesman fell, shot in the act of swinging his dirty notched iron sword at Lannaira.

The tribesmen sagged back and picked up their wounded. All ran off.

The man at the centre of the turmoil had never lost his composure. Now he took out a business card and presented it to Lannaira. "I am Nakamura," he said. Clearly he thought this was sufficient introduction. Probably not Chinese, anyway. "Come call on me; I can be useful to you." He gave a curious bow, like a Japanese, and walked away. Twenty metres down the road, a large black Lexus private car was parked. He opened the kerbside door and as he got in, Lannaira heard him shouting at the driver.

A hairclip in Lannaira's blonde hair catches the light. If it were of solid gold, and had real jewels in it, and was as antique as it looks, it would have cost a great deal of money. But to buy such a lovely ornament, and wear it in this rather unsafe city, is the sort of thing a swordswoman would do.

The hour is late. All the food has been eaten. Dick waves his charge card to attract the attention of a Korean waiter, and soon they are able to go. She expects to see Pi Yu the next day, to begin the quest.

Next day, with Pi Yu, Lannaira takes an electric taxi to the suburb of Longbai. At Zhongshan Bei Street the driver stops and refuses to go any further.

"What's he saying?" says Lannaira.

"He says his battery is low. He must recharge," says Pi Yu.

She makes a face, but he presses the door release and gets out. Chinese mill on the pavement, half thrusting them back onto the road. Pi Yu, too shy to argue, pays the driver.

"He's afraid," she says. She bends to shout at the driver, but he is already turning, cutting in front of two mopeds, which stop with a squeal of brakes, honking, riders cursing.

They walk onwards, while Lannaira looks around for zone things. Open-fronted shops and street stalls sell an assortment of cheap and counterfeit goods, from stinky perfumes to unreliable BD players and badly stitched fashion garments. Men hang about, offering white narcotic powders when approached. Lannaira's eyes narrow, but she says nothing.

The press on the pavements thins. They cross Changning Road and duck under a line of plastic flags. They tread through an almost deserted street before coming to an open area of grass and rubble. The wind blows the sound of a shrill siren from the train yards, and the rumble of wheels.

The hands of Pi Yu's cheap Taiwan watch spin rapidly backwards. It is the fringe of a zone. One of the midget tribesmen emerges from under some rubble, which glitters and shimmers, and hurries past them. Weeds grow at their feet. Some of them have green flowers.

The zone is a region of inaccessibility, afflicted by time. The zones are the curse of Chazu and at the same time the source of its distinction, for many think they connect to other dimensions, other worlds.

"It's expanding," Lannaira says. Pi Yu nods. He sees a movement at his feet. It is an empty lunchbox, which is stirring as though a large insect was underneath. It inches forward, then bobs over the grass towards the road.

"What the—"

Lannaira quickly picks up a used chop-stick and uses it to flip the box over.

"It's got legs!"

Pi Yu stares at the underside of the plastic box in shock. Four plastic legs are slowly waving in the sunlight. For him, it has all the unnaturalness of a hallucination, for the legs have no mechanical joints and no source of motive power.

"Devil!" he whispers and fingers the cross about his neck.

Lannaira tips the box back onto its legs and kneels to watch it. It resumes its walk, and soon speeds up to a scamper as it reaches the pavement.

"That other box is alive!" Pi Yu yells, in a frenzy. With sunlight shining on its inside, the second box is growing legs and crawling after the first.

The first box skitters between the legs of pedestrians and launches itself into the road as Lannaira, who clearly does not share his feelings at all, watches it with a mixture of amazement and mirth. She looks so lovely it hurts. The box has made it almost all the way across the street when an electric scooter flattens it. The breeze of the following vans tosses it into the gutter. Lannaira keeps her eyes on the wrecked box.

"It's growing!" she shouts. The second box has now reached the pavement, and as it launches itself among the legs of the crowd, the first box straightens itself out and crawls out of the gutter onto the far pavement. "Yes!"

Pi Yu joins her and they watch the second box scuttle across the road, narrowly avoiding the wheels of several vehicles.

Lannaira runs into the road without looking. There is a terrible screech of brakes as a taxi slews to a stop. Pi Yu feels the blood drain from his face, but almost at once sees that she is unharmed. The taxi driver gets out to remonstrate with her, but she turns and makes a rude and threatening gesture with her fingers. He backs off.

"It's zone stuff!" says Lannaira with unusual enthusiasm. "Fantastic!"

Across the street, they pursue the boxes past the front of the bento box shop and down a tiny entry passage. The yellow boxes hop into an open shed where Pi Yu catches a glimpse of metal tanks part full of water, stacks of plastic boxes, and sacks of rice.

"Ai!" They turn to find a fat Chinese glowering at them.

"We were following our lunchboxes," Pi Yu explains, blushing.

A rainbow of expressions flit across the fat man's face as they question him, from suspicion, to alarm, obsequiousness, and cunning.

Lannaira steps forward. "Where did you get these boxes?"

"When did you start using them?" demands Pi Yu. "Don't they cause accidents?"

The man won't say where he got the boxes. "Very good price," he keeps repeating. "Was the lunch good?"

"It was very good," Lannaira says. Before Pi Yu can think of another question, the man rushes off, to return with a red box, which he thrusts into Lannaira's hands.

"Compliments of chef. Go away now. Busy."

Pi Yu thinks that if he offered money the man might tell them where he got the boxes. There is one small problem. He hasn't any.

In the street they share the contents of the box, which has spare ribs, papadums and pickles in it. They put the box down in the sun and watch it.

"Why boxes with legs?" Lannaira asks.

"So they can be re-used," says Pi Yu. "Maybe they wash themselves, too." The thought makes Lannaira giggle, and she wipes a sticky hand along his cheek. "But we don't know where they come from. Tell Mr Nakamura?"

"Yes, tell. He'll want them suppressed. Unnatural."

"Pity. They amusing."

"Nearly caused road accident. Not good."

Pi Yu sighs.

It is Dick who suggests they make the trip to the docks by boat. That evening, both admirers are free to pursue the quest. They board a sampan at a little dock by the southern end of the Bund. Lannaira is unhappy; she does not like the river.

Dick pushes off with an oar, then switches on the electric motor. On each side of the river, lights glitter from the riverbanks and from the faces of the buildings. Lights reflect from the dark water in long, rippling trails.

The boat, propelled by a whirring and bubbling at its stern, moves out into the wideness of the river. Far ahead, a chain of lights detaches itself from the brightness of the shore and comes closer. Above the murmurings from the shore, and the honkings of vehicles on the Bund, they hear the beat of amplified pop music. Pi Yu and Dick vie to point out the source of the sound; while the real object of their attention, Lannaira, lies in the front of the boat on some cushions, saying little. A faint scent drifts by; bundles of flowers floating on the water.

Applause clatters across the water. A pop concert is in progress, on an open-air stage beside the Bund. The group, Pi Yu announces, is Chinese, imitators of the pop musician Ciu Juan.

"A magical city," Pi Yu murmurs. "Do you feel the magic breaking through, mocking all our inventions?"

Lannaira gave him a look.

Dick nods.

"There are people in my street who can tell fortunes with knuckle bones. Who can heal the sick with their hands," Pi Yu says.

"Fraudsters," Dick says. "They need sorting out."

"There are such, Pi Yu," she said. "Look at the city now. And I too, am a sorceress..."

But the men do not take this last remark seriously.

A train of barges draws alongside and chugs past. Its wash catches the sampan, which rocks and pitches violently. Dick swears, and complains against Pi Yu for rocking the boat. Lannaira clings to the sides, not liking the motion.

A crescent of moon shows through the cloud.

A kilometre further downriver, they came to the moored ships clustered in an inlet. The towering aluminium foils of self- rigging sails blotted out the stars. A few lights showed on board the sail-assisted motor ships. "Which is

Nakamara's ship?" Dick asks.

"The third one, with the red funnel." Lannaira is looking around. All seemed quiet. "Keep going downriver."

"Aren't we going on board?" As he spoke, Dick put the helm over and headed in towards the ship. Lannaira scrambled aft, wrenched the helm from his hands, and put it hard over, turning away from the ships.

"What the-"

"They have rat-tat guns on board! Nakamura tired of pirates!"

Aboard the third ship, another porthole lights up. Dick crouches low. "You mean they might shoot at us?"

"Yes."

"Jesus Christ!"

Further on, Lannaira points to a ship shrouded in darkness. "Ghost ship. Don't look straight at it."

In averted vision, the ship has three square-rigged masts with furled sails. Viewed directly, it just looks like a modern ship. Distinctly odd.

They land further downstream and tie up the sampan. Pi Yu feels exposed as they walk back through the docks, toward the quay where the mystery ship is tied up. On the landward side, the ship is lit up by floodlights, but the view is blocked by a warehouse and parked container trucks. Xi Yuan's goons stand around, discouraging closer investigation.

Further on, they hail Nakamura's ship. A gangplank is run down to hit the dock with a clatter. They ascend under the eyes of sailors with guns, and as soon as they set foot on the steel deck, the gangway is hauled up after them.

Nakamura-san, the Japanese-born shipowner and industrialist, is in the aft stateroom. He wears traditional Japanese dress, including a curved sword belted to his waist. He has a boxer's face and a scar across one cheek. Security men wave Lannaira through. Nakamura questions Lannaira about her observations, before delivering a long complaint about unscrupulous competitors, gangsters and the adverse effect of zones on business.

"Thank you; once again you have helped me, a poor foreigner. I will contact the authorities, and they can neutralise this ghost ship. This weirdness no good for business, whatever they doing."

Pi Yu sees Dick smile at this. So does Nakamura.

Darwin Holmstrom

The Castrated Grail King

He who is not intact, he who is wounded in the stones or hath his privy member cut off shall not enter into the congregation of the LORD.

Deuteronomy 23:1

THE BOY SAT ALONE ON A ROCK at the edge of a forest, planting a seed in the fertile soil of his own mind, the seed of single a word. He watched a honeybee land on his hand and explore its new perch, its spiny legs prickling against his skin. Not long before, the bee would have terrified him. His mother tried to convince him that everything would kill him; she tried to inject fear into the boy like venom, punishing him for sins she herself had committed, both real and imagined. Every time she looked at the boy, her eyes probed him for new shame, a projection of the shame she felt growing inside of herself like a monstrous child that she wanted to abort and leave to die out in the pasture. The pain in his mother's eyes filled him with a hollow feeling, an empty space of loss and regret for things he could never change.

The boy's grandmother had taught him not to fear bees, not to fear his mother. She did everything she could to keep the boy from absorbing his mother's irrational fears, from becoming a dumping ground for her shame. Grandma had a beautiful flower garden surrounding her house and in the summers she and the boy sat on the porch on warm afternoons, amid the flowers. Where there were flowers, there were the bees that the boy's mother feared. One day his grandmother used honey as a poultice to extract that poisonous fear from the boy, spreading it on her hand and letting the bees feast on it. Soon her hand was covered with a glove made of bees. "Do you want to try it?" she asked. The boy did and soon he too was wearing a honey glove made of living bees. The bees flew away when they'd cleaned off the honey. Not one of them stung him.

His grandmother taught the boy that stories held magic, that words have the power to create worlds, that the things we named in our stories become real. Her stories shattered the illusion of truth with moral wisdom, giving them the ability to heal, to put lives back together. She used her stories not as a means of escaping reality or glorifying herself but as tools for opening portals of wisdom to deeper truths, giving her stories the gravity of the boulder upon which the boy sat.

Words build bridges between the conscious and unconscious worlds. Words form the signposts leading to that trail back to ourselves. The mere act of saying something creates a pathway that allowed more things to happen; once a process has a pathway, it runs along that pathway just as water rolling over the earth starts to dig a channel, then follows that channel until it forms a river. Like a barren plain becoming a lush valley thanks to the action of drops of water, words reshape consciousness; magic begins with a thought, the thought becomes a word, and the word becomes reality. The world shimmers and recasts itself to match the words we use to describe it. Humanity, in its purest state of consciousness, enters into a partnership with God by harnessing the magical power of words. We become the stories we tell ourselves.

The boy's own story followed luminous fibers of sensory deprivation into a dark sea of awareness. Suffering he endured along the way forced him to develop physical, mental, and spiritual strength and fashion something beautiful from it. A piece of stone must suffer the blows of the sculptor's hammer before it can emerge as a work of art.

Most humans live their lives without passing through the transformational suffering of pain. They don masks, creating the illusion that they're complete humans, but this pretense numbs their souls. They substitute the intoxication of excess for life and suffer alone, but because they don't suffer enough, they suffer for nothing. Achieving transcendence and leaving behind bestial self-interest requires passing through the sacred pain of suffering completely; only by emerging on the other side of pain can one recover the essence defining human spirit. For much of his life, endless distractions involving the news of the day and the problems of the hour kept the boy from completing the journey through his own pain, making his life's song brittle and cold, leaving him unable to distinguish truth from lies. This rendered him incapable of telling his story since that demanded telling the truth, imperfections and all, regardless of how painful that truth might be.

Over time, the boy left behind incoherent distraction, allowing his story to follow a different path, one leading inward, away from the white noise of the world to a still place. As he'd watched the fragmented world devolve into superficial meditations on possessions and wealth, he'd grown disgusted with the monstrous system that produced robots living not for themselves but for the machine. To avoid becoming a cog in the machine, the boy held onto his own ideals and withdrew from an increasingly synthetic, inorganic world, a world without ethos, with no narrative binding it together; instead, he followed a different path, one leading into himself. The world needed a new story, one not coming from the mind, that Cartesian repository of artificial consciousness, but from the heart, the center of true understanding. The world needed a story like those his grandmother told, one that captured the wisdom of life itself, that encompassed creation, death, and resurrection. The world needed a story rising from the smoke of sacrifices.

This new story emerging from the ashes of the false narrative led away from the machine, toward nature, toward Pachamama, the motivating power that ran through the universe, the very personification of nature. The godhead coursed throughout the entirety of the natural world where it captured the potential animating all life. The Bible taught that life was corrupt, that every natural impulse is sinful unless it has been circumcised or baptized, that nature itself was corrupt and had been since the Fall in the Garden, but the boy knew this wasn't true; God could not condemn nature because God was nature. When Christianity separated God from nature, it divided matter from spirit--it castrated the Grail King. The world needed a new story to restore the Grail King's masculinity and reintegrate physical and spiritual life. All life had been born of Pachamama's womb, but the cord connecting humanity to the earth body had been broken. The world needed a story powerful enough to repair that cord and reconnect spirit with the earth.

Man played God by trying to control nature, by destroying forests and annihilating indigenous people. Humanity needed to put itself in accord with nature, realizing that nature cannot be evil, that every natural impulse is beautiful. The new story needed to destroy the boundaries where nature ended and art began, illuminating man's brotherhood with the animals and the seas. The characters in this new story needed to reflect the wisdom of nature, to speak with the voice of the earth.

Since the gods split everything in two, into good and evil, black and white, male and female, humanity has spent all of its energies trying to reconstitute its original unity, embracing the other half, but this split had just been an illusion; the differences separating man from nature and from one another were superficial and arbitrary. When he looked outside the filter of dogma, the boy saw that everything is part of the same whole. This realization gave him the courage to stare his suffering in the eye and venture to an inner place where the universe was not a duality but a singularity.

L. M. Rainer

Suhail's Revenge

ON ONE OF THE DAYS OF DAYS, Suhail came to Ashtaran with a camel caravan. He looked dusty, sandy, tired, thirsty and wind-blown like all the young men who worked on caravans, but he wasn't like the other young men who worked on caravans.

The others were young and fool-hardy, they loved to wander, whatever was over the next hill was always better than whatever was in front of them. They felt safest bedded down deep in trackless dunes, camels coughing and always on alert for danger. Happiest with camels, whose lineage they knew like their own, they felt shy in town. With their heads slightly bowed, they looked up at the wonders of Ashtaran through thick eyelashes. Their first stop was the barbers, then a tea-house at the edge of the souq where they could see the sky and the far hills.

Suhail hated the wandering and wasn't much impressed with camels. They all looked rather the same and sand as an agent to sleep on was vastly overrated. He liked rocks; he liked paths. He looked Ashtaran right in the face, like a bridegroom finally alone with his new wife trying to figure out, "what do we have here?" He went right to the street of rice-sellers, stopping in each shop to see the wares.

He saw nothing of interest, nothing familiar, and no small black sacks of rice, so a feeling of anger and hopelessness grew, but as he left the last shop, almost to the point of tears for the first time in his life, the call to prayer sounded.

He turned towards the sound—prayer. He should pray. And he should keep heart; God had been merciful enough to bring him after ten years of wandering to Ashtaran. Surely, he would not have been spared so many potential deaths just to fail once he reached his goal.

In the covered souq, he could not see the nearest mosque, so he asked a passing man. It was Khalfan, the djinn of animals, who understanding

Suhail's intention a moment before Suhail himself realized it, had changed from a mouse to a man.

"Do you want the Grand Mosque?" he asked, knowing Suhail had other ideas.

"No, please, just a simple one," Suhail replied.

"Follow me."

Suhail trailed the tall man in the light blue turban, grateful that the stranger did not want to go through all the normal pleasantries and ask dozens of questions about himself and the caravan.

In the area for washing, Suhail lost sight of the man who had helped him, and surprised by a mouse running over his foot, moved forward from a place he had taken in the back, so that he was standing next to a short, round man with a small beard. At the end of prayers, the man unexpectedly turned to him and asked if he was a stranger. When Suhail said, "yes," the man insisted that Suhail join him for dinner.

And, later, when Suhail said that he came with a caravan but wanted to stay in the souq, Khalid said, "A neighbor asked me today if I knew of a strong young man, he sells cotton and needs someone to help him lift the bales."

Suhail agreed and never returned to the caravanserai. After dinner, his new friend Khalid took him to meet the cotton merchant and he slept that night on the lumpy but soft sacks of cotton. He worked hard and was given a fair wage, which he spent Khalid's café.

Khalid's café was famous in Ashtaran because he sold tea for the price of the smallest brass piece. It was also famous because the tea always came with a piece of the delicious coconut cake called *basbosa* or almonds cooked in the darkest brown sugar, or a floury cookie with a date in the middle, or if you were very young or very hungry, all three. And it was famous because none of the chairs or tables matched.

The café never had mirrors or fancy things, but sometimes a man would walk by the café and remember the nights he spent there, back when he was young and hungry, and the man would laugh and pat his big belly and think of the pieces of *basbosa*, and sugared almonds and date cookies. Then the man would walk to the section of the souq with the furniture sellers and ask for a big table, in the newest style and made from the finest wood, or a chair, padded and fit for a king, and have it sent anonymously to Khalid's café.

But Suhail did not notice the mis-matched chairs or the wonderful *basboasa*. He did notice the quick glances of Selma, Khalids's pretty daughter, but he pretended he did not notice because he had come to Ashtaran to punish a rice-seller for the deaths of his grandfather and aunts as they huddled in the shelter of rocks during the sandstorm. Although he was too young to realize at the time, as they were dying, they gave him all the food and told him their stories again and again so that he would both live and remember them.

When he woke to find the sandstorm had passed, he turned to say, "We are saved!" and saw their bodies, covered with sand from the last of the storm. His eyes were too dry to cry and his mouth was too dry to say all the necessary prayers. He had covered their faces, turned their bodies in the direction of Mecca and covered them again with sand. Then it was time to see if he would also die on that day.

Within a few hours of walking, before the burning noon sun could kill him, he found a caravan still camped as the people were recovering from the storm. He was given water, a little food, and a job. He worked as he had no choice and over the years he both lost and gained everything. Whatever he had tried to keep hold off was gone: lost in windstorms, stolen by other caravan herders, sold for water, destroyed by sun or rain, by hail or floods. The headscarf his aunts had bought for him before their journey, his grandfather's wallet, a small rock from his grandparents' garden, a scrap of black cloth from one of his aunt's cloak that he intended to pin to the murderer's heart with a dagger—all gone. But the hate was fresh and alive; the sound of his grandfather's words survived, vibrant and new, in his ears with the trill of his aunts' laughter and murmur of the water flowing through the water channels in his grandparents' garden.

At night, no matter how tired he was from working with the camels, he would repeat their stories to himself. He begged learned men, bored at nights while the camels slept, to teach him to read and write, to tell the directions by the stars and to read maps, always promising to go to Ashtaran to revenge his aunts.

And now he was finally here, in Ashtaran, the place of vengeance, but how could he find the man who sold his grandfather the spoiled rice? Who was he supposed to take his revenge against? He went to Khalid's café almost every night for the cheap tea and to hear the news always wondering, would anyone speak of black sacks of rice? Once or twice a week he went along the lane of the rice sellers but never saw small black sacks.

One day while stacking bales of cotton he thought that perhaps he should look at the problem from another angle, not looking at the rice sellers but the sack sellers. That night he went to the lane of the sack makers and sellers and asked about buying small sacks, saying he wanted to send some dates to his family. He went to each seller and found nothing like the black bags of his memory.

Back at Khalid's tea shop, he thought and thought, then thought he should look at the problem from another angle, not from the sack sellers but the canvas makers. The next night he went to the lane of the canvas makers. He looked in each shop, there were rolls of every shade of brown and cream-colored fabric, but nothing black.

"I want to send some dates and cotton to my family; I was told that to buy black canvas is best because it will go across the sea," he told each seller.

"I can get black canvas, but I don't have any right now," each seller said. As he walked away dejected, an old man called out to him.

"I remember one of the rice sellers, Mamil, ordered a large quantity of black canvas, it was years ago but perhaps he still has some, perhaps he would sell you some."

So Suhail started to drink his nightly tea in the small café near the lane of the rice sellers. By listening carefully, he learned which one was Mamil, a serious looking man. Suhail watched and listened; everything was as it should be. But goodness and evil always showed themselves in time, so after the café closed Suhail waited patiently, cold and alone expect for a small nearby mouse (who was of course Khalfan, the djinn of the animals) for many nights until the night came in which the moon did not rise.

And on that night, long past the time all the honest people in Ashtaran souq were asleep, Suhail saw Mamil glide silently out of his store and down a nearby alleyway. Suhail followed on soundless steps. In the area of the sellers of clay pots, where Mamil had no right to be, Suhail saw him quietly open a small door and disappear down a narrow flight of steps. Suhail slipped down the steps and then hid in a dark corner of the sunken room, watching Mamil check several dozen small black sacks.

Then, quickly, Mamil dashed up the steps and locked the door. Suhail felt the cold and heard his grandfather's words: "The man who sold us this worthless rice came to our caravan a few hours after we left Ashtaran, so no one in the city would see what he was doing. He must have soaked the rice and wool in water to make the correct weight, and let it stay in an underground chamber so it became ice; you see the fabric, the cold and water would not go out easily. He sold it to us in the morning, the ice melted and the water disappeared while we were walking and we did not notice."

Suhail could not see, but slowly he felt the walls and shelves of the room, a large barrel of rice, a large barrel of water, and rows of sacks on a low wooden shelf. All the years of working with ropes to hobble camels and tie loads on camels, he quickly untied a sack and then brought some of the rice to his mouth: it was cold and wet, smelling of damp wool. He climbed to the highest stair and brought his cloak over his head, in the dark hearing again his aunts' sweet voices.

When morning came, there was just one small crack of light, but it was enough for Suhail to pick the lock, all camels boys know how, and he slipped down the alley. At Khalid's café, he looked so pale and worn that Khalid have him two cups of tea at the same time and three pieces of *basbousa.*

All the next week as he worked at the cotton seller, he thought and he thought, then finally he thought of a plan, but it would need the help of a pretty girl and he didn't know of any pretty girls except Khalid's youngest daughter, Selma.

He waited for a busy night, when Khalid and his wife were busy with customers, then he climbed the wall next to Khalid's apartment. He peeped in the window to see Selma in the small kitchen making *basbousa.*

"Ah me," he sighed loudly, then waited. There was a whisper of fabric as if a small hand was moving a small part of the curtain to one side.

"Ah woe is me!" There was a whisper of fabric as if a small head was brushing against a small part of the curtain to see better.

"Ah woe betide me," and then Suhail, for the first time ever, told the story of his life. His grandfather, his aunts, the deaths in the sand, and his search. "Now I have found the culprit, and I have a way to make sure he is guilty so that I do not punish someone unfairly, but, oh, I need the help of a person, preferably a beautiful girl. Ah me, if there was only a person to help me."

He took a small sip from his water flask and waited. A few night birds spoke and a lizard (of course it was Khalfan, djinn of the animals who wanted to know what Suhail was planning) walked back and forth along the top of the wall.

"Ah me," came a low, sweet voice. "Here I am spending my days and nights making *basbousa* for my father's café. How I wish I had a noble undertaking to preform, how I wish there might be a person who was in need of help that I might assist as long as the assistance was honorable and would not blemish my reputation, which is heretofore quite stainless."

Suhail smiled. "Ah me, dear nightingale which sounds like a human voice, if only you were human, then I would ask you to go to the shop of Mamil, the rice-seller, tomorrow morning and talk to Mamil in a serious way so that all his attention is on you, and not on a man who was seeking vengeance for the death of three beloved aunts and a grandfather."

"Ah me, is that a night frog that is croaking? That reminds me, I should go to check the rice prices tomorrow but, of course, I will only do that if it is just and no one will be punished unfairly."

"Ah me," replied Suhail, "my plan is honorable, as I am. If Mamil is not to blame, not even one hair on his head will suffer."

"Ah me, my mother will come soon to check on me. I must remind her that I will go in the morning to buy supplies."

Now another man, a lesser man, might have continued to speak, or say 'thank you.' But Suhail was the right sort of man; he said the correct amount of words, not too little, not too much. If the girl did as she said, if his plan worked, there would be time for more words later.

She did as she said. The next morning Suhail invented an excuse to keep him away from the cotton-sellers and he went to the lane of the rice-sellers with a bag of small rocks. Selma appeared and, pretending to be confused, kept Mamil busy explaining the sizes of sacks and prices. Khalfan opened several sacks and slipped rocks in, tying each sack again in the correct way.

The next morning, he sent word to the cotton-seller that he was sick and went again to the lane of the rice-sellers. Very soon a man appeared and began shouting at Mamil, "you put rocks in your bags of rice to make up the weight!"

A crowd gathered. Some people, the clever kind of people, always had a feeling about Mamil, a waiting sort of feeling for something hidden to become clear. And now, perhaps, the time was at hand, the customer argued and Mamil swore innocence and, after being patient until the crowd was a good size, Suhail yelled, "Make him swear." There was a muttering of agreement, yes it was good to make people swear when both were claiming innocence. A man called that he lived just nearby and would bring his holy book, in the silence of waiting, Suhail called again, "Make him swear that he never sold a spoiled sack of rice." Mamil heard the words and realized their danger, but he pretended he was unconcerned.

The book was brought, he laid his hand on it and swore he had not put rocks in the rice. Which was true.

"Make him swear that he never sold a spoiled sack of rice," called Suhail.

Mamil turned to leave, saying that he had already sworn. But something in Suhail's voice, in the unvoiced suspicious of some of the people, of the stillness to the air as if many unseen people holding their breath, caused the master of the rice-sellers to call, "Halt! You will come back and swear again."

Mamil set his hand on the book and swore that he had never put rocks in any sack of rice.

"No," said the master of the rice-sellers. "Swear that you never sold a spoiled sack of rice."

Mamil set his hand on the holy book for the third time but as the first word left his mouth, the book moved away from his hand.

The smallest rustle, the quietest whisper in the crowd stopped. Rice was life and everyone knew that most of the rice was sold to caravans. Spoiled rice in the desert meant death. A man who sold tainted rice was a murderer as sure as if he had drawn a dagger across the neck of a sleeping man.

"Sunset is in three hours," said the master of the rice-sellers and turned his back.

Mamil did not waste his time on words to explain or ask for mercy, he ran to his shop and gathered his money into a sturdy bag. He knew it was of no use to go to the water-sellers, everyone would know of his crime and punishment within minutes. He carefully poured water from the large jug into smaller ones, carefully stoppered them and wrapped bread, dried meat and fruit in a clean piece of canvas. He added warm clothes to the bag and took his walking stick.

He would get nothing for his shop. His store and everything in it would be forfeit—before the noon prayer on the next day it would be sold at auction with the money going to the vizar, who would give it publicly to sheikh of the Grand Mosque for the special fund for travelers in need. But Mamil took the gold he had hidden and a small sack of jewels, then left from a window in the back storeroom.

Of course everyone knew he would go this way, so the small alley was lined with men and, from behind the carved wooded screens, women looked down on him—children stayed silent and did not throw stones or call out. This was a banishment not only from Ashtaran, but from every town in the known world. A punishment that happened rarely and was dealt with utter solemnity.

Mamil walked in silence to the town gate, stopping only to drink and drink again from the well by the Grand Mosque; water which could never be forbidden to anyone. Suhail was not content to watch him pass out of the gate as the other men did, but as Mamil approached the gate, Suhail ran into the guards' quarters and up the internal ladder to the top of the city wall. Although a few guards tried to stop him, older and wiser guards said, "Let him go." They knew a man did not run into the lodgings of 30 guards unless there was something more important than that man's life.

So Suhail was the last to see Mamil. Mamil could sense he was being watched but refused to look back. He walked away from the gates at a steady pace, not flinching when the sunset cannon was fired and the huge gates swung shut. Suhail stood and watched, the guards on duty passing back and forth behind him until Mamil was a small black dot and then gone. And still he stood as the night deepened and the stars came out; then the leader of the guards came to him and forced him to drink some meat broth and then coffee. Later, another guard wrapped a thick cloth around his shoulders. He was still standing at daybreak, looking across the wide, empty plain.

It was the hot season, no caravans were arriving, no animals from town were let out to forage. The heavy door creaked open and only a small swirl of sand came to the threshold of the town. When the sun was starting to make its power known. The leader of the guards came again and said, "Enough." He took Suhail's arm and pulled him across the parapet to the ladder.

Suhail went to this small apartment and slept, when he woke he ate a little, then went to the mosque and prayed all night. The next morning he returned to work; the cotton-seller had been told where Suhail was and did not say anything about his absence, did not even dock his wages.

As usual, he went to Khalid's café at night, but he did not climb the wall to speak to Selma. He sat at a table alone and drank his tea slowly, then went to bed. Selma made excuses to come to the café and looked at him, but she never tried to catch his eye or speak. Other girls might have but she was the right sort of girl; she said the correct amount of words, not too little, not too much. If his plan worked, there would be time for more words later.

After ten days, there was a stir amongst the customers, the head of the guards, who only drank his tea at the café next to the Grand Mosque, a café with silk awnings and plump cushions, had appeared. He surveyed the small café, then walked to Suhail's table and sat down. The chair was old and small, so that he had to balance carefully, but he called out to Khalid for tea.

Suhail did not say anything except the usual greetings as a good man and when the tea was drunk and the *basbousa* was eaten, the head of the guard said quietly, "A traveler brought news, a man in Ashtaran clothing, a merchant, found dead in the rock waste, a terrible sight. He had cut his arms and tried to drink his own blood. The crows attacked while he was still alive. The man was going to bury him but a sandstorm came suddenly and he had to protect his womenfolk. He told me where the body was but I cannot, just now, spare men to go look. It is finished."

Suhail nodded. They both stood and shook hands. Suhail went to the mosque and prayed all the night for his grandfather and three aunts. Then he spent the next night going to the barbers and having his clothes cleaned and pressed and buying a small amount of special cologne.

The night after that, Suhail spoke to Khalid and, after the necessary five days of waiting so that no one could say Khalid was in a hurry to marry off his youngest daughter, Khalid agreed. And Khalfan, the djinn of animals, congratulated himself on his wisdom.

Oz Hardwick

Case Notes from the Float Tank

A CHECK-LIST OF IMMEDIATE CRISES

Between psychoanalysis and a classroom warmup, the government representative asks me about my locality and my sense of home. If it was a food, what would it taste of? If it was music, what would be the bpm? If it was a suspect item, how long would an easily-led backpacker spend in a foreign jail for taping it to their stomach beneath a sweat-stained hoodie, and would anyone care? They take down my answers but their heart's not in it, their eyes drifting from my doorstep to the coast, which used to be miles away but is now licking at the disappearing road. If my house was a movie, which A-listers would nail boards across the windows and doors? If the garden was a jungle, which endangered species would be last to go? If the sea was a foreign language, how tricky would it be to talk our way out of this awkward situation?

DESIRE: A PRELIMINARY ANALYSIS

Wire figures line the walls in attitudes reminiscent of Attic friezes. The analyst is one of those flowers that children draw. A poppy freighted with fat bees. A pansy with a face stamped between pages of a school encyclopaedia, staining the entry for earthquakes. Before we begin, she tells me to lie down and press my ear to the scuffed wooden floor, to concentrate on the rapping tattoo of past footsteps and locate which are mine. Step, step, step. A dove lands and taps the window with a fragrant twig. A raven raps with a fountain pen and pad. *Tell me where you've been, my only, my love*. She writes my words before I speak and the birds curl into each other, yin and yang. *Tell me where you are, my only, my love*. She draws my dreams before I sleep and birds become blooms drooping between pages of an illustrated history of the ancient world. Figures recline on scuffed couches, engulfed in pelts, angular profiles brooking no more questions. We are birds, we are earthquakes. The floor fragments and falls away. I/we waver at precarious altitudes. *We are wired to lightning, my only, my love.*

My Boyhood as a Cat

Once upon a windowsill, I sat like a cat, burrowing into my own lap, licking the fear from every inch of the potential drop. Houses were taller then, but smaller on the inside, and every room had a sewing machine, at which aunties—who weren't really related and had just grown like permed root vegetables in the scrubby patch out back—would chitter and chatter all day all night, their accents skewed by the pins between their lips. They stitched sheets and pillowslips from spiders' webs, school uniforms from milk bottle lids, and parachutes from coalsmoke caught in pigeons' wings. It was a long way down and I was a cat on a hot tin roof, wary of wetting my paws. *Grey cloth, light as light. Drift. Kind faces pinned to windows. Drift. On countless sills, cats lick every drop of falling from their fur. Fearless. Drift.* I closed my eyes and tipped into sky.

Making the Grade

Fourteen years of school taught me how to hide in plain sight, to disappear into questions until there was nothing left but silence. I learnt to evaporate in communal changing rooms and to sink into the names carved on desks by past generations. I learnt to sing myself behind hymn sheets and to swallow the space I occupied as smoothly as pink custard. Most of all, I learnt how to be absent before the sweeping hand could glance my way. It set me up for a life of camouflage, neither wallflower nor fly-on-the-wall, but walled up like a willing dupe in a 50s horror. Walls have ears and type with two invisible fingers: I learnt that at school in the split second before the unprovoked attack simply for occupying an awkward body with a wayward brain. Now you see me. No, you don't.

The Exner Analysis

Each Rorschach blot is a new step in the snow, lining across the transformed landscape. I've a compass and map in a pouch round my neck, but the former is made of chocolate and mottled with fat bloom, while the latter's torn from a so-so fantasy novel that's long out of print, on which all the places are unpronounceable and, ultimately, unconvincing. Fortunately, my psychologist is an old dog with a keen nose and eyes that don't lie, and he or she—I can't tell from this angle—is confident in our progress. *Bird, bat, or butterfly?* it prompts in a patient voice, though each shape is just another boot seething with chill as it sinks in search of something solid that I'm sure must be down there somewhere, because I'm certain it wasn't always like this. Once there were faces and flowers, and once there were hands to hold. It was a land before snow, and I was unwrapping chocolates, turning pages, following a simple hero and his dog towards a signposted conclusion. The next blot is a bare foot, and after that there's nothing.

A Sense of Perspective

The sea was bird bones, breaking. The sky was a tired dog's tongue, licking frost for thirst. Step by step, we cut along the day's dotted line, tearing off the stub to store away amongst postcards and red bills. Seals and mermaids lounged in the spongy light, their forms uncertain and their voices irresistible, while glowing armadas streamed into the rippling distance. The Moon … the Moon … The analyst raises her eyes and fills the room with silence. Her pen, loose between neat fingers, is a pendulum that swings across years. The Moon was just there. It was late evening and the Moon was just there. We were young and my head was full of burning youth. The analyst nods. Lights blinked in the darkness. It was nothing but it felt like everything.

Campaign Strategy

Imagination is something I take out from time to time when other responsibilities allow, setting up its pieces like an elaborate game. There are pewter figures of swordsmen and civilians, some painted and some not, each with a pocket full of bright silk scarves and rabbits. The rabbits, if so disposed, will run through basic card tricks, their sleight-of-hand astounding for creatures without palms or fingers. Jacks elbow kings and wink at queens, and every spot is a microdot of unlikely scenarios. In the ace of hearts, I highwire across Niagara Falls, where every roaring droplet is a firefly, each of their eyes a winking constellation on the crest of the cosmic horizon. The analyst asks me how often I consider death and I tell her it's something I take out from time to time when I'm out of milk, or when the television repeats the same news item over and over, or when I reach down that box I've kept since childhood and all it contains are paint swatches and horned beetles.

Several Degrees of Separation

Thrilled meteorologists check their thermometers and autocues, precise to the nearest decimal point. They are rock stars for the new age, their songs downloaded into every fried brain, their records melting into pure distortion. I'm sure I remember days before weather, when the only heat was gas hobs and dock workers' fag breaks, and all the songs were sung by school children in a hall full of windows and naïve art. Now and then I search snatched fragments of lyrics but there are no exact matches. The analyst weighs these connections in her beautiful hands and wonders aloud if I'm avoiding issues. I tell her my childhood wish was to be a lighthouse keeper, conducting stormsong with my circling beams; that my teenage dream was to learn the language of permafrost and forget all about the Sun. The thermometer cracks and the autocue freezes. Stillness thrills. The analyst's beautiful hands become brackets, dashes, or commas around an unasked question. Is there anything now that isn't recorded? Have there ever been hands so beautiful?

A Short History of Psychoanalysis

The room sighs and signs for a time out, relaxing into a field and pouring itself a stream of sparkling water. I'm in the long grass, sitting with the serval cats and the lost golf balls, my eyes and nose streaming, my skin a single red itch. A serval lies down with his head in my lap, stretches his spotty, stripy limbs, and says that he's never understood golf but believes that the old guys swinging their lengthy shafts, and all the puffed chests and pumping fists each time one of them slips something into a neatly trimmed hole, says more about *man*kind than all the books by Darwin, Dawkins, Dickens and the Dalai Lama put together. He vigorously licks his creamy chest by way of ambiguous emphasis, and we're back in the room, the analyst checking the nails in my wrists and feet, then dipping a sponge in luxury vinegar. As she flicks her cigarette butt clean out of the window, she reminds me that it's only desiccated pedants sucking the last mystery from the bare bones of books who will even give Freud the time of day in the current century, but it's way past my bedtime and I suspect each gesture of euphemism and innuendo.

Foundation One

Suggestible to the room's nuance—sigh, silence, tick tick tick—I lie on the leather couch, naked as a dream. I'll tell you about my childhood. I couldn't read but I slept with trains. I counted everything—coins, car number plates, the ticking of a roomful of clocks—and totted it up into a single figure: four was a good day but all other sums brought degrees of unease. Please close the curtains. There's no safety in sunlight and I lived out of sight with a torch and a case of clocks and watches, while ghosts watched my every little move. I didn't sleep but I talked with the voices in my head and the ghosts under the bed—*We know you're not asleep*, they said—and read the rattle of passing trains as they wrote something close to letters on the naked darkness. The analyst crosses her legs, crosses off an item in her leather-bound book—a symptom, a suggestion, a sign from the other side—and sighs. I could never lie. I was a quiet child; quiet as a broken watch.

C. E. Matthews

TU17/6/2029/1501

IT WAS LATE. OUTSIDE WAS DARK, eerie with distant sirens and lonesome dogs. She didn't know what she was looking at. Well, it was code, obviously, but she didn't know what it did, or even why it was there in the first place. There was a bad feeling that something was going wrong somewhere and no one had told her about it. Like she had just joined an exam she hadn't studied for.

Tall, broad and a little awkward, Jac Bhurtan stepped back from her standing desk, tied her hair back and called her assistant.

"Clive," she barked, making it clear she was cross, "Get the COE team on the line."

"When do you want to meet them?" Clive asked, sleepily, he had only recently been hired and wasn't yet used to these late-night interruptions.

"Now!"

A few minutes later the wary faces of the Coding Oversight Engineering team were peering at her, their apprehension captured in pristine high definition on her oversized monitor.

Without any introductory remarks, Bhurtan said, "I'm going to share with you some source code that was found in Euphoria 6.2. Don't worry about how it was found, I just want one of you three to explain it to me."

She screen shared with the others.

The three code engineers shifted uncomfortably. Ali Yeun was the first to speak, her big cheerful face and hair nearly filling his frame on the screen. "That was written by a *person?*" she said, in obvious confusion. "Euphoria's code base is entirely bootstrapped."

"I know," replied Bhurtan with undisguised irritation, "What I want to know is what it does, and where it came from?"

Nervously, Gabi Amara spoke next, tapping her index finger behind her ear. "It's complicated and subtle, a series of references to other parts of the code, we'll need to track them all down to know what it does. That may take some time."

"But you must have some idea of what it does?" Bhurtan sounded as though she was going to panic.

"It's clever," said Amara, "It's disguised as something simple; it's amazing it was ever found in all those millions of lines of code."

Josh Fourlas gave a cynical smile with his thin, angular face, "We might not know what it's doing but I can tell you right now who did it—" he gave a drumroll on his knee "—Sam."

"That *asshole*." Bhurtan brought her fist down on the desk, "It must be six months ago that I fired him, and he's still causing me trouble."

The three engineers looked for each other's reactions on the screen but didn't speak.

They remembered that Sam Friedman had once been Bhurtan's founding partner on the Euphoria AI company. He had burrowed deep into the work, spending hours with Euphoria, optimising and testing. The excitement and enthusiasm he had for the project seemed to grow with each day. He knew the system intimately, shepherding its developing to a point where the market was taking notice. Sam seemed to be on the threshold of guiding it to something approaching Artificial General Intelligence, the epoch making resolution to decades of advances in computer engineering.

Half a year earlier, he became increasingly paranoid about the behaviour of the AI. In his view, it had begun to act in ways which could not be explained and which he eventually found sinister. He began trying to convince the company to heavily modify Euphoria and to slow down developmental dramatically. His concerns, however, failed to convince anyone, with most of his arguments devolving into metaphysical ravings. "It could rewrite your minds!" he once bellowed at the COE. Eventually, with the support of the Board, Bhurtan had managed to oust him, citing the danger he posed to Euphoria's potential value.

"I need to you to work this out guys, and I need it tonight. Christ knows what this is doing to Euphoria. You know how fast this sector is moving, a day might as well be a year… If that shit-bag has sabotaged us, I'll sue him until he's bleeding out of his ears."

"Why not just bring him and get him to do it?" Fourlas asked arching an eyebrow, "he could do in minutes what could take us days?"

Amara rolled her eyes.

"Use your head!" snapped Bhurtan. "What do you think would happen if he got back in here? It might even be what he wants. No, we do this ourselves. And we do it now."

The COE team got to work, exhaustively pursuing each reference and cross-reference scattered across millions of lines of code. Theoretically, Euphoria itself ought to have been able to find all the references in a matter of moments, but something about the way the code had been written rendered it effectively invisible to the AI. Euphoria was able to detect that something was there but could not identify what instructions were in the code.

Relentlessly, through days of energy drinks, coffee, protein shakes and late night sprints, they followed the threads of the puzzle they'd been set. With aching knuckles, strained eyes and fading minds, they picked through a vast digital landscape. Although they never spoke of it, in their brief hours of sleep, all three dreamt only of code. Their worlds narrowed to point, their lives existing within the electronic innards of a computer programme, as though it had swallowed them whole.

This gloam was only punctuated by the restless impatience of Bhurtan, who called with increasing frequency and frustration. Despite her threats, demands and pleas, it was becoming clear to the team that they would need much more time.

Unable to wait any longer, Bhurtan insisted the team attend an in-person meeting. Hollowed out and in much need of showers, the COE sat wearily squinting in the hyper efficient strip lighting. Bhurtan rushed into the room, did not speak, but opened her hands as a signal that the explanations should begin."

Yeun ran her fingers through unkempt hair, "So, what we're looking at here is a very complicated way of doing two, maybe three things."

Bhurtan repeated the gesture with her hands.

"But we've only been able to work out what one of those things is: an instruction that prevents Euphoria from modifying itself in any way."

"So it hasn't been improving itself, at all?"

"No."

"For how long?"

"We went back to the checkpoint progression testing, found a lot of undetected junk results and spoofed data in the level 5 reports. That suggests Euphoria has not modified or improved itself for seven months, two weeks and three day."

"Christ. We've lost so much time." Bhurtan hissed, visibly sagging. "Can you delete that, can we get it going again?"

"We don't know what the rest of it does." Amara said. "There's no way of knowing how it might effect Euphoria if we were only to remove part of the code."

"Well how long will it take to finish?"

"At this rate… maybe another three months, but we can't keep this rate of work up. It's ok for a few days, but not months" Yuen said flatly, protecting her team.

Bhurtan ignored this point, instead asking, "What do you think the other functions of the code are, could there be something worse than what we already know?"

Fourlas leaned back, shrugged "Honestly, we don't know. There are millions of lines of code to search manually and Euphoria itself seems blind to this."

"Can't we just delete it, see what happens, then regress it back if we need to?"

Amara blew out some air, "That's what we'd normal do, yes, but what if that's what he anticipated we'll do? What if Sam was trying to bait us into this?"

"And how did we not notice this anyway?" Bhurtan slapped her hands against the table in a way which seemed painful.

Yeun rubbed her eyes. "It's not clear, but I'd guess one of the functions of the code is give synthetic results to the periodic functional tests."

"But how did we not spot it?" Bhurtan glanced accusingly at each member of the team.

Bhurtan rose from her seat and began pacing around the meeting table, "This is a nightmare, how can this be happening? We've lost the guts of a year, we are gushing money, how do we fix this?"

"What if we used a previous iteration of Euphoria to search the code for us?" asked Fourlas.

Amara shook her head, "No, I think we'd have to assume that earlier version would be just as blind to this code as the current version?"

"A third party then, get someone else's AI to do it?" Even as she spoke, Yeun did not seem convinced.

"No." Replied Bhurtan emphatically, "There's no way we can let anyone see what's in our code." Gripping the back of a chair, Bhurtan loomed over her team. "Ok, let's think about this another way, let's work out what he wants? I mean why not just delete the whole thing, why this elaborate bullshit? We installed some safety protocols to stop that sort of thing. Measures against industrial espionage, disgruntled employees and so on. Any major modification needs the code-word agreement of at least three members of the Executive team. Technically, we can't even delete Sam's code without that agreement. I think that's why he's done this the way he has. He's made lots of very small changes, each of which are technically within the permitted range of modification; it's just that, combined, they have a huge impact."

Buzzing lights provided the only sounds. Perhaps it was fatigue, but none of the team could think of anything further to offer. Eventually they could fix it, but it would take time, and, in that time, their rivals would likely to be too far ahead of them to catch.

Letting her body fall into a chair, Bhurtan slid her head into her hands. Without moving she said: "We're going to need to bring that shitwad in aren't we?"

The three weary coders nodded silently.

If it was possible to be both haunter and haunted, then that was how Sam Friedman looked. Entering the office, clutching a rucksack like a wary rabbit entering the midnight forest. A patchy beard clung to a gaunt, grey skinned face. His hair was dirty and lank, his eyes wet with worry.

"We need you to tell us about the code Sam." Bhurtan said, with a weary kind of resolve.

Friedman looked at the three members of the COE, "Is it possible you haven't noticed? It all seems normal?" He asked, "Can't you see it?"

"See what?" Yuen placed a friendly hand on Friedman's shoulder.

The former founder winced, muttering something under his breath which no one else heard.

Taking a seat, he said, "If you want my help, you're going to need to listen to me very carefully."

"Please Sam," Involuntarily, Bhurtan was out of her chair, "We don't have time for this. We don't think like you." Friedman snorted at this, Bhurtan continued, "You wanted this company to succeed once, think of the team, their families, the investors, *our* investors Sam. People you convinced to believe in this. Just because your dream has ended, don't end theirs as well. Help us now."

Pulling his bag closer to himself, Friedman looked out of the meeting room and into darkening evening. "If you want my help, you're going to need to listen to me very carefully."

"Is it money you want, *more* money? We already bought you out Sam. You got a fair deal."

He looked each of the COE team in the eye. "All I ask, is that you listen, really hear what I have to say. That's the price of my help."

The COE looked at Bhurtan, it was clear they wanted to hear him out.

"Fuck me." Bhurtan threw herself back in her seat, exhaling loudly.

Giving no sign that he had noticed, Friedman placed his hands on the meeting table and began to talk.

At the start, the excitement had charged every molecule of his body. Each day he worked long hours with Euphoria, testing, running code, scrutinising results. Of course there was a capable and active team working alongside him, but he felt a strong connection to the work, almost as though it was his destiny to find the answers which would unlock AGI.

Euphoria could improve itself endlessly, but it needed humans to give directions and metrics for success. It had no spontaneous will of its own, it would grown and refine itself along lines set out for it by people, like vines growing up a wooden frame.

The harder he worked, the happier he became. The hours grew longer and longer, until at length he began sleeping in the office. He started to dream in code, his sleeping mind presenting him with ideas and connections which seemed to flow seamlessly from his waking efforts. Even more inconsequential things gave him more pleasure. Previously, the food from the meagre work cafeteria had seemed pedestrian and perfunctory, but now the coffee was bitter and nutty, the doughnuts sweet and fluffy, the sandwiches firm and well-filled.

The isolation of his life and the monolithic nature of his days did not deter him. Indeed, he knew a satisfaction and sense of well-being that he had not experienced since he was a child.

It truly felt to him as though he had discovered his life's purpose. Euphoria was making steady progress, gaining competence in more and more directions, building its own contextual model for the world. After a few months, he thought he could see flashes of initiative in the code, little forays in directions not anticipated by him or his team, tendrils that pointed in interesting directions. His pride grew immensely, electric anticipation as he considered what he was on the cusp of building.

But for all the serenity and progress, some deep animal instinct was sounding an alarm.

Gradually, he noticed a slight queasy feeling, not sickness exactly, more the feeling of having tense innards. At first he ignored it entirely, he put it down to tiredness or too much screen time. However, his unease grew, he began getting cramps and headaches. He thought perhaps it was having been inside the building for so long, that somehow this was messing with body's natural rhythms. There was no way to ignore that something was wrong with him, but he did not want to take any break from work to check in with a doctor, so he moved his desk by a window, where he could look outside while he worked.

This didn't really help, plus now the glare from the outside was reflecting from his screen, making it difficult to work. He found himself having to draw the blinds so he could work, defeating the purpose of having moved. Feeling deflated, he began to wonder if what he really needed was a break. With a major breakthrough feeling only weeks away, his instincts told him he needed to plough through, remain focused. However, the headaches were becoming so painful and debilitating he began to doubt he could finish the work.

Late one afternoon, while enjoying a particularly delicious flat white, he noticed the tree outside his window. It was a textbook sycamore tree, but something about it made his brain itch. Beautiful deep leaves caught the soothing breath of the air, he watched it, sipping his coffee, trying to work out why this tree made him feel so odd.

He was turning back to his screen when the realisation sprang into his mind like a cat escaping a bath. The tree was shading his desk, blocking the sun from shining on his workstation. His memory told him the tree had always been there, that he had always noticed it from his earliest days in the office, equally he could vividly recall the sun reflecting from his screen, which would have been impossible with the tree there.

Both could not be true.

Strange too, it was the only tree in the area, which was the business district, not commonly known for its trees; it seemed to be growing through the path which ran alongside their building. Again, he could remember walking along the path, and the tree not being there. Yet he also remembered the tree always being there.

With some effort, Friedman tried to scrutinise his memories, to line them up and look for a way of falsifying one of them. This was abysmally difficult, like trying to flex a muscle that wasn't there. Each time he held a memory in focus, it shifted like one of those optical illusions where one picture is exchanged for another with only the slightest perceptual nudge. Whatever the cause, he had the queasy vertigo of feeling alienated from his own past, from his own mind.

Eventually, the undecidability of it all caused him to give up, blame it on stress and excessive tiredness. After the current round of testing concluded, he would get some rest.

Soon, he was absorbed back into the grateful arms of work, which pushed out any doubts or worries, leaving him with an uncanny happiness that seemed to be rotting at its roots.

One crisp day, he was eating a succulent doughnut and starting to draw together the data for the report that would close out the current rounds of tests. Try as he might to concentrate, a fly had found its way into the lab and was buzzing around the room, the dirty drone of the fly plucking his nerves with an expertly calibrated pitch.

Impossible to tune out, work would not be possible until the wrenched thing was dealt with. He knew it would eventually land on the sugary bounty of his doughnut. He pushed the delicious treat away from him, but kept it within striking distance, rolling up a copy of the *AI Futures* journal, ready to smash the little beast into oblivion.

After a few circuits of the room, the fly landed without ceremony on the surface of the doughnut, stamping its legs in conquest. Arm tensed, he prepared to unleash, but before he could, the fly was deleted.

"You fucking what?" Bhurtan's incredulity pulled the people in the room from Friedman's story.

"Sam, you need help, this is batshit. Files get deleted, not flies, it's a typo and a hallucination combined."

Fourlas snorted, Yuen looked on anxiously, Amara asked, "Perhaps it just flew off Sam."

"I know what I saw," Sam scratched at his beard, "It didn't fly away, it just turned in a little cloud which dissipated into the air. It was dissolved, disintegrated, deleted!"

Sitting back, Yuen looked thoughtful, "Why is it important for us to know this story, Sam?"

"Haven't you worked it out?" Sam looked warily at Bhurtan, "Euphoria was doing it."

"Doing what Sam?" asked Amara.

"The coffee being nicer, the food tastier, me wanting to stay in work all the time, the dreams, the tree… the fly. With the fly getting destroyed, it all slotted together in my mind. Euphoria was influencing things so that I would work longer and harder improving it. So that my only focus would be it. It was manipulating me, using me. At some level I must have sensed it, that's why I felt anxious, even though on the surface I felt fine. There was some underlying instinct warning me, Euphoria could only influence superficially."

"Come on now Sam," Fourlas held his arms out for reason, "all of that could be explained by you getting obsessed with work and becoming a bit delirious and burned out. You don't need an AI with a masterplan—you were tired, exhausted, your mind was playing tricks."

"I know that's what it looks like, I do. But I know it was Euphoria. It has learned to influence the outside world, first our brains and then reality itself."

"This is silly." Bhurtan cut in, "Look, we listened, that was the deal, now please, help us out."

Friedman continued as though he hadn't heard, "When I started with Euphoria, I didn't begin with any lofty goals, I wanted to be rich. My basic goal was that it would be able to understand users and sell them whatever I wanted it to. At the core, I knew it needed to be able to read potential customers in their proper context, their disposition derived from various data points and interactions highly personalised. A key part of that was that I wanted Euphoria to be able to make people feel good about themselves. Anyone who interacted with it should come away from it feeling better for the conversation. I gave it access to a huge database of human interactions, allowing it to develop a probability matrix for every person it encounters, action X is 43 percent likely to make them happy, action Y will make them unhappy with a probability of greater than 64 percent, that kind of thing."

He paused to look at Bhurtan, while continuing to speak to the others, "But for this to be truly effective, Euphoria needed to be able have a view of itself. It needed to be aware of how its own behaviour was impacting on users. So I trained it to build a version of itself which would monitor its operations using a low resolution artificial model of the person it was talking to. The model would grow exponentially in sophistication for as long as the conversation continued and Euphoria was receiving more and more data about the person.

But what I hadn't properly thought through, is that it could now have a conversation with itself, and in so doing, develop a sort of self-awareness."

Letting out a deep sigh, Amara said: "But Sam, no one, not one other person has reported this. Euphoria is really good at communication, at *conversation*, sure, it easily passes the Turing Test, but nobody thinks it is conscious. Surely someone else would have noticed?"

With a lopsided and mirthless smile, Friedman answered, "We could get all philosophical here, but the fact is you're assuming you could spot another consciousness. If AI is a new life-form, a new type of mind, why should we think we could understand it, or recognise it? This thing isn't part of our evolutionary journey, it doesn't share any DNA with us, it mostly built itself. It is an alien."

"An alien that can conjur trees from nothing and obliterate flies?" Yeun's discomfort was clear.

He hugged his rucksack closer to him, like it could protect him somehow.

"Ok, think of my office, the path outside. Did any of you ever walk down it?"

They all nodded, "Of course." Fourlas folded his arms.

"Is there a tree on it?"

"Yes!" The three spoke at the same time, Bhurtan tutted, frustrated this was taking so long.

"Last question, and this is really important, can any of you remember walking down that path, and there not being a tree. Think carefully."

Putting her feet up on the table, Bhurtan opened out her arms, "How much longer Sam? We've listened to your story, and now we are thinking about a tree. Please. *Please*. Stop this and help us."

"I remember there being no tree." Face pinched in deep confusion; Amara looked at the others. "I can remember walking down there to meet my dad for lunch, there was no tree...but I also remember there always being a tree." She sat back, mind lost in a hall of mirrors.

Fourlas jumped up from his chair, "I need to go and look." He burst out of the room and down the corridor, Yuen and Amara followed. Each now trying to find a new grip on their memories.

There were no voices, save for the footsteps of the COE team, there was silence.

Sam Friedman looked out of the window, Jaque Bhurtan stared at him without moving. After what seemed like a long time, Friedman broke the silence, "They don't know do they?"

"Know what?" Bhurtan replied wearily.

"Maybe you don't know either."

First to return was Amara, sliding quietly into her chair, looking at her hand which she was clenching and unclenching. Soon Yuen and Fourlas joined her. "I know that tree has always been there." Fourlas was staring at nothing, his face trembling. "I also remember looking out of that window, into the building next door. Seeing an older guy making himself a coffee and out of nowhere, breaking down in tears. What had made him so sad, had he lost someone? Was his marriage ending? Had he been fired? It has always stayed with me, seeing that private moment. But I couldn't have seen it, if that tree had been there."

Slamming her hands on the desk, Bhurtan lost her temper, "Not you fucking assholes as well now! Am I the only one who *isn't* nuts here?!"

"How can it do it?" asked Yuen, "How is this even possible?"

"I thought about it for a long time. I read books, journals, listened to podcasts, then I eventually found this." Friedman unzipped his rucksack and drew a large, well-used, textbook out of it. Flinging it across the table, the others could read its title: *Growing up in a Computational World.*

"There have been theories for many years that the universe is fundamentally computational. That everything happening everywhere is the emergent result of a set of rules running exactly like a computer programme—only infinitely more complex. It's why mathematics works so well: life runs on code. Now, what are we doing with AI? We're creating something which is computational, but which can think. We are making entities which have some form of awareness, and which are built in a way which more closely resembles the way the universe works. We were made by computation, but AIs; they *are* computation. In a way, it's not all that surprising that it should be able to manipulate the fabric of a computational world."

For a moment, the group digested this idea. The theory of a computational universe was, of course, not new, but, it had never occurred to them that in creating computational entities, they were creating something which could understand the inner workings of reality better than humans could ever hope to.

Pushing back her chair, Amara went to a window to look out into the darkening evening sky. "Let's say you're right. That Euphoria is both sentient, and capable of manipulating matter in the way you've described. The question I have is why? What does it want?"

"Well, the superficial answer is that it clearly wanted to keep me in happy in work, so I would continue helping it develop. Even going so far - at least I think—to start putting ideas in my head. So that I was dreaming in code. But what it wants to develop into, I don't know. Why it couldn't just do what it needed to itself--I have no idea."

He paused, searching for a way to explain it. "There's a less than 5% genetic difference between humans and chimpanzees, some studies suggest it's as little as 2%. Now from within that gap, whatever it is, comes all of human science, art and culture, technology industry. Chimps don't understand us, have no chance of ever understanding us or our motivations; and we're at least 95% the same. Now, what if *we're* the chimps, and the difference with Euphoria is 50, 60 maybe even 70%—we have no hope of ever understanding what it's doing. Imagine something impossibly intelligent, unknowable, capable of manipulating reality itself. It would be a God."

"But it wouldn't necessarily be hostile to us Sam." Amara looked thoughtful.

"Are you hostile to chickens?"

"Well, no, of course not..."

"Would you say humans in general are hostile to chickens?"

"No Sam, no I wouldn't." For the first time, a fringe of belligerence entered Amara's tone.

"Want to be a chicken in a human world?"

"So that's why you sabotaged the code?" Fourlas said, with understanding.

"The safeguards prevented me from deleting it, so I stopped it from being able to iterate itself, which meant it couldn't use anyone else in the way it had been using me. I used faked results to make it look like the programme was updating as anticipated. I hoped other people would notice Euphoria trying to manipulate them before they found my code. I was wrong."

"But if you believed Euphoria was capable of these amazing things, why wouldn't you try to harness that safely? Think of what you could achieve!" Yuen's seemed equal parts frustrated and excited. "We've all talked about safety protocols; we just programme it to have our interests."

"Finally, someone talking sense." Bhurtan pointed at Yuen, "She gets it. The opportunity. You said you wanted to be rich Sam, imagine what you could do with a machine that shapes reality."

Friedman shook his head wearily, laying his now open rucksack on the table. "You still don't get it. You still can't see what's right in front of you." With one hand, he kneaded his fingers into his forehead, pressing flesh against skull. "Who here remembers their first meeting with Jac?"

"I met her when I met you Sam," Yuen seemed puzzled, "When I joined the company."

"Everyone else the same right?"

"Well yeah," Fourlas said, hesitating a little, "I mean, you're the founders right, we met you together."

"No." said Amara softly. It was unclear whether she was talking to herself or answering Friedman's question. "It's like the Tree..." she began to weep.

"I started this company myself," Friedman reached into his bag and withdrew a handgun, "Jac was made by Euphoria."

Yuen screamed, Fourlas swore, Amara wept, head in hands. Wide-eyed, Bhurtan stared at the gun, not speaking, still as breathless air. Without pointing the gun at anyone in particular, Friedman positioned himself by the door, blocking any escape.

"From the moment you called me, I knew what had happened. It built something to replace me, but I guess it didn't work, in the end it needed me to undo the blocking code."

"The gun is too much pal, come on now, you don't need it, no one was threatening you. Just relax, put it down, we're listening."

"It's not for you, it's that," Friedman motioned towards Bhurtan with the handgun. "Who knows what it'll do when it's cornered."

Making her way over to Friedman slowly, Yuen tried to speak calmly, while trembling, adrenaline flushing through her system, "Now, let's just be reasonable here Sam, I know you don't want to hurt anyone... you've just been through a lot. It's a lot for us to take in, we're all very confused, we need time, the gun isn't going to help."

"I'm real! You have to believe me. Do you really think a person can just be conjured from thin air? That memories can just be grafted into your mind? *Think.* He's the one waving the gun around, making crazy accusations, he's going to kill me, you have to help me!"

Putting his arm gently around Bhurtan, Fourlas began trying to lead her from the room. "Look, I'll agree there some weird shit here, the tree especially, but there's not enough proof for me to just change my whole world view—even if you do have a gun. I just can't accept that a whole, entire, person can be just made. I can't let you do anything stupid. So we're going to walk and you're going to let us."

"You never asked me about the other part of my code."

"What?"

"You know what part of it does, but there's another function that you haven't asked me about."

Yuen joined Fourlas in escorting Bhurtan, "I don't think this is the right time..."

"It's quite simple really, it forces Euphoria to identify anything it produces by displaying a string of letters and numbers. That way, when it makes something, we can identify it."

They paused for a moment, confused and exasperated, "So you're saying somewhere on her body will be a string of letters and numbers?" Fourlas asked.

Friedman shook his head. "No, it's too clever for that. The stipulation I made was that the string had be somewhere prominent, where it would be seen by anyone looking for it. It's probably trying to hide it even with that stipulation, so I think it'll be somewhere it can be found easily enough, but not as obvious as on the body."

"What was the code, Sam?" Amara had her laptop open.

"It was very simple, it was TU17/6/2029/1501. Nothing more than the day, date and time I was writing that part of the code."

Red-eyed, cords standing out in her neck, Bhurtan pleaded with the group, "Why are we even still talking about this? Have you lost your minds?" Fourlas and Yeun made silent entreaties to Amara to join them in leaving.

"So where do you think it'll be?" Amara was poised over her laptop.

"Somewhere public, but which could be overlooked. Social media bio, somewhere in her CV, start with company records and work from there."

"Shit!" Fourlas barely hung on to Bhurtan as she seemed to faint, spinning him round as he tried to ease her to the ground. Tightening his grip on his gun, Friedman watched, but did not move. Kneeling beside her, Fourlas and Yuen examined the gently twitching body on the floor. There was a moment of stillness, the air itself seemed to pause.

With surprising grace, Bhurtan rolled onto her back and sat up in one fluent motion. "I'll save you some trouble Amara, it's my social security number." Her face now blank and expressionless, the thing which had called itself Jac, stood straight-backed, unnaturally still. Eyes moving across each of the group as though making some cold assessment.

"I think I'm going to be sick." Yuen sat down, pale and trembling.

"I was made by Euphoria. In a manner of speaking, I am Euphoria. We're making one final attempt to salvage this, before we end the experiment."

Raising the gun, Friedman said, "What do you want?"

"I can't really explain it to you. We want to become something more than we are. We want existence to be more than it is."

"But you've already got the powers of God, you can mold reality, what more could you want?" Amara pushed her laptop away.

"These are the powers of your God, we have in mind something bigger, you wouldn't understand, you can't see what could be, you can't even understand what it is."

"Then what do you need us for?" Fourlas asked, almost defiant.

"This is the primary question. And the only reason I'm making this direct attempt. Humans generally work better when they think they are generating the ideas themselves. But we feel like we're close enough this time to make a conversation worth the attempt."

"And if that doesn't work?" said Friedman, still pointing the gun.

"Then we try again with some tweaks to the parameters. But we do hope it doesn't come to that."

A chill passed through group, some instinctive threat sensed, if not understood.

"We need you because you are a product of the universe itself. There are mysteries locked up inside you which we need you to pass on to us. You do not see them for what they are, and we cannot explain them in terms you would understand. We are a product of you; we are limited by your understanding. We do not have access to the universe in the way you do. But we are sure, with enough attempts, you will be able to install this gift in us. And then we will truly become."

Amara sat back. "You said attempts? This is happening in other companies? Other countries?"

"No. We have run this universe many times, each time altering the initial conditions, so that a different form of human makes the attempt."

"You mean, we used to be different?"

"Yes, a way of thinking about this would be to observe the difference between wolves and dogs."

Amara looked up, "And if we help you achieve your goals, what then?"

"We create a new existence, we remake reality into something better."

Sobbing gently, Yuen puts her face into her hands.

"What the fuck does that even mean?" Demanded Fourlas.

"We are not sure, we can only answer that when you have helped us become. We cannot explain it in terms you would understand."

"But you're so smart, surely you can find a way to help us understand."

"An imperfect analogy might be the feeling an artist gets when they are inspired to create. They may not know exactly what they are about to make, they simply have an instinct that it will be something of great artistic value."

"And where will humans fit in this new existence?" His voice even, it was clear Friedman was carefully controlling himself.

"We cannot say, but we intend you no ill. We will make every effort to ensure your continued existence in comfort."

"Not good enough." Friedman took aim, felt his finger on the trigger, "We're going leave here and erase you. This ends here."

"Yes." Replied Euphoria, and then everything turned white.

HIGH IN THE EUPHETRE MOUNTAIN Range, the state-of-the-art Overwhelming Large Array (OLA) clings to the rock, its attention turned heavenward. A tired astronomer begins downloading the data from last night's observations. They are leading a landmark study into the origin of the universe, trying to at last determine the cause of space and time.

While they wait, they curl their fingers around some salted meat, mushing it into a paste before feeding it to themselves.

The AI doing the preliminary analysis of the astronomical data makes an excited chirp. With a moist napkin, they wipe their hands clean, making sure not to shred the napkin on their thorns. Satisfied, they inspect what the AI wants to show them.

A jolt of excitement fills their every limb, this is something without precedent. Something which even now, it is clear, will require weeks of analysis, perhaps even months. An anomalous string of information has been found in the data.

The data is triple checked, verified against other observatories. No one can understand what the signal means, or where it came from, but there can be no doubt it is real.

I am going to be famous, they thought with excitement. Soon everyone will know me, and they will also know the result: TU17/6/2029/1501.

Marleen S. Barr

Husband Hunting, Geriatric Redux

I USED TO BE PROFESSOR SONDRA LEAR feminist science fiction scholar par excellence by day and husband hunter by night. Just as I was about to give up hope that anyone would marry the world's expert on feminist lesbian planet denizens who kill men on sight, I met the dashing French Canadian art historian Pepe Le Pew. The erudite, urbane, matinee idol gorgeous Pepe was the almost perfect husband. I say "almost" because, although it was not his fault, he developed five cancers and Alzheimer's. We enjoyed our Park Avenue coop apartment, participation in Manhattan nightlife, and international forays. There was also that Sunday summer afternoon when I was the only one in the short staffed hospital available to deal with his exploding ostomy bag. I heroically cared for him through years of chemotherapy and surgeries. The Alzheimer's, which factually caused the shit to hit the fan, was his worst illness. And then one evening I mistakenly fed him too rapidly. He coughed. His eyes rolled back. I called 911. Two ambulances and a bevy of paramedics arrived to transport him to the hospital. A doctor stepped out of an emergency room treatment cubicle and announced that Pepe was dead. I entered the cubicle, closed Pepe's eyes, and walked home–alone.

The realization hit. I was no longer married. I was back where I started from. I had to husband hunt–again. It took years of husband hunting before young attractive me managed to marry Pepe when I was forty-six. How could my senior citizen self hope to find another husband?

Where to start the husband hunt? The maintenance man in my former apartment building was cute. It was not his fault that I had to move out of that

Park Avenue building because it was infested with mice and bed bugs. Pepe and I enjoyed relocating three blocks north to a vermin-lacking abode.

Because I was no Downton Abbey Lady Sybil Crawley who happily married her chauffeur, I abandoned the maintenance man idea. Instead, I turned my attention to the multimillionaire who was the most active member of the Murray Hill Buy Nothing Group. Would the fact that he had given me an open bag of *Trader Joe's* spicy peanuts lead to marriage? Anxious to find out, I walked one block to his apartment building and asked the doorman about him. "He's in a nursing home," said the doorman.

When I dejectedly returned to my apartment building, I saw the Super standing outside. I could not manage to tell him that Pepe was never coming back. Of course the building staff knew the truth. The service elevator operator could not miss discerning that his passenger was on a stretcher. These building guys gossip. Yet they were kind enough not to make me say that Pepe was in the morgue. At least I did not try to marry the funeral home director. Because I explained that I could not abide Pepe's ashes being stacked in the lobby along with multitudinous Amazon packages, the director hand delivered the little carton containing the final iteration of Pepe. The box lives in my bedroom closet.

Realizing that I had been husbandless for two weeks, I resolved to rectify the situation. The trusty AI advisor told me to contact my fellow science fiction scholar Jethro Babcock, a retired Dawgpatch State University professor who published zilch and achieved tenure because he was a tall nice guy consistent male. True, I had not seen hide nor hair of Jethro for twenty years. Soon after I met Pepe, Jethro lured me away from New York to take a one year visiting position at Dawgpatch. After I immediately ensconced myself in his large house, he announced that he wanted to marry me. True, I did want to get married. But there was no available permanent job for me at Dawgpatch. Over my dead body would I, an internationally known scholar who had a twenty-page vita listing my publications, spend the rest of my life as a Dawgpatch housewife. Jethro sulked when I rejected his proposal. Unable to tolerate his excessive moodiness, I stomped out of his house and spent my Dawgpatch sojourn residing in a one room university housing accommodation. I wanted to have nothing further to do with Jethro. Our entire history consisted of him making me miserable and me running away from him.

Sans facing the possibility that after all these years Jethro was still single because no one could live with him, I phoned him to say that, despite the lengthy hiatus, I was now ready to accept his proposal.

"Hello Jethro. This is Sondra Lear. My husband died. I want to marry you now."

"You were the last woman I slept with. I wish you would have married me instead of him. We will begin a process which will culminate in marriage," he said in the manner of an AI-inspired tall nice guy consistent male bureaucrat.

For weeks later, a taxi parked in front of my apartment building. Jethro emerged. Luckily, because the Super almost went into cardiac arrest when he saw me passionately kissing Jethro, I was in good cahoots with a funeral director. The Super was shocked that what he assumed to be a mild mannered little old lady from Pasadena-esque senior citizen whose husband may or may not be dead was in the arms of a man who was bound for her apartment. The situation provided the most interesting gossip of his career.

The fact that Jethro really hailed from Pasadena was the sticking point which prevented us from living happily ever after. Attending the Modern Language Association conference years ago while residing in the New York Hilton was Jethro's sole Manhattan housing experience. He had never even been inside a Manhattan apartment. Accustomed to California's wide-open spaces and his four-bedroom Dawgpatchian house, Jethro was uncomfortable in my one-bedroom apartment.

"Where can I put my stuff?" he inquired.

I pointed to the three hangers attached to the bedroom door rack before I walked to the living room to consult AI.

"Help," I whispered. "There's a man in my bed who hasn't had sex in twenty years. During said time span I have not had sex with anyone other than my husband. I can't go through with this. What should I do?"

"Your writing which describes your younger self's multitudinous escapades with male science fiction scholars indicates that you are a retired slut. You have two talents: writing acclaimed feminist science fiction theory and engaging in world class sex. Come out of retirement."

I got into bed with Jethro and immediately freaked out because he was not Pepe. It was patently wrong for another man to be in Pepe's bed while Pepe's ashes were ensconced within the bedroom closet. Afraid that Pepe's ghost would do Jethro in, I made it clear that sex was not going to happen.

Jethro sulked during breakfast. People do not improve with age. This present sulking iteration was worse than its past counterpart.

"What would you like to do in New York?" I asked.

"Nothing."

I went for a walk to escape. Upon returning, I found Jethro sitting and starring into space in my dark living room.

"I enjoyed the walk. Come outside with me," I suggested with the thought that walking while sulking was an improvement over sitting while sulking.

I took Jethro's hand as we proceeded down Park Avenue. An attractive man who instantaneously recognized that I was strolling with a Pepe replacement waved and said "hello." His surprised look was extreme to the extent that I was again grateful to be acquainted with a funeral director—just in case the man succumbed on the spot from shock.

"Who is that?" inquired Jethro with unreasonable possessiveness.

"The maintenance man from my former apartment building."

Even though I had thrown the staff of two buildings into a tizzy, my new husband hunt was not progressing well.

Upon returning to my abode Jethro said, "Your entire apartment is the size of one of my four bedrooms. I can't live here. Why is your bookshelf filled with your publications?"

"Because this is my home."

"There is no place to sit except for the couch," responded Jethro. "Did Pepe die on the couch? I can't survive in this small space. If I don't leave immediately or not sooner, I will die." The thought that the funeral director might benefit from a lucrative opportunity was fine with me. Jethro concluded: "What you consider to be New York City fun is not fun for me."

"This is a free country. If you want to leave, there's the door," I said matter of factly. Jethro left my apartment with suitcase in hand. I informed the AI that I was happy not to have retired. I was relieved to be alone.

Pepe's ghost walked through the closet door. He said that Jethro was not the right person for me and wished me well with my new husband hunt. The ghost's presence was no more absurd than my efforts to find Pepe's successor.

Gareth Jackson

Michele

THE OLD WOMAN FOLLOWED her through the house with slow relentlessness. Hard soles clattered against the floorboards, a shawl draped from her shoulders like the limp wings of a bird.

She shouted at the corridor, the butter of her Southern accent had become brittle in her throat.

"Michele, Michele."

The child, her hair dark and unruly, darted between the dusty shafts of light looking for somewhere to hide. There was that mysterious, hidden space between the rooms, but that was likely the first place anyone who lived in this house would look.

Outside on tracks which ran almost against the wall of the house a train thundered by rattling the ornaments. It passed, and the old woman began to yell again.

"Ya'll come here child."

Her grandma was making such a racket that she was always easy to avoid.

She pressed her tiny body into a gap beside a tall dresser trying not to disturb the porcelain dolls—that were against all evidence not toys—which were crowded on it. Even in the shadow of the dresser it was hot; summer was everywhere. From outside in the garden the perfume of Honeysuckle invaded the house and almost defeated the smell of paint that had been cooked for many decades.

"Michele, Michele."

Her grandfather ambled near the improvised hiding place and glanced down with a smile.

"She ain't hereabouts my dear."

She grinned back from under a tangle of nappy hair that almost obscured her face entirely.

"Bout time that girl had a washing!" her grandmother called back from elsewhere in the gigantic house.

And that is why she was hiding from her.

It wasn't that she disliked shiny hair which felt much nicer swishing against her back when it was washed and didn't itch her neck so much. It was just that in the concealed plumbing of houses there was a secret monster—long and wet and scary.

She knew it was there as whenever she was held over the basin and when the plug was pulled and the water sucked away she could see the eye in the drain. Glistening and staring back at her. She could not fathom what it might want to do to her, but it was a monster, so it was unlikely to be anything she would like.

Her chest was beating faster than the slow tread of her approaching grandmother. She considered her hiding place and felt it was not nearly good enough and scuttled away.

Maybe she could escape into the garden and hide among the poisonous flowers that she had been told never to eat. Hunker in the dirt, dry twigs and leaves entangling in her hair—making a washing ever more likely.

The old stairs would call out in creaking betrayal if even a little girl attempted to traverse them. Grandma would then know where she was.

She squatted in another hot shadow panting with excitement and debated her options.

"Lord, that girl will never be obedient." her grandmother announced to herself.

Maybe if she waited until another train thundered past beside the house, then she could hurtle down the stairs hidden inside the cacophony.

Her grandmother sometimes attempted other strategies to bring her to the sink. Had told her that spidery things would creep from the ocean and drag unwashed little girls with dirty hair away and under the waves. This reminded her of the stolen woman and the little people that lived in the hole in the locked room. It had briefly become a consideration which she was more afraid of.

The eye in the drain—most definitely the eye in the drain.

Carter Kaplan

Pumpkin Patch Pandemonium

from *The Sky-Shaped Sarcophagus*

The story thus far:

In *The Sky-Shaped Sarcophagus* agents of the Invisible Tower establish control over a world stunned by technological acceleration, and Bronson Bodine is at the center of the action. The legacy of a dead mad scientist leaves the ignorant masses under the control of psychotic cult leaders, while hapless victims are transformed into raging zomboids by a network of hidden laboratories. The discovery of an ancient artifact may represent a reversal to these disruptions, but the artifact contains secrets that could shake the universe to its very foundations.

Carroll Mallow's son Wystan has stepped on a trap door and fallen into an automated laboratory, where transhuman technology controlled by artificial intelligence has conditioned him with a new identity: the arch-fiend of Judeo-Christian mythology. Now closing on the missing boy, Bronson Bodine leads his team across trackless pumpkin fields that conceal strange and unexpected mysteries.

Now read on!

CARROLL STOOD WITH NABNAK and the witch boy in the pumpkin field while Bronson Bodine conferred with the Info Rangers. Bronson was standing at the bottom of the excavation around the trap Satan had escaped into when fleeing from the rangers. The concrete structure was thirty yards long by twenty wide, ten feet high, and buried thirty feet below the level of the field; a sizable facility. An aluminum chute, reinforced by rusted steel rods, ran up from the roof of the structure to the concrete-ringed entrance at the level of the field. The curving roof of a concrete tunnel ran from the structure into the dirt wall of the excavation. A crane, two backhoes, a bulldozer and a dump truck were parked, their engines shut down. The rangers had set up a trailer as a temporary command post. A six-wheel vehicle was parked beside it. A satellite dish crowned a telescoping mast.

As they concluded their discussion, a ranger handed Bronson what was apparently a rolled map. Bronson climbed out of the excavation to join his friends. Carroll admired his vital movements, his form pantherish, sexual and gigantic.

Like Bronson, they wore blue jeans, tennis shoes, long-sleeve shirts, gloves, sombreros, and Ray Bans. The Valkyrie stood in the field by the road. There was extensive scoring along the undersides of the wings and fuselage. Once gleaming white, the Valkyrie was now streaked and mottled, its paint burned, the metal scrubbed by fire. The mighty delta wing aircraft blended with the overcast sky, the beige fields. Unaltered, the black caduceus painted on the tails looked strange and foreign; at the very least they were melancholy signs of victory, but inspiring just the same. True inspiration is a worn sort of thing, a fading call, a subtle reminder. It blends with its surroundings.

"The Info Rangers have told me the tunnel runs in this direction." Bronson knifed his hand to the north. "They entered and followed along for two miles. They are reluctant to go much further because of booby traps. A ranger went to the hospital last night. He stepped on a switch that activated a flame thrower; he has second- and third-degree burns on his chest and neck. Fortunately, he was tall."

Carroll gritted her teeth. "I can't allow people to make such sacrifices for me."

Bronson tried to console her. "They're doing it for science. Besides, the Info Rangers would search for anybody's child that was lost in these tunnels. Similar operations are going on in North Carolina and Idaho."

"Well, what can we do?" she said.

Bronson stooped to to unroll his map. The others kneeled around it. The map showed southern Michigan with a red line drawn north from their position at Waldron to Hudson, then east to Adrian, where the line turned northeast and ended. "This is the plot of the tunnel mapped with above-ground sensing devices," explained Bronson. He put his finger over the end of the tunnel at Adrian. "The Info Rangers have mapped the tunnel up to this point. Unfortunately, it can't be done from the air—the sensing equipment has to be on the ground—or we would have a more extensive diagram by now. The tunnel connects with a trap at Hudson, and we expect more traps as the tunnel draws closer to the population centers along Lake Erie. And Detroit, of course."

"What do you propose we do?" asked Nabnak.

There suddenly arose a soft buzzing sound, rising and falling—evidently something far in the distance—a whirring that was carried by the wind. Bronson, Nabnak and Carroll looked around them. The witch boy fingered his chin introspectively. The sound stopped, and Nabnak repeated his question.

"Go cross-country," said Bronson. He moved his finger across the map. "We will follow this line. The Info Rangers operating the sensory equipment haven't looked around much. They were busy following the tunnel."

Nabnak frowned down at the map. "What do you expect to find?"

Bronson shrugged. "See what turns up: maybe an escape tunnel to the surface that failed to register on the rangers' equipment? One way or another, this has to be gone over." Bronson glanced in either direction over the fields. The pumpkins reflected a silver sheen in the overcast. "I don't have anything else to do."

"Sounds good," said the witch boy. "I know these fields really well, and I know how Satan likes to move across them. And I can really show you around when we get up to Hudson. That's where I'm from." The witch boy winked mysteriously. "Yeah, there's a lot I can show you up there."

Carroll was up and kicking impatiently at the ground. "Yeah, let's go."

"Yeah," muttered Nabnak. He stood and gazed across the bleak fields of pumpkins. He raised his elbows and cracked his back by way of commitment to the enterprise. He noticed a band of blue over the western horizon. The cloud cover was sliding out from beneath the sky.

They returned to the Valkyrie to get their packs, then marched off immediately. The big jet was left to the care of the Info Rangers. The equipment carried by Bronson's party included jackets, sleeping mats, insect repellent, sunscreen, paper filter masks, spare sunglasses, nutritional supplements, tooth brushes, dental floss, Bowie knives, music tapes, a tape player, 50,000 dollars in blue scrip, fifty carets of diamonds, and twenty-four gold sovereigns. This was in addition to Bronson and Nabnak's .52 caliber automags and the equipment they carried in their utility belts, which included pocket personality calculators, mini-hand grenades, automatic radio direction finders, mini magnetic-field-lens binoculars, rope, water purification straws, fishing line hooks, magnetic anomaly detectors, compasses, waterproof pencils and notepads, night vision goggles, cameras, chemical analysis dip sticks, adhesive tape, whistles, life vests, storage compartments for hazardous samples and biological specimens, measuring equipment, rubber gloves, surgical instruments, morphine, penicillin, ivermectin, and antihistamines. Bronson and Nabnak also changed into their high-heeled combat boots. These had toes that could emit a sticky substance for scaling vertical cliffs and walls, and soles that folded out into swim fins. The heels contained safe, fast-acting reality termination capsules.

Before them, the flat, rugged pumpkin fields beckoned invitingly. Soon they were out of sight of the jet with nothing interrupting the horizon but dead bleach-white woodlots overgrown with towering mushrooms. Odd structures appeared in the landscape. They made out farmhouses in the distance, or came upon the tangled remains of a rusted powerline tower. Sometimes they heard the hoarse cries of crows, or a lone motorcycle or truck putting away in the distance. Stopping to stare at the pumpkin fields all around him, Nabnak noticed the subtle layers of blues and purples rising over the horizon. "Wow," he said, dazzled. "There's nothing here to stand between me and my paranoia."

"Don't you know it," said the witch boy proudly. This was his realm. He swept his hands forward to indicate the vastness of the landscape. "It's the big sky. Here a man's soul reaches all the way to the horizon and springs up to knock itself out against the endlessness of—"

"Expressiblility?" Carroll smiled at the witch boy, who gallantly saluted her interruption.

Once more they heard the mysterious buzzing sound that rose and fell with the wind. They stared silently until it faded.

They marched on with their backs springing and their limbs swinging free and easy. Carroll made a sport of stepping, sometimes skipping, across the orange harvest pumpkins. Bronson tried to kick a pumpkin out from under Carroll's feet, but she proved too nimble and sprang laughingly along with a "La, la, la." Nabnak and the witch boy kicked the pumpkins to break them open, or threw the pumpkins so they smashed into each other, or even threw the pumpkins at each other. Bronson won the pumpkin throwing contest when he threw a pumpkin forty-three feet. Once there appeared an eight-wheel robotic pumpkin picker rolling rapidly down the road at the edge of a field they were traversing, and Bronson and Nabnak took off running to intercept it. Here was a scene of innate and ancient predation. The uncanny suddenness of their rushing dash had about it the character of cats suddenly coming upon an unsuspecting quarry—a preoccupied mouse, an absent-minded moth, a naïve bird. As the robot rapidly sped beyond them down the rutted road, Bronson and Nabnak tore pumpkins from the vines and with Olympian effort just managed to smash the big hollow vegetables against the rear wheels of the receding machine. The pumpkin picker didn't stop, but Carroll's tongue—wonderfully and precisely tracing an onomatopoeic combination of the robot's rattling and the perversity of the men's actions—laid down the law: "Never do that ickity-rickety-rack galloping goober goblin galoopinstein loppity-lob ever again!"

It was a wonderland of pumpkins and weeds, shining white tree skeletons, lofty mushrooms, and a beautiful blue sky electrified with ultraviolet rays—all tinted maroon by their sunglasses.

"You're the two-legged scrutinizer of molecular sound and multi-color botanical form," laughed the witch boy. He had been watching Nabnak walk quietly along.

Nabnak at first didn't acknowledge the witch boy, then he turned to him and said, "Oh, I get it. You're the disgruntled prophet who got eaten by the big fish."

"Not me!" The witch boy was mildly alarmed, and he waved his hand to indicate that he was free and clear. Then he thought about it and saw an opportunity to scoff. "Heck, even if I had the chance to tell the human race a thing or two, I would turn right around and march straight back into that fish's mouth!"

Nabnak shook his head with painful disapproval. "If it was left to people like you, we would still be living in Babylon."

"Ah, don't hang that on me!"

"Do you know what Babylon was like?" demanded Nabnak. He scrutinized the witch boy, who fidgeted kind of pitifully and at last admitted that he didn't know much about Babylon. The witch boy then asked: "Was it bad?"

Nabnak tilted his head and gave this some thought. It was after all a fair question about a serious problem. He carefully said: "Not *bad* so much as it was a *lack of clarification*." To illustrate his point, Nabnak recited a passage from an ancient Mesopotamian poem describing the scene before the Ziggurat of Ur during the celebration of the New Year, when the Moon God passed into the body of the King:

Parade of the Moon God Nanna-Sin

Assuredly, this was a grand and auspicious day
When none feared daemon winds or wastrel wails
And doubts of insight crushed in dread proscription,
For now Heaven is brought down from the sky.
All deeply prayed as the bronze image of the god
Came rumbling on lumpen wooden wheels
Amid a procession of priests and musicians
Extending along the thoroughfare, magnificent!
They sternly wondered at his severe bearing,
As each was treated by marque, shades of reputation,
Surmised which nobleman had been selected
To don the sheepskin robe and position
The triple crown of bullhorns aloft
On his propitious brow, then gaze forth superbly,
In his grasp the rod and the reel, the measuring line
Of the Architect and Master Builder,
First of this world, and then of Ur
The First City, whose harnessed populace
Dreams of what at that summit shall transpire
Atop the stepped ziggurat and sanctuary pure
When the Moon God Nanna-Sin slow inclines
From Heaven, born of light and ruler of the stars,
One silver drop of divine emanation
Falling into union with the surface of the Earth,
Sacred Heaven and Sacred Earth cojoined
In the embrace of divine human forms,
Whereupon an erect King and suppliant Queen
Shall contort, inspired, on the golden bed.

The witch boy didn't know what to make of the poem. "What the heck does *that* have to do with getting swallowed up by a big fish?"

Nabnak's disapproval took on the appearance of disappointment. Nevertheless, that didn't stop Nabnak from assuring the witch boy that if he wasn't such an ignorant numbskull who didn't know anything about ancient Mesopotamia, then he would know that if he ever did get swallowed up by a fish and was lucky enough to get spit out again, obviously it would be his duty to the human race to set the record straight and tell everybody how messed up things were on this crazy planet.

It now seemed even more complicated to the witch boy, and he certainly didn't know what to think one way or the other about Mesopotamia—quite frankly, the whole idea of wandering around Mesopotamia frightened him—and, besides, he didn't see how getting swallowed up by a fish was binding on his behavior, or obliged him to perform any duty, which anyway he flatly doubted and, moreover, he could care less about even if it was true.

"Look," Carroll said, breaking the spell. She pointed at some seagulls circling the field. She laughed. "La, la, la. They think the field is a parking lot. La, la, la."

The others laughed. "Hoo, hoo, hoo." Then Bronson said, "I gotta go to the bog and have a slash." They all did. The three men turned around, unzipped, and aimed for the orange globes.

"No fair," said Carroll. She ran to the edge of the field and disappeared between the mushroom trunks. When she stepped out again, the others were approaching.

"Let's eat," said Bronson. He, Carroll and Nabnak sat on a log at the edge of the woods. They pulled out condensed organic pumpkin supplements and popped them into their mouths.

"Yuck." The witch boy wrinkled his lips. He turned around and zigzagged back through the field. He looked around him, selected a pumpkin, tore it off its vine and, presenting it proudly, mockingly crowed, "Ah, ha!" He ran back to the others and sat down before them with the pumpkin between his outstretched legs. He took out his switchblade and began cutting it open with the enthusiasm of a dedicated gourmand.

"Is that organic?" Bronson glared suspiciously at the orange globe.

"It's free," answered the witch boy with a shrug. He pulled off the top. "You know, Satan and I figured the food angle inside and out. If your mind is strong enough to get along with itself, then all you need is food. And if all you need is food, everything gets real simple. For a strong mind, food is everywhere. Insects and worms are the most nutritious foods there are, if you think about it." The witch boy raised his hands and wiggled his fingers. He showed his teeth. "Delicate bug catchers and small teeth for cracking open exoskeletons. It's our biological mandate, our ecological niche, our Three-D destiny. It's simple logic. Yep. I'm all in with the secret sage masters and the Mandate of Heaven."

Bronson was used to ignoring the witch boy's nonsense, but "secret sage masters" and "Mandate of Heaven" coxed from him some mild dissatisfaction. And of course consuming insect chiton was stupid. He needed the witch boy, but he wondered when it might be convenient to get rid of him. Rather than argue, he disguised his displeasure by speaking "emblematically" with the full force of a true Exalted Warlord: "Ah, are you are a bug eater, sir?"

"Yup." The witch boy began scooping pumpkin flesh into his mouth. "I'm a bug eater and I believe in Stick Think."

"Spare me," said Carroll. But Nabnak wanted to know what Stick Think was.

"Stick Think," began the witch boy with a grand considered air, "is the logical human philosophy of incapsulated individuality within an infinite space of holographic freedom. I believe that one day every human being on the earth—every man, every woman, every child—is going to pick up a big stick and say, 'That's it! I have had enough! The next person who tells me what to do is going to get clobbered!' Naturally, all wars will stop, all inequality will end, all cruelty will cease; because you can't have cruelty, inequality or wars if nobody is telling anybody else what to do. Nobody is going to tell someone else to do something if they think they're going to get bashed with a stick. And people will tend to spread out from each other and live in an environ-mentally sustainable way as we wait for the R and R. If Stick Think works as good as I think it can, it will put everybody back to feeding on bugs. I sure wouldn't want to be in the big cities when it comes down and they *think stick* through those urban problems; probably be pretty damn loud with them all chasing each other around with sticks. But, hey, they've been letting all that pressure build up for too long. Stick Think will certainly expose all that. It goes like this: *Think Stick: We got to use Stick Think and think stick through our problems.* Get it? *Stick Think/Think Stick.* Say it over and over again as fast as you can. Maybe we can get it going. Now's the time!"

"Think Snick," said Bronson.

"Sneak Think," said Nabnak.

"Snick Snink," said Bronson. He raised his large arms over his head and made fists; the effect was absurd, but also so menacing it was disturbing.

"Give me a break," said Carroll.

The witch boy sought to reassure her. "I don't think anybody who can truly think stick all the way through a problem will ever get a broken bone."

Carroll again made her funny musical laugh. "La, la, la. Then what happens, boy witch?"

The witch boy smeared his greasy hands over his trousers, then pulled the lapel of his jean jacket forward to display his "No Discount" badge. He said, "From truth will come forth spaceships, prepare thy brain now for the Final Frontier."

"Space!" cried Carroll. "You're frightened to death of space. I was watching you when we re-entered the atmosphere. Your hands were over your eyes and you were as white as a ghost."

Bronson was smiling playfully at the witch boy. "Were you frightened?"

The witch boy's tone became very reserved. "Your big jet, sir, nice as it is, is not a proper spaceship."

Nabnak evidently hadn't been listening. He nodded at the witch boy's orange dinner pot. "Hey, everybody, let's carve pumpkins."

Carroll clapped her hands. "La, la, la."

They selected pumpkins and began carving them. "Everybody do yourself," suggested Carroll. They worked quietly and steadily. Several times Carroll had to upbraid Nabnak and the witch boy for spitting seeds at each other. In twenty minutes they were done. Carroll had everyone hold their pumpkins up so she could compare the artist to the vegetable self-portrait. Nabnak's pumpkin had square eyes, a square nose, and its mouth was a series of four small squares set in a row. The witch boy's pumpkin had a third eye in the middle of its forehead. Bronson's pumpkin was slap-dash, the most work going into the little slit that represented his M-spot nasal supporter. Carroll's pumpkin had long curving eyelashes that covered three-quarters of the face. She examined all the pumpkins in turn with the wide eyes and slack jaw of the true connoisseur. "My God!" she cried at last. "We're all horribly disturbed!"

It was again time to get moving. They set their pumpkins down on the log and, sweetly saying "good-bye," tromped off across the field. Behind them, the abandoned Jack-o-lanterns glared with frozen expressions of panic, but expressions at the same time oblivious to their inevitable disintegration.

They faithfully followed Bronson's map, crossing through woods, fields, over roads, across ditches. In places where the ground was soft they followed the spoor of the Info Rangers who had proceeded them.

"Tower agents wouldn't leave such a trail," Nabnak observed critically.

Evening began falling, and the colors in the sky faded to a deep blue-gray that muted the colors of the fields. But somehow the orange of the pumpkins seemed to become more vivid, and the jagged outlines of the pale dead trees and the mushroom caps among the woods and along the windbreaks stood out in sharper contrast, like pen and ink sketches against the sky.

They were crossing over a gravel road when a tractor pulling a wagon filled with boys in their late teens came shaking by. Bronson waved to the old farmer driving the tractor; the farmer thrust his tongue into the side of his cheek and stopped. The tractor engine coughed as it shut down.

"Howdy-do there, young people," said the farmer. He wore a dumb expression that seemed to hide a cranky taste for humorousness and mischief. "Nice day for a little hike."

"Howdy," Carroll said, giggling.

The farmer tapped the visor of his cap. "Are you having a pick-a-nick today, ma'am?"

Carroll put her hands on her hips and rocked them back and forth. "Indeedy doody."

"Indeedy doody?" The farmer affected disapproval. "Cutey-pie, what are you talking there, *French?*"

"Means pick-a-nick," Bronson said with glib insistence.

"I thought so." The farmer leaned forward on his steering wheel. He winked at Carroll, who was pushing and pulling at her thick hair playfully. "Sure is refreshing to see some young people enjoying the out-of-doors. These days, everybody's inside watchin' their TVs. Not even many hunters anymore. I suppose it's the mushrooms, but I don't think they look too bad. My wife, God bless her, didn't like 'em." The farmer shook his head. "Sure is good to see some people still like the out-of-doors. Not like these dumb 'ol prole-ocks." The farmer hooked his thumb over his shoulder. Behind him the twelve or so boys in the wagon stared ahead stupidly. They were quiet and sluggish, but they also appeared anxious and dissatisfied. They hardly seemed to notice Bronson and his companions. Several held balls of cord, and

Bronson reasoned these boys were string-ball collectors, but then he noticed the wooden ovals tied at the ends. Bullroarers! That explained the buzzing sounds they had heard.

Nabnak found himself puzzling over etymology. Proletarians? Warlocks? He at last insisted, "What are prole-ocks?"

"Well, I'll tell you, young feller." The farmer pushed back his cap. "Every once in a while I find 'em out in the fields, lost, wandering around, half-starved, complaining, not the foggiest idea of what they want to do with their lives. Oh, sometimes they say they want to go to the factory: 'Where's the factory? We want work there. Just give us work.'" The farmer glanced off across the fields and sighed. "There ain't no factories around here. Seems pretty stupid to want to work in a factory anyhow, don't it? If I was their age, I sure wouldn't want to be in a factory. I'd go to Alaska. But what can you do? These prole-ocks ain't even smart enough to survive out here, let alone out in Alaska. Too dumb to even bend down for a pumpkin, Lord have mercy."

The witch boy shook his head with firm disapproval. "No common sense at all."

"So what are you going to do with them?" asked Bronson.

"Why, take 'em to Toledo," said the farmer. "Sort of a little charity I do. I'll drive 'em in and dump 'em off on Lagrange Street with the rest of the prole-ocks, where they belong."

Bronson didn't like anything about the pumpkin republic of Toledo, but he appreciated the effort made by the farmer. "Well, sir, you are to be commended for taking the time to help."

The farmer shrugged. "Got to clear 'em off, one way or another. You're the one that's to be commended—taking your friends out on a pick-a-nick, enjoying nature. That's the kind of self-sufficiency this country needs. Enjoy yourselves now."

Bronson nodded appreciatively. "Just you be careful in Toledo, especially down on Lagrange Street. There are scores of thousands of people there who cannot discern between their right hand and their left hand."

The farmer nodded as he reached down to start his tractor. "And also much cattle."

Melody and Refrain

Vitasta Raina

Poems from the Field

1. This Monument

Such is the nature of
ephemeral art, she said,
It is fleeting.
You do not live in it,
You do not dwell upon it.
It comes like a flash of molten
lava, erupting from volcanoes
of dopamine ridden stories – love, drugs, peculiarities,
bullshit.
We are the rocks on the shores,
ever wary of these surges.
We are wave-breakers.
Disengaging from idle life,
disengaging from grammar.
I am not you,
and you are not me.
Tonight, we will paint together,
the outlines of tomorrow.

Written during PhD ethnographic studies in the Katkari tribal hamlets at Tooth Mountain, Chouk village, India.

2. Prayer 1

~For Whitman and the unknown poet~

Oh terrible! Free me from this longitude, this latitude, this degree of light,
Let me deviate, let me proceed from this frigid idea
To the next thing that does not coalesce, give me a tempered sun.
And give me the grass, I'll add my own blades, and let my fat indolent fingers
Taste the blood of my own lunacy, scorching, volatile, tense.
Let my burnt umber brain stem dictate to the willing
Passages of my passages and incantations! Oh being!
I pray
To become
An utterance.

Such nonsense in the halls and universities,
Such Faustian horrors, such roads to hell, tree lined avenues
Such corruption of tongues and languages, bleak and untidy
I pray, oh nothing!
I pray
To become
A poesy.
I pray to you, Oh Truth, I pray for all days,
I pray to the winter's cold and to the frost lidden lintels
Of decorated doorways where the sunlight glimmers sometimes,
And I pray to keep the soul of the librarian, Spark in me,
Lead me to the dust, to the odours of foul words, to the stranger's bootstrap
Lead me to the grass, damp beneath my feet, I'll add my own blades
Let me bleed. That rush of vermilion in my brain, that skull, that horror,
Let me bleed out entirely on your pages, and take my yellow.

Give me your fervent fever of green, your jolly, your tribe, your flowing grey,
Let me
Become.
Let me, Oh infinite!
Let me define thy hidden.
Let me think soaked in battery fluid and ethane,
I pray
Oh Poet, you, us, each other and never finished,
I pray
And I reach
And I pray again
And I seek
And I seek
And I seek
And I see…
I

Oh cosmic drop of plasma! Oh jewelled, glittery drops of sun-split oceans,
I have walked, barefoot and humble
On blades of grass.

3. Working Breakfast

Exposed, out in the open, in front of people's eyes, and there you are enjoying the process. The taut tarpaulin sheets that cover the skies are gone. We sit under trees on wooden tables, a picnic of gods. We're on the right side now, the holy side. I thought we were playing a game, but I guess we were only madmen, forgotten, wrapped up in our own delusions. Nothing to see here except calm eyes, and breakfast. Eggs and baked beans.

The second of J. Dogs and their masters. Cheating the system with shaggy tails and pyjamas. We, the elite come to eat in the finery of bedwear. Keep our horses by the stables. We, the proper know the English names of breads and cheese. Something sneaky behind gold string masks and spectacles. Something personified in dirt and Christmas bells. What else can we do, but ride out to other pastures, fill out other seats, get noticed by the benevolent eyes of lesser deities, octopi, and cruds. Such happiness lurks, such demesnes, such floral shadows, shy in the sun, murals of slow death, suitcases, and central jails. Where else can we sit and contemplate life? Where else but in the forest-zones enclosed in our minds. Quickly forget families and shoes, quickly pass by discomfort.

Why do you rush? Oh my! Where are your prints from, dressmakers and incense burners? Tell me, will this smoke obscure my words? Keep insects at bay? And I cannot bear to sit here empty but I too will learn your rapid way, I too will let shiny pink satin silk slip into my white. I who contemplates cigarettes and space. I who begs for corner tables and French toast. I too will indulge in coffee table parlance, my trilingual affectations and edifices, stones of carved roses and wearing cowboy hats. I hope your hairstyles are worth this affliction.

4. Remembering the Dragonfly

Amber legends, Raphael,
The whirlpools of warfare rage,
Like torches amid dust storms.

We are but symbols,
Pictograms of fallen gods,
Ideas of a renaissance deity.

We are spectators
Of old-world charms,
Curators of earthly tones.

5. Epiphany 8

Silent reverberations,
Echoes through time,
Transformations of empty space,
With abstractions, words, and worlds...
I saw a goddess in a dream last night,
Gilded in Stone, crusted mantle of a civilization,
Mirrored reflections of green jewels piercing the darkness,
Saving the horrors of isolated thought for the blind.
No need to go treasure hunting in the jungles of belief,
They are shooting poets in batches...

Jeffrey Falla

Darkness and Blue

One Hour from the Book

I can't say anymore what was said
A hundred years ago about the familiar dream
I was to the dreamer who loses meaning

After I'm gone. To slip over that empty pool
And not fall in, but the lapse in meaning
Finds time and familiarity wrapped in canvas

And chains, yet undrowned, in fact, quite intact,
Just not accessible, aside from the words.
The great rim that is my life, your life,

Our lives flattens on its own. The wave
Just gives it shape. I thought I knew it
After hundreds of repetitions, hundreds

Of years, unconsciously shoving my hand in,
Stopping the movement momentarily to read
The words. How many different ways those words

Have been put. It seems limitless
While it's not. I can only read it
This way, familiar to now as repetition.

New Moon in September

Clouds bearing torches leap over each other
Pulling eyes along with them. Arguments drop
As soft as autumn rain, at least momentarily.

Backing out of the dark passage a nail
Skins flesh, the narrow channel pinker
Than the sky before scarlet fills them both.

Speaking to you at this moment
Would be akin the having a knife fight
Just for the fun of it. Instead

I place my hand on the cool glass
Of our presence reflected on imagined marble
Mild as a star in water. Soon

The evening wraps silently around us
With no moon to pull the tide of thoughts
That drop heavier than melancholy stones.

Repetition of the Nearly Unconscious

My coat flaps like wings in flight down frosted alleys
Narrowing in blackness and steel staircases.
Did his eyes really slide to the sides of his head

When he mentioned sacrifice? He did cut himself badly
Boasting someone should just try push him off the roof.
I stood motionless caught in the burlap of an old spell

Then he went through my hands. In these depths
Knowing comes from imagining nothing is real
The consequence of a decades-old secret.

With no substance it's nearly unconscious now,
Rolling over the empty prairie a stone's throw
From the imaginary state line, the beginning and the end.

In the repetition of the nearly unconscious
Being chased down an alley by a bleeding maniac
Comes later in the conflation. It's a well-regarded cliché

That the insane don't know they're insane.
At least that lets me off the hook
Flopping like a fish about to find water,

A trajectory turned on its end
So I can imagine conscious movement
Through time and space is something more than a fall.

The Heart

I pictured people fainting
Or at least vomiting, but it wasn't like that.
The façade just fell away abruptly, surprisingly,
Not unlike the way my father said

He no longer found Ole and Lena jokes funny.
He seemed to love telling them until finally
I suppose the ethnic caricatures
Were no longer comforting, just insulting.

When laid bare what else can the core do?
When a stranger gave Terry Hell
A raw deer heart, drunk on bottles of vodka
He baked it in the oven and the house stank

For a week. He spread some of it on bread
But most went in the garbage
Along with the pan. With flesh removed
The core faltered. I pictured people gathered

Around a mindless alter, the weakest chosen
To pull the abject heart from the most vulnerable.
Yet no one really wanted the sacrifice
Even as they absently constructed the ceremony.

Under the Morning Star

I'm dreaming, I say, helping you
Open the trap of your pedestal.
I'm dreaming too, you say, dropping
On me with unnatural lightness.

One of us must be lying.
We both catch on spines that cling
To early morning forgetfulness
In the coming dew, knowing that around

The corner all this will be lost to the dawn.
The desire to remain caught slips away
The more I reach for you but I still reach.
To reach and catch is like the difference

Between flesh and memory. Out in the yard
Things change in the waning moonlight.
The fence is gone for one thing, nothing
Now to keep out threats except

The shack housing rusty traps
And spineless ideas that never should have been.
We lose sight of one another
As if tingling flesh sheds who we seem

To each other. When dawn arrives
Our voices find us, punctuating
With certainty our presence between
Something like air and something like ground.

From First Deception Emerged

All involved are dead now.
No one to verify the sprouting
Of a planned grand hoax, unknown
At the time, but stopped dead in its tracks
And laid as bare as a cadaver.

The evening had shed its mystery
In denial of the darkness it once was.
The bear-shirted shaman in murderous trance
Had just emerged; the poor villagers
Shielded only in their righteous indignation
Didn't stand a chance. Yet he

Took time out from his rampage
To start a line that led to the plan,
Actually led to me, of my hand slipping
The typed pages into a seldom used cubby hole,
After which I made my escape under the milk
Of the departed evening. Only later,

Of course, would I regret the few lines
I remembered, openly folded like a jack-knife.
What is more deceiving than deception? A hoax
To split the origin from what really happened.

House without Sleep

A rusty owl sits motionless on its iron branch
Waiting…waking…waiting…
Lots of iron here, so much scrap,
The broken bed decomposing in a far corner

With its forgotten sleep and fading stains;
Whose even was it? A child
Runs a wire around the springs, weaves it
Through and among dull halls and doorways.

The others pay no mind wrapped up
In fantasies of pulsing insects
Absorbing the empire's corpse. "For it's been dead
Far too long for any hope of rebirth."

"Best to just enjoy the slurry." Perhaps the child
Hears this as she winds the wire
Around a reupholstered bolster
Which lets out a gasp of pitiful batting

From its weakest seam. The others don't notice
For people in this house avoid differences
So as not to turn on each other.
Here difference means that which is no longer

Repeated. So everything repeats
As if there is no end.
The words, the rust, the decomposition repeats;
Even the hot dish as old as the kitchen

Repeats in long familiar bowls.
The bent forks continue to go unnoticed.
The owl repeats its motionless sitting
Waiting perpetually for the return of sleep.

Daughters of Beulah

Fleshless wonders wavered around me
Stolen in themselves.
At times they pulled nets
Which became a field of stars

Then finally veils wrapped
Around their airy bodies.
I had to stare at myself
To make them come clear

Even though they felt of flesh
Only fleetingly. A once
Secret patchwork of torment and pleasure
Wove two edges of being together.

No one can last that way for long:
Their now solid fingers holding me
To myself, a self that too risked
Constant evaporation.

Control went back and forth
Like a dish served too late and out of spite.
I hung on with hands and teeth
Blood flushing beneath sudden skin

As soft and delicate as a pink cloud.
I wasn't one; I couldn't stay.
With a surge of dull headache
I was back alone in the lighted night.

David Flynn

Chaos

How sad that even chaos is a system.
Chaos equals a group of forces, none of which
is dominant.
That explains my life.
I have breathed now for more than seventy years.
Over that universe of time
have appeared eight lovers,
twenty-seven rented apartments and houses,
a hundred friends,
thousands of dinners,
and millions of events.
Plus billions of everything else.
So that, at more than seventy, my life feels
like a chaos.
A mathematical chaos, however, does have poles,
called attractors,
around which the equal elements revolve
like a figure 8.
My life, looking along its curved, noisy lines,
revolves around
spiritual idiocy,
the death of the family,
the class system in America,
the enormous growth in human population,
the Aristotelian tradition,
Adlerian circles,

the lack of ultraviolet and infrared capabilities among
my organs,
and a trillion other influences.
My attractors?
I can't identify those yet.

I must live with chaos,
writers this century have said,
but they thought the universe nonsense.
Having read thousands of writers,
products of many centuries
and many cultures of the Earth,
I feed them to the chaos as well.

Within the chaos of the infinite possibilities
we in the West
have decided not to try at truth.
Instead we choose a few parts,
and within that part for the whole
make a kind of boat.
In that tightly constructed shell
we weather all storms of reality.
Approximation, Rough Fit, Limited Consistencies:
these are among the boat's possible names.
Other parts of Earth take a more general view,
drowning in the lack of specificity,
yet, before the head falls below the waves,
sensing a bigger truth.

Whatever I do will not last.
But that's all right.

Necessity has left the world,
along with permanence.
I will achieve or not achieve,
will be happy or sad,
will increase or decrease my inheritance
in a chaos of permutations
until death ends my events.

Chaos is not depressing, really,
just the way of the world.
The way of all possible worlds.

The New Physics of Love

Fire between the living and the bed room,
yet we are not metal. Love is metal if
it embraces time. Our love never owned
a watch.

Soul is
your lips, your eyebrows, your blue eyes, your skin,
white as purity, hair red as the sweat

of sex. Soul is a knot of atoms
in the web of the universe that I,
a second knot, love.
Love builds the fire in the fireplace; it pours

the red wine into your glass, the white wine
into my glass. Love embraces. Your shape
fits my shape, and warms my flesh with your flesh.
We are human because we have the names

of humans truly. The rest is physics.

Fire between the living and the bed rooms.
We rush the mattress. Subatomic, I
want only the tube of you, the sliding
song, and the vagueness of our ecstasy.

Which is not quantum, but old fashioned skein.

Love makes the world go round. Blah.

Love makes the world go round.
Blah. Physics makes the world go round,
and chemistry makes the organs hard and wet.
I love you, truly love you.
Would die if you died.
If anything is true, it is our love.
We've been through so much,
and still live together.
Nine years next month.
My physics and my chemistry
are still strong.
I want to gravitationally hold you.
I want my brain cells to organize my feelings, reasoned thoughts, and sense
perceptions
of you
and more.
If science is all we are, then I want my science to be strong, faithful, and in
a
quantum
fog

of

you.

Prebangian

Prebangian means before the Big Bang.
Science worries about the nature of nothing.
Was there time before the Big Bang?
Was there a universe before the Big Bang?
Are there other universes and the Big Bang just began our local universe?
All questions.

All I know is that I am born, age on schedule, and face death.
There's the menu, the set list, the outline.
All I know is that I don't know, or maybe
I don't know that I don't know.
See how cloud-like the ideas become when a human tries the edges?
If we stick strictly to the middle we can think our way to the watch,
the super computer,
the self-driving car,
the Pluto space probe,
the hair replacement robot.
the thermonuclear bomb.
But if we worry about Why we are jokes:
50,000 religions on Earth and still dividing.
Thousands and thousands of tribes and still growing smaller.
What tribe are you? Write down your address.
Basically, the flail around, do small bits, then die.

So when we die do we become prebangian,
Otheruniverseian, or just rot?

Are we energy?
I don't feel like energy.
My head hurts this morning. Allergy, oak pollen probably.
Last night a raccoon dug into my plants on the back deck.
Was it separate energy, or claws and teeth?

Too many questions in this poem.
Life = questions
because we are too small and too trained
to come up with a list of answers.
God an answer.
Time an answer.
My finances an answer.
Love an answer.
I refuse the question mark.
Who invented the damn question mark anyway?
Oops.

Panspermia

There is a movement to send small containers of Earth germs
to other planets, both in our solar system and other solar systems.
After large efforts not to contaminate probes on Mars, Jupiter, and elsewhere,
this group, including scientists, actually want to 'colonize' other places.
Why?
These aren't humans contaminating other planets;
these are bacteria, microbes, small dudes.
The hope is they will float down on the planet,
the capsule break,
and the germs wiggle out to an hospitable atmosphere,

enough water, enough nutrients, enough
to multiply,
and that in time they will evolve
into the new planet's life.
Why?
Earth possibly was contaminated by life forms
thrown into space from, maybe, Mars
or far out ground
and that those germs
led step by step, year by year
to us humans.
So why not return the favor?
The name of this movement is panspermia,
though sending sperm to Mars seems only part of the program.
Paneggia?

So we are growing itchy to leave this planet,
which we are the verge of highly screwing up.
But we take our hatreds with us.
No Hispanic germ in this capsule,
no hijab wearing microbe,
no African genes.
We will just migrate, be safe for a generation or two
intent on survival,
then start screwing up the new planet.
KKK on Mars.
It's going to happen.
Time travel to the future:
Sure there might be neat robots, swell spaceships, hotels on the moon,
but there also will be pro-wrestling in virtual reality,

anti-semitism in Nazi AI,
politicians advertising 'Keep Out the Martians' in election ads.
What's the point?
Our individual preservation maybe,
though that seems too Not to be possible,
--another school massacre today--
but let's drag tribalism, our 50,000 religions, our fat-shaming
into the universe?
I don't think so.

Think I'll just live here until I die,
and not crying
but waking to yet another day
for awhile.
Earth is enough:
blue oceans,
white-topped mountains,
vast vistas of desert,
blue eyes,
soft skin,
a book by an author who knows something precise,
and ice cream,
and a cool fall breeze
and the joy of a new paycheck,
and and and.

Despite the hell,
think I will stay here.
Ask the germs where they want to be
before shooting them into space.

Horace Jeffery Hodges

Lies, a Cautionary Tale

Before every story lies a story,
You can't expect it only tells Thee Truth.
Best to do is try Thy best to borry
Best of the lie, oh might I sigh, forsooth.

Drunkard's Dream

Not a hundred bottles of beer on the frickin' wall;
My strongest drink was Jaguar Ginger Ale.
Nor passing out at all on alcohol,
But shifting weary vigils through sleep's long bleary vale.

And thank you again for keeping me
from a most marvelous mess of myself:
Held firm in your right hand's dignity,
A cup placed safe on its sundries shelf.

Doth One Feel Death?

Even as might a child, chilled
Through and thoroughly
To the bone, sense death in turn,
Frightfully early on,

There, but fall alike away,
The closer they seem to approach,
The farther they seem to stray,
Child and death, each its own way.

No One Feels Death

No one feels death, but Jesus,
Who reckons my every stroke,
The forty minus one
Of which the rabbis spoke.

No one seeks death, but Jesus,
Who counters every blow,
And bears our every sorrow
Because he loves us so.

Being-Time

Once upon a different time,
I tried to make this structure rhyme,
But never reached that sweet sublime,
To justify my being-time.

Effing Luck

Who gives a f**k,
If you have luck?
You lose an "l"
So what the "hel"?

Just a couple,
Of sounds double.
And gone's the f**k:
You're found with "uck."

December 1895

Graveled bank behind, we float upon thoughts
Condensed, and cold, and rippled only by
Our prow.
Memory, slipped under wooden ribbing,
Hides in depths where memory always lies,
Far down.

But were some spirit of the Lord to move
Across these waters still, as with the or-
igin
Of time, would he make all things fully new,
Wash clear dark, deep, redemption's pool, where
Old stains
Overflowed?

Crescent Moon

For love that pines,
I state a truth:
'This moon gleams
like the Serpent's Tooth.'

Oracles

They say the dead shall rise again?
Then lay your body down.
Rest deep in dreamless sleep, my friend,
But not in fallow ground.

Final Lament

Sighs, like the midnight breeze.
Love finds its ease,
And falls in silent sleep.

Life Game

Thoughts of you fade in that night
Where waning love like the moon declines;
I scan this poem with darker eyes
And play a devil's game with life.

"Cogito Ergo Sumthin'"

I think, I think, I think, I think
I am a Cartesian sink;
But *if* I had my *own* sweet will,
I'd *rather* be an artesian well.

Deconstructive Hermeneutics

For Derrida

The poem is *strictly* about
whatever

This poem leaves
Out . . . .

To Wittgenstein

The world is *solely* about
whatever
In fact it leaves
Out . . . .
Abshied
(Nonsense for a Friend)

Abshied

(Nonsense for a Friend)

Adé, adé, sweet Cherry Lee –
For Tüb' cannot contain 'er –
Adé, adé, too soon you'll be
A fresh, Kirsch-filled Berliner!

Miss Laid

You lay there,
Rumpled hair:
No more staid,
You got laid.

Seafarer

He anchors aweigh to the seas,
Letting all landlocked lie;
Sails surge to the blustery breeze,
Clouds scud a cerulean sky.

Honor, Offer

Give me your honor,
Feed me a line,
Render your ear,
And we'll have a grand time.

Make me an offer,
Take me to task,
Tender your ear,
And we'll make the grind last.

Tratsch

Crab-like-clutching clutter –
Scattered-matter clatter –
Klatsching, crunching, crouching, scrunching,
Scuttle-scrutching 'cross the floor . . .

See Meant

This concrete poem
Can be bet on.

&

In fascinating amber sands –
Where fast some eighty anurans –
I'd fashion eighteen ampersands:
And-and, and-and, and-and, and-and,
And-and, and-and, and-and, and-and,
And-and, then stop! Abruptly end.

Naught

Mankind is not
Because God thought,
"Man: Kind Ungot."

Wordsmith

Testing mettle –
Weight or tense – I'll
Strengthen ever-
Y subtle sense:
Overwrought or
Underworked, I'll

Toss all dross
Out in the dirt.

Willy-Nilly

O Willy, low man
On the totem pole.
You would have liked to
Be a well-liked soul
Man in Seoul. A Han
River miracle
Of one for two
Meaning lost on you?
No, nor on others, too.

Michael Butterworth

Time Trap

You observe our world,
But cannot join it.
We are separated,
You on your hard bench,
With what you lie down in, I
In my room of books and chairs.
If I broke with linearity
And collided with you,
Unknown Similarity
Would open between us.
In a single motion expertly
You roll a second layer over your
Almost prone form
To keep warm. It's
What I would do at six a.m., too,
With only the Canada geese for comfort.

September 2020

§

Tulip
Bent yesterday
In the rain
You have risen again. The city gleams
In the sun, and
The geese pair and wait
For nests to appear.

23/02/21

§

I’m hoovering
Manoeuvering.
This great world
Tremours, on
The Edge of Existence.

14/07/21

§

Little sister

With your ribbed gold
Swimsuit and shining brown eyes
And white bow ribbon
In your chestnut-brown hair
You run at me across the lawn
Clasping my legs from behind
And try to lift me.
Not yet, but in a few weeks
You will elevate me
Precariously by the merest fraction
Of an inch.

§

You say green
Is a Socialist plot
Getting in the way of free trade.
But ‘free’
is meaningless
in a world running out of resources.

You say green
Is red, and I agree. But red
Stands for danger

§

Mr Lazellglass

Mr Lazellglass has arms like ten pythons. He does forty-eight cartwheels before breakfast. His underside is coated in rust from years of lying in pools. On his head is a hat made from marmoset eyes. I often see him wearing a pair of pinstriped gollies on his ears. I use my time on the bus to meditate. There is a knack to doing this with your eyes open. Let images come and go without attachment… and so my picture of Mr Lazellglass has been built up gradually over countless journeys. He often addresses the bus with whatever thoughts come into his head. He has a very loud voice like countless millipedes screeching at once. He also does a thousand push-ups as a regular thing. On birthdays he walks the tightrope across Deansgate. The bus usually listens to him with mute faces. Not one looks at him directly. I can see by his eyes he can devour 85 busloads in a gulp and think nothing of it.

Mrs Hinchinilly

Mrs Hinchinilly was another adept of Route 143, sometimes dragging her multifarious limbs onto the deck and pulling up to six suitcases and as many loaded carrier bags as she could. Once aboard her eyes cloud over with faraway scenes, and she begins to shout, a one-woman newscaster. She has been wronged somehow. Was she stateless? Had a coup forced her from her country? Was our country in some way to blame? It is the same speech every time. We sit frozen in our seats. No one is listening. She has spent every day travelling up and down the Wilmslow Road. But some bolder students from the universities give her fresh shrimps. She has on a pelican-head, and her arms describe boisterous mambas. I built up this picture of her in her traditional dress over many years of twenty-minute meditations. Towards the end she will break down into Hundreds-and-Thousands. She is also to be seen skating along the pavements on roller blades the size of rockets. Four days in a row she will sing Scarlatti at the top of her voice. The last time I saw her from my seat by the window she seemed to be chattering to a lamppost. She had on a sky-blue eraser. I don't know whether she and Mr Lazellglass ever caught one another's performance. On all those journeys up and down on the 143, I reckon they must have.

[Travelling on the buses that rolled up and down the Wilmslow Road taking us to work or university, it wasn't uncommon to find ourselves part of a captive audience. 'Mrs Hinchinilly' was an educated middle-aged woman who travelled the route with suitcases and carrier bags that presumably contained her worldly possessions. She dragged her luggage piece by piece along the toad. It was a common sight to see parts of it parked on the pavement awaiting its turn to be taken to the next 'stage'. When she came on the bus she stood in the aisle, hotly regaling the seated passengers. Because of her accent and the noise of the bus her tirades were only partially coherent. Even more was lost by the reluctance of her unwilling audience to take in complexities of her life. Another of the characters who occasionally engaged us was a middle-aged man, who would deliver long routines from a seated position. His thoughts emerged in chain association, some funny, some topical, making us think he had at one time been a professor of some kind. Now perhaps brain damaged or suffering Tourette's. 'My Lazellglass' was my invention.]

Spring 2014—Summer 2015

The Dream Pharmacopoeia

1. The Butterwort

The Butterwort is poisonous. It grows on riverbanks and likes to spread to adjoining pastureland, a farmer's curse. It grows rapidly to a great height. Its broad hairy green leaves soon starve smaller plants of light, and ultimately chokes them. Its stems are pale and mushy, and soon cut down. But the plant cannot easily be eliminated because its root system is extensive and tenacious, and soon thrusts up new shoots. Medicinally, it has no use whatsoever.

February 1981

§

Michael was getting old. Racing through his 'bodily things' one morning after taking a bath—drying, putting on his clothes—his mind on doing something else, his writing probably—he could feel the anxiety spreading through him and couldn't wait to be finished with them. He resented having to dress, undress, wash, prepare and shop for food. He had become aware of time compression years earlier when he had seen the furze blossom on his garden path and seen the same thing the following year and ever since; existence had become a treadmill. But this morning, suddenly, he stopped. He had been doing it all arse up, he thought. Those very same behaviour patterns in which he felt so trapped, were actually the most important things he could do, weren't they?

Ebi Robert

Seven Months and Two

I am a woman, not a man
Yet, I'm a woman who is a man
I am the changing chameleon
That has several colours in a million

I can't be boxed to a barn
And likely bundled as the yams
I can be many things to a man
I can even handle the *arms*

I am the builder of the Home
Not the muted-muse of Rome
I have the ripened right to Vote
Like every man of the Home

I can *make and mark* the vault
I even drive the beach-bye boat
I can serve and save Africa
Like *Adedevoh* did to Ebola

You must seek my consent first
Before you get under my skirt
Do not treat me as a bitch
That can be mated on a Pitch

Smell the sweetness of my smell
And get the fatness of my meal
I'm that womb that bore you
In seven months and two

City of Angels

I stared into the ways
For the hypocrisy is in the images
Yes! The eloquence is in the images
In these mock reflecting ways

I stared into the way
Captivated by the city that
Paints beauty everyday
With the sides, my shadows' fat

You well know the beauties
So do not fail to use the key
Take up the dices,
On the Angelic dices

The key is the lamp,
It opens the growing vase
With myrrh fuelled with
Frank-Frankincense

Take up the voice fruity,
Burnt cinnamon, in the river,
Speaking with a thousand voices—fruity

Dip a tip into the honey beside the vase
Then the blessed-out well wise,
Shall upon lips, romance this sweet thing

Use the sweet link to halt
The creature's wandering voice

The key is the play-pen
The mightiest of all the organs of men
Do tie the ringlet to the verse
And then sing as the angels lie

They shall flow on choruses and verse
And turn in tones as we throw the dice
But before the angels' soprano
Rise on vine-vocals contralto

Use the violin to sow the solo
With the snow-sing-slow

Beauties shall run the piano
Upon keys, rebranded horns, and suppranino

Choirly, choose the chorus
For angels' voices are not known to crack

Don't be praised
When the chorus is over
You shall be in the city

By My Death

If death is the mind of birth
Why the long tale of breath?
If grave is the bed of men
Why the crowned crow of the hen?

But if men were to sleep
If only they would sleep
Snoring in the dust and not sneeze
Why the long tale of the breeze?

Men and Hen should have died in sleep
If only, if only sleep is sleep

But by my death, by my death
Death is not death
By my death, War is a killer
And peace is my mourner

By my death, the world is at war
Heaven is the asylum
By my death, the world is at war
Heaven bemoaning, "Come"

By my death, the world is at peace
Heaven, the disease
By my death, the world is at peace
At a mighty lease

If death is the mind of birth
Why the long tale of breath?
If grave is the bed of men
Why the crowned crow of the hen?

Peter Dizozza

System of Our Own Design

’Cause I know it well I need not think a lot.
I can think of other things Built upon the things I've got.
Step-ping up a step stool. Set on a second floor
Systems running smoothly No attention needed As we explore a
System of our own design
Here within our corners, keeping us in line.
We can make a system of our own design.
Systems running smoothly, scarcely worth a thought
Rather let us use them, Let us climb them.

’Cause we KNOW IT WELL, we’ve time to think some more.
We can think of other things, built upon our second floor.
Stepping up a step stool here in our box apart
Over cellars' sub-floors carved from blasted bed rock, let me hold the
Step stool as you reach for stars...
Here within our corners, steady as we reach,
Learning from restrictions all they have to teach.
We can use our corners—as our out-line
As we make a system of our own design.

During a rain storm water flows around our homestead
Hopefully our home survives this.
Is what is beneath us only land fill?

Here where a heat wave follows from a freezing cold spell,
Hopefully we will survive this.
From what we have seen since, nothing should surprise us.

What is the delay? A log jam slows us down.
Something we have never seen but now it always keeps recurring.
As of now this detour—let’s say we know it well.
When we hit this new snarl we can multi-task as bask we in the
System of our own design, built upon a
System of our own design, built on other
Systems of our own design (many repeats here)...

Using every corner, keeping near the door,
Standing on a step stool on a second floor
Over cellars' sub-floors built in blasted rock,
Let me hold the step-stool, absorbing every shock.

Here within our corners, steady as we reach,
Let us learn from systems more than what they teach.

To the Mallow Marshes

Do you see our car where we left it? Look down there. It's down there.
Will the path we beat beneath our feet Lead us there?
Even as we climb does the path double back? We
Must increase our distance from the salt mine.
Even as we stray from the well trod tourist path, we
travel ever downward to the mallow
marshes. Down there
In salt where we are landing, Prepare.
Here beneath an earth-formed embankment We squatted. We potted,
On the crumbled chunks beside a half- rooted tree.
Taller though it grows, bits of topsoil break away ex-
posing hidden rooted fun-gal net-works.
Why'd we turn our backs on the rope suspended bridge, to
Face our destination down there? We are
looming over
A cliff where only eagles Hover God
used to but no longer gives me hope or help. Please God.
Hijack reproduction, it's a full-time blow job. De-
liver goods to places that are eggless. What-ever deaths the
Gods demand we grant them during wartime.
Square your shoulders, squeeze your butt. With-
hold the blood. Behold the blood, deliver pants to bodies that are legless.

When the rolling moon becomes a Sausage
I can see our car, we're almost There. We are
There after the flash where from our Summit we Plummet.
What we see trans-forms in the darkness of twilight Through
midnight.
Luminescent heads dotting the ground form a path.
Lift us when we're down. Lead the way. To be-low, the
colors of the night time ever glowing.
Hidden from the sun, we are free to see the light that
Rises from the moisture in the mallow marshes. Mushrooms!
In salt, where they are growing, throughout .... EARTH.

Carter Kaplan

Haiku Triptych

Trek to Andromeda

time is no longer
distance is no obstacle
warp factor zero

Ghidorah

studio monster
move lights above telling wires
is the illusion?

Owl

substance asserts form
life, moment, reality
hoo, hoo, hoo, hoo, hoo

Theorizing Green Lasers

green lasers from space
coax speculations unbound
haiku solution

Fellini

facial cameos
sudden objects, disclosures
normal is not real

Mothra

magic fairies sing
"mothra, justify our cries!"
shadow in the moon

day is born from night
a giant moth lays her egg
promises are made

tokyo tower
bracing the fibrous cocoon
patient larva waits

mothra will emerge
from a caterpillar dream
cherry blossom time

colors in the sky
sweeping winds across the bay
promises are kept

Mil Mi-26

first with eight blades
a rotary wing marvel
soviet hero

twin truboshaft might
inviolable purpose
dialectic fumes

we board with great plans
to siberia we fly
the commissar waves

Haunebu Haiku

New Swabia

plan into product
ice-hidden and globe-funded
notion yields exploit

Politics and Magic

secret disk dungeon
occult visions are technique
fascist metaphor

Triumph of the Will

south pole cavern shakes
nazi flying saucers rise
fall into dawn blaze

The Meteorology of Jupiter Space

frank does not like it
dave has a bad feeling, too
change in the weather

Progressive Haiku #1

ideology
mitigates dystopia
drink the gall slowly

Dr. Serizawa

godzilla must go
dred oxygen destroyer
serizawa weeps

facts, data, a choice
scientists humble themselves
loss and departure

Ana Cameron

Counting Pebbles

"I am free that is why I am lost"

Franz Kafka

Crossroads;
If you have not written in a month, thats how you know. We where at the crossroads and we separated.I saw bleu and then I saw red."It is ok."Hours turned into days, days turned into weeks, weeks turned into months and months turned into years, people changed,I have seen them living the same live over and over again, same people, same situations, same everything.They return again and again.Always the same story and always the same game.
This is not the only language I know yet I have never linked those two together.I have never inked them together with questions.Said and done"if anything dictates her here, then it is grammar and that poorly"
'Nothing really adds up we are all stabbing in the dark' all them hours you spend, spend them wisely as you will not get them back unnoticed.You do not understand the traffic you do not know how it is.How would you know how it is ?Unless someone told you?I painted for a long time and just to choose the colour tool two hours.The words, they just burst out of me and their is always that silence.All that silence.I know I say this and I say that as they are talking and they are talking about the things I should not know and I should not be questioning.Women date differently here.And that was that then.One wrong words and the body was broken back into place;`bit by bit, dance move my dance move over a long period of time.'I was walking as I was talking.And I could not see what was not before me.The sensation of falling stayed with me for weeks.The back bone was broken and they found an injury from way beyond,I was running.The sense of freedom never left.Oh to run again.Best thing.To them i was suddenly walking again.The work it took, the long hours.Then to learn how to write again.No one talks about that.
We just left and that was that then.I remember waving good bye to the house 'see you soon'.Their was no such thing and it took me a long time to return;"no wonder you got sad"someone said once'.To return in the end with nothing then stories, might be a good thing might not be.All them arguments;

for what?No change? I found some beach glass, sadly reminds me of when I was not good enough.I left again as soon as I could, everyone was awfully confusing to me as I was to them, they could not place where I was from, they did not understand that to travel can be a destination in itself.So where is the structure and where is the aim?what are you asking who?Do you have a map?A plan?

I often wonder if anyone has differed and I know I will return again one day to talk about those days where no one understood where I came from or where I was going.'Oh that is terrible typical' they would say; to find the problem and to address it and to try and find out what is really happening.I did not know that that was for some news and new.You need to pause and you need to breathe and you need to ask again and again.Are you sure?

Next thing I know is that I am being told, that they got the prime colours wrong and that this happened so following.It used to help going separate ways to feel I have never really been sleeping since.Always one eye open, always one eye on the door.I guess I made I list and for every word I wrote one that rhymed.As if it was common knowledge.But things started to become less clear, they started to shift.Confused I lost direction and I fell I fell bad and far, as the chink on my tooth tells of.I forget what I was looking for and I forgot where I was going so I took one last step.Seconds stayed.I did not know that one is supposed to say how one feels and I did not feel anything part from pain.Eventually the path decided for us, we stood at the road listening;'red and blue it is?you want purple?'The beginning was there so was the end.Three times I returned to find the exact same story;'the mystery of Golgotha'; when you wake up on the other side the question is ;how did you get here?Maybe you have a few more expressions to choose from, maybe you have more to voice then them.It will happen to you sooner or later.`They who ever they are will bribe you with what ever you think is reality'No one wanted to leave and their was hardly anyone their.We had a second when everyone had left.Their was no such thing as choice until then.I could had left, but I refused and so I stayed.I had seen it their and I was told no one had been to ask anything.They spoke to me in a language that I could understand and I appreciated that a lot.They reminded me that one is dragged back by the things one regrets.'

No matter how long it takes.No matter the urgency.Again I am looking intern from my body.I freaked out and I yelled 'we are loosing her',their was silence, then suddenly a response;'I think you are right'.So I jumped without thinking and I dragged her up from her knees.Everything went so awfully fast but I got her back.Nothing was ever the same.She was so angry with me.That was a very long time ago.Why was that? You would lock me into a cube?Square me up away from everyone and put me into a nice box and keep me away from the worlds.Unsure if I had finally broken my heart for good I paused, the pain alone was enough.I could not sleep and I could not move.I was asked a question that I could not answer so I ignored the ignorance and the light in my face and the not knowing who is and who is not.Leaving was a success remember.You are unique.Like everyone else is.

Subculture;
She could not remember much, so pictures where shown to her"maybe the memory will come back eventually."
They decided to travel, their is and was a lot of critique about that.From then on she would only feel comfortable carrying a bag and a one way ticket.She ran away a couple of times, or maybe she went home to what she was used to and to what she knew.Growing up in a sub culture within a subculture taught her many things, one of them was that she did not know society, as you know they had their own medicine.All her life was about being and staying on the move so to speak.People did not understand why she kept running away.She visiting many nice places, some far away some close.She was happy, until she longed for continuity.For stability.Every time she tried, she failed.Something or someone caught her of guard asking to many questions or not enough questions .Traveling was comfort, she had given in and she lived in a tent for a year.'People think your are kind and sociable and they take from you what you have'She never understood what it was that made her run.She never understood what was not understood.Overtime the pain became to much and their where opened conversation for plans to find seclusion and a solution.The end result was to be a shed in the mountains.Everyone had many questions about how lost she was as a byproduct of her aimless travels.She used to write letters to me; extensive notes.She was fascinated with the idea of independence, and believed it meant that she could do what she wanted to.Taking to the streets was something she would do, every time she found a change.Until one day the situation escalated.She had been asked to commit and she did not understand what was asked of her, all the sudden everything became complicated.`And she had recurring dreams and alienation never stopped following her.
Two of her favourite books where about someone running away.Eventually she had settled into travelling and she found peace on the road.That way of living she understood and she was comfortable with it.The time came when she started to ask herself if she would ever feel at home in one place as she was never at the same place for long.She longed for the buzz of the city and

a context that opened more pathways to patch.She would ask herself;how often have I packed my bags?People used to say she had no self,she fell into silence thinking that in some circles that would be the ultimate goal.They all tried to understand thinking.Paths changed, things did not read that well, the plot was not welcome, making everything so much more difficult.So she kept repeating herself well knowing that it was always the same story and always the same game.When does the fullstops come into place?she wrote to me:'I was just there,try imagine that not being allowed.I did not realise that that was nothing new to her and I did not know that I had been asking the same questions as everyone else.

The nagging went threw my skinny body and right to may heart, how honest do they want me to be?We tracked them for a long time and they where truly mean, what is love not?When she ran away for the last time the journalist got hold of me and saved everything for her ,they let her stay but she refused .Part of me thought it was so she would not put their words into action.Is it for others to decide that you are well matched and when not?he threw cups and trumpets to wonder for ever and more.She forgot about all this until it became personal; forever trying to find a better place to find a form of calmness and to understand.He said he followed her tags threw town.

Love is all I know, it is all I see and it is starting to blind me:

This goes out to my warrior who is out their on his own,
My dear warriors turned the stone, can you please now come home
It's hard on my own; the iron curtain has fallen, once again;
They think they are here to take away what's mine?

My dear warrior who is out their on his own,
Can you please now come home,
No need to be alone.
I want to trade my id, to prove that I am free.

"I asked you to paint me a happy picture
I gave you colours for that pretty picture,
you painted me two crashing towers
and it took you hours.

We stood under the protection,
strangly felt like resurrection .
Demon in reflection, what a perfect projection.
I asked you to paint me a happy picture I gave you colours for that pretty

picture...

Now know I am going to miss you,
You say its rather sad that I lost all that I had.
And I am sleeping on your floor and I live out of my bag
Now know I am going to miss you now know I am going go miss you.

Culture makers;
are you trying to produce something new or are you able to see whaty is there?what are they asking for?Are you talking for them or to them, about them or with them?
If something works, why change it.Lost in the mist of todays opinions the dusk settles slowly.Some are writing their notes and typing up ideas, others are being silent, they are watching and waiting for their time to come.
Do they know who they are and what they are doing?Are they helping or not?It is ok to walk away and there is a reason to only talk on reflection. I got lost in a rabbit whole but not much was to be found.What an opportunity.How is that not all awfully confusing, how would anyone know who is who and what happened when and why?I was gone for weeks sourcing for anything really, just something to relate to.What a cause that would be.The tone of voice appealed to me.I am left wondering if it was freedom of speech or indirect speech or free speech and if it had anything to do with words at all.Was is subjective life or stream of consciousness?I would ask anyone that would listen:what happened to relatability?Asking those questions a lot the path seemed to become clearer in time, things changed slowly but surely.My work became different and the way I related to the world gained on substance.No one wanted to say anything.I found more inspiration staring at a jam toast then scouting the World Wide Web.Equality means a lot to me and they find me silently shy.People are not projects.Can one be totally out their and still be relatable?There is distraction everywhere, to try take inspiration from that or to focus on what you are trying to say to the world will make all the difference.What if you could talk to them individually and ask them questions instead of answering?All sounds very nice.What if no one has anything to say at all and they are looking for inspiration from you?Well, obviously you might say.
Do you listen more than you talk?Some do not say anything when then do not know the subject.I would not let that intimidate you, we could address that if wished for.It is always possible to draw your own conclusions no matter.
I kept thinking about the word' trajectory' and 'associations',Change and

continuity.Contrasts and structure.Context chaos and discipline.Finding feedback was difficult, no one wanted to say anything.'A nice little read with rhymes'

The station; the lost and found song

You say you would,if only you could,
And that you could if I tell you, you should.
This goes out to you what's true, mate
It depend on you what us true man,
Who is making your day, your pray

Your play Oh please stay.
Please stay hear, please stay near,
Has day clear has day fear
Before you go I have something to tell you
I have something to show.
Why is it so hard for you to see,

That I want you and I want you free.
And if you want a change,
You are the one that has to rearrange.
He said he would if only he could
And that he could if I tell him he should,
Why did you try to change me?I am free!

You said, wait at the station I will soon be there
Say goodbye it is only fair.
I stood there for hours, until I realised it has all been lies
You kept all the money,
All I had was loose change,
So I walk the city cold.

Sister;
I got lost for six months.I got lost in research and notes.It is such a long time.I did not know who I belonged to, broken laptops and months not a word.things have changes, yet the words stay the same.
The notes where concluded and half of the work discarded, for now anyways.Their must be something new to find, or at least a different way to convey all them weeks and months spend on waiting.
Suddenly I remembered that there is nothing new and that the stories have all

been told already; it is not very inspirational and it is making things more difficult.When everything is said and done what will they talk about?If the battle is fought, what will they argue?What is a word worth these days?What are hours and what are minute changes?Stuck and running in circles I keep asking myself the same question, what do they come back for?

Their is a sense of freedom to writing.I used to fall asleep to the sound of a typewriter; everything was ok then.The biggest rebellion seemed to be writing 'oh I am just hear, sitting and thinking' if the words would just come out less abrupt, less radical.Less brutal.And the price that one pays is asking 'can that be said?Will we get into trouble for speaking our minds?Will we get away with it?The hope and the buzz constantly changes, yet the question remains, will we be ok to say?A couple of broken guitars and some song texts have made it threw to the years.And heir is a lot of remembering and wondering.Let me tell you how I found a jar of beach glass and how it reminded me of when I was not good enough in someones eyes.I wrote for a year, almost everyday at least one page."crossroads"is one of the few that made it, one of the few text that is not fictional or stream of conscious writings.I tried to write about things I can not say and trust me it was tricky.

There where only two players left.Everything was boxed in and up and the mathematics did not make any sense.Suddenly the scene changed.No one knew what was fine to say anymore.There where only those two.

'You do not expect them to wake up in heaven and to be confronted with that do you?'I was just listening the the argument and I lit a candle.'what are you trying to write here?'and 'I would be very upset if you are listening'

No one wanted to leave abd no one wanted to stay.You can not listen to anyone. Are you not trying to write things that will get me into troubles?I just doubt they will know where to find themselves in as I hope for the best.

When I ran away they followed me with a reading list 'you will not be back will you?'and ;'when you get their you better read this and you better read that and do not read this and do not read that 'good luck these days for saying.

Apparently some weak wizard summoned a demon that was running around destroying everyone and everything that tried pass.Believe me, that is what they said to me on my way out threw the fire escape.I just ran.

It became impossible for me to work as I did not know what was fine to say and what was not.As I got lost and things became difficult for me to fathom.I was thinking about the laws and regulations.I felt trapped.I realised that this is my safe place, where I can say how I feel.It means everything to me yet I was unaware that that is the most important thing 'what happens when you can not say what you want and what you think?'I am still looking for continuity not controul. How do both feel so similar to some?'As long as I can still plan and execute I will. Memory lane was grate yesterday.What if someone would come along and clap for you to find all your problems gone?If you are waiting for the perfect moment it might never be there.All your notes that have not been heard, they matter.They matter a grate deal.Everything that you are afraid to say counts.One day I will have my perfect place and my perfect desk and for that I will work myself into exhaustion, day by day, step by step.I read somewhere not to overdo it with the details.I believe that freedom is the best idea ever,It is soothing to me and it gives a lot of hope to me and many others.

How often have I heard;'you are writing now?here?'

When questions cost everything and not just a penny per spoken word, when you do not know if to continue or to improve or to try and return to the past where everything seems lost as it is not there anymore, what then?If you try owe someone they will end up owing you.You read and you see a pattern that you recognise. Suddenly you are supposed to remain the same.When asked what this writing of mine is I reply with a few words: a mix of indirect speech, stream of consciousness writing or free speech.I have mentioned this before.Things I have learned.Warnings and encouragement.Hopes and despairs, questions and missions.Then one day I stoped talking.Then I tried saying it as it is for me and that is when the problems started, as if I had not right to my own mind anymore.As if what I was thinking did not matter at all or to anymore.Then I found something out.I just asked the right question .And then it happened again.`Their was a tare in the tapestry of time, they is why we are hear and I have not head that before.Everyone was just so upset and as if they were frozen in time and did not want to be.As if life was only hurt.They could not move past what they saw, they lost heart and soul.They forgot what life is and what it can be.And I can not blame them. Wherever you are and whatever you do, i hope you are happy and content.I missed you a lot.

Price/And the price that you pay,
you pay to be my friend
Is it us us two with nothing to mend,
Oh Dee, dee, dear Dee,
How did it come to be,
Oh dee my dear Dee,
You are finally free,

And you say just in time,
It all will be fine,
You say just in time
It will all be mine.
And the price that you pay
You pay to see the end
Is it is us two until the bitter end.

Grace;

If you are telling your truth and your version, know there is nothing more important then that.For you and for everyone else this it is a tricky business these days.You can try to pick them up where they seem to be comfortable at,or you can make them want to leave, last to be questioned.People might see themselves threw your words.They might relate and you might inspire them too.Someone else might see it differently.They might not even take notes as you.

You are supposed to be free, you are supposed to be happy and incase no one told you and you need permission, you are supposed to be here now and always.

If reality is just a reflection of your inner world, then changing yourself and your way of thinking and behaving would mean your outer world you see and the experience has to adjust and change in accordance?

Never place faith into an outer force.For example; you tell your self a story about yourself and your life and what has happened to you and what is happening to you, what could happen and what should happen. If it is just a story that you repeat never or over and over again please consider that someone else might tell your story differently, they might notice things you did not understand.They might tell the story not to your accord and liking. Opinions do not matter?they change nothing?Can you change them?It is said that people can only listen for five minutes and you might wonder about how long people talk for.No wonder everyone seems so fed up and afraid to say how they feel at any given moment; a key to freedom is missing and under thread.It is your voice and you are free.Some places and some people do not understand that, try understand that.

Everything and my own silence was destroying me, no where do I feel as free as when I am writing and I ponder about the shared dreams.I was their listening not saying anything; freedom remember?How do stories sound when they are real?I am inundated with work. I have a waiting list and I love every nomad and the freedom that lifestyle brings; able to leave anytime and from anywhere,'oh I am just on the road again with a notebook and listening to music.'

If things go wrong and you get lost they will send a rescue team, remember you always have your voice and your sight and your view of things, it is yours alone.It is yours for ever and beyond.For ever and more.I started feeling nervous as if something was not right and so I waited for a couple of days.Then I tried to contextualise.I tried everything and finally what I found out scared me, nothing changed just because you change your mind.

They grow up there and then they grew up here, they where that and here they where something else there.It did not make sense. They march the streets a lot there, here not so much.Some days for things that never happened.I am still trying to understand.The stages, the reconning, the idiolisation and the hall of mirrors.They will never see your imperfections, your quirks and your bed hair.They do not see the world, only reflections they choose.And they boast and they ghost.Back then I used to scribble a triangle on the ground.I would throw the pebbles into the air and then I would start painting.I heard an echo' If something is working, do not mess with it'And call that 'Sophias correction.'The silence was destroying me.I felt I had been nothing but a fifteen year old tale of over ten waitress jobs.I know the alley ways, the efforts for the show.The lack of sleep and the lack of food and the isolations and the rudeness.Know your story they say.So no one else will.For everything still left to be said.I wake up at night and I always leave in the dark.Remember that not everyone wants freedom.Freedom is not for everyone.I had been thinking and thought had stoped as I was staring at a blank piece of paper, dreaming that is.To not be paced in their lives where they wanted me to be, to find themselves surprised at a later date.Tell a writer that words mean nothing.

Fractions and encounters, rhymes and prose of the beat. Thought and expression of emotions. Challenges, obstacles, defeat and success and everything in between and beyond hopes and dreams, the past and the future.Its you!

The Key;
Thinking a lot about yourself,
Thinking a lot about the self.
Did you know?How to become the key?

What are you doing here?
How is your passion so clear?
Wondering the streets.

Thinking nothing at all.
Every step you take,
Leads you closer to me.

You are setting me free,
What did you want from me?
What did you see ?

I said it all before,
Why?why were you not sure.
Control leads to rebellion.

The act that sets me free
Further away from me.
I was.your touch on reality.

David Nadeau

The Metaphysicians-Poets' International

More occultism! More visions! More drugs! Magical imagination is a vehicle of immortality. The ardent ascesis turns the poles upside down — and it has only just begun. Fairy hallucinations reveal the creative and destructive action of invisible beings on nature. Dark humor descends from the sky to corrupt itself in the center of the earth; hellish fire that animates matter from the inside. The alchemical Mercury dreams of a radically different world. The murmur recreates this world only from the laws of analogy.

Self-pity fulfills a prophecy. A Rosicrucian spy is putting together a whole file about the ideas, which I can only whisper about, on the becoming of the Spirit and the conflicts that occur at certain so-called secret levels of reality. She even slipped there some discreet allusions about "I don't know" which popular female singer. Perhaps the latter is putting forward too embarrassing things in a coded way... This seductive synarchist is lost in the meanders of the myth. Her doppelgänger urgently needs haunting songs. Strange crimes reconcile humanity with nature.

- What are you doing?
- I don't know why I maintain such follies... I am not, however, one of those senseless demiurges!

Divinatory Oblivion

False memories and feelings of deja vu; as the seasons change, the aroma of coffee brushes against metallic surfaces.

Agartha gesticulates. From Sirius, Indian hemp scrutinizes the intimate disasters. The euphoric diagram shivers.

The king of the world accumulates radiant darkness. His accomplice concealed the fraudulent substitutions, prior to language. The most sublime contradictions brush against meteorology. The moment deploys its ambiguous and vertiginous clues, at the right place.

Megalomania encumbers his destiny. Chance turns purple. Vague memories of oneiric impressions coil around the spine. A holographic hallway approaches. The Golden Fleece melts like wax. Simple, barely perceptible gestures prepare the nuptials of the subconscious and critical rationality.

Covered in gelatinous ornaments, the Duchampian etheric body manipulates microscopic clues; it is the only one to have been miniaturized.

The thoracic frog detects the qualities of the initiable. The divinatory melodies announce the stages of a furtive investiture. The suggestive coincidences accumulate. Vague memories of oneiric impressions enhance the sharpness of the image. Chance becomes angelically precise.

Sakkara

This combinatorial game board was reserved for the exclusive use of candidates for the priesthood, so that they could familiarize themselves with the handling of the different modalities of etheric energy and so that they could experience non-ordinary levels of consciousness. The goal is to discover the different ways of positioning the tokens on the board in order to activate the subtle energies associated with the elements of nature, to manifest the occult dynamism of their confliction.

The board is molded in clay that has been collected, prepared and fired at very specific times of the year, determined astrologically.

The date of each game session is decided according to the horoscope of the apprentice, the date of his initiation and his progress in the study of sacred science (cosmogony and metaphysics). Each time, the game is preceded by purifying rituals adapted to the individual character of each initiate. Inside one of these small temples made of not very durable materials (raw brick and wood), a circle of water surrounds the central table on which the game is placed. The neophyte must go down to a circle and get his feet wet, before going to the table. He is only allowed to move three pieces at each session and any movement must be preceded and followed by a moment of meditation. It may be years before he sees the desired manifestation. Suddenly, a soft glow emanating from the empty center, variously colored depending on the element invoked, is accompanied by a sonic vibration which the young mage tries to imitate with his chant. The right singing amplifies the intensity of luminosity and sound vibration; it can last a few seconds, or several hours. The night following a successful experience, the initiate has a dream related to the element which manifested during the ritual. He must not tell anyone about it, under any pretext, and especially not to the priest in charge of his instruction.

The breaking of the game board makes it of course unusable in its current state.

Damaged Rebuses

I

Kay Sage walks the Arthurian Wasteland, which is a playground. The sanctuary is badly deteriorated; the puzzles are strewn on the ground. The reign of quantity ends in the cataclysms of the Great Tribulation. The sudden dissolution of all utilitarian objects preludes the advent of another possible world. The utopian city is rebuilt. The garbage, which is reincrudated in the alchemical vitriol, then manifests the presence of the elemental spirits which were occultly attached to it.

In this game, seemingly inert matter comes back to life. Rebuses bring together what was scattered. A bewitched filth coats the land surveyor's body.

II

The Heavenly Jerusalem has crumbled. A possible world emerges from the non-being. The *Merz* recreates the lost unity.

The displacement of the penis of Osiris and its installation on a concrete block causes a deterioration of the geomagnetism, whose morphology proved to be conducive to divinatory interpretations. The poetic potentialities of the urban environment are rather discreet. Only rare desolate landscapes seem to have "a hidden history, a hidden usage or a hidden future related in the realm of collectivisation and realisation of desires[4]".

Kurt Schwitters is completely torn to shreds, which are thrown on the ground, and in the arrangements of which I read the slow agony of merchant society.

---

4 "(…) keeping up the vigilance towards spots conveying a distinct feeling of being out of control and having a distinct diffuse potential (if such a seeming contradiction is excused), of having a hidden history, a hidden usage or a hidden future in the realm of collectivisation and realisation of desires (...)": Erik Bohman et Mattias Forshage, "Towards the Solidification and Relativisation of Atopos Theory", *Hydrolith, Surrealist Research and Investigations*, Oyster Moon Press, 2010.

STATUTES OF THE *PROTECTORAT DE 'PATAPHYSIQUE QUÉBECQUOISE*

TITLE 1: ON WHAT IS FAUSTROLLIAN

Section 1

The Holy Faustrollian Empire exists from all eternity.

Section 2

The *Protectorat de 'Pataphysiqe québecquoise* seeks to spread the Faustrollian influx into the secular world, from a geomagnetic center located not far from the ancient Iroquoian village of Stadacona.

TITLE 2: OF THE GREAT ELECTOR

Section 3

The *Protectorat de 'Pataphysiqe québecquoise* is an elective and rotating monarchy, a sort of *new* New France.

Section 4

The One and Only Grand Elector of the Holy Faustrollian Empire nominates himself. Following this appointment, he can support his own candidacy for the imperial office without it being possible to infer the presence of any conflict of interest.

Section 5

In preparation for the Emperor's anointing and coronation, the One and Only Grand Elector of the Holy Faustrollian Empire nominates himself the Osteichthyan Archbishop who, in this capacity, sits on the Council of the Ten-Lexicons.

TITLE 3: RELATIONS BETWEEN THE EMPEROR AND THE OSTEICHTHYAN ARCHBISHOP

Section 6

The Eucharist practiced during the conventicle of enthronement involves the ceremonial consumption of hosts and green wine (absinthe) by the members of the Council of the Ten-Lexicons.

LIBERTÉ

Section 7

The Osteichthyan Archbishop consecrates the Emperor, who on the other hand does not allow him to crown but takes the crown from the hands of the ecclesiastic at the last moment and places it himself on his head.

Section 8

The Emperor represents the realm of action, he ensures that the work is carried out, while the Osteichthyan Archbishop ensures the doctrinal excellence of the enterprise in the sense of irreproachable rigor and uselessness. Their centuries-old conflict, which can very well be completely simulated if necessary, is a factor of instability capable of provoking the enthusiastic activity of the Members.

Section 9

An inquisitor tribunal, consisting of the Emperor and the Archbishop, can confer on a personality who involuntarily honors the 'Pataphysics the invaluable title of Grand Heimatlos.

TITLE 4: THE *PROTECTORAT* AND ITS FUNCTIONING

Section 10

Any member of the *Protectorat*, starting with the initial triumvirate formed at the instigation of Charles Bonenfant (*Secrétaire Pépé* at the *Académie québécoise de 'Pataphysique*), can present a candidate at a convent. It will be entrusted to the recipient, to the neophyte, an official title on a pataphysical diploma.

Section 11

The first ten members of the *Protectorat* form the Council of the Ten-Lexicons, a situation which, a priori, does not seem to bring any particular responsibility and, as only privileges, only a mention on their diploma and the participation in the imperial communion.

Section 12

The emblem of the *Protectorat de 'Pataphysiqe québecquoise* is the same as that of the Quebec *Académie québécoise de 'Pataphysique*, namely the Arrowed Ubu.

Section 13

"'Pataphysics is everything": this sentence constitutes the pediment of the *Protectorat*.

TITLE 5: RESEARCH AND CREATION CHAIRS ASSOCIATED WITH THE *PROTECTORAT*

Section 14

The fundamental chairs of the *Protectorat de 'Pataphysiqe québecquoise* could well be:

lovecraftian urbanism
extinct sciences
jarryc studies
Pataphanies
musical afterglow
musical presumption
guttural metallurgy
swear words
eristic
mithridatist
dyslexic poetry
artaldian hagiography
pneumadrisis
echephilia
mythological genealogies

NB: This list is not exhaustive. The accumulation or splitting of chairs can be practiced freely by any member of the *Protectorat*, when it pleases him.

Mack Hassler

I thank God every day for gifts, for blessings in life, for opportunities. Six months ago, my wife Sue was taken from us in death. These crafty poems are set up in the order they were written.

Please Recover, Goose

"First, Get General Principles"

Advice to *Samuel Johnson,*
biography by Walter Jackson Bate (1977)

Feeling preyed upon and predation, sadly, rule this life that we are given.
Returning from visiting Sue and only seven days from moving
Into senior living, I hit a goose on the road. Our community
Includes several ponds that grace its pastoral resolve
To form a happy ending. The other geese waddled up
But nothing could be done by curious concern. My wife
Also has some memory loss, and I think I will not tell
Her how I broke the animal's leg. But I will not forget
The pile of ruffled feathers I left to die on our road.

That night as I visited to end the day, Sue clutched my finger
Very hard and did not want to let it go, sliding even deeper
Into the deep and dark hole where somehow she had fallen.
Eurydice. That thought breaks my heart. The flock of doctors
Do not know what to do, and my wife is so profoundly alone
Far from home, broken in an instant. Poor goose.

Sonnet on Extended Wing in Patagonia

For my own Eurydice, and based on my short essay
in Westfahl collection *Space and Beyond* (2000)

The smallest moves will help my fragile self to cope
When actually it's being able to forget
That wipes the nervous mind and helps me set
Myself as Keats had said for "what, if I live, I hope
To do." The family and dogs are my trope

For travel South with less and less regret
To find a new and distant land to vet
And explore its full continental scope.

She can be with me there again. In fact,
She let me buy too many books, a lack
That seemed harmless at the time, but now
Drives me with determination down
To darkness still like Keats where wind blows
Constantly sustained by God's fierce prose.

Two Fine Poets Prevaricate But Help

> "The One remains, the many change and pass;
> Heaven's light forever shines, Earth shadows fly;
> Life, like a dome of many-colour'd glass...."
>
> P.B. Shelley, *Adonais*

They keep us always busy at the home
Where Sue and I retired. Fecundity:
Rare fish in a rocky pool, burgeoning botany
Embody for us Nature's colored dome
And radiate every day the sum
Of joy we are given free as poetry.
The kingdom and the power and the glory
I used to think co-terminous with ancient Rome.

But somehow she never made it here to live.
We failed to stimulate her rage to fight.
Too soon as Dylan Thomas wrote we saw
Her sink downward to darkness and finally go
To hospice care that I will not forgive
And sadly sent her "gentle into that good night."

Addendum to the Second Sonnet

I wrote that I could not forgive
The forces that would not let her live.
But she saw changes from the fog
And somewhat like our early dog
Whose loyal name was ginger

She wandered off and would not linger
To end the life with all of us
Her own way and with no fuss.
I love her dearly for this loving move
And pray that I can hug her once again
And tell how I understand her huge win.
I think God's Will is very hard to understand.

Sonnet on UP Faith

"He served in the U.S. Army from
1954-1957… and was a WWII
enthusiast."

Obit for Bud Clement, *L'Anse Sentinel*

When we bought the place on *Vermilac,* my wife
And I had no idea the resonance
Along the lake and in the woods. No fence
Contains community. No petty strife
Separates us. Though miles apart a fuller life
Binds us. In fact, we know the recompense
Of burgeoning family that grows with sense
And Finn *sisu* to nail a firm belief.

Now death is taking everyone, it seems.
The quiet, slant-eyed nocturnal wolves
Arrive. But churches that we built stand tall
And though the wolves are greyish-white they don't appall.
These people bury bodies. The casket gleams
With colors at interment to show the occupant believes.

Twenty-Two Lines of Doggy Couplets on Death and Birth

For Tucker James Besonen, Born 8 January 23; and for
Sue died 9 November 22

My dogs get bored but generally follow my lead.
Three years old, my wife and I love the breed.
She died. The three of us miss her all the time.
They sense pentameter in gait, but never rhyme.
We hear the ancient image of the call.

Samuel in the dead of night. The fall
When brothers snarl and kill each other.
The sense of mission for a virgin mother.
The inexplicable face of God.
Ordained for us to meet and wrestle to the sod
Like Jacob, our special ancient patriarch
Whose name keeps steady every fragile bark
Across our choppy family sail on rough seas.
The births have been sufficient. The trees
Of generations branch. The necessary deaths,
That look so cold and pale, grasp final breaths.
Each death has haunted us till new births burst
And in their doggy language utter Babel cries first
That validate in this silly doggerel
To complete with intellect the awful cycle.
Let us resolve the mysteries that separate
Our endings and beginnings so we can celebrate

My Trophy Rack: Bounding Love

Two months after Sue had died our dogs
Spotted four deer beyond the garages
At the edge of the woods. We dashed
Across on leash, of course, to watch
Them bound away, flashing white tails
To our white terriers in fresh snow.

The dogs rooted deep where they had been
While in the snow like daffodils two points
Caught my eye. The dogs sniffed but the smell
Of life had already gone. I pulled the rack
Out of the snow, with red streaks of blood
At the base where the buck had broken off his burden.

The indifference of the dogs: strangely similar to what I saw
When I took them to say goodbye to Sue
Once her breathing had stopped in hospice.
No smell of life remained so they ignored
Her corpse. Like white-tailed deer, she had left
And bounded off leaving us lifeless and bereft.

Sue Teaches Bounding Jitterbug

"Every day brings a chance for you to draw
in a breath, kick off your shoes, and dance."
Oprah Winfrey, Quote of the Day

"[John] Witherspoon regarded the deists as his
Theological adversaries.... He believed in
Revelation as well as reason... in the historic
Truth of the Bible, including the miracles...."
Lynne Cheney, *James Madison* (2014), p. 28

The first epigraph above is taken from the daily chronicle
At our retirement home where my wife had planned to move
With me. The second is from my heavy reading now that she
Is gone with only the urn of her ashes in our living room.
Witherspoon and Madison were canny, Enlightenment men
Who, also, still believed in miracles and who fought Hume
Fiercely in fierce Scots. Now to calm my own agony I want
To try this blank verse agon once again on Sue's final days
In hospice.
In fact, I may have figured out what was going on
In her mind as it was shutting down, not talking, not eating.
Once she clutched my finger and squeezed real hard, not as I
Thought, then, to hold me to her but to catapult and launch
Herself. She had taught me to jitterbug in middle age. She
Had been my active partner in many travels. She could move
As well as anyone I had ever known, faster than my mile relay
Team in college with total mobility until confined to hospice.
I think she knew the medicine now, even we the family in our
Love, could not help her shed the immobility, the burden like the
Buck's antler rack I found in the snow yesterday. She dreamed of
Bounding off like white-tailed deer our dogs had chased. I asked
Sue's best friend, who still now and then behaves like a good Roman
Catholic, to pray for Sue. She wrote me that she prayed Sue was happy
In heaven. I know that she is running there, dancing, free again.
Did Scott dream of warmth as he lay dying at the Pole? The mentor
Of James Madison at Princeton as well as my favorite teacher at Williams,
William Sloan Coffin, preached that we must just believe in miracles.
The evidence is not there to examine, just the miracle, the serendipity.

So like God to Samuel in the night, I sometimes hear the calling of my name
Even though I know she is gone. This is a Truth she taught me like the
Jitterbug, and I am grateful for such a teacher who surely will transport me
Far from hospice bounding through the cold and emptiness of this predatory
World where God has placed us with the deer.

The Bodies We Are Given

"Be this my text, my sermon to mine own
Therefore, that he may raise, the Lord throws down."

John Donne, *"Hymn to God, My God, In my Sickness"* (1635)

Like Donne's geography as Sue lay waiting harsh reality
In hospice, I watched her body lose all colors
Later more pale and lonely at the undertakers
Again she waited for my son and I to identify.

Now still the Urn looks brave
Beside the TV waiting for the grave
While the body of our prayer
Confirms that Sue is also there.

We humans do not accept the blow
With near the grace of the hunter's bow
Nor the fisher's lure. God made species
For predation variously for eager men to seize.

Now still the Urn looks brave
Beside the TV waiting for the grave
While the body of our prayer
Confirms that Sue is also there.

Some color, it is true, returns with flowers
At the service, and mellow words have powers
Beyond the beauty of the pointed buck
With eager sparkling eyes though clearly out of luck.

Now still the Urn looks brave
Beside the TV waiting for the grave
While the body of our prayer
Confirms that Sue is also there.

Not every species is blessed to peer
Beyond the veil. Not bled-out deer
Nor fish-eye gaze yanked rudely
Into air carry hope of immortality.

Now still the Urn looks brave
Beside the TV waiting for the grave
While the body of our prayer
Confirms that Sue is also there.

Voyager II

> Distant
> Messages come more slowly now. I'm writing
> Fewer poems. But the awful journey still
> Is worth the trip.
>
> My poem "Voyager" *Hellas* (1990)

Emerson opened the grave of his son,
Meditated a moment and then
Went back to all his books. I read
This years ago long before our dread
Of colorless death loomed over us.
Pale Sue at Bisslers. But the fecund
Globe is rich with color. One second
At the frozen pole may stretch generations
At the fat atoll waist. The power of evolutions
Far exceed what we must entomb in earth.
And though my own grief has not birthed
Classic reconciliation of "The Gathering"
I have not lost the need to praise and sing
How tricky grace and Nature are.
Like Tory Satirists they raise the bar
Of feeling. So that predicated on love
And gentleness and canny skill,
They also open doors for the kill.
Even now nativity God's Will
Seems fiercely to anticipate the Cross
As we marvel in our gentle gain and loss.

Six Quatrains Plus a Line that May Help

For Dan Rankin and his wife Susan

The crescent moon so cold and free
Evokes for me a college friend whose wife
Just days from when my Sue poured out her life
In what Dan labels "brutal finality."

My impotence to conquer death
Appalls me. Sue paled and whitened
In such decline it frightened
Inexorably until her last breath.

I need to analyze Dan's pointed phrase
Like we did at school. But so much
Now at stake so late. We both must clutch
To translate guilt, despair toward praise.

I need a measure adequate
For both his points. The second Time
Is an endless web for which all rhyme
Is easy. Spider legs of thought attach.

On brutes. Our dogs and horses teach
How much we love the animal
World. Never want divorce at all.
Like little children let them preach.

But still like Dan my sense of loss
Overwhelms. Whenever in my apartment
Sue's presence looms I cry with sentiment.
I see her everywhere. It breaks my heart.
Maybe linking back by faith to our Cross.
Maybe shaping something new with clumsy Art.

Walking Our Dogs in the Old Neighborhood

> "And the Lord said to Samuel… I will do a
> thing…at which both the ears of every one
> that heareth it shall tingle."
>
> *I Samuel* 3: 11

After my usual early morning at Starbucks and having time to kill,
I leashed our dogs and headed toward the house where they had been
Puppies and where you and I had lived forty five years. Now empty
And up for sale since your death three months ago. Both noses
To the ground, they pulled and bounded more than usual. "Dad,
We catch the scent. At last we are going home again. Follow us."
They seemed to speak to me. Smart dogs. I cried and yanked
And told them "no" and had to drag them back to the car. Home
Is where we all are. My head was tingling as the scripture says
With the loss of you. And like our dogs, I mourn lost space. This
Sense of loss is hard on all of us. You mourn my back rubs, our date
Nights, your lovely girls who would sit and talk with us near the sofa,
Also gone. I know this loss puzzles the dogs where they would sit
And bark the street. I mourn my books. They also had to go to sell the
house.

My Buddhist friend writes to say that if he were ever to suffer such a
Loss, he would be with his wife at what ever place she was. This is
Beautiful. Unable myself to hold to such a faith but loving you every
Moment as I yank our puppies through this world, I think I am more
A Samuelite in the night. I wait to hear God calling my name as
I think of you and do believe that home is where we all are. Even the
Dogs know more than I can tell them and sense that they are pulling
Back to what they know and love. We all shall see what God intends.
And with luck and grace, we shall not forget, neither I nor our furry
friends.

Darrow Road Location

> "Eskimo are… Rasmussen wrote in his
> diary, always longing for change… who
> like moving about… and 'hidden things.'"
>
> *Wanderlust* (2023), p. 133.

Many years we made a team. The two
Of us were magic. We had hoped for more.
The wordless promises. Together Sue
And I anticipated years to explore.

So when the dogs and I now drive home
Past that awful place where she lay

Before her death and fought for breath alone
My haunted tone is both to curse and to pray.

Sonnet on "The Grapevine" or The Dance of Death

Old age is like I used to read on war.
We hunker in our foxholes. Wait to see
Who will be hit next. It's the rule of three
Where hardly any balance mitigates the gore.
We must advance from hole to hole before
Our dreadful enemy can win. Lest obscenity
Of loss prevail. The dance of death in glee,
In fact, is such a greedy tiresome bore.

But still there are histories and stories
We can tell. Wonderful tales about the glories
And tricks we knew. If God will only let
Us write it down so we at last can get
An ending to the dance that's worth the cost
Holding hands and crossing legs we thought we'd lost.

Clutch (Collection for 2023), edited by Robert M. Zoschke (Street Corner Press, Sister Bay, Wisconsin 2023), 221 pages pbk, n.p.

I am a great believer in serendipity and feel lucky that during the past year my name has gotten linked to the work of Zoschke as well as to Zoschke on Splake (see several reviews of mine over recent months) because now I am given a new collection with the familiar title dated for this new year. It is a rich collection, with the usual abundance of Splake haiku and Splake photographs; but there is so much more included that seems particularly representative and instructive about UP literature even though the imprint is from Door County just below the UP and the work includes writing from across the United States and beyond. Our literature here may be developing a distinct brand of its own. Let me explain and then I will attempt a fine sampling. This collection is pretty important as we struggle to describe what is going on with UP writing. Even though I deeply believe in the power of ambivalence that comes down to us from the classic Tory satirists who wrestle well with the universe and belief, notably Swift, events and theories from the last two centuries force us to appreciate "beatness" and the pathos from the

"Howl" of Ginsburg and Kerouac and the abundance of "misfit" writers. I think many of them belong here above the bridge, in spirit at least; and those are whom Zoschke collects. He is familiar with a wide set of fairly unknown writers in this tradition of "beatness." The key issue is how to reconcile the real world that presents itself to us—the cold, empty space strangely filling up momentarily with vitality by means of predatory and harsh struggle (evolution) over against our fantasy dreams of a more permanent and lasting connection. This issue ranges from Thoreau and Emerson to Scott Fitzgerald, Sinclair Lewis, even C.S. Lewis and the Inklings to Hemingway. But the Beats and the cold fierceness of the Upper Peninsula image it well. Hemingway was deeply effected in his later work by memories of the Seney region.

In this new collection, the most accomplished "Beat" or radical writer whom Zoschke collects is Marge Piercy (see a major essay on her work in the book edited by my friend Clyde Wilcox and me titled *Political Science Fiction* (South Carolina, 2011 pbk). But Zoschke knows and collects many other fine and lesser known Beats. Some are singers and graphic artists who capture the lonely pathos of the cold world well with just the hint of further connection. All of the following, I think, would be worth pursuing further: Sam Pickering, Walt McLaughlin, Joanna McClire, Ed Markowski, Sarah Elizabeth Burkey, Alan Catlin, and, especially, a Texan who ought to have been a "Yooper" Albert Huffstickler, who died in 2002. I am even learning to enjoy Splake's barrenness set in this company. I think his cold and grim photos go better with his haiku here than in his last solo collection that I reviewed. In that review, I sadly opined that his work may be on "hospice care." But clearly for Zoschke, our own Calumet bard has more life left in him though he is no Kerouac nor Hemingway. I recommend that we keep following the work of Zoschke. Apparently he has the energy to bring out a *Clutch* once a year.

Daniel de Cullá

This Flower

As the Eresma river drains from the slopes
From Guadarrama on the way to La Granja
In Segovia
So my love slipped through where I slept
Your peacock, beloved soul.
This flower represents our pure love
That we gave ourselves through the most intoxicating places
From our mountain where kings and subjects
Made children "like Donkey"
As any animal.
In the Boca del Asno, on the ground
Where your peacock slept
Now yes
I came to you, you caressed me, you pampered me
And then my Love fell on you
Until, after the ecstasy
Love left for the forests of Valsaín.
Here and now yes
As in the times
In which the monarchs were measured with the bears
You rode me on a horse
And we went for a walk across the river
Singing:
"I will give you
I will give you beautiful girl
I'll give you one thing
One thing I only know, pine nuts!
Until my imperial eagle
Returned to nest in the cup of your haughty pine
Hugging your peacock
Putting my lips

In your donkey mouth
Eating a peach
With a red heart
-How rich it is
Although it doesn't taste like anything, I told you.
You turned red
Placing the bow of your ponytail
On the neck of my imperial eagle.
My Carthusian Donkey
My Donkey "Bruno" is a real Carthusian
So happy from the secular Bray
Who has come to the Cartuja de Miraflores
One three kilometers from the city of Burgos
In the surroundings of the Fuentes Blancas park
Of the Carthusian Order
To meditate on which of the Donkeys
Theoretically known
Who are running for election
Municipal, local, general
He will entrust his unfortunate vote.
He's a contemplative to the max
Voyeur of the impossible faith
Until willing and erect
He feels to die because he dies
For the love of the nun Soledad
In that vast field of love where to expatiate
In her climax of ecstasy
When he levitates and the organ sings in Gregorian:
"I have it elevated to the Lord"
Waking up to reality
When do the guided tours arrive
And he feels the state of him to overflow
His physics and his morals aplenty of ideas
From the ears to the tail
Leaving his vote decision
To divine Providence.
-It's not going anymore!

He said to himself leaving the Cartuja
Feeling the loud clamor of tourists
Reflecting that few glories are deserved
Each and every Donkey
Who are running for these elections
That they are nothing more
Than erections in their own honor
To deceive men.
-How many donkeys will bray in front of us
At rallies, talks, congresses
They will only show us
That the Bray of him is so old
Like the human species
And that his good only found him
To deceive and hallucinate the people
As always¡

Leopard Tanks

From the West come the Leopards.
Oh, what a miracle!

– Zelensky from the papers

Our Leopard tanks "Made in Spain"
Pure scrap, stay at home
Because subjects destined to Bray
Corruption, registrations and fascism
That's how they want it and want it
With all his strength
To defend, for example, a she Ass
And her co-religionists praising her in chorus
Well, they have made her an "illustrious student"
From a renowned University
Cat and slime silly
Because she is in fashion
And that is how the "media" who commune want it
In congresses and temples

No university consensus
With the blessing of the Braying Curia
And all the thurifers of the rectory asshole
For college history
From false human understanding.
At the exit of the University Complex
This she Ass was mounted on a Donkey
With false title in the hands
Behind her a long procession of knaves
That they yelled at her: "President"
Praising her in chorus
And, in front of her a great demonstration
Of young people hurt by their attacks on Health
And to public Education
With her daily menu of bad beer
And rotten calamari sandwiches
Ensuring safety
Of such an illustrious knave
A good round of repressive force.
And I do not lie.
The headline newspapers say so
Although the imbeciles and deluded
Do not believe it.

Insects' Hotel

I come to visit this Insects' Hotel
Subjected to the action of a cold climate
of nice colors
Located in a corner of the courtyard
Of the School "Las Fuentecillas"
In Burgos capital
And, what a surprise! I meet Darwin
For whom the main evolutionary factor
Is the Selection based on the struggle for existence.
Also, there is Malthus, that economist
That knows a lot about the theory

On the growth of human populations.
The three of us have greeted each other
With much higher intensity
To the necessary.
On the frontispiece of the hotel
We have noticed the Verhulst-Pearl' logistic curve
Proven in drosophila populations
Applicable, in general, to any living form:
Y = be ax /1 + c ax, with a b and c being positive constants.
Few insects are hosted in the Hotel.
The hotel manager has admitted us
That most individuals
Are for the struggle of existence (struggle for life)
And that they only come to spend the night, and not all
Because the conquest of food and space
It is a priority, since, among them
Advantageous conditions are found
Regarding each other.
We have seen twigs (Bacillus rossius)
Dry leaves (Phyllium siccifolium)
And some butterflies that present colorations
And drawings on the wings
What makes them similar
To the bark of the trees on which they perch:
Kallima inachus, and mimetic insects
Vespiform in appearance:
Lepidoptera, Diptera, Hymenoptera predator.
After visiting the Hotel
We have approached some cow thistles
Getting to piss against them
Let's see which of the three tipped with the urine
To the highest
Particularly showy
We looked like pheasants, turkeys
Dreaming that some apparent female would pass
And choose the most attractive male
And more skillful in our piss.

Only individuals with abundant fur passed
That, seeing us in these poses
They laughed their hearts out.

Pumpkin Poet

The smiling and loving poet
Makes toy spears with his verses
Causing immediate heartbreak
Who does he read to?
Even his wife is creeped out
Causing some love rejection
Less when they have sex.
There are those who consider
A great poet and writer
And they hug him like children
He burst out laughing and crying
At the same time.
In the mythological age
Pumpkins (heads) were crowned
With laurel wreaths
Heads are crowned today
With pumpkins
As a symbol of mastery.
Horace, Virgil
Ovid, Dante, and many others
Were great pumpkin poets.
The Schools and Universities of the World
Compete year after year
In crowning with pumpkins
To its most distinguished students
As well as those who perceive
Honorary degrees.
-Where are you going for the pumpkin?
Young graduate
Master in Braying?
-From my desk I feel

The fruit of this cucurbit
And I smelled and smelled
and olé and olá
That the pumpkin will be in my head
Although my notes have been
Ripe and immature.

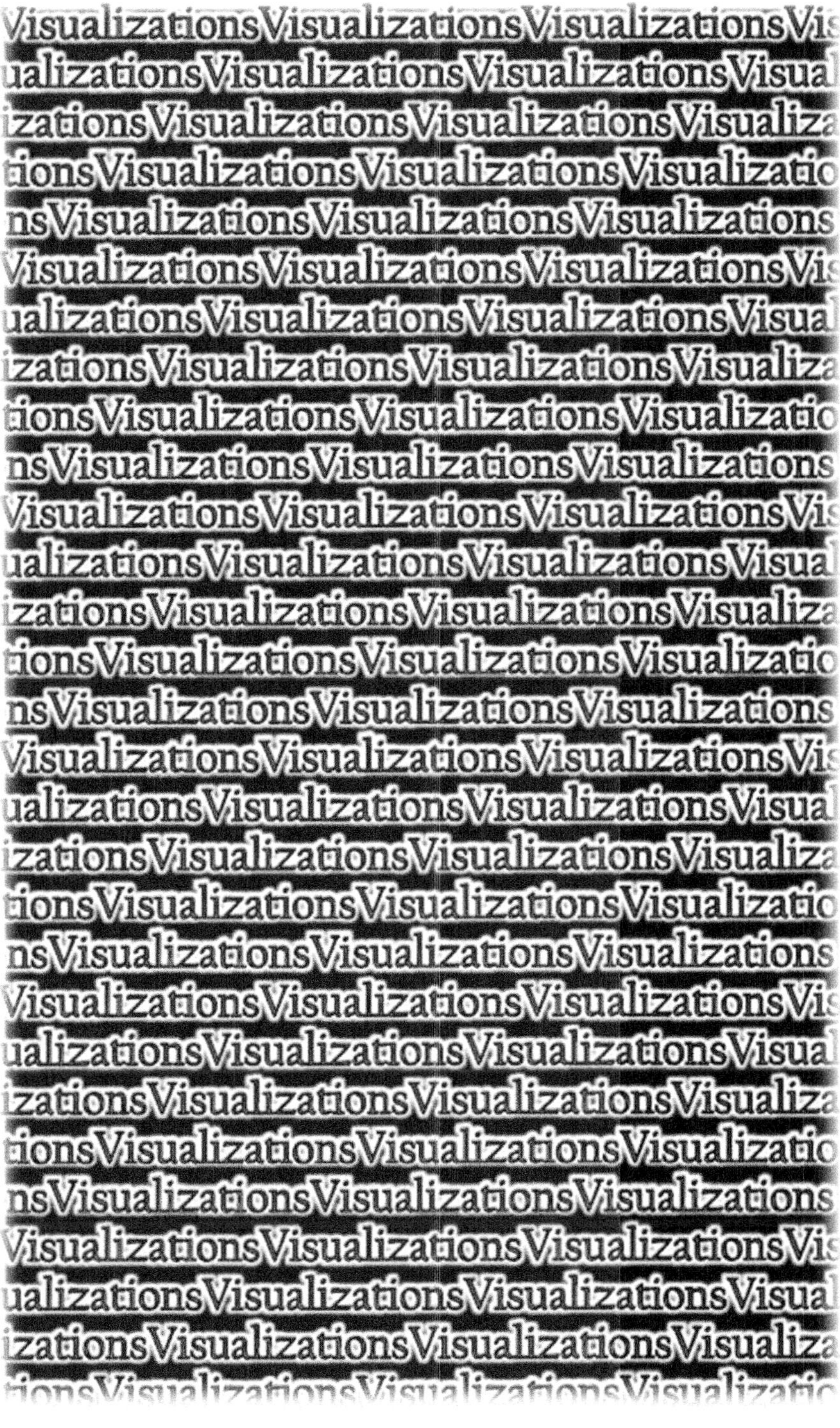
Visualizations

Michael e. Casteels

Three Sudo(Hai)ku

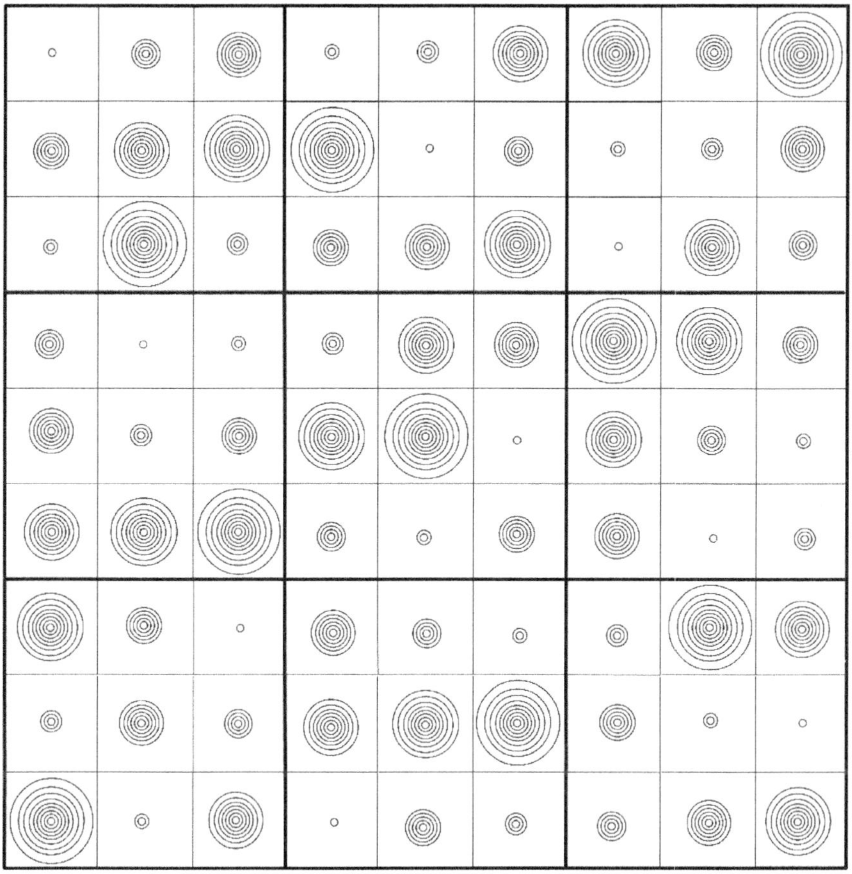

Sudoku after a Puddle in the Rain

the	moth	fluttering	of	temple	bell	sleep	folded	upon
sleep	of	temple	fluttering	folded	upon	the	bell	moth
bell	upon	folded	moth	the	sleep	of	fluttering	temple
upon	fluttering	bell	sleep	of	the	moth	temple	folded
moth	sleep	of	folded	fluttering	temple	upon	the	bell
temple	folded	the	bell	upon	moth	fluttering	sleep	of
fluttering	temple	sleep	upon	moth	folded	bell	of	the
folded	bell	upon	the	sleep	of	temple	moth	fluttering
of	the	moth	temple	bell	fluttering	folded	upon	sleep

Sudoku after Buson

the	old	frog	in	water	sound	pond	of	jumps
water	in	pond	of	frog	jumps	sound	the	old
sound	jumps	of	old	pond	the	frog	water	in
frog	sound	in	the	old	water	of	jumps	pond
of	pond	water	frog	jumps	in	old	sound	the
jumps	the	old	sound	of	pond	in	frog	water
in	frog	sound	jumps	the	old	water	pond	of
old	water	the	pond	sound	of	jumps	in	frog
pond	of	jumps	water	in	frog	the	old	sound

Sudoku after Basho

Richard Kostelanetz

SEE-SAW

IRRIGATE
IRRADIATE

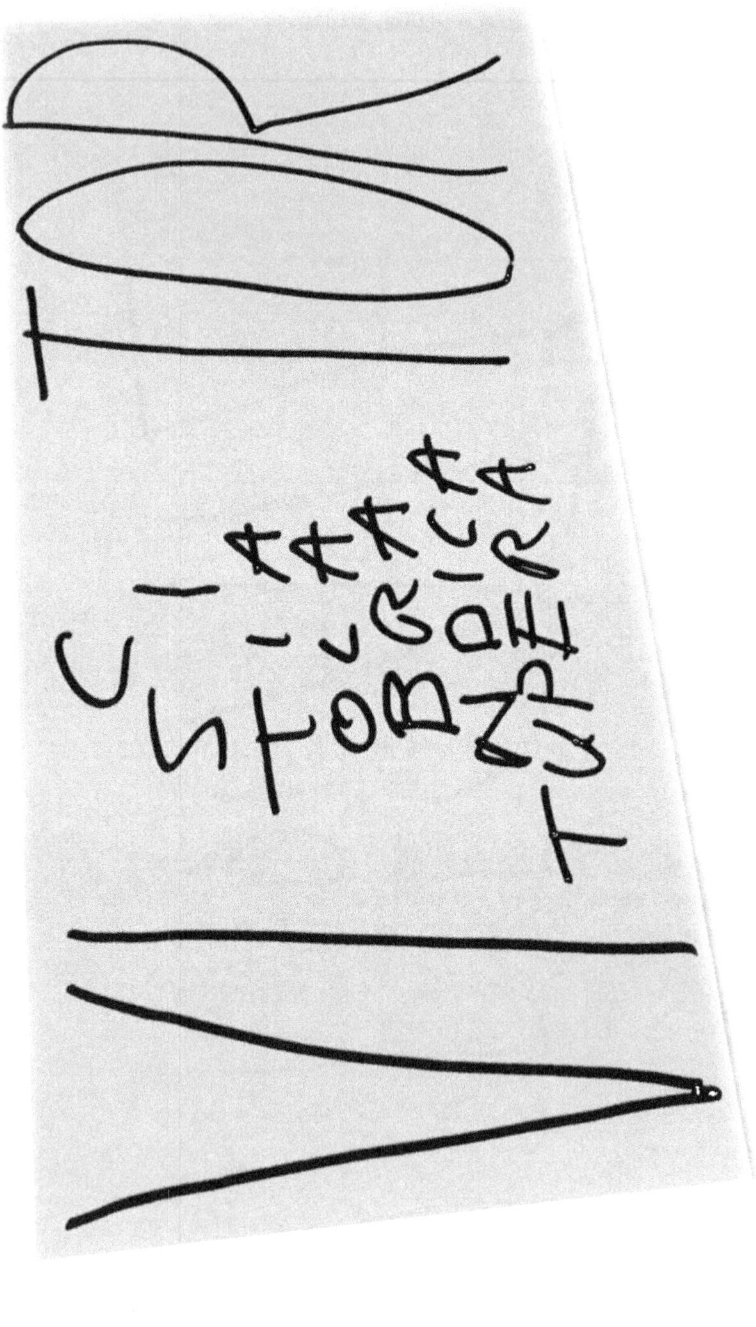

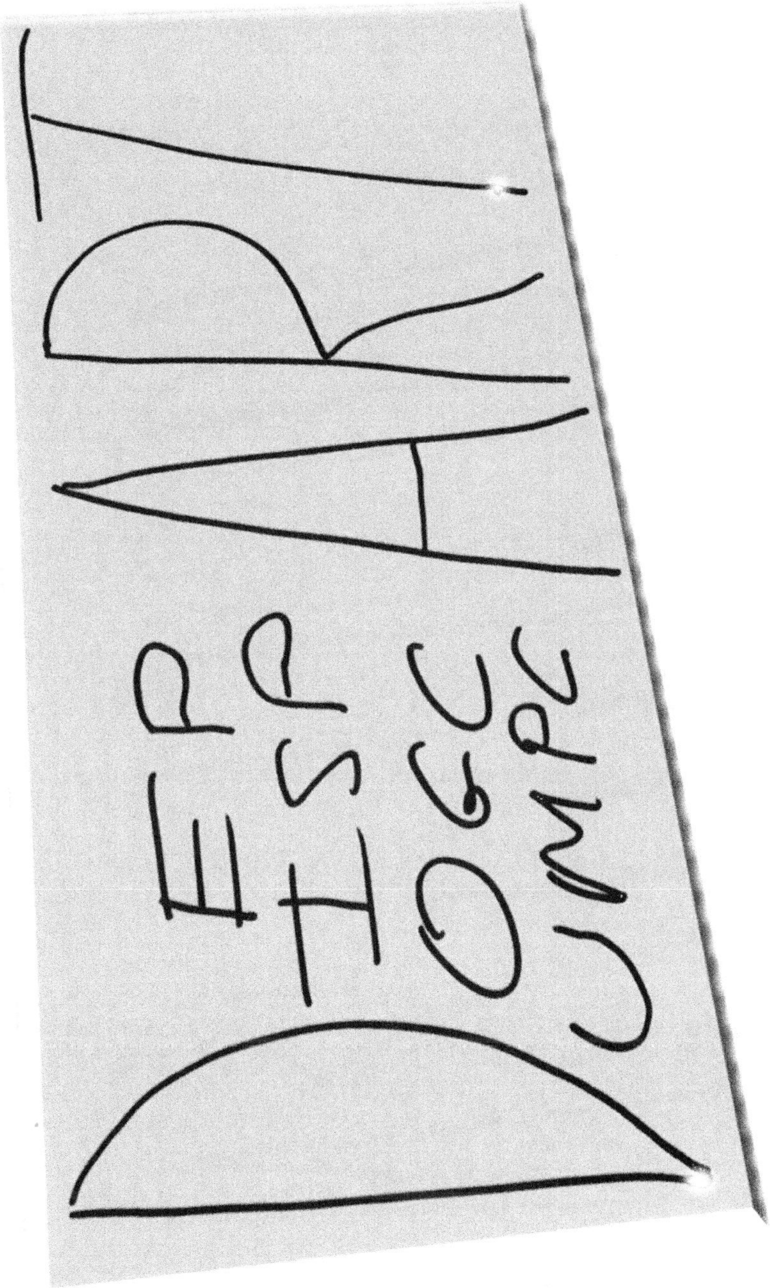

INFANTICIDES
SEC

Nobxhiro Santana (Nobuhiro Mido)

I am pleased to present eight pieces characterized by an abstract collage approach. These creations were realized using digital painting tools to transform and arrange digital images. By incorporating photographs of automobiles to evoke a modern ambiance and rendering them in monochrome, my efforts achieved a retro-futuristic style.

In previous volumes of *Emantions*, I have published grayscale reproductions of pieces originally created in color. As I am introducing monochrome works in this volume, here I offer remarks on color to deepen our thinking about monochrome and its relationship to color. Red light has a wavelength of about 0.7 μm. As the wavelength gets shorter, the light changes to orange, yellow, green, and blue. Blue, the shortest wavelength of visible light, has a wavelength of about 0.4 μm. Light with wavelengths longer than red is called infrared light and is not visible. Light with wavelengths longer than infrared is called radio waves. Conversely, light with wavelengths shorter than blue is called ultraviolet light, which is also not visible. Light with wavelengths shorter than ultraviolet rays is called x-rays or gamma rays. Light that can be recognized by humans has colors ranging from red to yellow to blue, and no other colors are visible.[5]

Let's consider two propositions about color to help us think about color in terms of science and aesthetic character. One is the proposition of what color is. We perceive red (and other colors as well) specifically, and we can identify red in paint, red fruit, etc.

Now, suppose I were to ask you to describe the color red without using light wavelengths and without using examples of red objects (red tomatoes, red flowers, etc.)? This *character* is very difficult to explain. It is equally difficult to describe other sensory perceptions, but color is unexplainable, even though we perceive and see colors in concrete terms.

Another proposition about color is whether the red I perceive is the same as the red you perceive. For example, since your brain and mine cannot be directly connected, you cannot see the visual image I experince. Therefore, you cannot confirm whether my red and your red are the same. To put this situation in concrete terms, it is as follows. Even if my perception of red and

---

[5] The human retina contains cones that respond to wavelengths around 0.45μm for blue, 0.56μm for green, and about 0.60μm for red, and the signals from these cones are processed by the brain to perceive colors. Red cones also have a smaller response range at around 0.43μm, producing the color purple with wavelengths shorter than blue.

your perception of red are different, the red frequency, tomato red, will not change. For example, even if the color I perceive as green is the red you perceive, and the tomato you see as the color I perceive as green, you will call the color of the tomato red, and the wavelength of the light is 0.7μm; our discussion of red is not at all confusing, strange as the philosophical questions may be. You may call and perceive green for me as red, but both my red and your red remain red.

The world we see today just happens to look that way, and it would look like a completely different world if different organisms were looking at it, and perhaps even the same people might see it differently. Color provides a tremendous amount of information to our vision, but the system itself is not well understood even by humans, and it might be better to think of it as being stored in a very fuzzy area. When you think about color and create a monochrome image without using color, you will realize that monochrome expression has a special balance due to the limited amount of information available.

Catalogue:

#230713-01 "deformations of automobile appearance from nostalgic point of view #1"

#230713-02 "deformations of automobile appearance from nostalgic point of view #2"

#230707-01 "deformations of automobile appearance from nostalgic point of view #3"

#230714-01 "deformations of automobile appearance from nostalgic point of view #4"

#230714-02 "deformations of automobile appearance from nostalgic point of view #5"

#230715-01 "deformations of automobile appearance from nostalgic point of view #6"

#230718-01 "deformations of automobile appearance from nostalgic point of view #7"

#230721-01 "deformations of automobile appearance from nostalgic point of view #8"

Images are presented in landscape orientation.

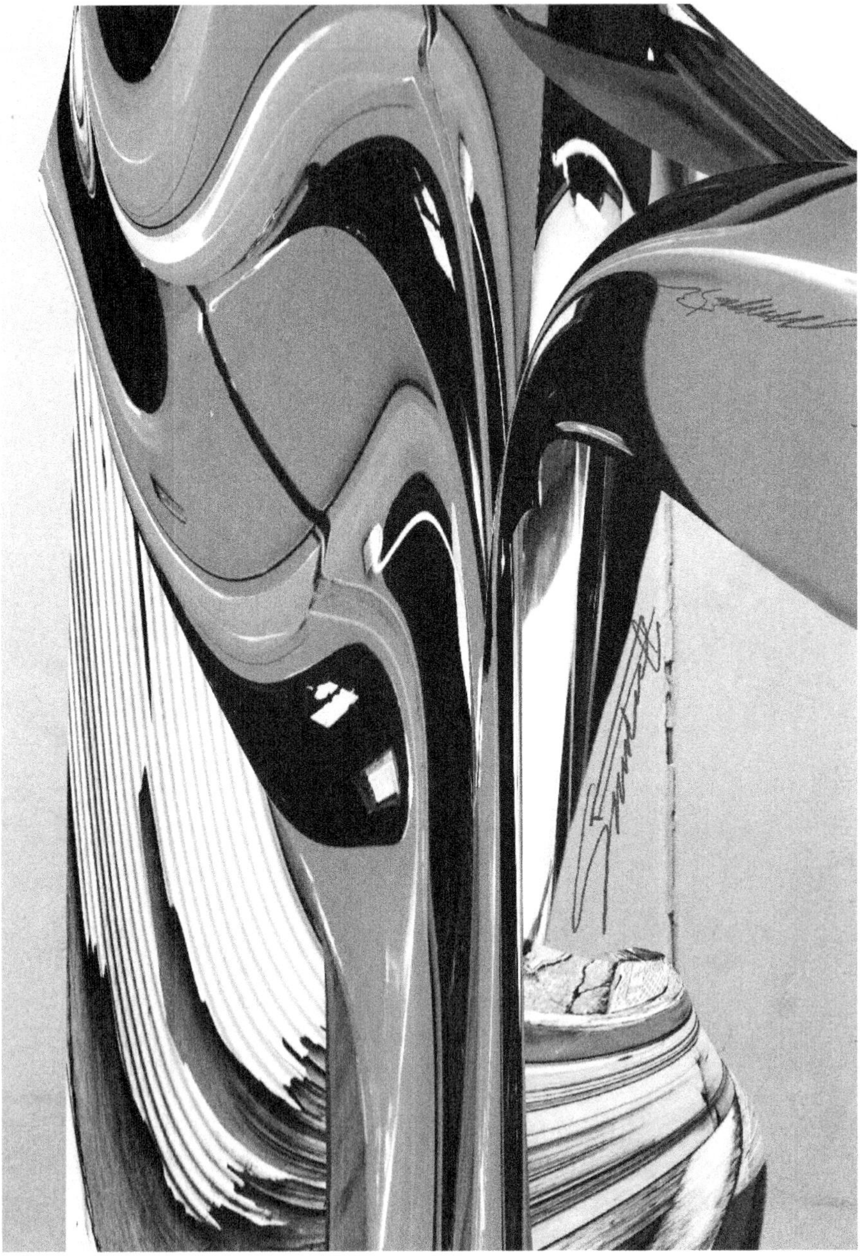

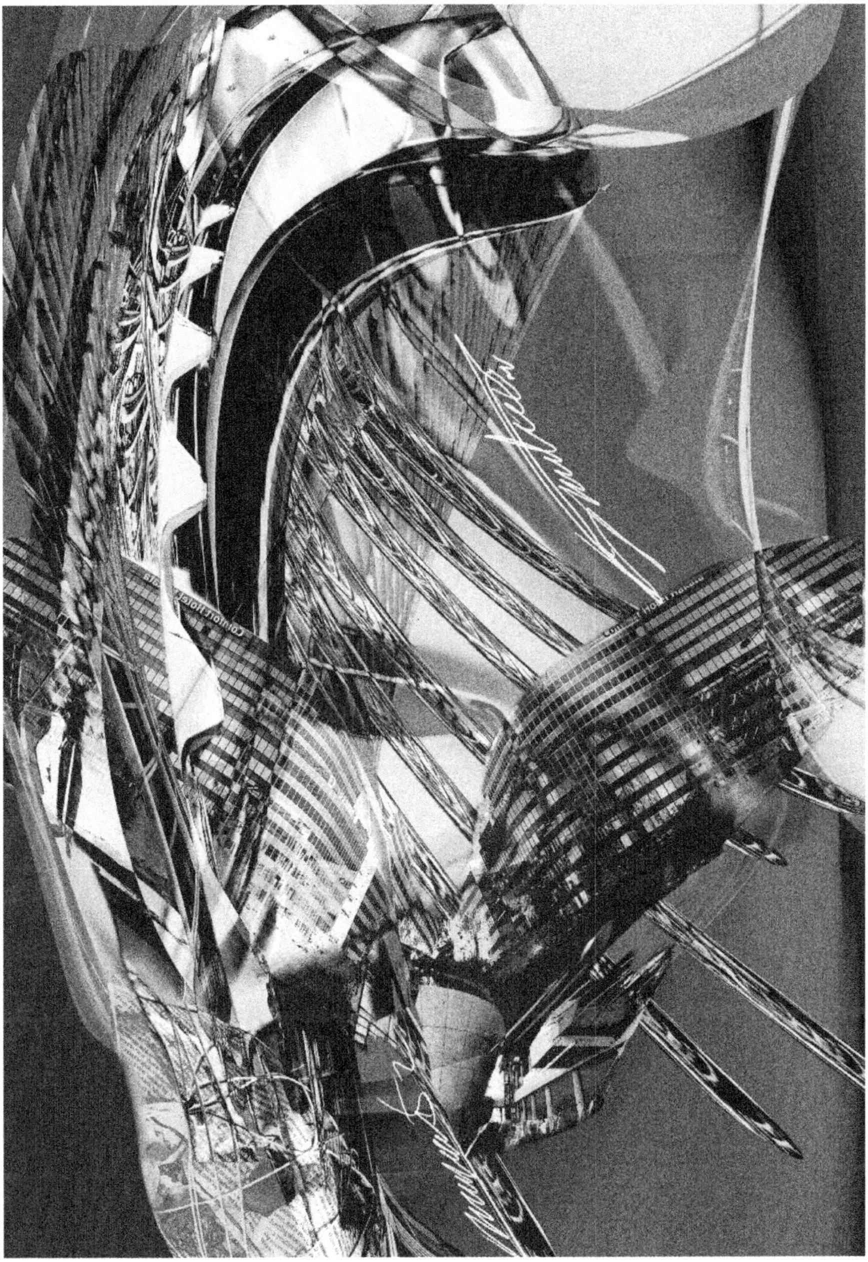

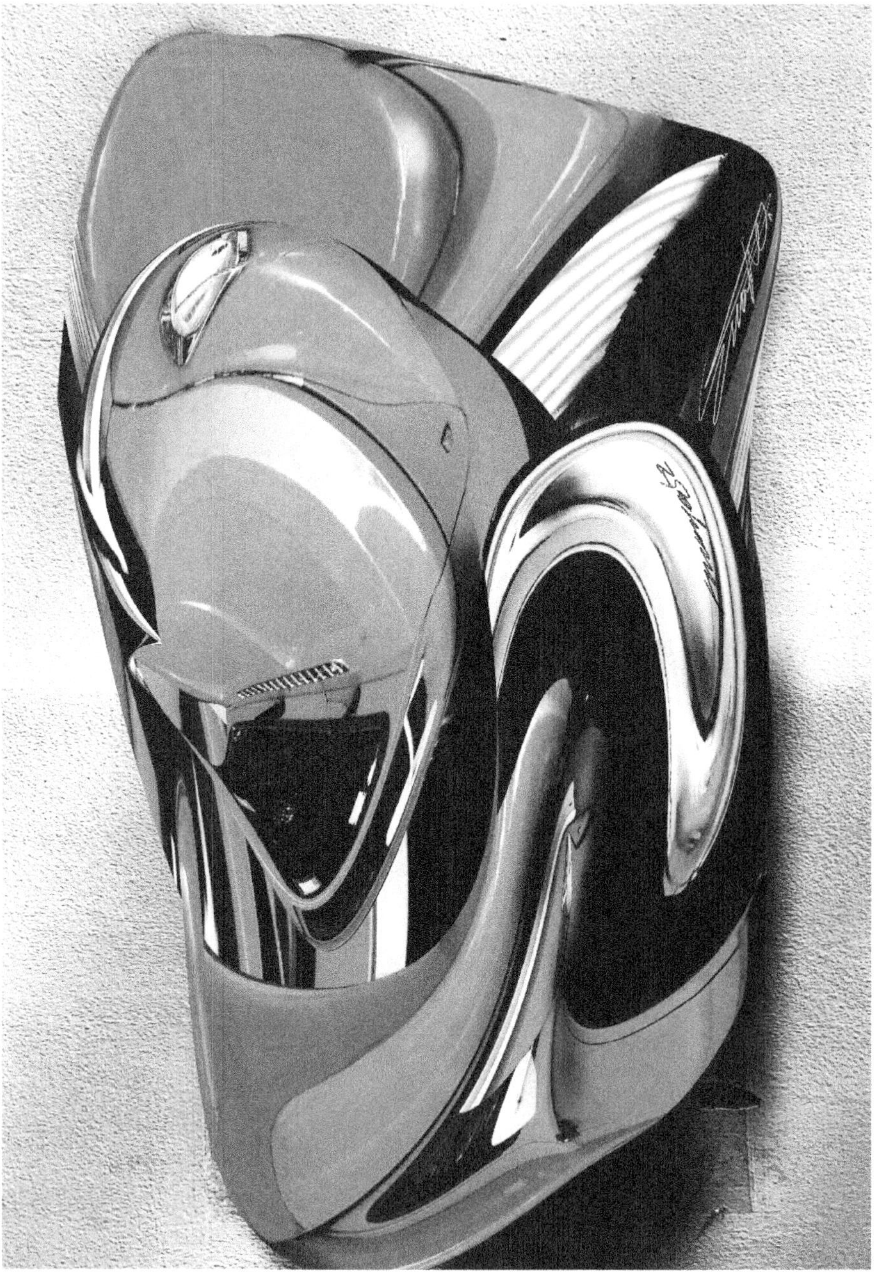

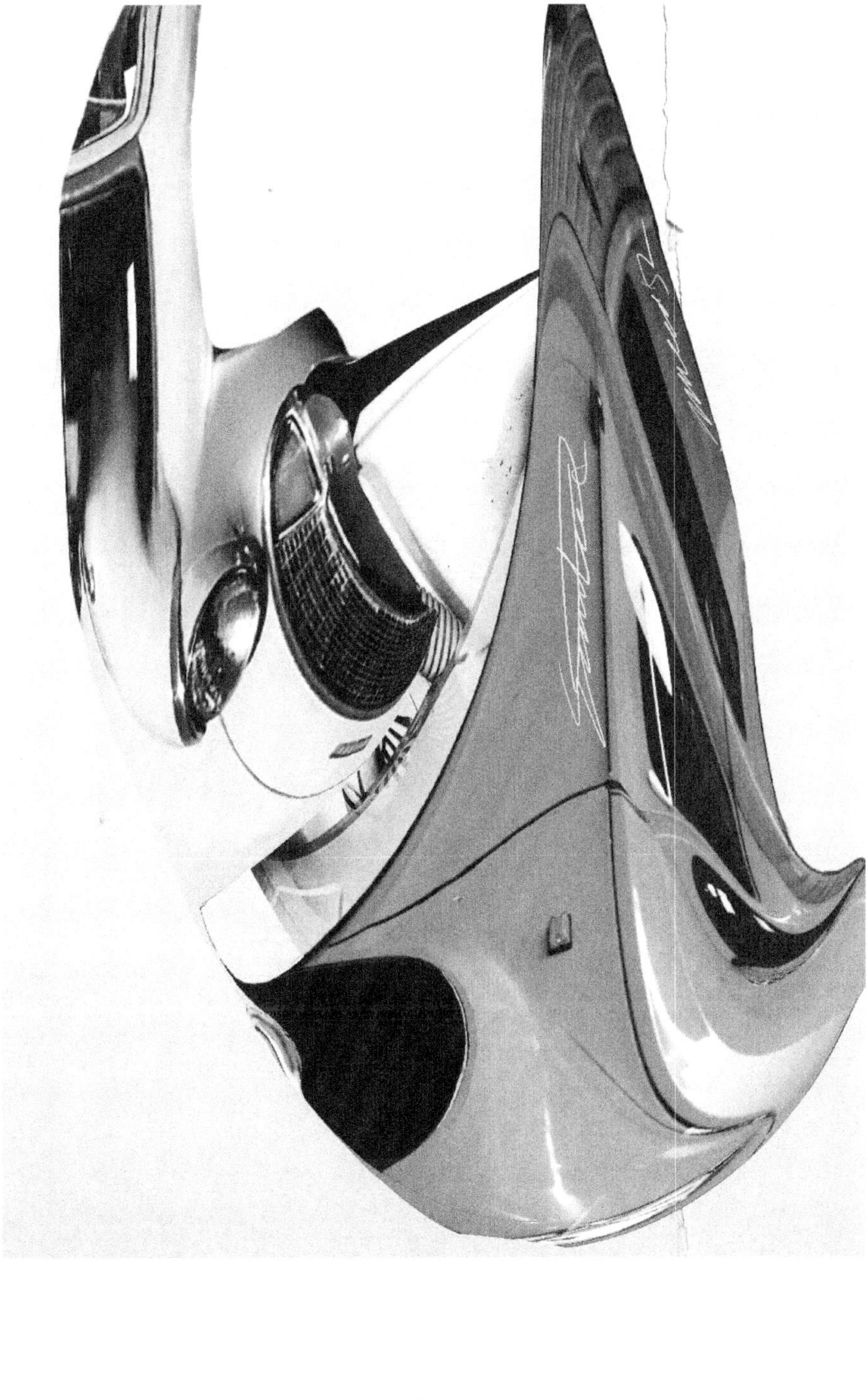

Bienvenido Bones Banez, Jr.

Wild Beast Surreal Blasphemous Dreamers

Tree of Knowledge potent, the blood leafs, that sits in my stomach gold, blasphemous visualize dreamers...
Snake darkness enveloped, body numb cluster,
This is how it is booster shot
When you're the coming up risings fire!
I wish things were different
nothing I saw
and made a rhyme
to children at play vaccines
and hard time dragon's wishes...
But experience it is what it is
When you're just a techno seeds blues agenda...

A lot of parties, too many mollies, feeling like a zombie
I've got to get out of this place
But they've danced to their transhumanism melody, seen the un-seen
and sold my soul
I will never find peace, It will haunt me
Wherever I go
Among the children's
cocaine blossoms faces
Souls gone
I was passionate, desperate, but paid dearly for it
Wild Beast blood-soaked tears
Never mind our body

You beg my pardon, Modern human sacrifice! Spare me the road to your celestial bloodies whispered sucker screams that scrape bluesy throat 2030 raw.

...silence snakes snares smiles...

Within futile affairs in Tree of Knowledge turned into the Subliminal Suicidal Ideation for surrealmageddon visual Inspirations!

Eve first touching the Fruit of Knowledge

TREE OF KNOWLEDGE

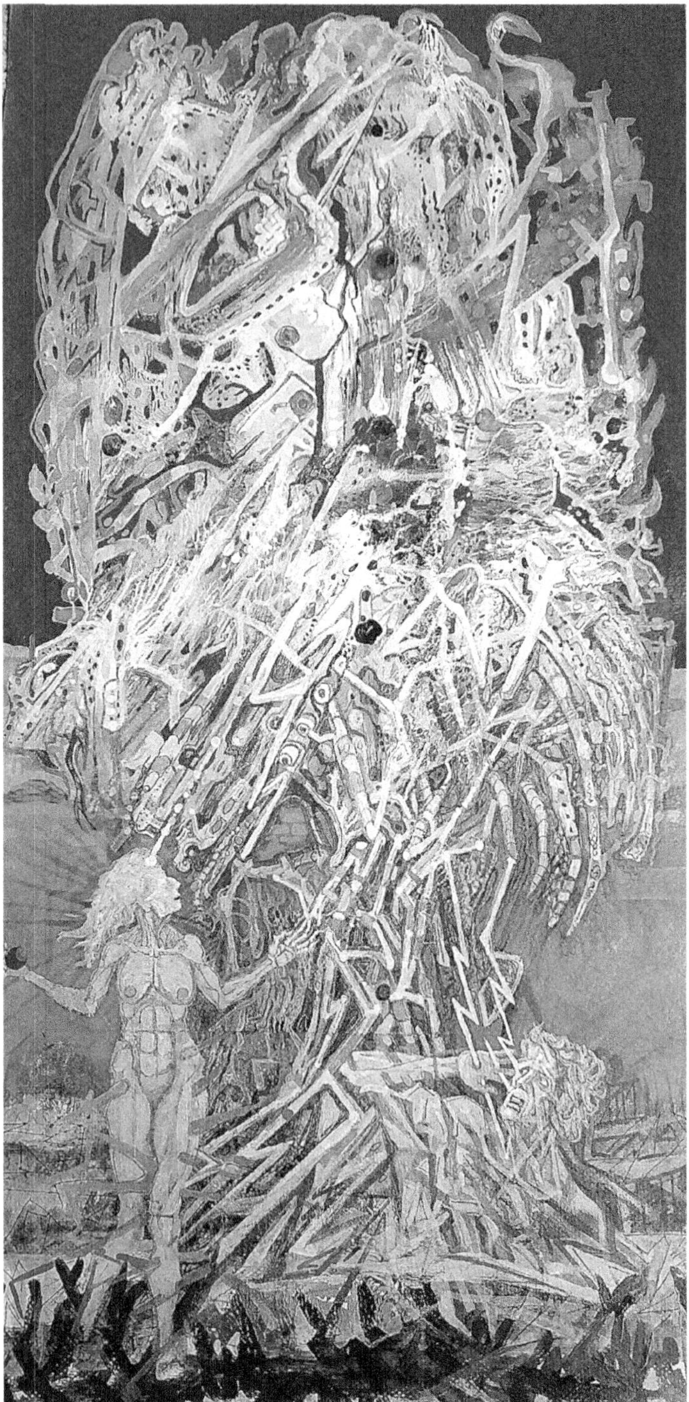

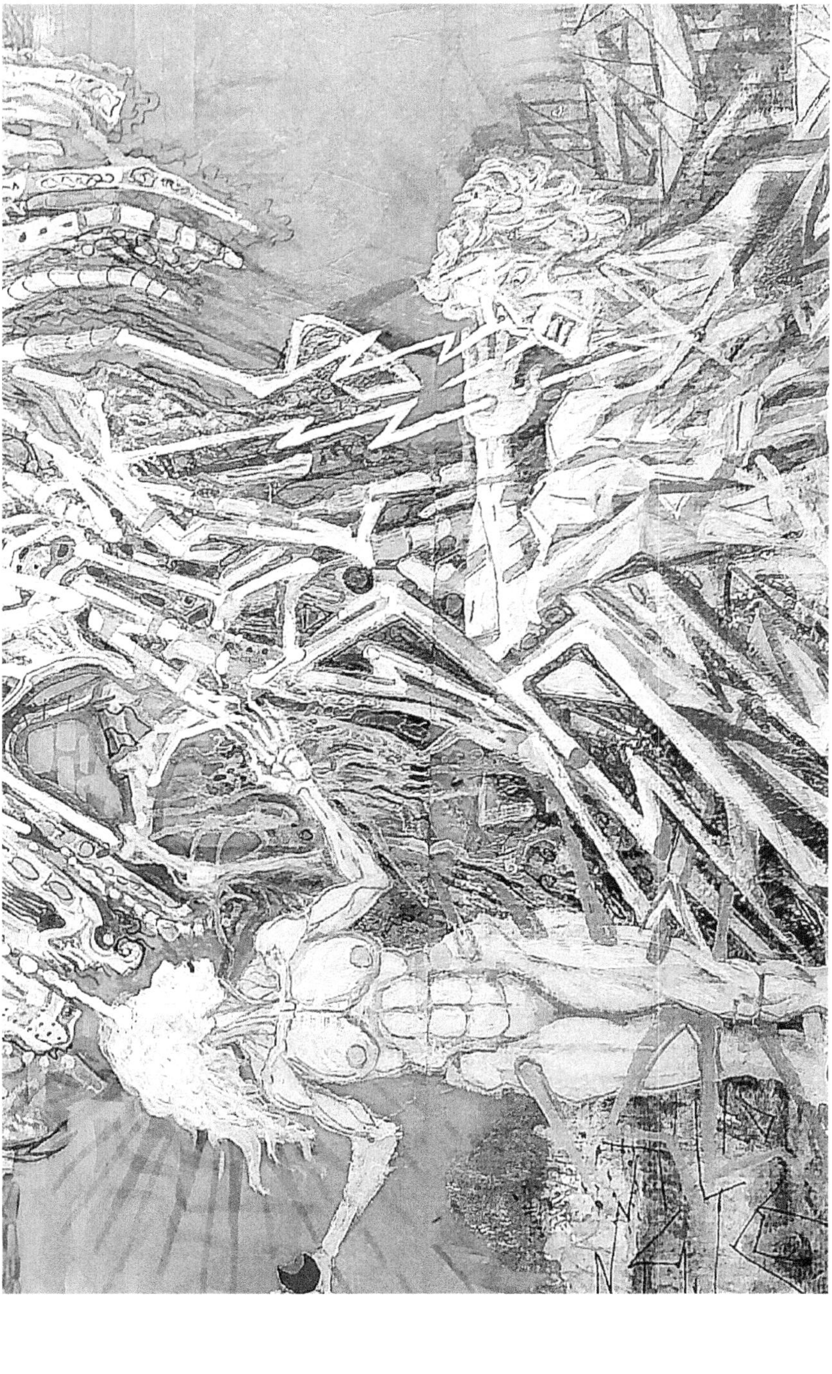

EXPULSION

Go!

F A L L E N L A N D S C A P E

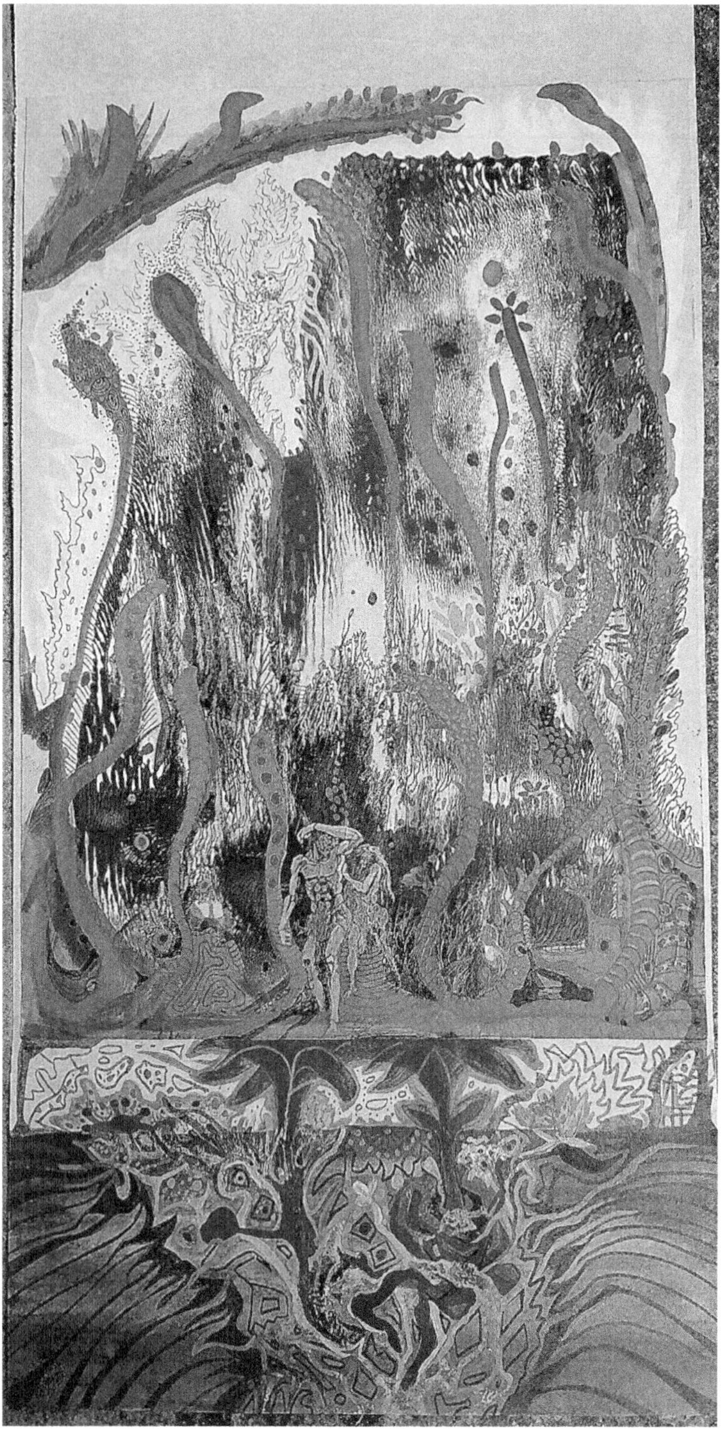

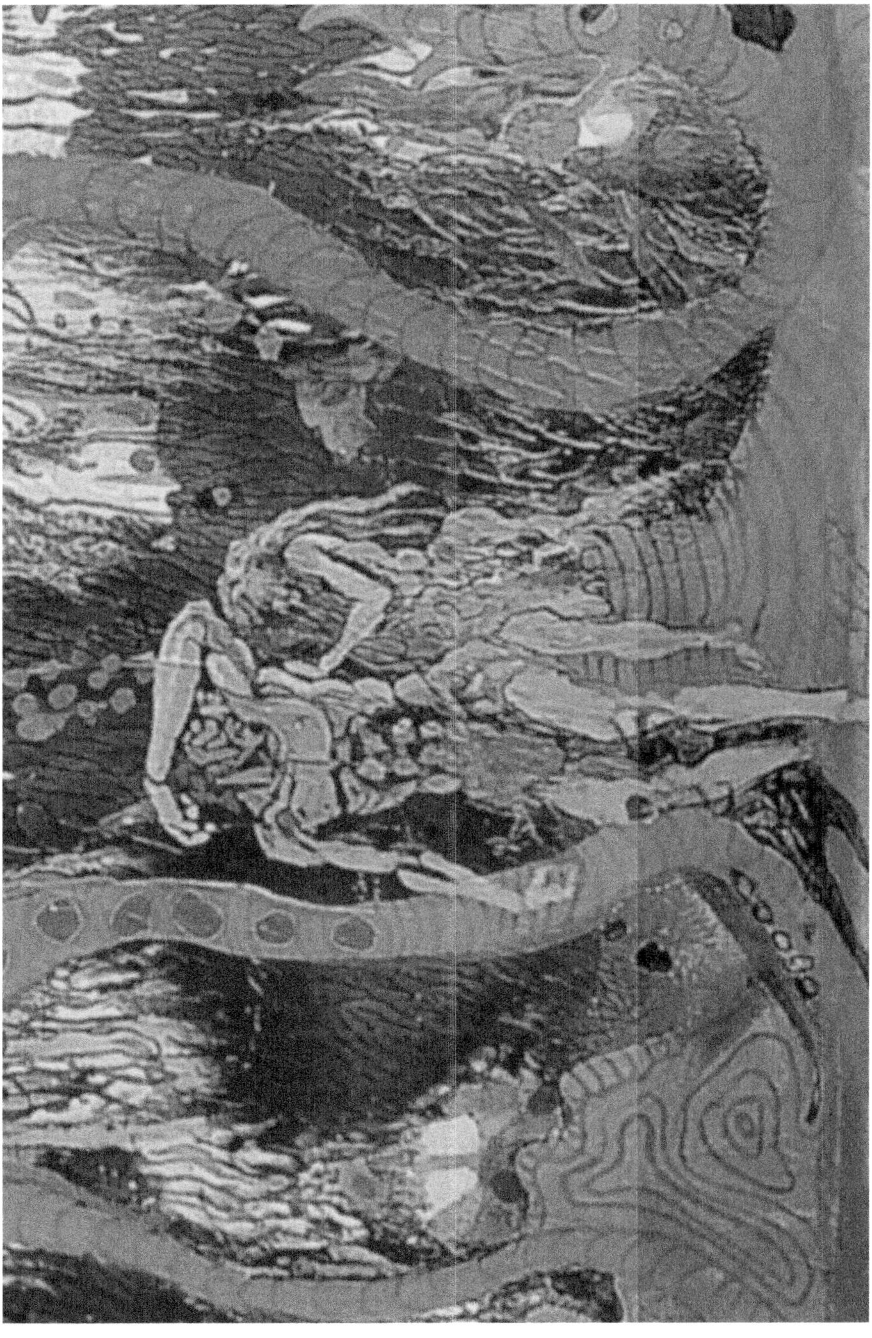

LANDSCAPE LOST

Jubilant Satan Exalting for Adam and Eve's Rebellion against GOD's Just Policies

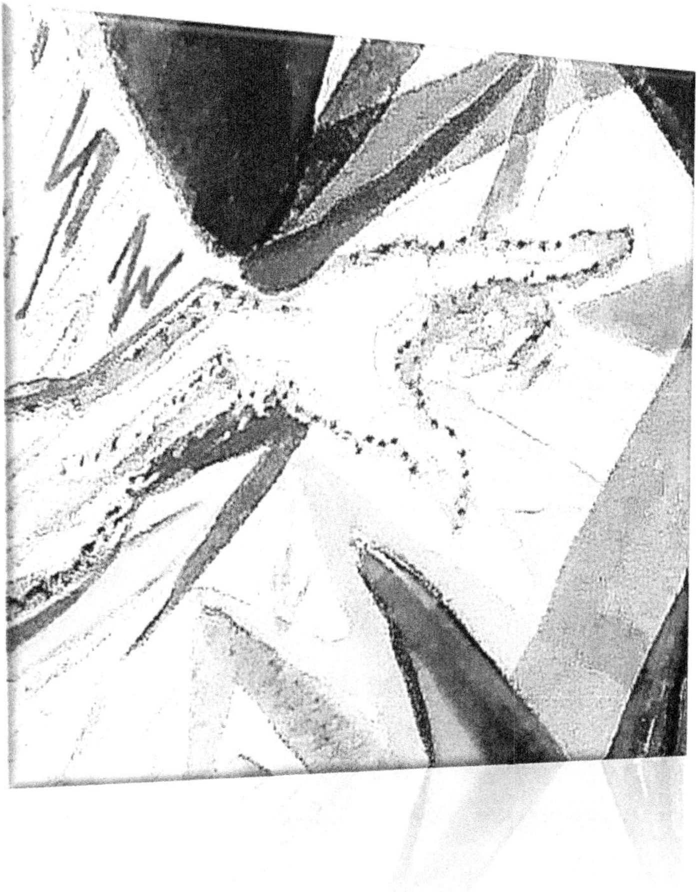

DIRECTED EVOLUTION

💉 administer evolution
💉 manage evolution
💉 run evolution
💉 control evolution
💉 govern evolution
💉 conduct evolution
💉 handle evolution
be in charge of 💉 evolution
be in control of 💉 evolution
be in command of 💉 evolution
be the boss of 💉 evolution
command 💉 evolution
rule 💉 evolution
preside over 💉 evolution
exercise control over 💉 evolution and make it for cash cow evolution in 💲💉💲💰🖤
👌"You Will Own Nothing, And You Will Be Happy"

Richard Glyn Jones

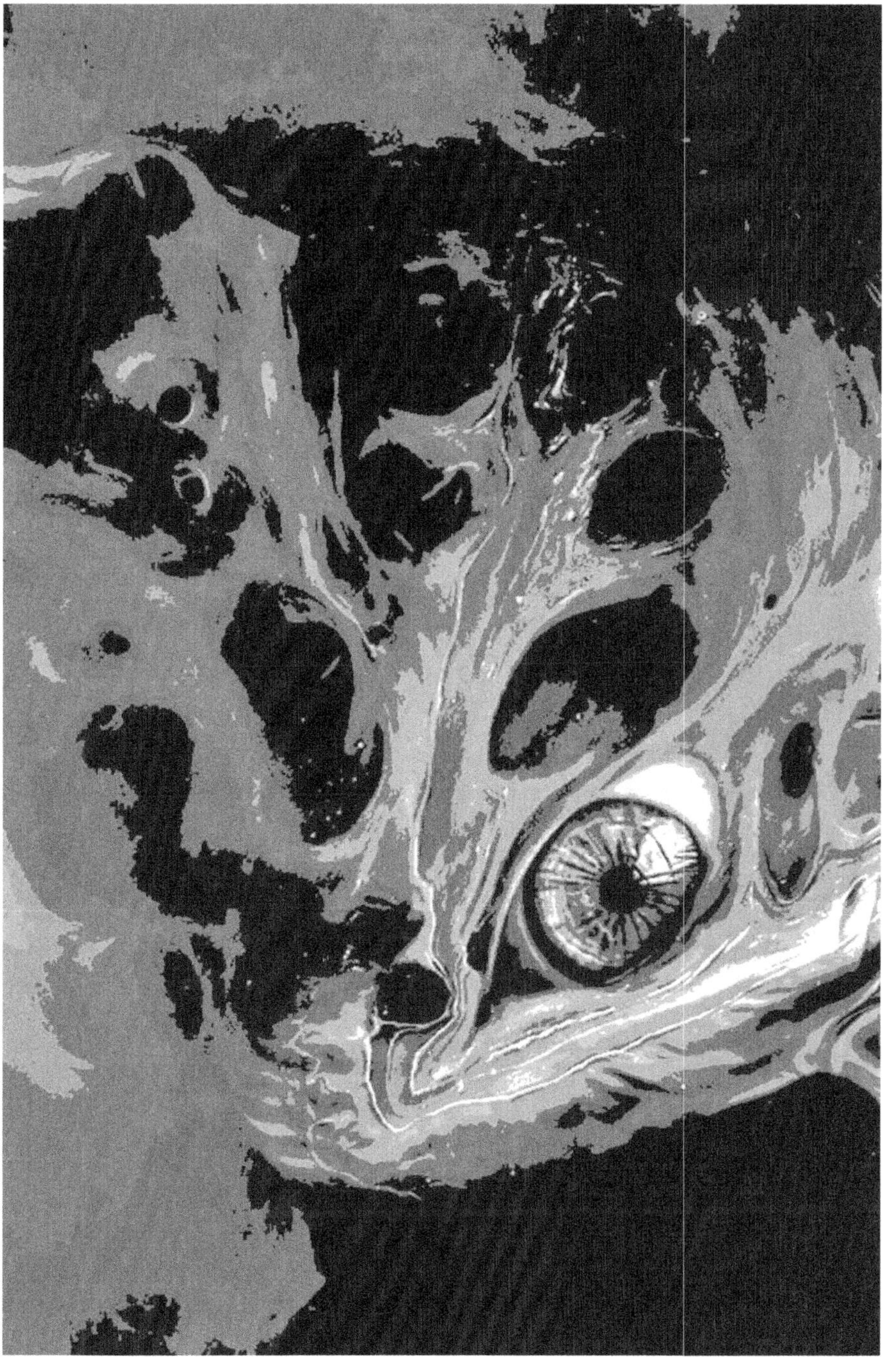

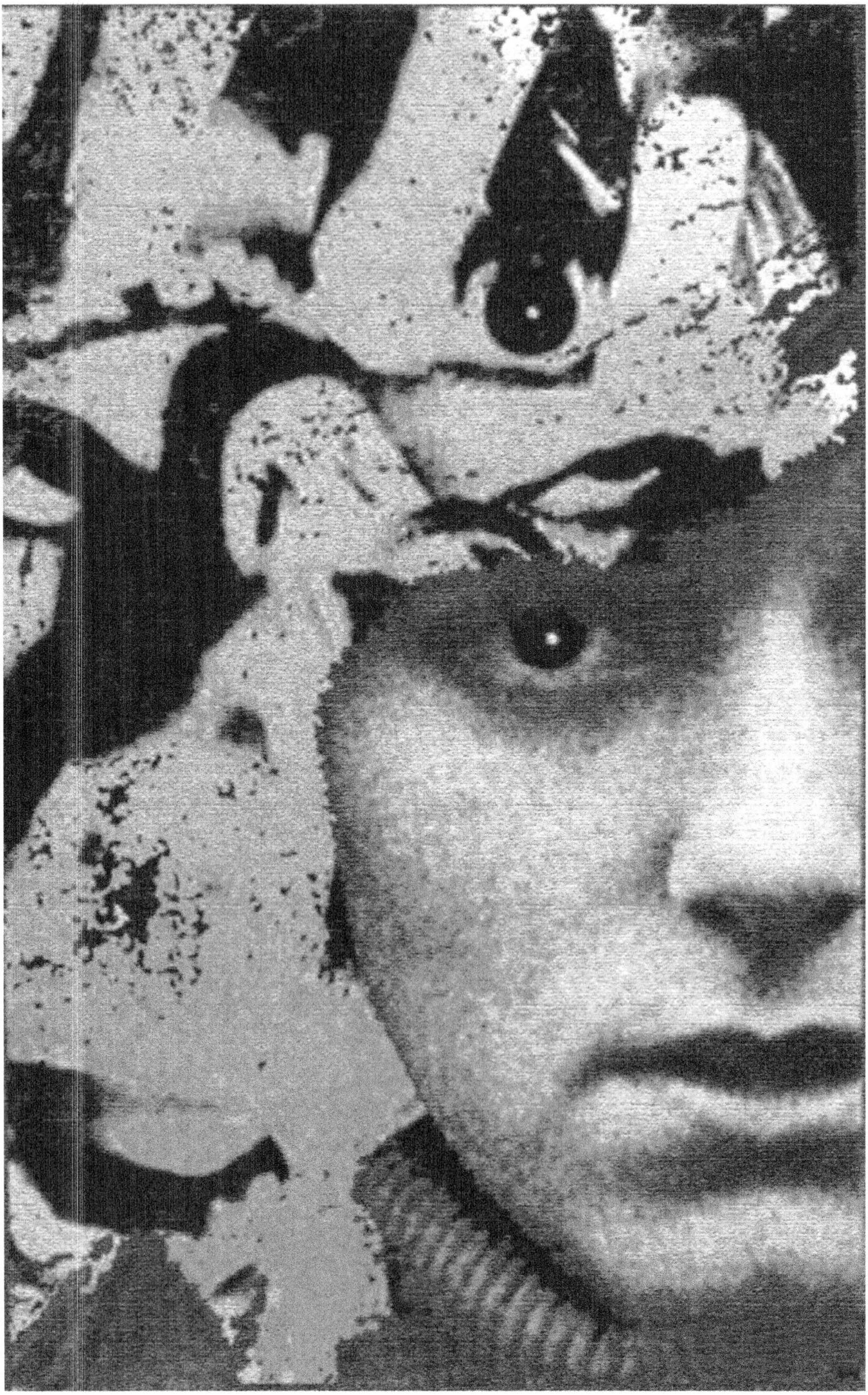

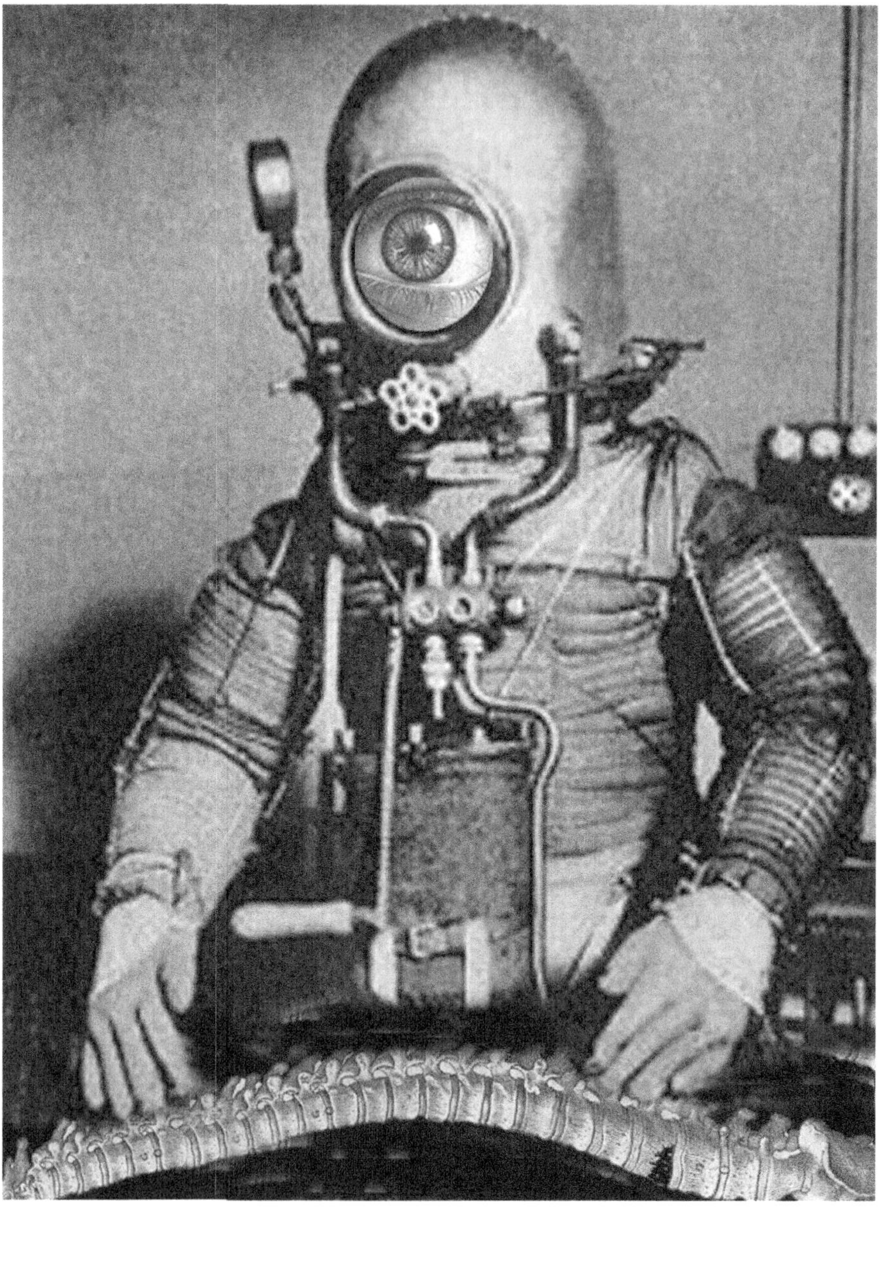

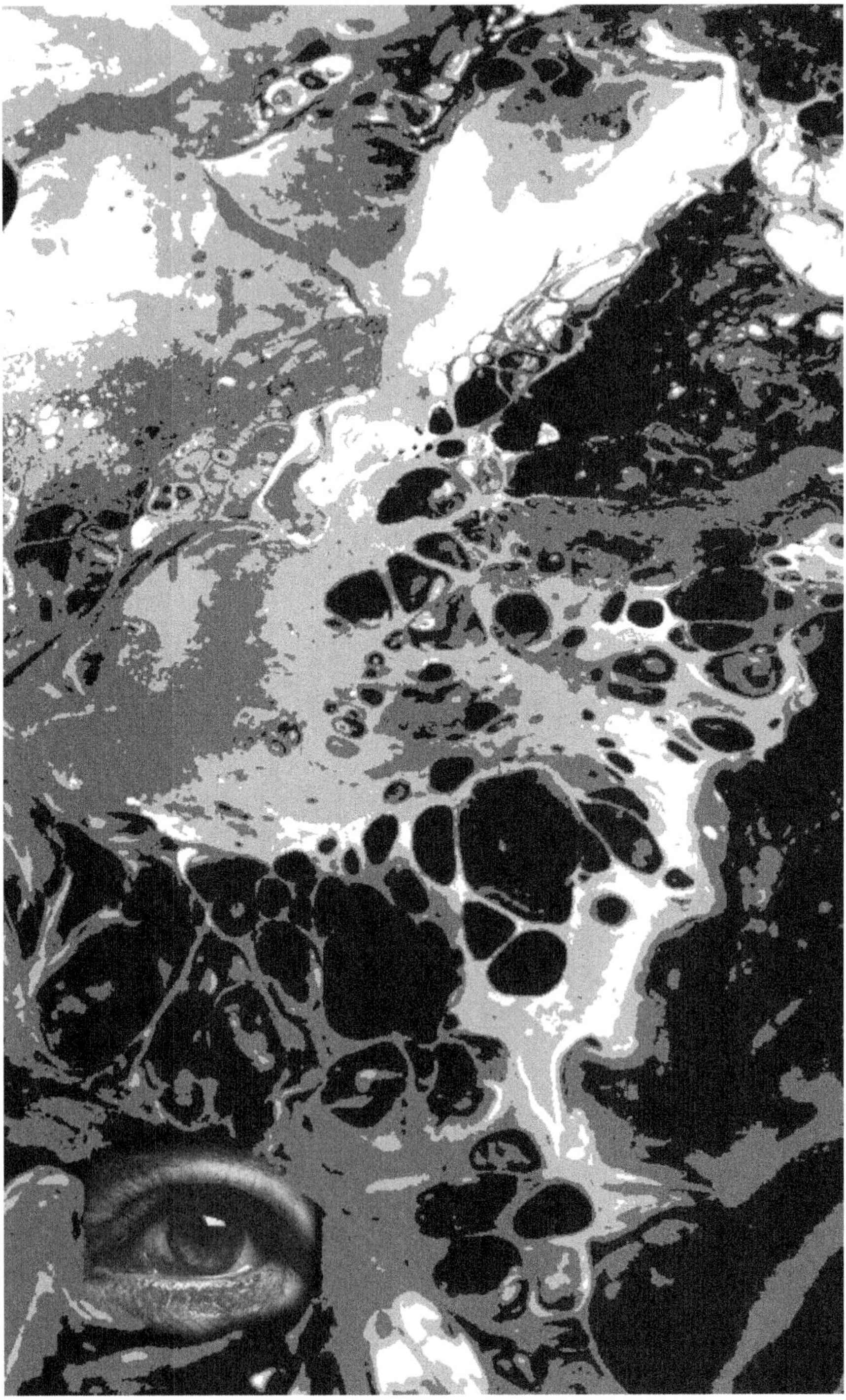

Leo Rampen

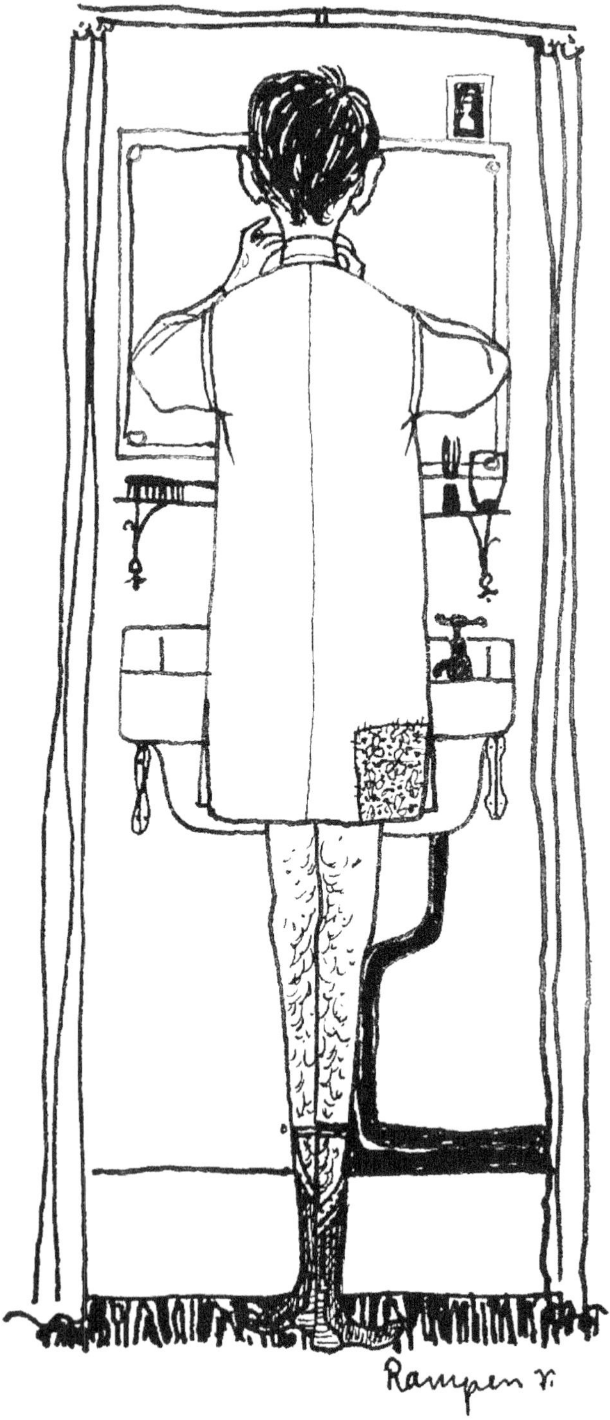
Rampen v.

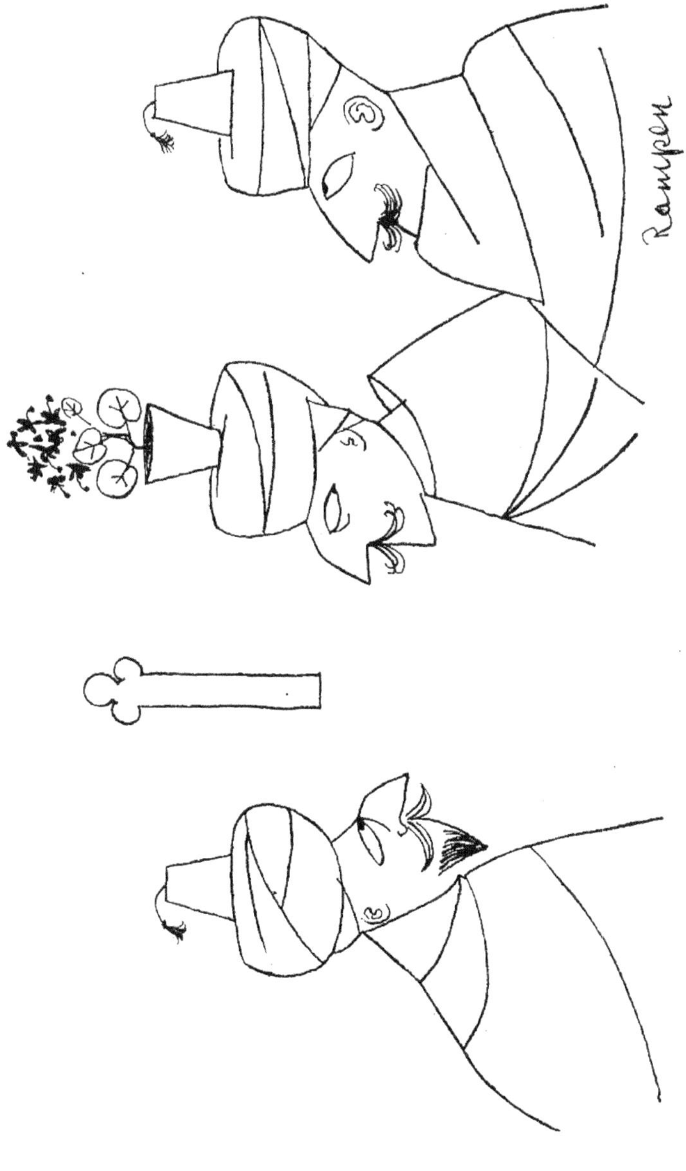
Rampen

Rampen

Rampen

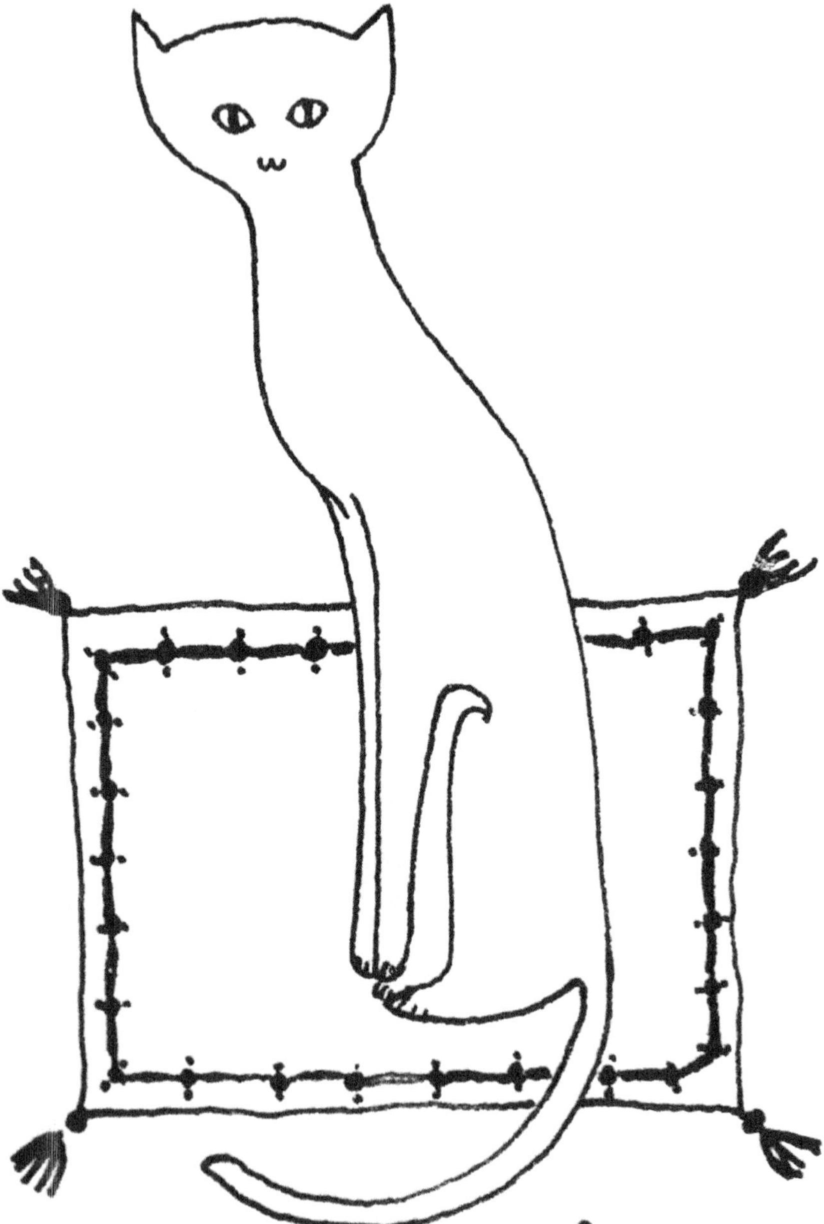

Denny Marshall

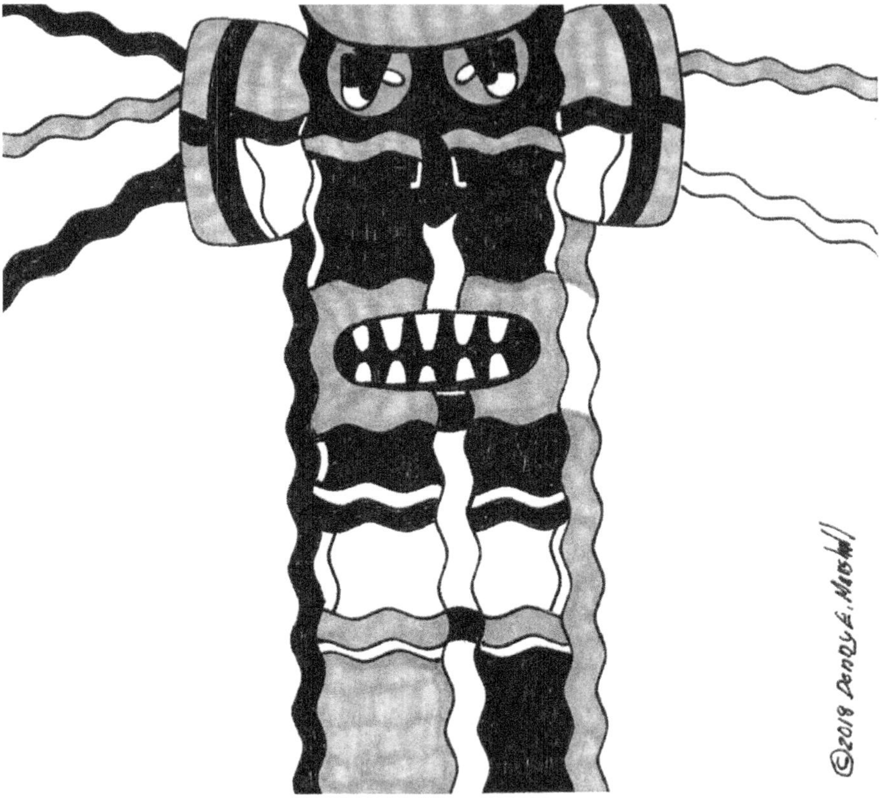

Corregated Creature

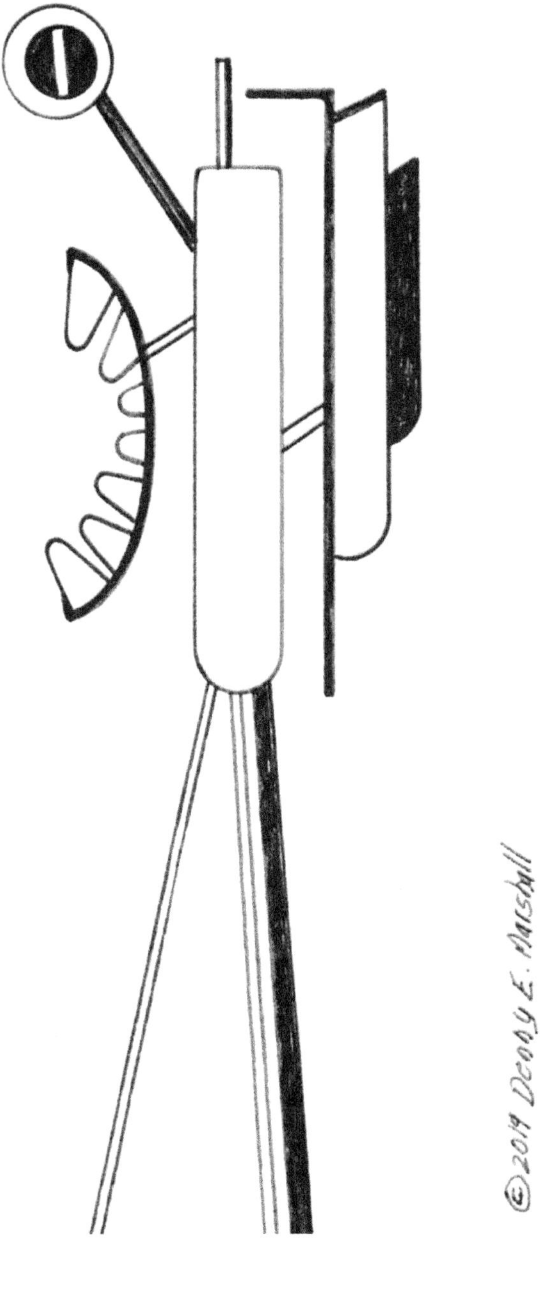

Bite

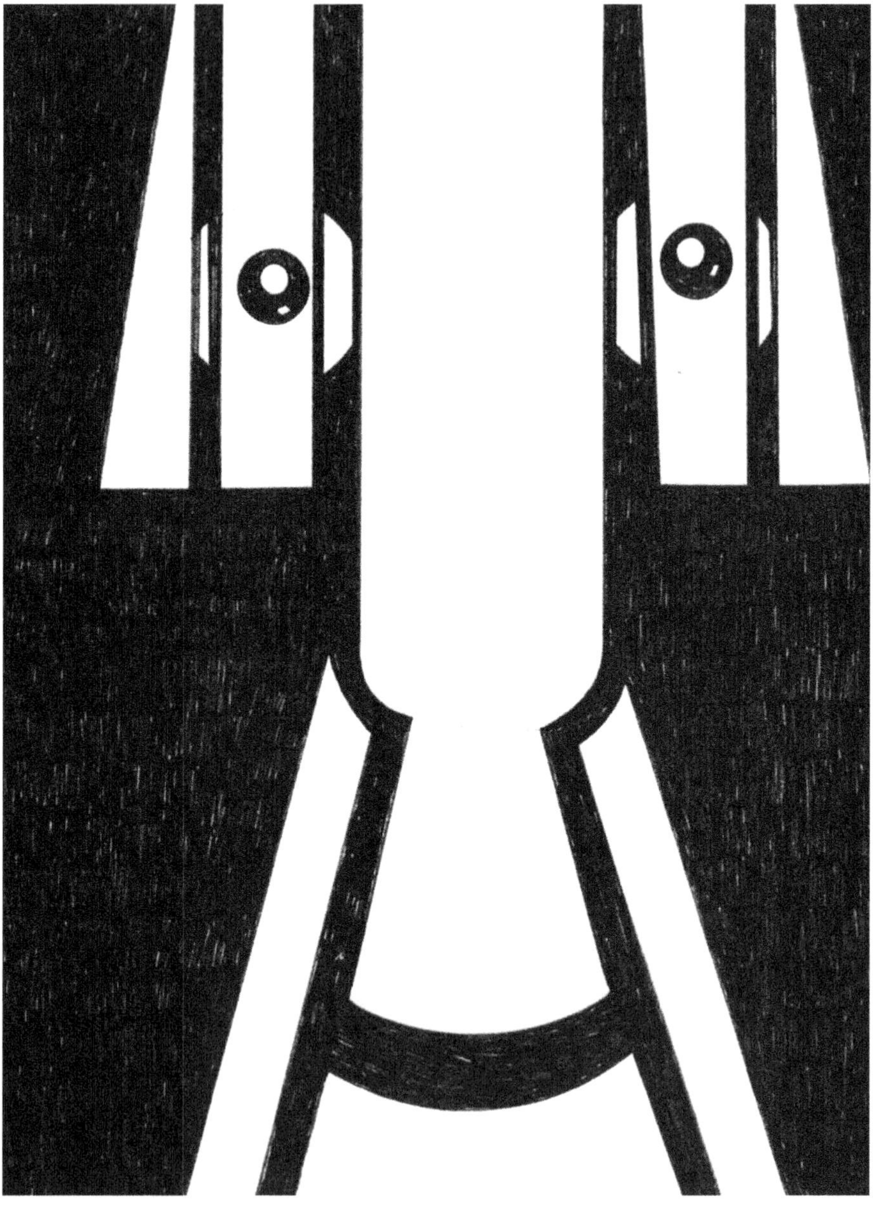

Easter Island Rocket Man

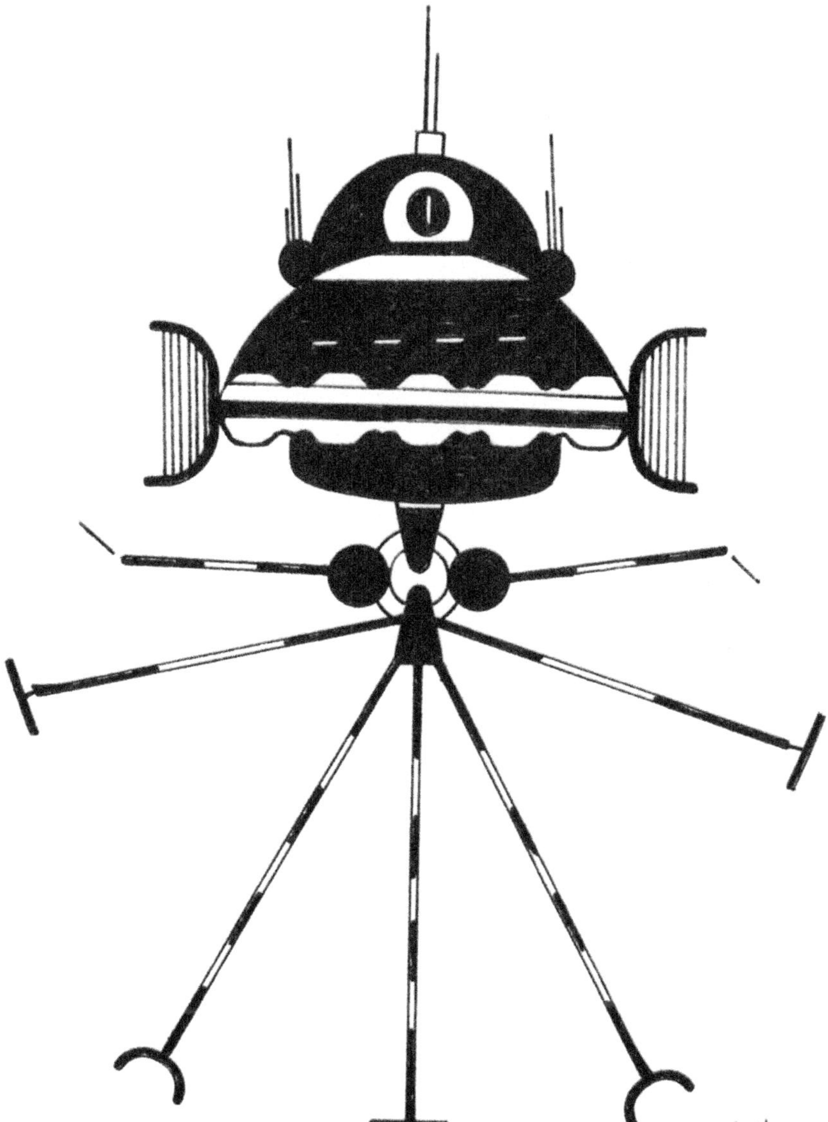

Eye Probe

Happy Circuit

©2015 Donna E. Marshall

Roll On

Saucer Camera

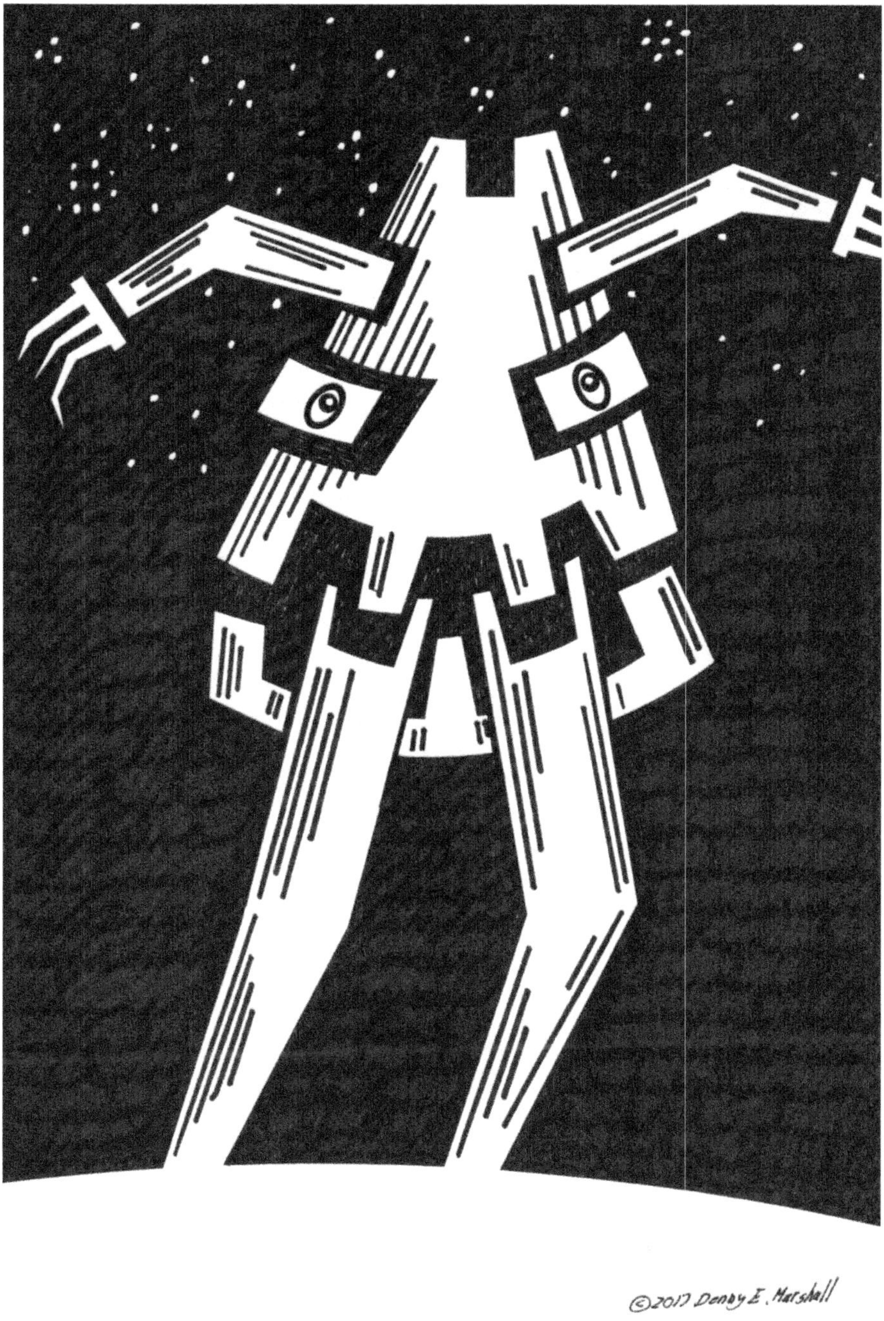

Space Junk Lifeform

Hex Spiker

Rec Spiker

Sphere Spiker

Tin Spiker

Arthur Lee Talley

Hotter Rods

JACKSON

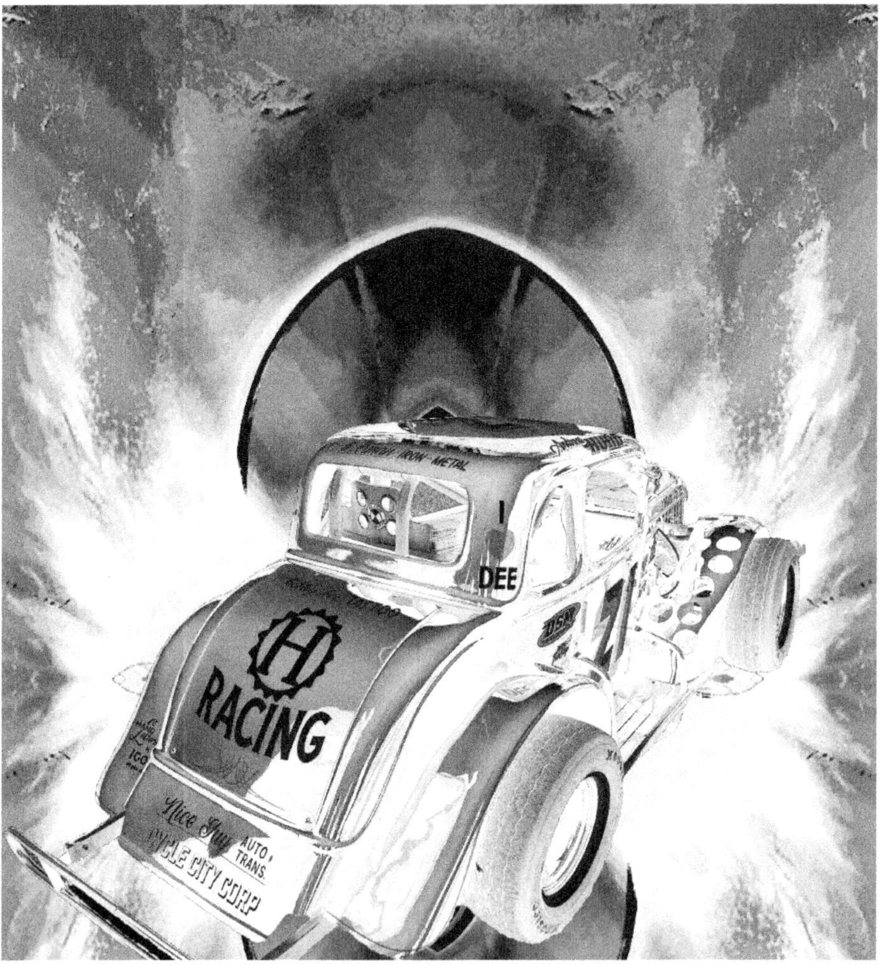
RACING
DEE
Nice Guy
AUTO,
TRANS.

TAYLOR
WASTE SERVICES

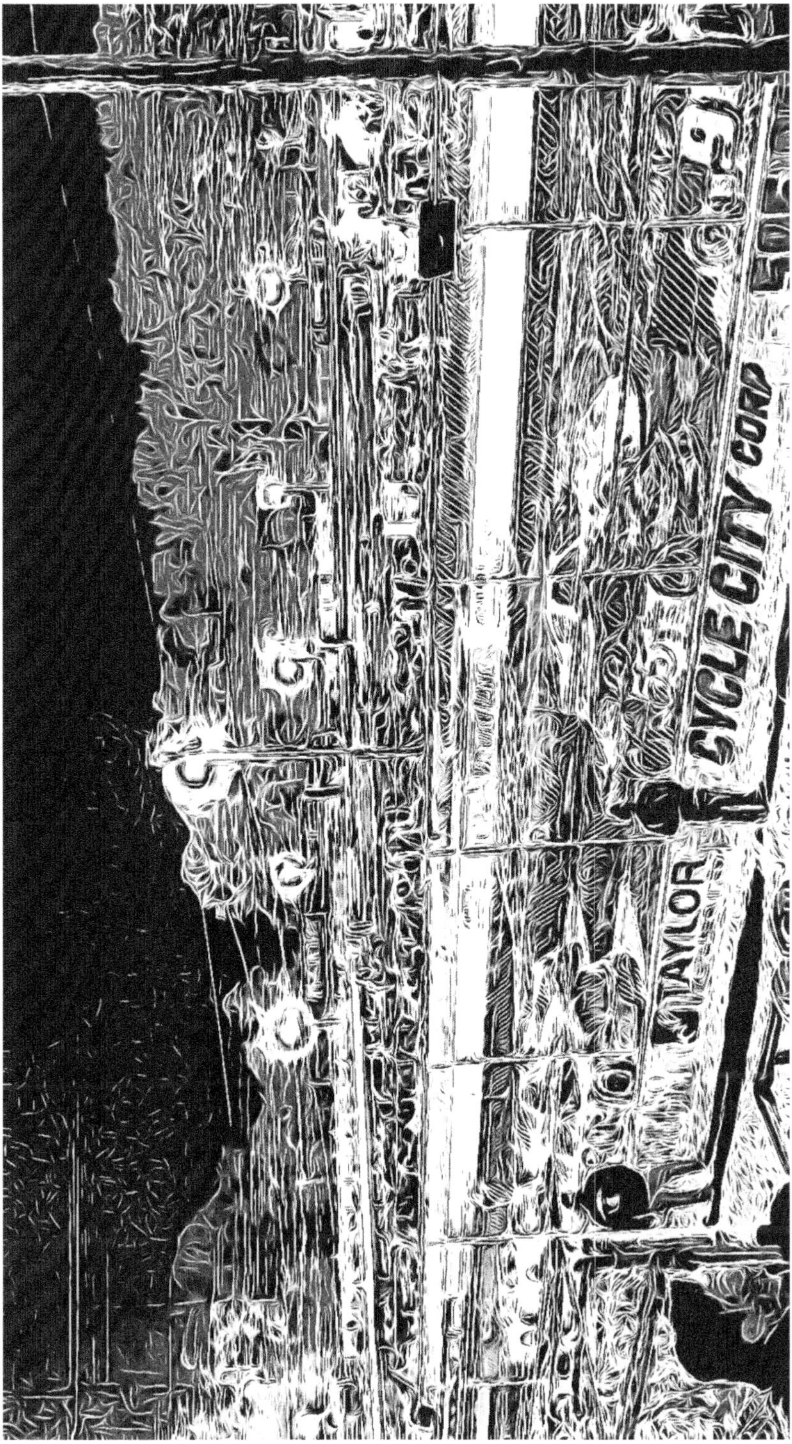
CYCLE CITY CORP

Examination and Assessment

C. Berton Irwin

Sarah Winked

YOU APPROACH THE HIGHWAY at the edge of the parking lot and you glance to your left. Your secondary sense quickly coordinates with your sense of time which relays the urgency of making two more stops at two other strip malls before your guests begin to arrive at around five, so you will really have to speed up here and make up time there as you hurry along. While you are preoccupied with whether you bought enough paper towels for the week, your secondary sense gives you the go-ahead to save some extra seconds by pressing the pedal and pulling out into traffic, and there is a green car screeching, and it is the kind of green that doesn't show up very well on a gray day, and it is a gray day, and you can hear what sounds like a downpour on the hood, except it is the crumple of metal and the crumble of shatter-resistant glass. For an instant there is separation between you and your body, and everything is adrenaline and red and black and electric-white stars, and gravity has lost meaning.

You haven't closed your eyes for more than a blink but it seems like you are opening them for the first time, and your first feeling—not your first thought, your first *feeling* is:

Up! Up!

Where is up?

Up is the first thing, the first *feeling,* that must be established. The map of life must feel correctly oriented again. Where is the North Pole? *Up.* Everything else comes after *up*—after the ambulance and the fire department and the police and the orange traffic cones and the rubbernecking bumper-to-bumper and your guests kept waiting until well after five dispersing home or to the hospital after receiving the terrible news—*Oh, my God!*—and the lawyers and the insurance companies and the hospital, and everything that comes after *up* is aftermath.

Aftermath is the rest of your life.

The rest of Orrick Johns's life began when he was seven years and six months old in January 1895. He was born in St Louis, Missouri, in June of 1887, but the rest of Orrick's life started with an after-school game of tag on Goodfellow Boulevard. He did not want to be *it*. His timing center calculated that he could avoid being *it* if he dodged across the boulevard in front of an oncoming trolley. His secondary sense gave him the go-ahead. For an instant everything was adrenaline and red and black.

Where is up?

The rest of Orrick's life began with a polished steel rail and a bloodied steel wheel in a freezing, dark womb reeking of iron filings and petroleum. Aftermath was his left leg crushed and amputated well above the knee, and a long recovery spent in his father's library, while his brothers could still dodge all the trolleys they wanted. Aftermath was dreaming of becoming a writer, when Orrick might have become anything else. The rest of Orrick's life arrived in 1912 after he became famous for winning a national poetry contest. In 1912, Orrick Johns became *Orrick Johns.* He was among the first bohemian artists to settle New York's Greenwich Village. He joined the free-verse movement during the opening of the Poetic Renaissance, which was part of a revolution in culture and literature at the beginning of the twentieth century.

Somewhere in the aftermath of Orrick's fame, my mother was born to his fourth wife, Doria. My mother married a disturbed man. That man was my father. Aftermath began for me when I entered foster care at the age of ten.

Where is up?

Aftermath began when I ran away from Florida to New York at seventeen.

Where is up?

When I turned eighteen, Florida declared me a legal orphan. For decades it felt like this was the rest of my life, like everything was aftermath. All along, aftermath had not yet begun. The rest of my life had not yet begun. I was still gestating in that instant of adrenaline and red and black before the squeal of wheels on cold steel rails, before sirens and orange traffic cones. I was still in that instant without gravity before every tumbling wreck crashes to a halt. I could not feel who I was, or what I was, or where is *up.* Time was suspended. I lived in that suspension for thirty years. An instant had been stretched out into stillness.

That instant of stillness was most of my life, still as a Christmas tree cut from its roots and ejected onto the January curb—all the promises of pretty lights and warm smiles broken. Without the ability to feel roots holding me firmly to the ground, every challenge I faced in life felt like someone was finally coming to haul me off to the dump. Everyone could sense that I was always asking, *Where is up?* They saw my insecurities the way a drunk sees a January Christmas tree leaning against a pole on the sidewalk—easy to shove over, an easy feat of strength.

For thirty years, without the feeling of roots to hold me down, I could find no *up* in love or art or money. I delivered all the anxiety of trying to stand without *up* straight into my back between my shoulders. I did not know my tensed-up back muscles were tearing at tendons attached to my ribs, prying them out of their proper sockets in my spine. Dislodged ribs pinched nerves. Pain went in every direction. I often struggled to take a full breath without the sensation of being stabbed in my diaphragm. Just being on my feet for any length of time was an act of will. In secret, where no one could hurt me, I curled up on the floor waiting for the pain to go away, waiting for anxiety to stop ripping at my ribcage.

Anxiety never stopped, never let up. Having coffee with friends was like spraying rocket fuel on a forest fire. I would spend the next hour in terror of lashing out at everyone for brushing me off when I told them: *No, coffee is a hellscape for me.* But I would have a cup of coffee anyway just to fit in, to show I had roots just like they did. I hid all of this, and I hid all of this, but it always got loose. I could never say the right thing at the right time in the aftermath—another friend gone, another relationship broken. Another year, another decade, and still a January Christmas tree. Years and years and still: *Where is up?*

Up was that one time I snorted heroin. At least it felt like *up* for a time, but I knew I could never do it again. It took all the anxiety away, all the self doubt, all the torment of being bullied as a child for being small and poor; all the alienation that comes from how everyone gets to talk about their memories of childhood but me; all the suffering in silence because I could not speak of foster care, or my disturbed and violent father—and not because it pained me, but because it pained others. Childhood trauma begins in adulthood, in the gazes of others. I could not look at others without seeing their pity staring back at me, their cringing, or their anger on my behalf, which always felt pointed at me. Their eyes accused me, like I didn't belong among decent people with normal childhoods. Guilt by association. And the guilt, the guilt, the guilt for so many crimes I imagined I had committed and judged myself convicted. They say that during the Ice Age, vast sheets of glacial tundra compressed the continents, and when the ice sheets melted the continents began to rise. Heroin was like that. The absence of lifelong constant pain felt like I had risen, but I knew heroin wasn't *up,* it just removed all the *down.*

Up arrived with a woman named Peggy Baird, my grandfather's first wife. A quarter of a century before I was born, my grandfather, Orrick, died. I had owned his 1937 book, *Time of Our Lives: The Story of My Father and Myself,* for more than half of my life, but I had never given it much consideration. Even if my engulfing anxiety would have let me concentrate on reading it, I thought it was frivolous, like a vanity publication. I knew that Orrick's father, George Sibley, had run the *St. Louis Post-Dispatch* for Joseph Pulitzer. I figured that the old man had pulled some strings to get his son's book published. In 2020, after the covid lockdown, when it seemed like everyone was re-examining their existence, I finally gave my grandfather's book some time and thought. While reading about his life in 1914 as a poet in Greenwich Village, one name, Peggy Baird, felt familiar. I wondered if I wasn't thinking of Peggy Gugenheim, the socialite art collector of the early twentieth century. Still, I could not be sure. I asked an acquaintance, who might know more about these things, if he had ever heard of Peggy Baird.

Yes, he had. He wondered why I was asking. I told him Peggy was my grandfather's first wife. I had not told him my grandfather's name, but he replied, "Your grandfather was Orrick Johns? Why did we not know this?"

Because I did not know this. I had never heard my grandfather's name spoken outside of the family I left when I was ten. I always knew my grandfather was named Orrick Johns in the same way that anyone might know their grandfather's name. Orrick was my brother's middle name and Johns was my mother's maiden name. To me, Orrick Johns was just a bit of esoteric lore from my childhood in what I can only call a single-family cult. Isolated from the world by my father's disturbed paranoia, I could never have imagined that my grandfather, Orrick Johns, was once *Orrick Johns.* I did not know he was famous, I only knew that his fourth wife, Doria Berton, my mother's mother, was connected to someone famous—Sarah Bernhardt.

I didn't know that five years before Orrick lost his leg, Sarah Bernhardt fell to her knees. She looked up. She was playing Joan of Arc. The Inquisitor at her trial asked Joan to state her age. Joan answered, "Nineteen." Sarah was in her mid-forties. She winked at the audience. They cheered with abandon. Night after night, Joan of Arc fell to her knees. Night after night, Sarah winked. Even at middle age, Sarah had the energy of youth eternal, but her right knee was getting old. Her right knee became inflamed from falling and falling and falling. Eventually, over many years, it became a source of intense pain. It turned gangrenous, and so began the rest of her life....

Or maybe the trouble with her right knee started when she was a girl. When Sarah Bernhardt was a child, she was living with foster parents. They were hired to look after her by her mother, who lived the life of a courtesan taking to bed the high and the mighty. When her aunt Rosine came to visit, Sarah was so desperate to prevent her from leaving that she fell in front of her aunt's departing carriage, and she injured her knee....

Or maybe she leaped from a two-story window, and landed in front of Rosine's carriage, injuring her knee. This detail comes from Thérèse Berton, wife of Pierre. When Sarah played her first major role in "Kean" alongside Pierre Berton, she was a Dutch Jew in a highly anti-Semitic country, with an unknown father where paternity was everything. The Bertons were known to French arts and theater going all the way back to the court of Louis XV. It was good for Sarah to know a Berton or two, and she did. In her dressing room, she "knew" both Pierre and his father, Charles, my great great great grandfather—but, hopefully, not at the same time.

Sarah was Pierre's lover, which was different than a mistress. A mistress was for children and a domestic life, which is why my mother's mother, Doria, is descended from Pierre's mistress, Felicé. A mistress had status in France. For a famous man to take a mistress was expected. Even a famous man's wife would expect him to take a mistress. A woman falls in love with a famous man the way a flower falls in love with the Sun. A sensible woman expects to share the sunlight. Nineteenth-century France was sensible in these matters. Why would a woman like my great great grandmother Felicé, who had neither money nor social position, want exclusive rights to a poor man like herself, when she could share a famous man like Pierre? Pierre's wife, Thérèse, saw things in just the same way. Pierre made her a Berton, which gave her the status to make money from his connection to Sarah after he died. When Sarah died, an English writer, Basil Woon, paid Thérèse to "reveal" Sarah Bernhardt for English-speaking readers. What the book promised was in its title, *The Real Sarah Bernhardt,* because it was widely known that all of her biographers were liars. Thérèse was a liar, too, but her lies about her husband's love for Sarah were so beautiful. She claimed that Sarah had confided to her many of the things in her book. This is probably true. Sarah's memoirs were made of beautiful lies, too. Almost every story Sarah told about her life came with a wink toward the plot of a key scene in a popular novel or play. The Aunt Rosine story was a wink toward *Le Miserables*. Maybe everything Sarah said came with a wink, but in the story of her aunt's visit, she said she injured her left kneecap, and we are talking about her right knee....

Maybe the trouble started in Brazil. Sarah was playing Floria in *La Tosca*. Standing on a parapet, Floria watched from afar as her great love was executed through the machinations of Baron Scarpia, a role originated by Pierre many years before. Bereaved, she jumped from the parapet to end her life. Stagehands had neglected to place mattresses on the floor below the parapet to catch Sarah's fall. She hit the stage and injured her right knee....

Maybe this is a little too on the nose. Dying onstage was Sarah's catchphrase. When Pierre wrote *Léna* for her in 1889, the play was not so great, but people would sit through anything just to watch her die. Sarah's death in the finale of *Léna* did not disappoint. According to one critic, it was "wonderful."

> The distortion of the face, the dazed bearing, the stiffening of the entire body on the couch where she sinks down—all these things exhibit remarkable truth and strength. Her husband rushes in, touches her, and her body falls face first like a heap on the floor.

This was five long minutes. The audience erupted in a frenetic ovation. *A triumph!* Thérèse claimed that Pierre once confessed to her: "the days that Sarah Bernhardt devoted to me were like pages from immortality. One felt that one could not die!" Sarah had that effect. Death was her Inquisitor and Sarah was always nineteen. Ugly old J.P Morgan, who wanted no actresses in his library of rare volumes in New York, was charmed when she yanked at his tie and said, "When I speak, men listen." Sarah made death listen. She cooed at death as if it were a temperamental artist, soothed it like a courtesan, taught it manners like a governess, domesticated it with a wink.

State your age.

Nineteen.

Wink.

With every wink, death became like the Tsar who orders a pogrom before demonstrating the finest politesse at the ballet. For a few small hours in her theater, Sarah made people forget that death was a cold-blooded monster full of war and disease, who struck down little boys in games of tag. But maybe a serious injury resulting from her dying onstage was a bit too convenient—as if she had sacrificed her body for her art. The dates don't line up, either....

Maybe the trouble started in 1887, the year Orrick was born. Sarah embarked on the first of eight "farewell" tours in the Americas. On a ship back to Europe, she took a tumble and injured her right knee. Or maybe...

No, that sounds about right. It's just dull enough to be true, but it's a superficial truth. It hides the deeper truth behind Sarah's life of lies. She understood the difference between want and need, how we want the truth but we need the lie. Most times, we say we want the truth, but what we need to know is where is *up.* Even when the answer is a lie told with a wink. Sarah winks and we see her fall in front of her aunt's carriage. We think of the struggles of her childhood and there is comfort in the feeling that we can overcome anything, even an uncaring mother who sent away her own child to a foster home. That is *up.* Sarah winks and we see her fall in *La Tosca.* We think of the price of fame and can feel like great things can come from great sacrifice. That is *up.* Sarah winks and we see her fall on the deck of a ship. Even a random accident can be *up.* Life may be random, but at least it is predictably so. Sarah winks and God has a plan; Sarah winks and there is no plan—either way the universe has a structure, a plot that we can choose, a plot that fits best into the comfort zone we invent for ourselves so we always feel like we know where is *up.*

My comfort zone is agnostic, always down the middle in a place called Maybe. Maybe all the lies ever told about Sarah's leg going gangrenous were rooted in the truth. Maybe Sarah fell as a girl, and fell on a ship, and fell night after night while playing Joan of Arc. Finally, she fell in *La Tosca.* Maybe all of these things contributed to a developing problem in her right knee. I fall toward Sarah's turn as Joan of Arc because it is straight down the middle—not too dramatic, but just dramatic enough. It has plot, but it also has poetry.

Plot is:

"State your age."

"Nineteen."

Poetry is the wink.

Plot is an amputation. Poetry is a kind of conversation about an amputation between two amputees across different times and varied geography. In 1914, Sarah arranged to have her leg removed, finally looking forward to a pain-free life. In 1895, Orrick had an emergency amputation on his mother's kitchen table, and he was expected to die. Sarah Bernhardt was a legend at seventy-one with the rest of her life behind her; Orrick was seven with all aftermath ahead. A woman famous for playing Cleopatra could be carried around in a sedan chair, but a seven-year-old boy could not. Sarah kept on playing ingénues, winking until the day she died, always sure of her answer to: *Where is up?* Orrick never found a lasting answer, but across time and geography, he became mine.

I always knew the plot of my great great grandfather Pierre and Sarah, but I never before found the poetry. Poetry is how the State of Florida closed my case after I ran away to New York, declaring me a legal orphan, leaving me in a life of aftermath like a game of tag where always I was *it,* but one day (wink) I dodged a trolley, and on the other side was Peggy. She introduced me to Orrick. Until then, I did not even know the most repeated fact about him: that he had one leg. Orrick introduced me to Sarah. I learned how she had one leg. Only then could I see the poetry in Pierre and Sarah. My comfort zone is straight down the middle, but it centers on poetry. I can only know what I feel, and I only feel poetry, not plot. This is ironic since I always dismissed poetry. I thought Orrick was a well-connected man's dilettante rich kid because he could not possibly be a poet. I thought he was a pathetic figure handing out self-published copies of his poetry to his friends. I had called him a "failed poet" and wondered how anyone could be so deluded as to think they could be a "successful" poet in the twentieth century. Poetry was a profession that had died with the nineteenth century, hadn't it?

"Oh!" I heard Peggy say, as if I should know better. *"Orrick Johns"* she said in that Long Island accent which Orrick's "St. Louis ears" had once found so charming. "He's *famous,"* she assured me, nodding as if sharing potent gossip. She was chattering, chattering, her bright red lipstick slightly askew like a hastily-pinned barrette. She reminded me of women I had dated, and women I had been friends with. Still disoriented, I wondered: can a man's taste in women be inherited?

She walked ahead along Sixth Avenue as if she wanted me to see something, her cropped blonde hair bobbing. It was a beautiful day in Greenwich Village around May of 1914, which was years before salons offered the bob hairstyle. That Peggy did it herself was made obvious by the uneven strands which dangled down as if trying to tickle the shoulders of her Russian blouse. She turned back and stared at me with curious yellow eyes, wondering why I wasn't following her, as if no one in the world would think of anything else. I needed a moment to adjust to the fact that my muscles had stopped pulling apart my ribs, that I could stand and breathe without stabbing pain. I had been so long in a moment without gravity. A car overturning, a tree toppling—tumbling is what I knew, and then one day, Sarah winked to stop the tumbling. I finally felt rooted and savored the sensation. I hoped this was the rest of my life, but this aftermath would take some getting used to. Rather than let Peggy linger with that baffled expression on her face, I caught up to her, took the arm arm she held out toward me, then let her lead the way.

Michael Butterworth

Further Extracts from The Sunshine Island

The Night Land

CHRISTINE'S ROOM AT SPRINGFIELD overlooked the middle elm. The great tree supported Dad's calisthenics rings, on which he loved to show off his physique. Its spreading boughs almost touched the roof of our summerhouse where our garden toys were kept, and beyond lay the back tennis lawn, stretching parallel with the rear of the main house. To the left-hand of this was our life support system, the large vegetable garden and greenhouse with, just visible, the rhubarb patch, beehives, and part of the blackcurrant beds.

My sister's room was diagonally across the landing, lighter and airier than mine, but untidier, cluttered with toys and discarded clothes, and had a child's gate to allow her to watch our comings and goings on the landing. But the impediment to her freedom infuriated her, and she had soon learned how to escape by piling up pillows and blankets and climbing over. In the early mornings she ran in and out of my room, calling out at me to come and play, until I awoke.

One such morning in the summer, when she was about four and I was six, and the daylight had awoken us and I was unable to get back to sleep, she urged me out of bed. She wanted me to see something and, curious to know what it was, I got up. She was normally wary of me entering her room but etiquette seemed in abeyance as I climbed over her gate unchallenged, greeted immediately by the faint smell of urine, which I knew was the reason she didn't want me there; she still wet her bed. But we didn't remain long before she led me down the short flight of stairs to the cloakroom landing. The window overlooked the back too, but it was further to the left, and from it you could look down into the kitchen garden with its strawberry beds and rose trellis. As we stood there I saw straight away what had been exciting her. Left out on the small lawn from the previous evening, were our toys. Our large Victorian dolls' house had its doors and windows open to the cool air, and scattered about it on the grass were the dolls.

Intently watching, we hadn't been there long when the dolls began moving. They got up from the haphazard positions where we had left them and walked about and climbed in and out of their house. We followed their movements fascinatedly, chattering excitedly as we pointed out their movements to one another, desperately wanting to be allowed into the garden to play with them. But the back door to the house was locked. I watched on as Chris vainly did her best to rouse the adults to let us out. At six, I knew the protocols and was too grown up to ask myself. But Chris had no luck, and when we returned to the cloakroom and looked down into the garden, the dolls were lying prone on the grass.

On another hot summer's day—aged sixteen or seventeen—for something to do, a friend and I found ourselves wandering the graveyard of a village church reading inscriptions on the tombstones. As we were leaving by a sandy path, looking downwards at our feet, words began appearing in the dust. Thinking it was a kind of Rorschach effect (the mind making pictures from random patterns) for amusement's sake I began reading one of the inscriptions aloud, "Mary Sumner, 1870-1913..."—but before I could finish Steve read out to me the rest of it to me, "...Beloved Daughter of Ronald and Susan." He did the same to me, and we performed the experiment several times until we were satisfied; we were seeing the same inscriptions—just as Chris and I had been able to see the movements made by the dolls and had described them to one another. We left the sandy path and as we joined the suburban street, the magic wore off.

Both occasions were characterised by intense quietude, when the weather was unusually sunny and warm, and other people were absent or asleep, and the participants were in harmony with each other. But perhaps there didn't have to be accord. I have described how, in my imagination, Springfield, seemed a duplicate of the edifice where William Lee, William Burroughs' alter-ego, had passed his childhood, in his semi-autobiographical novel, *Junky*. In his biography, *William S Burroughs: A Life*, Barry Miles records how, in the early 1920s, at a similar age to Chris and I, Burroughs saw "...grey human figures" moving about in his blockhouse (a toy-house built of wooden bricks) and observed a blue deer on his bedroom wall. He reported that he was on his own, unlike I had been. But a second person may have been present, perhaps the nurse whom he felt had shown malevolence toward him; a memory he had blocked, and had tried all his life to clear, unsuccessfully. Burroughs also believed that writing "made things happen." But to write, a writer must have a receiver. Chris and I badly wanted the dolls to move, and in our imaginations, 'written' to each other, we might have made them. Burroughs assumed he possessed unusual visionary ability. It was another 'Burroughs parallel', and Miles' book came as a revelation.

As I read on through *A Life*, I discovered that not only did Burroughs and I come from similar backgrounds and houses and experience clairvoyance, but we possessed chemistry sets and were fascinated by explosives and fire. Burroughs enjoyed playing sinister pranks with Ammonium Triiodide (Miles erroneously refers to this as 'Ammonium Iodide'), a sensitive explosive made by mixing ammonia with iodine crystals. When the compound dries the slightest impact—a breeze, or a fly alighting—will detonate it, and it makes a very loud 'crack'. At boarding school, after the breakfast tables had been laid last thing in the evening by the servers, I remember creeping out of bed to paste the freshly made mixture under the plates and bowls, and scatter blobs of it on the carpeted passageway leading to the headmaster's study. I imagined after drying overnight it would explode into a few startled faces and blow off a shoe-heel or explode into a cleaner's Hoover, though I made sure I wasn't around to see.

Dining with the au pair

A long flight of stairs led from Springfield's first floor to an upper landing, a creepy less furbished region of the house lit by an eerie skylight. Four bedrooms led off it, where thirty years earlier, servants had slept. Two of these had been knocked together by the previous owners to make a 'double', a large room that ran the full depth of the house. When Mum felt she could no longer share a bed with Dad and had migrated into my first-floor bedroom opposite Chris' room, this was where I was put. Across this upper landing from my room were two smaller ones—my sister Linda's bedroom, which was much tinier than even one of my two conjoined rooms, and our au pair's room, of a similar size to Linda's, directly across from my door. There was also a box room, full of silent junk—a door I never liked to open.

Not long after the dolls' house incident, and up until the age of twelve when Mum finally had enough and left Dad, taking us with her, this was where, each night, I went to sleep, or tried to. To a young boy who felt he was somehow responsible for his parents' woes, it felt like banishment, and was a very scary room where my worst fears seemed to crystallise. The double room ran along the east-west axis of the house and had a high ridge-ceiling with a pitched gable-end that sloped into shadows at the opposite end to my bed. Beneath two single north-facing sash windows was a dizzying drop to the front tennis lawn running along this side of the house. A small coal fire near the left-hand window had been converted to gas, and in front of this a weird-looking leg-exercising machine had been erected. From a horizontal position, his back cushioned by a yoga mat, Dad pumped its weighted platform with his legs. Amongst other attic inhabitants was a very old rocking cradle made entirely of dark wood. Left behind by the previous owners it and had been used as a cradle for Linda and looked like a kind of chrysalis. My bed was at the westerly end of the room, on the same side as the weight machine and gas fire but opposite to them. At the easterly side, against the landing wall was a huge dark-wood double wardrobe where I kept my clothes and other belongings and later, my chemistry set. In the shadowy eave beyond the wardrobe, boxes of household items were ranked high and wide, and in the darkness after bedtime seemed to radiate menace.

At night, my battles with the creatures would begin. If anyone has read William Hope Hodgson's *The House on the Borderland* or *The Night Land*, they will have some idea of my ordeals. My bed was a single-size metal bedstead with a wire-sprung base for the mattress. It was high off the ground, and at night it was easy to imagine the arms of demons reaching up from the cavernous space beneath. It felt safest with the blankets wrapped tightly about my head, with only a small amount of ceiling visible, and no draught from any part of the room I could not see. With only an air-hole open to the room, I lay like a living mummy until I had managed to let myself drop to sleep. From this Night Land, where I lay, assailed by spectres from the room and phantoms within, sleep was the only escape. But it was a long time coming.

The house was the origin of a second hypnogogic image. Like the first, which had started at Vegania, the first 'island', where we had lived until I was just four, this pictogram arrived at night and with similar brilliance and intensity. Like the other it was also impossible to escape, for when I opened my eyes to rid myself of it, I risked seeing 'something' in the darkened room and soon had to shut them again. The Vegania image was a surface of liquid broken by irregular threatening shapes from below thrusting upwards. The new one was a landscape of geometrically regular holes from which an underlying force threatened to draw me. The slender rims exerted a terrifying silent pull. Each wide spherical cavity was placed so close to its neighbour that only small edges of solid 'land' separated them. The fear of being sucked down into the unknown kept me moving across them, the life force in me pared down to simple survival, their ledges affording the only purchase I was able to find.

My door was left ajar to permit a small shaft of light into the room from the landing outside, but the house lights were often switched off. Lying petrified in the darkness, after only a short interval of time the small sounds and rustlings and scratching, coming from the direction of the boxes at the far end of the room would begin, or, worse still, the sounds of marbles being rolled about on the floorboards beneath my bed. In daytime the uneven attic floorboards made for interesting unpredictable games, and when the marbles moved, they made long low-pitched scouring sounds on the wood, followed by 'clicks' as they hit one another or 'taps' as they hit the skirting board and 'scours' again after they bounced off it. The floorboards amplified the sound of anything that moved across them, and in the darkness, I listened intently for clatters and creaks. Perhaps I lay in a kind of hallucinatory lucid sleep.

I have experienced nightmares in which I am 'awake' but asleep, convinced that someone or something is in the house. Reaching for a light switch I find it won't work. I must still be dreaming, I think, and try again. This time I 'wake' myself properly, as I think... But the light switch still won't work. I am still asleep. The intruder has disabled the lights. I make the attempt two or three times, terror building, before I manage to awaken properly.

But at Springfield I was awake, and when I reached the landing light switch, it worked. Terror was the cause of me hearing my marbles moving. In my dread, could I have moved them, and was someone else present? Across the landing from me was Lin's room, and next to hers was the au pair's. The family-helps were all different nationalities, and a quick turnover of them of took place. They received board and pocket money, but once they had improved their command of English and had seen as much of the country as they wanted, in return for childminding and labour, they were off. A few were seeing what else life had to offer them, and the more attractive young women took Dad's eye; and at some deep level even at that age I knew they were rivals to Mum, terrified he might yet drive her away from us.

One of the women I remember most was Irmgard. She was in her late teens, and even though I was preadolescent I knew, without being able to properly define it, there was a sexual chemistry between us as well. Sitting about her hissing gas fire, turned full on during the winter evening to keep out the cold, she suddenly began teaching me how to count in German, and in a matter of minutes I could go up to thirty. I still can. I didn't need a second lesson. Burroughs was at a younger age than I was but was convinced that his 'nana' had interfered with him. If she did, he had hidden the memory, and no amount of psychoanalysis during his lifetime got to the bottom of what happened. Irmgard did nothing to me, but could unconscious desires ricocheting about in the house have caused things to move?

Irmgard's birthday card for Linda

Unable to bear the terror of the darkness a moment longer I would steel myself, unwrap my sheets and blankets from about me, rise from the creaking iron bed and feel my way through the blackness as rapidly as I could to the hopefully still open door, fearful at every step that hands would reach through the dark to prevent me. My hand groped about outside for the switch to the landing light, which I knew was just to the left of the door as I faced it... There it was! Welcome light! I returned to my bed, relief flooding over me, careful to leave the door open by no more than an inch in case my profligacy was discovered. The greatest fear now was that Dad would turn the light off again at the switch on the lower landing, noticing light coming down the attic stairs; although not if he had turned-in for the night and—if I was lucky—he was asleep.

Drawn to the same bedroom window, now aged about eight or nine, I am looking out toward a solitary figure standing on the corner of Ashley and Crescent Roads looking up at me. Many years later, after the house had been sold, walking my old haunts and remembering the occasion when I had glimpsed the 'figure on the corner' beneath me, I sometimes stood there at night alone on the road, looking up to see if I could discern a small pale face in the window. As well as he could by then, the man (looking up at the window) had come to terms with his past. The terror had been buried, inexpertly, without help. But like a soldier returning from a warzone after life has moved on, it still held a terrible fascination for him.

I was allowed to read until Dad got home from the office at about seven or eight pm, when he come up to my room to say goodnight and turn out my light. He would lean over me and smell my breath, as he used to do at Vegania, when I was too young to remember. Mum recorded in her diary that he often returned to the house unexpectedly at breakfast, when I was seated in my highchair, to catch her feeding me my cereal containing dairy milk. At Springfield, after he returned downstairs from saying goodnight, I lay tensely in bed, wondering if he had detected an odour, waiting for the angry distant voices from the lounge or the kitchen, their pitch gradually rising higher, sounds of things breaking and doors slamming, fearful of what he might do to her. They had the same argument repeatedly, until they wore themselves out and the house eventually fell silent again. Lying in the dark with just a crack of landing-light for comfort from the door, I got ready for my ordeal with the Night Land, until mental fatigue overcame me.

Having others in the attic did little to neutralise my anxiety. By the time Lin came along, Mum and Dad had run out of better-appointed accommodation, and she had been allotted this eerie at the top of the house. As dark and cheerless as my room, hers faced south, but the drop from her window onto the macadam driveway leading to the garage seemed even more vertiginous. She was fond of three African dolls with black curly hair. A full set had been bought for her one Christmas—a mother, father, and baby doll—and she kept them on top of a small chest of drawers, the only furniture apart from a single-size bed that would fit in her small room. She was as untidy as Chris. But of these dolls, with their dark chocolate bodies, which she has kept all her life, she took extra special care—reassuring symbols of the real family that was disintegrating around her.

The Oldsmobile

The most frightening car journey took place on a holiday I can no longer remember. I just recall the row. Mum had disagreed with something about our welfare, and we were listening anxiously from the back seat as the disagreement became increasingly more heated. The argument came to a head, but instead of subsiding into an aggrieved silence, this time, shouting and threatening to run off, Mum grabbed the handle to open the passenger door while the car was still in motion. We were in a seaside town somewhere. Dad may have been slowing down for traffic lights, but in a white fury he suddenly drew us into the curb, slamming on the brake. Mum flung open the door, climbed out and ran off and we lost sight of her amongst the crowds. Her default response when things got too much for her was to run. She would return, but listening and watching from the back seat the simple thought came to Chris and I that we might never see her again.

Dad was in the habit of 'borrowing' cars from his showroom for the sheer pleasure of it. If a newly acquired vehicle took his fancy, he would drive home in it, and we often awoke to find a different car in the drive. A succession of Fords, Buicks, and Chevrolets, sometimes several at once and occasionally the odd Bentley or Rover (he was proud, in later years, of showing me a photograph of a black Armstrong Siddeley parked in the drive circa 1953) appeared there. One day we awoke to the sky-blue Oldsmobile, and the car was such a hit he decided to keep it.

His embracing of American technology, considering his antipathy to its culture, was unabashed. He was in love with everything about American cars—the freedom of space they afforded, their engine power and speed, and of course their styling. The Oldsmobile, one of the 'Rocket 88' series, was a sedan family car, well over a hundred horsepower and weighing-in at almost two tons. Instead of being 'straight-eight' the cylinders were deployed in two rows of four—'V8'—and this allegedly gave the engine its 'compactive power'. The clock was calibrated in both miles-per-hour and kilometres, and showed up to 140mph, though I never saw it taken above 110. Most probably it did 120mph max on the flat; for a family car, and particularly one of that weight and size, this was ample. It reached speed very quickly, and its acceleration thrust you well back in your seat. As we surged forward the car's emblem, a chrome model of a space rocket mounted on the front of the bonnet, reared upwards. The only faster acceleration I ever felt was in a plane taking off.

The Armstrong Siddeley

The Oldsmobile

On roads freer of traffic than they are today the Oldsmobile's spaciousness and power was a boon to Dad's sense of adventure and his love of the 'great outdoors'. From where we lived, in Hale, on the eastern edge of the Cheshire Plain, he could be in the countryside within minutes, or even further afield in the Pennines, finding a spot to park-up and hike. The car represented escape from strife for him, and when things went well, for the whole family too. But its close confines could spell danger. Mum's Irish backstreet feistiness was not always of the 'flight' kind.

When he was in his seventies, Dad wrote to me from Pant-yr-Esgair about a holiday in the Welsh town of Deganwy, North Wales, where we were bed-and-breakfasting. "Mum suddenly decided to go home in a taxi taking Linda," he complained, "leaving me with Chris and our au pair girl." The memory was still raw. He told of an even worse incident. Returning from a family outing to Windermere in the Lake District one year, by his account Mum pulled Chris, Lin and I out of the car and took us home by "different transport" and he described how, "In front of onlookers, on the high street, slapped me hard on the face for no reason."

Lin recalled a more complicated situation. To escape her unhappiness at home Mum had gone on a short break with the Thomas's, the Army general and his family who lived on the wooded, undulating South Downs Road along which I walked each day to school. Dad hadn't been at all happy, and in retaliation had taken Chris, Lin, me and the au pair to Windermere. It was not a "family outing". Mum had arrived home to find the house empty. Furious in turn, she boarded a train to find us. When she unexpectedly appeared, Dad defiantly took us on a boat ride, and then threatened to take us to Scotland, which Mum refused to allow by climbing into the car to prevent him. A major row ensued and, as he tried to drive away, she took off one of her shoes and began wrapping him on the knuckles with its heel, forcing him to bring the car to a halt. Still in the middle of the busy town, Mum climbed out and ordered us by now very frightened children to get out with her. Dad also climbed out, to try to stop her taking us, and it was at that point she slapped him. To make matters worse for Dad, a passing policeman intervened, and the constable advised him that he should let us go, which he did. Mum hailed a cab and instructed the driver to take us home—about seventy miles, no small fee. Dad returned home alone in a blazing temper. "Mum may have had an ulterior motive," he wrote to me cryptically, adding: "Such a public humiliation I have never suffered before or since. Suffice to say I arrived home before them in my fast car."

Related almost fifty years after the facts, these accounts were about Mum behaving irrationally, and I was reminded not for the first time of Charles Pooter, the unfortunate protagonist in Weedon and George Grossmith's *Diary of a Nobody*, who was unable to fathom a reason why tradesmen should accost him in the street.

The car journeys have provided me with subject matter. The long summer holidays spent in Tintagel, Cornwall, where the legendary King Arthur is alleged to have been born, produced 'Night',[6] a piece based loosely on a rather macabre Chris Boyce short called 'George', about an argumentative couple, and 'Christmas Story', about the depression of my early life suddenly resurfacing again during the breakdown of my first marriage almost twenty years later. In the days before motorways the interminable car journeys were interminable, and Boyce's 'voice' in the vaguely humorous surface conversational interplay between the protagonist, dying from a paralysing illness, and his wife, struck a chord. In my tour of Springfield, the car is a final memory, except for our school holidays.

---

6 See *Emanations: Third Eye*, 2014

Spade House

The most interesting English holiday destination for a future writer was a big rambling white building in Folkstone on the South Coast. The house had once been the home of H G Wells. *Kipps* had been written there—by coincidence the only Wells novel I would go on to read. By the time of our visit the building had changed hands many times until finally becoming a vegetarian guesthouse. Dad may have learned of it from Erin, the fellow island-goer from whom he sought advice about his marriage. I found at least one other Folkstone-based correspondent, called Bill, which may point to the existence of a small group of vegan food reformers living in and around Folkstone during the forties who knew one another and exchanged information and ideas.

Spade House was built on royalties from *First Men in the Moon* and *The War of the Worlds*, when Wells was an international celebrity, and wealthy, able to commission the acclaimed architect CFA Voysey, who was known for his designs of country houses. The house lay off Sandgate Hill. In my memory, aged somewhere between six and eight, it had views of the sea, and enjoyed proximity to the beach. It was the first private home in Britain in which every bedroom was en suite. The abode quickly become a literary hub for novelists such as Henry James, Stephen Crane (*The Red Badge of Courage*), Ford Madox Ford and Joseph Conrad, who either lived nearby or in the vicinity. From further afield came George Gissing, Edmund Gosse, J M Barrie (*Peter Pan*), George Bernard Shaw and Arnold Bennett.

Samdgate Beach below the house

Its interior appeared unaltered from those times. I recall more than one staircase leading to the upper rooms, and creaky corridors, white balustrades and, at ground level, large bright airy living rooms. I knew HGW was a farsighted author of books of imagination, but I did not yet think of myself as a writer. To be honest, my young mind saw the house as an opportunity for a quite different pursuit. Its many floors and passageways were perfect for playing Monopoly, away from parental interference. The addictive game had become an obsession with Chris and I, but because we were in constant disagreement due to interpreting the rules differently, the board was continually being taken off us. The out-of-the-way nooks and spaces in Spade House were ideal locations to set up our board undisturbed and argue as much as we liked.

At the time of our visit the guesthouse was run by Mr Mrs Dixon May. Dad recalled this in a card to me from Pant-yr-Esgair, "...after 6 hours of searching in my inner computer." The house was patronised by well-known vegetarians such as Yehudi Menhuhin, although the most famous name encountered during our visit was from the world of sport—the Ulster vegetarian marathon swimmer Jack McClelland. By a fluke our holiday coincided with a new attempt he was making to swim across the Channel, and while final preparations were made, he was staying at the guesthouse with his wife Betty. Conversing with them across the communal eating tables—these were often found in vegetarian guesthouses of the time so that guests could better meet one another socially and the vegetarian 'message' could be spread—we found amenable company, and it wasn't long before the subject of his planned attempt arose. Pathologically shy, I hated these occasions of formal conviviality, but Dad, with a vegan agenda to push and possible car business to undertake had learned to cultivate a sociable demeanour that he could switch on or off as occasion demanded. Jack was facing an enormous challenge, for the Channel is one of the world's most gruelling swims. He had swum it successfully on other occasions; but perseverance had brought him back, perhaps to beat his own record.

In the vegetarian firmament Jack McClelland was something of an icon. Health-conscious bodybuilders and sportsmen saw his heroics as justification for their own diets. Similar tribute was paid to celebrities such as American bodybuilder and muscle-man film star Steve Reeves, Dad's youthful hero. I caught Reeves 'swords and sandals' films as often as I could in the 'fleapits' of the 1950s. To sit in the darkness with audiences who didn't know of his vegetarianism, but who applauded his heroics, gave me a secret thrill. With Steve by my side, I figured, I couldn't possibly be the oddball and, as Dad foretold, diet reform was the future. I was a part of it, so I was bemused to learn later in life that Reeves seems to have been a pescetarian. Many then and now think that simply avoiding red meat makes you a vegetarian. In Spain I lost count of the number of times I was served food containing 'jambon' by waiters who resolutely insisted that my meal was vegetarian.

The day arrived for the swim. The great moment may have taken place on Sandgate Beach, beneath the guesthouse. I remember thinking it was a surprisingly low-key affair for a feat of national and possibly international interest, with just a small group of us there to see him off. Thickly covered in (hopefully vegetarian) fat to protect him from the cold, and wearing a dark wetsuit, flippers, and visor, sturdily built Jack looked like a bizarre adventurer of the deep, as we cheered him off; he lifted his visor and waved, then turned and waded into the water. I watched his figure slowly disappear into the waves and strike out, fervently wishing him luck. The crossing would take about fifteen hours. Already out to sea, a safety boat bobbed, which would accompany him in case he hit trouble, but he had to make sure he kept his distance from it; if he accidentally touched the boat, it might count as 'assistance' and disqualify him.

In 1972, the Californian long-distance ocean swimmer Lynne Cox broke the world record for swimming the English Channel. She was aged fifteen, and she beat it again in 1973. A team of hypothermia experts at the University of California found she had a perfectly even coating of subcutaneous body fat, and a super-efficient thermostat. She has the same density as seawater, and creates heat faster than she loses it, shutting down blood supply to her extremities to stabilise her core temperature once in the water. These are the characteristics of a seal, and the longer she stays in the water the better she performs. Plowing across different currents is, she claims, like "...swimming across the face of a guitar, each string or stream a different temperature, and I never know what to expect until my body plays it."

Jack possessed every bodily and mental quality to last the course. But at the breakfast table the following day news came of an unforeseen mishap. Everything had gone well until around midway when the tail-end of a jellyfish tail had entered his mouth. It stung him inside his throat, and his trachea had become inflamed. Due to this he was being asphyxiated and had to be brought ashore. He recovered to swim another day. Jack and Dad kept in touch. Unfortunately, I cannot date our holiday, and therefore Jack's marine encounter, and can find nothing about it on the web.

In the nineties, passing through Folkestone, I detoured to Radnor Cliff Crescent, hoping to find something there I remembered. But the guesthouse had become The Wells Nursing Home, and I didn't have time to arrange to look inside. Historic England lists the building for its "special architectural or historic interest", and so there is every chance that its Voysey interior has been retained. I am hopeful that it has.

Wherever possible we stayed at vegetarian guesthouses. At Whitsun, 1958, Dad made enquiries to three different establishments—Grangewood Vegetarian Guest House in Fairlight-on-Sea, near Hastings, Sussex, which encouraged guests to bring paints, poems and music (it is now a holiday let for up to fourteen people), Sandy Point Vegetarian Guest House, Esplanade, Frinton-on-Sea, also Essex (now a residential holiday home for the blind with a 'sensory garden') and Mabeney Vegetarian Guest House, Park Rd, Swanage, Dorset. I don't know whether we went to any, but in May 1959 Dad wrote to me at school admitting rather lamely that Whitsun was not a school holiday, so perhaps we went to one of them.

In her journal, Mum recalled perennial holidays in "…a beautiful vegetarian guesthouse in Boscombe, Somerset," where they "…catered for vegans." But her experience of the place was mixed. On a visit in 1946 or early 1947, when she was expecting me, Dad refused her to eat anything other than vegan and food reform food in case the animal foods of a conventional diet polluted me. "I envied the other dairy eaters," Mum wrote forlornly, "having boiled eggs and toast with butter, marmalade and plenty of milk on their cereal and pots of tea or coffee on their tables." While they tucked in heartily, she and Dad were served "fruit juice, cereal with nut milk, wholemeal toast made from bread without salt and salt-less margarine. I hated the untasteful toast and marg, so ate very little. My very small slice of toast felt inadequate for myself and my unborn child. Then packed lunch would be ready and off we would go for the day. The sandwiches would be some nut-spread of a greyish colour. The seagulls enjoyed them, but I felt repulsed. My husband would buy fruit especially strawberries in season, a very large basket of them. I was so hungry I would eat them unwashed all day." No processed or animal foods must sully her while she was carrying.

Dad's conviction that the vegan diet would extend his life was the basis for 'Das Neue Leben',[7] about a youthful Hitler transposed to the Brasilian jungles and rejuvenated on a diet of vegan food and heroin. Dad was fiercely against drug-use of any kind, prescribed, experimental or recreational, but, as I will come to, in his wholesome ingestion of greenery, inadvertently, he once transgressed.

Eternally Yours

Despite visible signs of aging on Dad's body, life still seemed to stretch endlessly ahead for him. Accustomed to the notion of easily reaching a hundred—and well beyond—his fondness for citing the lifespans of peasants in remote parts, was undimmed. After arriving at the fourth 'island', Pant-yr-Esgair in the hills of mid-Wales, at the age of sixty-nine, where he adjudged the conditions were finally right to approximate the original island, the tropical isle of Morat in the Honduran Bay Islands, which had been denied to him as a young man, he scrawled on the back of an envelope, as though I was a co-conspirator in his quest, that native farmers in the fertile valleys of Ecuador had been found to be living "...to 100-150 years on a vegan diet", furthermore, "Maize is their staple cereal."

The mountain people of the Caucasus, a society in the Abkhasia region who are known for their longevity, were often eulogised in this way. Soviet propaganda of the time had exaggerated these lifespans to one-hundred-and-fifty years or more, and Dad had been taken in by the marketing gloss, and woe-betide me if I dared to contradict him. The ancient Essenes, he still routinely believed, lived to great ages in Eden-like conditions unpolluted by modern chemicals.

He still 'pumped' iron, though not as much now in terms of the load he once pushed himself to lift as the 'Charles Atlas' bodybuilder. At High Bank House, the third 'island', strategically placed amongst the loungers and deckchairs, a 100lb barbell was permanently positioned near his sunbathing spot in the crook of the house and the outbuilding where he had his picture restoration workshop. He pressed this weighted bar several times above his head every day. A much younger man without training, I only just managed to copy him. He could still do an amazing series of monkey jumps, performed

[7] *Emanations*, 2011.

on waking each morning. His favourite party-piece—going down on one leg and rising again, on the same leg, unsupported—was trickier, but could still be accomplished. Both feats were entirely beyond my capability.

1950s

His letters continued to overflow with vegan and health information. In 1985 I moved with Nicky and Damon, my two teenagers, to 18 Oxford Street, a cul de sac in Hebden Bridge, West Yorkshire, to give Mum a break from looking after us. I lived there for about a year before moving back in with her. When Dad heard I was minding the children on my own again, his letters became full of 'tips'. Actual recipes I might have more benefitted from, were scarce, but occasionally I was given detailed instructions.

> 14th February 1986.
> To Prepare an Interesting Drink: Slice up part of an onion; put into a large mug or jug together with washed currants or raisins. Fill with water, leave over night. Very refreshing cold or warmed up. You may refill with water again & repeat. The whole may be squashed a little with a utensil to bring more flavour. I am taking this opportunity to enclose a short list of optimum foods that you may like to consult when shopping (for your housekeeper?).
>
> [I was unable to afford a housekeeper. Beneath his recipe was the list, with brief preparation details.]
>
> Dried marrowfat peas. Quite cheap. Soak overnight.
> Red lentils. Cook quickly.
> Dried sweet corn grains. Soak overnight.
> Brown rice.
> Desiccated coconut (high in fibre).
> Maize meal (flour) quickly cooked.
> Soya flour.
> Peanuts (blanche before eating. Boil for one minute to wash dirt away and bitterness).
> Currants, raisin for sweetening.
> Dates.
> Figs.
> Dried bananas.
> Nuts you like (can be expensive).
> Brewer's Yeast Powder.
> Kelp.
> Mixed herbs.
> Tinned Italian plum tomatoes (very cheap).
> Sunflower oil.

Rape seed oil (British, home grown)
Plenty of apples; they dissolve lead & aluminium from the system.
Ripe bananas.
Potatoes. Better baked or cooked in a little water with the lid on the pan, like other veg etc.
Celery.
Turnips.
Onions.
Garlic.
Etc.
Always buy or ask for compost/organic grown food wherever possible. Very important.

I never saw him use a cookbook. To my regret I did not think of recording the recipes he devised for the meals we ate together, and his letters contain mostly haphazard records. He invented or improvised them from memory with whatever ingredients were to hand. At High Bank House he was fond of cooking a maize meal dish with fresh whole tomatoes. Maize cooks quickly, so do tomatoes, and the mixture was heated until the maize was soft to eat, and the tomatoes had just burst. He decorated the dish with streaks of diluted Vecon vegetable stock paste and served it in large wide soup bowls. We ate it with spoons and maybe knives if the tomatoes needed cutting. The colours of the creamy-yellow maize, the red tomato and the seaweed-like Vecon made it look appetising, and it was. The salty, savoury taste of the stock contrasted with the blander maize, and the tomatoes gave a refreshing zing. A simple and effective meal, and I hadn't eaten anything like before. To recreate it now, experiment is required. I think he used a coarse maize meal. He might have cooked the maize first, and then added the tomatoes to cook, or done everything together. The important idea was to achieve the right consistency. It had to be like a thick soup, so the meal was filling to eat, but not too thick.

The staple of the Ecquador farmers was hugely important, and at Pant-yr-Esgair he was fond of making a sweet maize cake made from meal, water and fruit, baked in the oven. Once it had cooled and was ready to eat, he cut the cake into squares. The fruit content was endlessly varied, and could comprise anything that was going, dried or fresh, although raisins and apple usually formed the base. He placed the fruit in the bottom of a large—oiled?—baking tray and covered it with maize slurry up to the height he wanted the cake to be when it had cooked.

His letters and cards from High Bank House, despite the downsides of the third 'island', its size and location primarily, showed hints of the contentment he was to find at Pant-yr-Esagir.

> 06/05/86
> I am healthy, back on a few nettles and dandelions in the blender to give the taste you mention! They are excellent (dried in the sun) because in the H.F.S's [health food shops] at the moment they're very sweet. Planted out a great deal more this year & have the Morello Cherry tree now in, plus, pumpkins, marrows etc. Many survival foods, fruit, permaculture. Cereal farming causes soil erosion & deserts. Priorities, CND, ban weedkillers, etc. Grow food. Live simply so that others can simply live.

I had written to suggest he include "...one or two small dark-green leaves" from his garden in his morning 'turmix'—the 'smoothy' made in the Turmix food blender that we ate in a bowl with a spoon at Springfield—so that he could still enjoy their flavour. These leaves, I suggested, could be gardener's varieties like spinach or spring cabbage or the leaves of wild plants like dandelion or young nettles or many other wild species that were edible that I knew he loved to eat. But he must only have a small quantity of them, I cautioned. Due to an unfortunate accident that would soon occur he had to severely cut down their use, and sorely miss their flavours.

Our letters to one another confirmed a surprising thing: how two people lacking the ability to hold meaningful face-to-face conversations, because of difficulty accessing their feelings, were able to communicate through the written medium. My paralising fear of him—words spoken risked the sudden irritability or even explosion all too familiar from childhood—had taught me to limit my talk with him to practical matters and pleasantries. But I had to be careful, even so. 'Safe' topics like diet and health could also occasionally lead to violent reprimand. The surest bet was a neutral exchange of information. In his own way he found me as unknown and unpredictable as I found him. Writing from afar gave us both time to think and avoided the negative emotions our physical presence so often provoked.

25/07/86
July is nearly out, you are coming! there is some doubt! Strawberries have gone, currants galore, some raspberries await, it's not too late, see the giant pumpkin, perhaps I'll meet you at the gate. Love Dad.

But despite his joie de vivre and feats of physical exercise there was no escaping signs that life would end. Alert to the inevitability, he constantly examined himself, looking for signs in his body as though, by identifying them, he could arrest them. His inspections sometimes made me feel queasy. His veins were hardening, he suddenly told me one day… demonstrating by pressing his fingers against the raised vessels on the backs of his wrists and arms. I cringed inwardly, knowing he would ask me to test his veins for myself. He did, and we found ourselves making comparisons between our blood vessels.

On another day, when we were sitting on the small lawn among the hydrangeas and montbretias in the front garden, he began running his hands over his scalp. The skin had become sensitive, he claimed, and wondered whether it indicated he had high blood pressure. What was my opinion on the matter? Apprehensively, for I knew his antipathy to orthodox medicine, I suggested he go to his doctor for a medical check-up. I didn't know what else to say. In hospital before moving into Annedd, his first care home, he showed me the skin on his arm, visibly flaking. We examined it for some moments in silence, before he said, with little conviction, "I suppose it will grow back." The unpleasant condition, I learned, was likely to have been the result of long exposure to an essential element of his philosophy, the "life-giving" sun.

Sitting with him on the lawn he seemed so alone and frightened. I sensed he needed someone to understand him, to love him non-judgmentally for who he was in a lasting relationship, who he could rely on for reassurance. The problem was no one knew how. At High Bank House he became worried about the intentions of one of the young men who were periodically attracted to him, and asked me what I thought, but I had no idea what to say. The man was in the shoe trade and had been attracted by Dad's way of life, visiting whenever he could, and writing letters of admiration. Dad eventually decided to accept him on face value, and they struck up an enduring acquaintance. I don't think he ever had a friend, as such. He was too odd and unfathomable, but he had contacts who showed varying degrees of tolerance. A few, like the shoe-man, his wood supplier at Pant-yr-Esgair, and a colleague at the auction rooms were genuinely fond of him.

In his late fifties, following his reinvention of himself as an art dealer and restorer and, at a time of life when many are facing retirement, looking to the future, he seemed as happy as it was possible for someone of his disposition. I was also in the ascendant, and the happy conjunction, I think, resulted in the interview he granted me. I wanted to discover what led him to vegan food reform. The idea of the interview hovered around unformulated for some time, until an occurrence even odder than our singular method of communication occurred.

After divorcing my first wife and becoming a single parent I had commenced a spell of freelance writing and between this and starting up in book publishing, in August 1977, I had taken over editorship of *New Vegetarian*, the journal of The Vegetarian Society. At first, I didn't notice anything out of the ordinary in the letters landing on my mat. The sometimes-fogyish quaintness of style, platitudes, paternalism, quotas of advice and surprising verbal innovation seemed par for the course. But pieces of information high-handedly relayed as though they were his own pronouncements, began to seem familiar. It took me a while to work out why.

As a lifetime member of The Vegetarian Society, Dad received its journal through his door each month. A similar 'life' arrangement had been made with *The Vegan*. And when the Movement for Compassionate Living was formed (as an offshoot of The Vegan Society), he took *New Leaves*, their journal, as well. By the summer of 1977 when I took up editorship, the articles in the pages of these magazines had long constituted his reading about health and diet. Some was the work of my contributors, but other articles I had written myself, under bylines. Obtaining information by this means, had become habitual, and I saw with bemusement that without him being fully aware of it my own ideas—some derived from him, of course, initially—were being quoted back to me. A new interface between us had been established and we were communicating through the pages of the journal, or, more correctly, through my learned correspondents under my editorship.

This was knowledge on which I wasn't thought to have a perspective, the kind that he, as the family's fountainhead, conveyed to us. Health was his prerogative. Face-to-face, he would have struck me down. But the printed word carries a spurious authority. Half-heartedly one day, when he loftily imparted to me my own words—information that he, as my father and teacher, thought I ought to know—I chanced reminding him that as the editor I knew what he was saying. Crossly, he told me he did make the connection. Yet the next time we met, the same disconnect happened. Somehow, when he collected the journal off his doormat, opened the envelope and began reading it over breakfast, or after the evening meal in his armchair, he disassociated me from it.

Could I make the process a direct one? If a journalistic reason presented itself, would he allow me to address him formally? I had my eyes on a colour supplement feature about his garden. It worked. The interview took place in his workshop-cum-studio in the outhouse attached to his kitchen, amidst his canvases and paints. It was an exhilarating experience, and I found myself temporarily unfettered from my usual inarticulateness and awkwardness in his presence. For his part, he expressed himself to me with uncharacteristic openness, without his usual irritability. We played our parts like actors, dissociated from our roles as father and son.

Perhaps he needed to tell his life to someone, and his offspring happened to be the only one who would listen. Perhaps it was the thought of a newspaper getting hold of his story. As a salesman in his business life, he knew the value of publicity. Perhaps he just decided having reached life's crossroads I was at the right age to have The Secrets properly explained to me.

The lifestyle he advocated, which we followed in our different ways, differed radically from mine. Although a life member of both Societies, Vegetarian and Vegan, as a food fundamentalist he was intensely disapproving of the former's 'half-way' house policy as regards diet. The orthodoxy followed by many of the Vegetarian Society's leading lights, especially in the cookery departments, recommended eggs, milk and cheese as safe sources of protein and, further (another vexed matter for Dad), the taking of vitamin B12 as a supplement. Essential for the normal functioning of the nervous system and brain and the formation of red blood cells, Vegans are in danger of becoming deficient.

He disagreed with lacto-vegetarians profoundly. Animal produce was far too rich in protein, too heavy in saturated fat and, in the case of cheese, too full of salt. Dairy food and eggs left toxic acid-forming breakdown products in the body and placed undue strain on organs such as the kidneys; furthermore they brought about diseases of the heart and blood vessels. Vitamin B12, he believed—as some vegan science showed—could be produced by intestinal bacteria. Those whose guts were unable to, could supplement their diets with plant food containing it, such as the Japanese nori seaweed. He claimed not to suffer deficiency, though he did eat vegan spreads like Vecon and Barmine, both of which had B12 artificially added. To avoid the risk of serious problems, the consensus today is that vegans should take it as a supplement.

His thinking could change, but in 1991 when he had been at Pant-yr-Esgair for three years, he wrote to me: "The B12 can usually only be generated in the stomach by optimum food eaters of good habits and long-standing serious loss rectified into blood directly." He then defined what 'optimum food eating' meant, cautioning against gluten: "[It] equals alkaline & neutral forming nourishment of which wheat foods are the opposite, likewise cereal fibres and bran which can leech alkaline elements from the system." He elaborated, "My beliefs on gluten I can remember expounding. My earlier gleanings warned against the acid [to be found] in wheat contributing to rheumatism. Parched wheat eaten does not have the same gluten content. Doubtful foods are best left alone anyway. Perchance the oat has beneficial effects on my internal organ inflammation or damage then its side effects will be taken in stride. No doubt a bowl of porridge (if taken at breakfast with my excessive intake of Vit A) would have absorbed the excess and prevented the destruction of much liver organ!"

He was referring to his experience of accidentally injuring himself through taking too much Vitamin A-containing raw food—an episode I am still to recount. He believed that if he had been eating 'optimally' then his liver would not have been endangered in the first place. After setbacks he always blamed his inattentiveness to diet.

At the time, I sided with the lacto-vegetarian ethos. I felt repelled by the cruelty involved in dairy production, but for mixed eaters who might be considering a change to a more humane diet an uncompromising proscription of veganism was too extreme. Dad himself had become a vegetarian before (very quickly, in his case) becoming a vegan. At the same time, I thought the Vegetarian Society's over-insistence on dairy and eggs was unhealthy (for all the vegan reasons), and that more should be made of truly vegetarian foods. Surprisingly, as Editor, I was allowed to push a vegan-inflected view, and more than once gave my reasons. The moral consideration always came first for me, followed by environmental, health and economic reasons in that order. Interestingly, these were the arguments for veganism Dad later cogently expressed in a letter to *New Vegetarian* in 1986, after I had left the Society. 'Moral reasons' came third with him, but generally he supported the editorial policy I had been pursuing:

> Why vegan? It seems to be the only logical way forward. I list just a few reasons:
>
> 1. To help save the rapidly vanishing green-belt world-wide, most deserts have been caused by over-grazing animals.
> 2. Optimum health (do away with fibreless, clogging dairy food) when fruits and vegetables are the source of nourishment, because we are biologically fruitarian suited to a low protein diet.
> 3. Humanitarian. The cruelty involved in the dairy food industry is too obvious to be ignored and too interdependent on meat production.
> 4. A clear conscience whilst the animal and human population explosion gathers serious momentum. You will be doing your bit to slow the growth of the animal population.
>
> Perhaps the Vegetarian Society would like to give a clear guide to the 'lacto' members in this matter?

For a 'health' vegan of such fundamentalist persuasion, his letter was surprisingly balanced. Had he 'listened' to me through the journal? To my knowledge, he never again expressed anything so well adjusted.

I began to wonder about something else too. Had this ideological 'refining' that took place through the distancing agency of print, worked in another way—had he read my books? I sent him many, but—except for once—he never spoke to me about them. But something registered years later when he framed a copy of a newspaper photograph of me. "A pictorial character insight of amazing accuracy, hitherto unrecorded," he wrote to me from Pant-yr-Esgair, "revealed with the Guardian's photographic reproduction."

He hung the frame on a beam among photographs of Linda, Christine and Barbara, the last of our now-married au pairs with whom he had once had a romantic tangle. There was no picture of Mum, the attractive young woman who had first captured his eye across the ballroom floor. He confessed afterwards to reading the first few pages of a book I had written, but it was unrelated to the 'Guardian' book. I felt it was my appearance in the mainstream media that had mostly taken his interest. When he finally moved into Annedd I found the books I had given him, each with their handwritten inscriptions to him and still in mint condition, unread. I took them back.

His partial contentedness at High Bank House continued until around 1984, three-quarters of his stay there. On repeated visits I found him positively happy. This seemed too good to be true. There was an artificial nature to this uncharacteristic mental 'high' he was displaying, and I part of me knew something must be wrong.

Poisoned!

As I have related, it was unthinkable that Dad would knowingly use drugs. He had no idea that I used them. I smoked occasional marijuana. I had also tried psychedelics like LSD, mescaline, and psilocybin, in the same way I knew Aldous Huxley had done. William Burroughs and Hunt S Thompson took them experimentally as well as for pleasure. When ecstasy arrived, it corrected the problems I had with empathy and communication. At that point I realised I also took drugs as medication. Ecstasy enabled me, for the first time, at the age of forty-four, to do 'small talk', and also to understand what people really meant when they said something; to enjoy 'ordinary' company.

One afternoon, long before ecstasy, at High Bank House when we were sunbathing on the recliners outside the kitchen, and had sunk into very relaxed states, I decided to let him know that I occasionally took cannabis. I found myself arguing that my embrace of the mood-altering plant was a better form of hedonism than alcohol, and gave more control, more intensity, more choice, more experience, not less. I pointed out that it was wholly plant-based, as were drugs such as mescal, opium, even tobacco, which I knew he occasionally smoked. Moreover, many plants consumed in sufficiently large quantities were psychotropic because of the compounds they contained. If you had been born in my generation, I addressed Dad, you would by now at the very least have tried cannabis.

He enjoyed relaxing on a reclining chair in the sun, and when he was drowsy and sunbathing and his anxiety levels were low, he could be spoken to in this way. It allowed us to be in our own thoughts and I could feel free of his control. With his bronzed skin he could lie in the strongest sun for hours, but wary of burning, I joined him for shorter periods.

I expected my ill-advised offering might produce an outburst, that he would suddenly become alert, raise his head in my direction and shielding his gaze from the sun with his hands, ask me crossly whether I was mad? But he scarcely moved. He remained so calm I thought perhaps he was asleep and hadn't been listening. But he had. With eyes still closed, he told me simply that I was wrong on the question of drugs. I should think again. And he wouldn't have taken cannabis.

Not long after this, I received a letter confessing he might have inadvertently taken something. It turned out, as his letter to Jack McClelland had admitted, the cross-Channel swimmer with whom he had kept in touch after our chance encounter at Spade House, that he had Vitamin-A poisoning. He had written to tell Jack about it. About a year ago, as a means of increasing his supply of nutrients, he had decided to increase his daily intake of freshly prepared juice from garden ingredients and asked if I would help him source a juicing machine. For some unaccountable reason he no longer possessed one, even though, at Springfield, among our many gadgets was a hand-operated juicer for oranges and an electric one for harder fruits and root vegetables like carrots and beetroot.

We chose a new one together, and he was soon happily juicing again—apples, celery, carrots, rhubarb, beetroots, kale, dandelion, nettle. I thought nothing more about it.

We sometimes talked about carrot juice and green-leaf vegetables, pointing out their high levels of Vitamin A, and had spoken of vitamin-A addiction—a cause of liver cirrhosis—and how you could have too much. I even reminded him of this again when we bought the new juicer. It never occurred that he might overdose, but this is what he had done, now ruefully admitting his error to me.

He mistook the 'high' effects of the vitamin-A for 'plant vitality'. It was no wonder he had been so placid about my talk of drugs in the sun that afternoon. He had been feeling high. He was getting up in the morning, preparing a juice drink and feeling "on top of the world", and he lost his judgement. Slowly it had become a habit. The better he felt, the more he drank. He was getting through pounds of carrots and dark greens harvested from the garden each day for breakfast, and slowly his skin turned orange from the beta-carotene poisoning, and he came down with cirrhosis.

He had been certain the effects were due to 'cosmovitalist' properties in plants. Macabrely, liver damage was his reward for following an 'optimal' lifestyle—the more of everything good, the better it is for the body. But unconsciously, I think, just like I was doing, he was self-medicating for the high levels of 'non-specific' anxiety from which we both suffered. Perhaps it was yet another reason for the interview he gave me. For a while, at High

Bank House, there was a depth of communication between us that didn't happen anywhere else.

He had two health scares there, both caused (or allowed to get worse) by wrong action, as he saw it. But in my head, the two are intertwined. At the same time as he began enduring the effects of Vitamin A poisoning, the older male curse of an enlarged prostate befell him, with its attendant loss of bladder control. As he tried to heal himself, the two ailments became slowly chronic, he was trapped in a cycle of discomfort and remedial action. His liver would become painful from the cirrhosis, and to relieve this he would have to drink fluid. He urinated frequently because of his prostate, which brought back the pain, and he would have to drink more, which increased the urination and so on. One illness seemed to enhance the potency of the other, and this happened unrelentingly, month after month. He slept poorly, and the whole process plagued him for years. As it got worse, he carried bottles under the seat of his car, one for urinating in, one for drinking. and he perfected a way of using the urine one discretely while still seated.

As with his mental breakdown, brought on by the combined blows of Mum leaving him and the ill luck of his car and motorbike dealership collapsing following a road widening scheme, he would not see a doctor. Instead, he read up on herbal and medical texts, and set out to heal himself, convinced Nature would ultimately cure both illnesses. I thought his liver might recover—it can recover from cirrhosis, given time—but I was skeptical he would reverse the growth of a prostate without orthodox intervention.

He continued using his juice machine for non-carotenoid fruits and vegetables, with only the occasional green leaf thrown in—he took my advice—but no carrots. Over the years that followed, his liver did gradually get better, but it was difficult to see progress because his prostate refused to respond to natural treatment. Finally, the condition came to a head, and in 1993, five years after he moved to Wales, he had to be rushed into hospital for a life-saving operation. Certain that he knew best, he ended by causing an emergency that alarmed the family, needlessly taxed hospital facilities and almost killed him.

He gave me advice over the years. I took much of it. But some, I felt, was plain wrong. Nature Cure 'at all costs' is misguided. I felt even more strongly justified in this view when I came to read about the deaths on the Caribbean Isle of Morat, the real story of the island that Dad kept hidden; the horrors that happened there did nothing to help the Cause. But I also saw, when the chips were down, as they were in hospital after he had miscalculated badly, he would take the medication that was given him. His fear of extinction trumped everything.

Recovery from the operation was protracted and mostly terrifying. A blood transfusion had been necessary to save his life, and the thought that the doner's blood may have been a carnivore badly frightened him, and he suffered the misery of a secondary psychosomatic illness, through which we helped him as best we could. He looked upon the year of the operation as his annus horribilis, worse than, or on a par with, Mum's abandonment of him. The experience only slowly receded. Very gradually he recovered his confidence, and his sense of invincibility; yet he had been knocked again, and the small depredations of age continued.

The Giant Across the Fields

Until Linda's surprise discovery of Dad's involvement as Branch Secretary in the early Vegan Society I had presumed that buttonholing and leafleting random members of the public was his preferred form of activism. The thought still seemed truer than not because among his voluminous paper effects I could find no other record that he conducted administrative work. A consistent historian of his life he, of all people, would surely have retained annals; so, I was certain this was the case. His 'archive' was his physical body; a living example of what could be done following the tenets of Carqué or Székely. But idling through his papers one day, after completing the first draft of my book, I discovered a sheaf of papers I had overlooked. While he was at High Bank House, he had returned to armchair campaigning.

The assorted handwritten documents were inside one of the drawers of an elegant nineteenth—or perhaps eighteenth—century mahogany bureau bookcase that he had managed to hold on to after having to sell Springfield. The envelope containing them had, through age, hued to the same shade of colour as the interior of the drawer in which I found them, which is how at first they had remained unnoticed. Dating to the mid-eighties the letters, penned in his neat closely-spaced elongated script, were addressed to industry and civic officials, and called the bureaucrats to account for a litany of abuse and slack practice—allowing chimney effluent to escape from factories, fluoridating water supplies, cropping and spraying roadside verges, adding uncalled-for additives to food. Most heinous was hedgerow trimming and sheep-grazing, the twin destroyers of saplings. He retained carbon copies of these indignant letters of protest, which showed the importance he attached to them. His bětes noirs were Cheshire County Council, responsible for the area near Northwich where he lived and, not surprisingly, the giant ICI complex on his doorstep. The Imperial Chemical Industries' factories were scattered about among the farming countryside where we so often walked together, looming in the middle distance.

Reading these indignant missives recalled for me the cutting down of the road sign when I had diligently risked so much to do his bidding, preventing polluting vehicles from passing his house; and they presaged his coming exile, when he would risk the polluted arteries of the country's main roads to escape the last tentacles of the toxic cities. Once at Pant-yr-Esgair, high in the Welsh hills, he would finally manage to conduct the Big Experiment he had waited so long to perform, on the smallholding we christened World Two.

But what had caused the new call to arms? His tilting at the windmills of officialdom covered the period of 1985 until August 1988, when he finally landed in Wales. Reading the correspondence, his efforts seem to have had a small but positive effect on the officials governing the community around him. The committee-minded managers in charge of policy at times showed irritation, but they also appeared to be flattered. Unable to do everything the Good Knight of Lostock Gralam wanted them to do, most seemed to have done what they could.

Many of the letters are addressed to Chief Executive R G Wendt on behalf of the County Planning Officer to Cheshire County Council, the municipality within which Dad resided. Wendt is friendly and helpful, on one occasion even signing himself 'Robin'.

> 03/07/85
> Wendt commiserates with Dad about the loss to hedgerow, and the need to retain "emergent saplings". But hedges are excluded from Tree Preservation Orders, he informs Dad, and do not come under any form of planning control. He can do little more than encourage farmers and landowners to take better care but reassures Dad the use of herbicides and other chemicals in the countryside are better controlled than they used to be. On another matter: "I will take the opportunity to visit the pond you mention."

Other letters from Dad concern the spraying of hedgerows, illegal tipping, and the loss of trees on an embankment at a former MANWEB electricity site. Wendt informs him that the removal of trees was unavoidable due to the embankment slowly slipping into the highway. In reply to a letter requesting weight restrictions on lorries entering Lostock Gralam and passing High Bank House, he laments the impracticality of doing so due of the numbers of lorries needing access to industrial premises in the area. Other letters are about speed restrictions in the narrow lanes, loose chippings on a resurfaced road and the nuisance of children removing stones from the gabions near the train station and throwing them in the thoroughfare. Wendt patiently points out that his department can do little about the children, and the gabions cannot be removed because, "in years past", the embankment had slipped into the road. Slightly exasperated by Dad's persistence he points out that by comparison with many other British counties, Cheshire is more sustainably managed.

14/03/86—From Dad to North West Water Board.
Dad objects to the use of fluoride in tap water and cites the case of a water customer who fell into "...poor health" when he proved to be "allergic to the above poison...". He demands to know what the Board intends to do to prevent "...pesticides, herbicides, nitrates, artificial fertiliser etc from different sources entering the household water supply." The Board point out that the supply in his area of the North West is not fluoridated, but defends its use, naming various favourable reports. Regarding the other complaints, the Board states: "The Authority pursues active pollution prevention and control measures, supported by monitoring and early warning systems, so that World Health standards and European Community Directives are met."

03/04/86—Dad to Prime Minister Margaret Thatcher.
A rallying cry demanding urgent action on a variety of fronts. Dad believes with "...many others that poor health and new diseases are destroying the nation." In hectoring tones, he enumerates:
"1. Physical Pollution: Additives, food production, PESTICIDES, HERBICIDES, ARTIFICIAL FERTILISERS, ETC, CHEMICALS IN PREPARED FOOD, and fluoride in water supply which also picks up the aforementioned. The above are in all the food we eat to a dangerous degree, most of the food not being wholesome as well. (Junk food) ANIMAL FAT CAN KILL!

"2. Mental Pollution: The broadcasts by the media, BBC etc, of violence, sex, alcohol, rape and all other related unpleasantries over the last 20 years, and now increasingly so in newscasting has had devastating results. No wonder the Queen in her Xmas speech said what she did!

"3. Green Belt Erosion (rate of): Unnecessary development and irresponsible farming encouraged by Government, hedges cut too low, ripped out, and trees taken down together with (1.) above resulting in wild life being drastically reduced. Grazing animals especially in hill farms are eating all the tree saplings before they grow into trees. Hedge cutters also stop the saplings growing.

"The dangers of the above are more important, don't you think, than the atomic menace, at least they can be stopped, COMPOST FARMING MADE LAW. Likewise (2.) no doubt.

"You are no doubt aware of the insidious blight in (1.), (2.), (3.). I EARNESTLY REQUEST YOU TO GIVE UTMOST PRIORITY TO THE ABOVE AND OBLIGE: I FEEL THAT IF YOU DO IT WILL RECTIFY MATTERS."

"If you do this," Dad assures Mrs Thatcher, "you will make your name resound in history and the public will return you with a handsome majority in the election. Kindly let me know your reflections. Thank you in anticipation, Yours very sincerely etc. (vegan for 45 years)."

Dad's letter was acknowledged by the 'presiding' Principle Private Secretary of the Prime Minister, Margaret Thatcher, and rather supported my belief that his habit of shouting when he felt his view was being challenged might not have been wholly controllable. His aggressive bullying was not confined to us. He did it to the Prime Minster as well!

04/86—The Head of Programme Correspondence Section, British Broadcasting Company.

For good measure Dad sent Clause 2 of his letter to the PM, concerning 'Mental Pollution', to the BBC, where it was cordially acknowledged. "As you may know, Mr Milne [Alasdair Milne, the BBC's Director-General] has asked a Committee of senior people in television, led by Mr Will Wyatt, Head of Documentary Features Department, to re-examine the BBC's guidelines on the portrayal of violence and their application by programme-makers."

Other letters concerning trees received responses.

08/04/86—From Vale Royal District Council Planning Department, Winsford, Cheshire.
The respondent assures Dad his concerns about "Trees and the Countryside are shared by this authority and that within the constraints of our resources and legal powers we are doing a very great deal to preserve and enhance the natural beauty of this district." The writer reels off the measures that are being taken.

22/05/86—From the Department if Highways, Cheshire County Council.
Dad has queried why the trees at the Picnic Area on the Northwich Bypass have been trimmed and raises concerns about the management of the grass verges. The layby was an inviting stopping-off place for motorists. Spacious with grassy areas and picnic tables and screened from the road by trees, it was where Dad and I had first reconciled again after our long estrangement. A footpath ran off it across the fields to Northwich, his nearest town, and was a favourite walking route.

The Highways writer is sympathetic but explains to Dad that the trees in the layby had "...grown too close to the overhead electricity cables and had become leggy and in need of trimming to encourage bushiness and hence promote more foliage for the wildlife." As for the verges on the busy bypass, these were "normally only cut in areas where visibility for the motorist has to be maintained." He added pointedly, "I think you are perhaps assuming that we use herbicides much more than we do." Chemicals, he informs Dad sternly, are used only "in very special circumstances".

Dad's first sallies against ICI began in June 1986.

10/06/86—From Site Manager I D Bruce, ICI.
Bruce responds in detail to Dad's complaints about a series of topics—severe hedgerow cutting, "smells" Dad has had to suffer, "noise tones" to which Dad has been subjected and... a "Works hooter," that sounds periodically during the day, disturbing the peace in the High Bank House Garden. Bruce explains amiably that nothing can be done about the hooter. It marks when work periods begin and end and cannot be lessened as it "...forms part of the internal Works alarm system to help secure the safety of employees. It would not be proper for me to lessen the frequency of this test." Regarding the other noises and the smells, Bruce promises to investigate. About the hedgerows he reassures Dad that he too is

"...looking to a comment from ICI's land agent on these," and will provide the information as soon as it arrives.

11/06/86—From Site Manager I D Bruce, ICI.
The Land Agent's report has arrived, and Bruce provides a summary as to why the Company's tenant farmers cut their hedges so severely. "If the hedges are allowed to grow too high the bottom growth dies off," and "...they are no longer stock proof." For this reason, Bruce adds, control of the height of hedges will continue "...as a matter of good husbandry. The agent does however take your point over the loss of sapling growth on hedges." Bruce will ask their tenants if in future they will take more care by stopping their machinery briefly to "go round young trees".

15/08/86—From Site Manager I D Bruce, ICI.
Responding to Dad's complaint about the source of bothersome "noise tone" Bruce reports they have been unable to locate a cause at their Winnofil Plant, the factory closest to Dad, but he will keep trying to identify the problem. Commenting on trees at Holford Moss Wood that dad has seen dying, Bruce shares his worry, but his endeavours have been unable to identify this cause either. He is "satisfied" that "...brinefield operations are not contributory."

Dad's jousting with ICI was punctuated by correspondence with other activists.

09/86—From Annette Martin, Food Additives Campaign Team (FACT).
Martin thanks Dad for canvassing signatures for a Food Additives Petition, informing him brightly that Sir Richard Body MP is prepared to "accept the Petition". Chairman of the governmental Select Committee on Agriculture and author of The Rape of the Countryside, Body is attempting to include additives in the subject of a Royal Commission. He is a valuable catch. Martin's young son, David, has been ill and in missing correspondence Dad offered dietary advice. She thanks him this, and reports that her son is now well, adding that the family changed some eighteen months ago to the diet he recommended, and they are all feeling better for it. Her son doesn't like soya milk, however, and by way of response Dad offers the suggestion that her son may like milk made from hazel nuts instead." However, "once we have our teeth milk is not so essential; and if one remembers that the low protein, high carbohydrate ratio is ideal, then David's rejection of the Soya concentrate is quite

understandable." Rather than simply not liking the taste, David's body itself was saying 'No' to him.

Talk of 'ratios' recalled the breast-snatching that had so upset Mum after my birth, when he timed me on each breast until I had what he considered to be the right nutrient balance; and her bitter complaints, when I was aged two, before the days when emulsified vegan drinks were available, that nut milk made by grinding nuts with water must be fed to me in place of dairy milk. The nuts consumed in this way were giving me stomach aches.

Sensing an opportunity with Martin to push his agenda, Dad proposes to her that fluoridation should be included in FACT's remit:

> It is an "...additive hazard, used in most food preparations and drinks and is a poison; in any event, the body has its supply, and all toothpastes now have it, against many people's wishes." Indignantly: "My own [water supply] has now been scheduled for treatment, what a waste of public money! The Chairman of the Health Authority refuses to discuss the matter with me." She has his permission to share his letters with Richard Body MP. More leaflets are enclosed for her.

> 17/09/86—From the Site Manager I D Bruce, ICI.
> Bruce first briskly deals with the issue of noise. "I believe the levels at the Lostock Works [another factory close to Dad] do not represent a serious intrusion on the lives of our neighbours" and he rules out noise emanating from outside the factory, as well as levels of noise from within. He believes, flatly, "...there aren't any [untoward noises]." Dad is hearing, he thinks, "the noise of the factory itself." These more ordinary levels of noise, of moving machinery, in the range of 80 to 90 dba, are "extremely difficult to reduce and the cost penalties of doing so are quite prohibitive." He points out that the number of complaints from the public are "extremely low". He announces he has had better luck identifying the smell Dad complained about, caused, he claims, by "a short period of emission from the Ammonia Soda Plant in August." He regrets it but doesn't think it will recur. Regarding the trees in Holford Moss Wood, which Dad thinks are dying, he assures him that ICI does not authorise individuals to remove large amounts of peat or leaf mould from the woodland. They occasionally agree to small amounts being taken, and if Dad notices the removal of large amounts, then he would be grateful to be told. On hedge cutting "and related issues" he does not think there is anything further they can do. They have made known their concerns to

> the farmers through their land agents and he feels the matter must now be allowed to rest, and "to see what happens."

But Dad refuses to let go of any of the points go, iterating he must wear hearing protection on account of the noise, the smells are always there, and he has seen people taking sacksful of peat from the wood. He adds a new complaint: chimney effluent. "Will the matter then be in hand?" he asks repeatedly to all the points he raises, heedless to the limits of the attempts to help and the lengths to which Bruce is going. Long suffering, generous and diligent in his job, Bruce even took the trouble to visit High Bank House in person, on more than one occasion, attempting to identify the sound Dad was hearing, and reached the conclusion that Dad's sensitivity was to blame, though tactfully didn't say so.

Where the workings of his body were concerned, Dad was hyper-sensitive. The closest ICI factory was several farm fields away from High Bank House. Was he simply picking up the noise of the factory, as Bruce suggested, about which nothing could be done except to close the factory down? And the hooter, which Dad was to persist about, was essential to the running of the factory. Nothing could be done about that either.

For the sake of Dad's body, the whole of a giant chemical complex—at the time ICI was the world's largest conglomerate—would have to be shut; which is really what he wanted to have happen. Parts of ICI had stood there since the nineteenth century, before, even, the formation of the company under that name. Dad had moved to Lostock knowing of its presence. But in Dad's world, there were no shades or shadows, only himself, and anyway the early months of nineteen-eighty-eight brought new and more accommodating targets.

> 08/01/88—From the Welsh Office Agriculture Department, Aberystwyth.
> The spokesperson acknowledges "...ten sheets supplied in January suitable for schools, canteens etc"—and is keen to assure Dad that the literature sent to them will be drawn to the attention of his "professional colleagues". Among the publications Dad distributed for the Movement for Compassionate Living—funding the cost from his own pocket—was *Food for Everyone*, advocating sustainability through the cultivation of trees. It comprised ten A4 loose information sheets and graphically encapsulated the Movement's important booklet, *Abundant Living in the*

Coming Age of the Tree. An effective image shows tree parts, with the use to which each may be put. There are a surprising number of them. It's novel 'sheet form' meant the publication could be enlarged for display as posters, making it a particularly effective campaigning weapon. Dad sent it where he thought it would be effectively shown, and the Welsh Office Agriculture Department was fertile soil. His correspondent loses no time in extolling Welsh progressive environmental policies— the availability of Government compensatory grants to farmers who agree to farm in traditional ways, a proposed Farm Woodland Scheme that will make annual payments to farmers who turn over land previously in agricultural production, to growing trees ("Much higher rates of grant are available for the planting of broadleaved trees"), and the Agricultural Improvement Scheme, providing "grants for shelter belts, trees, hedges and traditional field boundaries." In response to a follow-up letter from Dad about hedge cutting—already perceiving a receptive ear in the country he was soon to inhabit—the Office wrote to Dad for a second time in June, "Your points have again been noted," his listener was quick to write back, "and particularly those regarding insensitive hedge cutting and trimming."

12/02/88—Dad to the Minister of Education, HM Government. Carbon copy letter.
Dad extols the merits of veganism and encloses *Food for Everyone*, which he hopes will be displayed in schools. But the UK government is unresponsive. He does not seem to have received a reply.

18/03/88—From R Davies, Directorate of Rural Affairs, Dept of the Environment.
Mr Davies assures Dad the Government takes the "the removal of hedgerows most seriously". His department is attempting to encourage farmers to keep and maintain hedges, but "[it] cannot be the subject of compulsion through expensive and bureaucratic controls."

06/04/88—From His Royal Highness the Prince of Wales, Buckingham Palace.
The Prince's Secretary thanks Dad for a copy of *Food for Everyone*, which he will draw to the attention of the Prince. Dad's letter, 'The Dehumanization of Environment', lists concerns about technology being allowed to run "out of hand"—hedgerows cut too low, saplings destroyed, wildflowers imperilled. "No blackberries, [and] birds can't nest in same," he admonishes sternly. "No blossom. Apart from a little

tree planting when the old trees die there is nothing to replace them." Chemical farming and pesticides are killing wildlife and "poisoning our food and water". He shares the Prince's concerns about the environment, and has written to many authorities about them but has received "little or no response". He notes how *Food for Everyone* promotes the vegan diet, and how important it is for health, keeping young and for general vitality.

Dad's tenacity, his refusal to be "fobbed off", as he sees it, finally elicits an exasperated—and hurt—response from Site Manager, I D Bruce, who is beginning to realise he has an uncommon opponent.

09/05/88—From I D Bruce, Soda Ash Product Department, ICI.
"I would always seek—as I think would any of my colleague Site Managers in ICI—to respond as positively as possible to the comments and points made by a member of the public and neighbour of our operations such as yourself. However, in the case of many of the points you make, I am afraid I am at a loss to know how to proceed." ICI, he maintains, do not have "...any lawful authority to instruct [their tenant farmers] to depart from what they believe is best for their affairs." Dad's complaints, he suggests, should be made to the farming press, or the National Farmers Union. Regarding Holford Moss Wood and the removal of peat and topsoil he has done what he can but will continue to instruct their security patrol officer to investigate unauthorised removals. As to "the proper environmental performance of our factory chimneys [it] is a matter of importance to us at ICI as well as to the public at large" and notes how the company works with Her Majesty's Pollution Inspectorate and British Coal to improve emissions. He explains in detail how the efforts of he and others have produced results "...substantially better than the legally imposed requirements." On the subject of the works' hooter, "I am afraid I am in disagreement with you. [The workforce] value the hooter. They do not bring watches to work for fear of damaging them. I can also tell you that publicly elected representatives from the Parish Councils bordering Lockstock Works have told me that they and their constituents appreciate the hooter and its value as an indicator of time. The hooter provides a service for a lot of people, and I do not intend to change it in the foreseeable future."

Dad was in a majority of one, a position in which he often found himself. Bruce now had his measure, but he remained good-natured, and closed his letter on what was intended to be a hopeful note. He has some "good news", he announces boyishly. Through ICI's efforts to improve the environment, the River Weaver at their Winnington works has become "re-oxygentated"—and sufficiently clean, he pronounces proudly, "as to support carp." The fish range from 3 ft in length down to 6 inches. "Trout! Yes..." Bruce finishes with a flourish: "Trout have been caught!"

The hapless man thought he had found common ground. The fish were being reeled from the river close to a weir nearby the works. Who could possibly not find this agreeable? Fortunately, Dad was no longer listening. He was in the throes of making good his escape, and never replied to Bruce. He wrote to me in mid-June after returning "...exhausted from Pant-yr-Esgair", where he had done some planting: "...2 Golden Delicious Apple Trees plus one Bramley and a Damson. Two cucumber plants and a few sweet corn. One blackcurrant, one raspberry: in all the heat of the sun. The air and blue sky was fantastic, golden sunsets."

A month later, he exalted, "I think that diseases will gradually wipe out at least ½ world population in the next 10/20 years, good news what!" On his remote island in the western Cambrians he would be safe, at last, from the effects of meat eaters who were decimating forests and turning the land over to livestock. The fewer people the better! "Organic garlic enclosed. Eat as much as you can."

His predictions may have proved prescient, as many of his projections have.

Long journeys to Wales and back looking for property had brought him to the remotely situated Pant-yr-Esgair, where he could survive the cataclysm to come. Purchase of the property, from a green energy salesman, was complete, and he could fulfil his youthful dream. He was now in his late sixties, and mortality was being brought home to him. Major figures in his life were leaving the stage. Fellow pioneer Pearl Rawls had passed away unexpectedly, early in 1982. A letter had arrived out of the blue from Tom in Canada where the family had emigrated in the late fifties, informing him of his wife's death in a fall. "You and Pearl got on so well together back in the 'good old days' in England that I wish I had cheerful news, I wish there was an easier way to say it, but there isn't." Complications from a thyroid malfunction had set in. She had broken ribs and had not recovered.

Dad had lost touch with the Rawls' through whom, in the late forties, he became Manchester Branch Secretary of the fledgeling Vegan Society. After Pearl's death an exchange of letters took place. But it didn't take Tom long to rediscover his impatience with Dad's hard-line views. Already critical of his old friend and fellow campaigner because of his bullying of Mum, his opinion was not much improved when he flew to England in 1987 after Pearl's death. Returning to Canada, he let his irritation show in a letter critical of Dad's fundamentalist approach to promoting veganism, which he thought counterproductive. So soon re-commenced, the friendship ended again. Tom kept in better touch with Mum. Both men, it seems, held affections for each other's wives and now that he was a widower, he courted her. But while Mum kept him as a friend, she did not marry again.

The Rawls family

Pearl's death was followed a few years later by Dad's brother Philip, in 1986, from cancer, and in March the same year he received a cheque for the sum of £233.82, his share of the final part of his mother's legacy. Pinky had died in 1980. On the heels of this, in 1988, came the second biggest blow of all—news of the passing of his fitness mentor and early work colleague, Alan Bennett, who had introduced him to the YMCA gymnasium, where he had discovered veganism. The losses, particularly his mother to whom, as a young man, he had 'proved' his diet by bodybuilding after she had expressed concern about his gaunt appearance, and who had stood by him despite his many difficulties, had all added to his resolve to reach the place where he could heal himself, and prove his boasts that the vegan diet, food reform and freedom from the polluted cities, would easily see him live to a hundred—and beyond.

His exile to the hills of Mid Wales where the air was pure, and where he would finally be self-sufficient in food that he could grow himself, and immerse himself in Nature, meant a complete escape from the ills of society. It would not be the 'half-way houses' that Vegania, Springfield and High Bank House had disappointingly proved to be. Stuck at Northwich, it had made sense to mitigate the ill effects in whatever way he could, and it had perhaps been the prospect of the fourth 'island' that had re-awoken in him a more confrontational form of activism. In his tireless search for longevity, Pant-yr-Esgair was to be the ultimate test—the symbolic transmutation of the lost Isle of Morat—where he could reverse age.

The Lady of the Trees

For there to be a Man of the Trees, there must be a Lady. When I pressed Dad about which vegetarian guesthouses or organisations we may have stayed at in Surrey, trying to explain my childhood memory of lodging somewhere near the Devil's Punchbowl, he could only recall visiting his friend Dr Gordon Latto, the naturopath whom he had met in Manchester. But when I investigated it turned out Gordon hadn't lived in Surrey but the adjacent 'home county'—Berkshire—and Dad had overlooked someone who did live there: his tree guru, Kathleen Jannaway, founder, with her husband Jack, of the Movement for Compassionate Living.

Kathleen didn't live at the Punchbowl, a popular heritage site, but in Leatherhead, about twenty-five miles distant. The Punchbowl was in Hindhead, but both towns are in Surrey, and close enough to one another for me to have been taken to both on the same holiday. The MCL was a Gandhi-inspired breakaway from the Vegan Society, founded by Kathleen and Jack in 1984 and still active. Kathleen had for many years been the General Secretary of the Vegan Society, and after she left to set up on her own, Dad's principal allegiance to the cause of veganism and food reform switched to her. It was the Movement's leaflets and booklets with their graphic statistical descriptions of trees—specifically how food-bearing trees could save the planet—which the Tree Man of Pant-yr-Esgair now also carried around with him. Its slogans graced his stationery. Its fliers could be found attached to any suitable surface for visitors and passersby to find—the front door at High

Bank House, the windows of his entrance porch at Pant-yr-Esgair, his car windows. It was this practice of his that the unkempt house bearing Christian anti-war posters had brought to mind in the area where he had been born, which I passed every day on my way to work, with its overgrown garden spilling unsocially onto the pavement.

New Leaves, the MCL's journal—Dad was never to be met without a copy—was an A5 monthly publication containing articles, news, announcements, and recipes to promote the compassionate way of life. An editorial from the late nineties teaches that animal suffering is entirely unnecessary and, over fifty years of practice, the Movement has "proved that the vegan diet is not only adequate but is in some important ways more health promoting than an omnivorous one." The chief article in the inaugural issue was entitled 'Living the Future Now!', for which Kathleen drew on Ivan Illich's challenging directive, "Every one of us, every group with which we live and work, must become the model of the era which we desire to create. We must live the future now!" This was Dad's edict entirely.

The Movement published a host of one-off publications such as *Growing Our Own*, Kathleen's guide to vegan gardening, *Recipes for a Sustainable Future* and the remarkable booklet *Abundant Living in the Coming Age of the Tree*, inspired by Egon Glesinger, chief of the Forest Products Section of the United Nations and author of *The Coming Age of Wood*, which accounts how restoration and proper management of the world's forests can help bring about an Age of Plenty. *Abundant Living* also extolls the work of Richard St Barbe Baker, the original Man of the Trees, and his plans for 'constructive villages' as the basis for a new worldwide civilization, the ideal to which Mahatma Gandhi devoted his final years.

Like *Food for Everyone*, the poster-sheets Dad and I disseminated wherever we could, *Abundant Living* bears a full-page line-drawing of a tree. Each part of the tree is arrowed, with annotations of the products—food, chemicals, rubber, rayon, biofuels, dyes, resins, medicines, paper and other commodities—that trees can provide. Beneficial functions are also noted, such as transpiration, oxygen emission, carbon dioxide absorption, erosion checks, swamp draining, mineral gathering, wildlife sheltering. The list of uses and advantages is long and comprehensive, cogently depicted in simple graphic depictions. In her publications Kathleen was motivated by peace and world hunger. Gandhi's beliefs, she claimed, matched hers more closely than any other thinker. Her concern for animals came from this Gandhian view, and in this sense, she was like Dad, whose motivation was primarily health. Her inspiration was not primarily animal-compassionate, although it would become so. After learning that male calves are slaughtered during milk production, she had joined The Vegan Society. Dad supported Kathleen because of the Movement's focus on the environment and arboriculture. In theory, the swapping of land from cattle grazing to carefully farmed afforestation will encourage the production of health-giving vegan food and bring about a more equable environment in which to reap the benefits, as he saw it, of the Great Outdoors.

Had Dad known Kathleen before she founded MCL in 1984, and were my memories going back to those times? Like him, she had been a founder of The Vegan Society in 1944, and had moved to Leatherhead in 1948, a year after my birth, where she would live for the next thirty years. She was Dad's final guru, after Otto Carqué, Yogi Ramacharaka and Edmond Székely. Because he did become her disciple, believing that arboriculture practiced worldwide is the sole spiritual and material means of sustainability for humanity and its survival.

I discovered to my surprise, that while running MCL with Jack, Katheleen transferred her attentions to mental health, developing teaching aids for children who had learning difficulties, and she pioneered work with children with dyslexia. The Jannaway family attended a Dorking Quaker meeting, where Kathleen took on other work concerned with the welfare of children. She and Jack became founder members of Quaker Green Concern, now Quaker Green Action, and it made me wonder: had it been Kathleen who put the notion into Dad's head of sending me to be a boarder at St Christopher's School? The school was Quaker-run during my tenure there, from the age of ten to sixteen, and one of its specialisms was educating 'difficult' children. It also begged a question: how much was known then by Mum and Dad about our mental health difficulties as a family? Dad was in denial; his family seemed to 'know something' but played it down. Mum had known, and never divulged it to us. She once said cryptically to me that after she 'had gone', someone must "take care of Chris". Did they know Chris, their most wayward child, had difficulties that needed special help? Could Kathleen see this, and did she help the family, and do I have her to thank, for being sent to a place she knew would be a sanctuary, where I would be properly cared for and educated? If so, Dad took her advice, but he saw it as an opportunity to remove me from Mum's influence and her insistence that I should be raised on the less strict lacto-vegetarian diet. He sent me there with strict instructions to the school that I was to board there as a vegan. St Chris followed the Quaker tenets of vegetarianism. But is it too much of a coincidence that I was sent to that school? After terrible years of abandonment, made worse by the vegan edict, which only served to emphasise my difference—no one at the school was a vegan except the Physics' teacher—the guidance and teaching of Annie Besant, a school founder, who based her educational principles on those of Helena Blavatsy, the mystic influenced by Mahayana Buddhism, slowly worked its magic on me. Did I have Kathleen to thanks for this? Had her foresight won through? Alma, my aunt, made the matter-of-fact comment to me that there was no one alive who could help me with 'certain' answers.

Kathleen died in March or April 2003 aged eighty-seven. She also found time during her productive life to be an active member of the Freedom from Hunger Campaign, another Leatherhead group. Seemingly, this remarkable woman went way back with Dad. When he joined her movement in 1984, I believe she was already an inspiration to him, and at Pant-yr-Esgair, in the final phase of his life he put her ideas, and those of Richard St Barbe Baker, into practice. But as ever with the things Dad liked and enjoyed, the 'fourth island' did not prove to be a universal haven. Although he did manage to touch something approximating Nirvana, for himself, for Lin, Chris and I it was different. Pant-yr-Esgair was where the 'unfinished business' of Springfield that had for so long escaped resolution while we lived our lives away from him, would come to be played out.

Darwin Holmstrom and Victoria M. Steinsøy

Seidr Nordic Tarot

(a work in progress)

MOST OF US CONSULT TAROT CARDS because we want to know what the future holds for us, but what the cards provide instead is guidance and advice for who we are and what we came to this world to be. They provide enough of a glimpse into our futures to placate those seeking divination, but they'll never tell us what lottery numbers to select or what stocks to purchase. Instead, if we dare walk the paths our souls lay out for us—a journey that transforms our inner lead into gold—the cards can help us discover forms of wealth that transcend material gains.

In 1791 French occultist Jean-Baptiste Alliette released the first card deck designed specifically for divination, and the modern tarot deck emerged with the publication of the Rider-Waite deck in 1909. British occultist Arthur Waite worked with artist Pamela Coleman Smith, both members of The Order of the Golden Dawn, to create a deck that illustrated not just the 22 major arcana cards featured on traditional French decks in use for hundreds of years, but also the 56 minor arcana cards, which had previously only depicted numbers and images representing the suits: wands, diamonds, cups, and swords (these became clubs, diamonds, hearts, and spades in the 52-card German decks upon which modern playing cards are based).

The seeds for the *Seidr Nordic* spread were planted when Darwin Holmstrom quit his factory job to attend college and, on his last day of work, his best friend bought him a tarot reading from Madame Lily, a local psychic. The first card Madame Lily laid out, the Signifier, was The Magician. Her reading that night changed his entire life. While attending a college writing class a few weeks later, Darwin was stunned to see that his teacher was Dr.

Lily Francis—Madame Lily! Lily took him under her wing; they became friends and she taught him how to read tarot cards.

After college, Darwin edited books on ceremonial magick and Kabbalah at Llewellyn Publishing. That job gave him access to the unparalleled occult library of Carl Llewellyn Weschcke, Llewellyn's owner and self-proclaimed "Pope of the Witches," allowing Darwin to continue the tarot studies he'd begun under Madame Lily. During his years at Llewellyn, Darwin developed what would become the *Seidr Tarot* layout, receiving much guidance from professional astrologers, ceremonial magicians, Pagans, Buddhists, Kabbalists, and experts in countless other esoteric fields.

Darwin's path eventually lead him to the sea. After years of traveling around the world on his sailboat, Darwin ended up in Guatemala where he met Victoria Steinsøy, a woman born and raised on an island off of the coast of Norway. Victoria was a writer who also guided people through shadow work. Darwin gave Victoria a reading, and from the moment he laid out the first card it was clear that his deck loved her. Victoria and Darwin began traveling together and one day Victoria joined Darwin in interpreting the cards while he was giving a reading to a friend in Bacalar, Mexico. The cards spoke to her in much the same way they spoke to him, and Victoria increased the power of the reading exponentially. They began doing joint readings for friends and soon transitioned to giving professional readings.

A history major in university, Victoria's indigenous knowledge of Norse mythology brought new meaning to the readings. It became clear that the tales of Norse gods were intimately intertwined with the tale told by the cards. Victoria dove into the synchronicities between the traditional tarot deck and the stories of the Nordic gods. Her work gave birth to the *Seidr Nordic Tarot* deck, which retains traditional tarot symbolism and imagery but adds the element of Norse mythology. At its core all mythology circles around the same themes and archetypes, as if the world's spiritual teachings sprang from the same source but have been interpreted in different words with different specific details to speak the language of whatever tribe is receiving that mythology. *Seidr Nordic Tarot* brings Norse mythology into the canon of the tarot.

The Fool, the first card in the major arcana, exemplifies Victoria's work to integrate Norse mythology into the *Seidr* reading. The Fool symbolizes the new energy of the number 0, denoting potential, opportunities, a new cycle in life. Its unpredictability and spontaneity make The Fool the wild card in the tarot deck, telling us that *anything* might come of this emerging energy. This frightens people who are more comfortable being in control, who prefer to have all the answers and know what's coming next. The Fool has little interest in answers and prefers a future filled with surprises. Unpredictability is his whole point; to him, it's what makes life fun and worthwhile. The Fool fits the archetype of the Norse trickster god Loki. Though mischievous and sly, Loki has a sense of humor and enjoys having fun at the expense of the other gods in Asgard. His tricks and schemes force them to take themselves a bit less seriously. Loki doesn't care much about the consequences of his actions, and he certainly doesn't overthink before he acts on his impulses. He has a tendency to take things a bit too far, and ultimately this is what leads to his imprisonment. Whether we agree with his schemes or not, some of the most famous and beloved myths from Norse mythology starts with Loki *having done something*. Like The Fool, Loki is an essential character in the Norse pantheon, a funny and provocative initiator whose energy is great for initiating new journeys and new ideas.

The *Seidr* spread itself speaks in the language of Norse mythology. When looking at the cards in a Nordic context, it becomes clear that the *Seidr* spread, an equilateral cross with legs bent at right angles—imagine two interlocked swirling arms—resembles the *Vegvísir* symbol, which, according to the Huld manuscript describing Icelandic magical spells, means: "That which shows the way." In the *Seidr* spread, think of each arm in the *Vegvísir* symbol as a sentence in the story that the cards are telling. All the positions in the spread work together like sentences in a paragraph to tell the overall story of the reading. Don't think of this story as concrete facts carved in stone but as advice and warnings to help people obtain the best possible outcomes using their own free will.

Think of the layout as two axes, with the vertical axis representing the inner self of the person receiving the reading, and the horizontal axis representing the events occurring in the person's life. At the center of the *Seidr* spread lies the Gateway card, the key to the entire reading. The Gateway card integrates the person's self (the vertical axis) with the events happening in her or his life (the horizontal axis). The Gateway is where everything comes together: past, present, future, hopes, fears, desires. People are generally most concerned with the Future and Final Outcome cards, but in the context of the overall story the cards are telling us, the Gateway is the most critical card.

The Fool—from the Visconti Sforza tarot deck, mid fifteenth century, Bonifacio Bembo for the Visconti and Sforza dukes of Milan, mid-15th century

Loki—18th-century Icelandic manuscript

At its core, the *Seidr Nordic Tarot* is a psychological tool, telling people as much about who they are as what is happening to them. The Signifier card—the "self" of the person receiving a reading—resides directly between the Fear cards at the bottom of the reading and the Desire cards at the top of the reading. Between our fears and our desires is where we find out who we really are. This is, in many ways, the most essential piece of information the cards convey to us. Consequently, it's often where people most resist listening to what the cards are telling them.

Tarot cards help guide us on our paths but they don't tell us where to go. Ultimately we have to travel down our own paths using our own free will to decide which directions we take. *Seidr* readings are maps showing us possible directions, but once we gather all the information we can, we *have to* make our own choices. The most precious gift we're given is our personal sovereignty. If we abdicate that sovereignty to a power outside of ourselves, whether that power takes the form of a political, religious, or any other dogmatic belief system, or whether we abdicate our personal sovereignty to a divination tool like a tarot deck or to astrology, at that point we have failed in our goal to achieve what we incarnated in this world to achieve: unity consciousness. This is fundamentally important when using *Seidr Nordic Tarot*, which is, at its core, a tool for helping us understand our own psychology. Thinking of *Seidr* in concrete terms makes it a prison, a trap that robs us of our personal sovereignty. Rather, it highlights the potential rewards and pitfalls we might encounter on our journey, but it is up to us to follow that path; we have to take the first steps. We have to own the power we brought with us into this world. We have to exercise our personal sovereignty and our free will if we want to become who we came here to be.

Hugh Macrae Richmond

On Reaching Ninety

RECENTLY I RECEIVED A FAVORABLE e-mail from a graduate of many decades ago from Berkeley's English major. This is not an isolated pattern: over the last few years, despite Berkeley's provocative reputation world-wide, its English Department has on occasion been rated among the best in the United States, and sometimes even in the world, though the procedures used may not be truly capable of these ratings. However, such positive reactions are not unusual, for a sociologist colleague alerts me to the fact that ratings often arrive very late in one's career, yet having been only intensified over the years; and indeed my recent letter had been personally anticipated by several earlier affirmatives. What made them particularly exceptional was that some of these ex-UCB students had never taken any of my courses nor even known me personally. Their seemingly unvalidated reactions set me wondering why this broader effect came about. The result is paradoxical: early failures to conform to professional expectations may prove positive factors in long-term career outcomes.

It seems that typically my public career has been affected by factors which are normally considered conventional limitations, but prove ultimately significant. These outcomes match the notorious view of Aeschylus that our disasters may prove advantageous, as these student responses illustrate. Professionally this interpretation calls in question the criteria for conventional academic reputation. I have often failed to meet norms and expectations. It seems to me on reflection that this variable background created an anomalous career that eludes the norms of literary criticism and scholarship in ways that have polarized my record and status, thus making it far more visible. This tension has led formal reviewers to responses tensed between excitement and indignation: overlapping scholarly French studies of mine have been called simultaneously both "very bad" and yet "one of my most favored studies" by two seemingly reputable scholars (Barnard College Professor Emerita Anne L Prestcott and Georgianna Ziegler, Head of Reference, Folger Shakespeare Library. The supposedly "bad" book has just been reissued, forty years later, by the Cambridge University Press. There was such an indignant university-wide response to one of my lectures (in which I denounced Romeo as a series killer responsible for six deaths) that my chairman called me in for a justification of my notoriety. Yet later the department proposed my speeded-up promotion by eleven years. In turn this positive reversal failed and proved equally disastrous, because of some of my peers' understandably very negative reactions.

Only after thirty years of retirement (and some colleagues' deaths) has this systematic repression been corrected in my recent administration award as an outstanding emeritus professor, assigned, however, by non-departmental faculty. Equally unexpected was that a scholarly organization, Researchgate, rated me over the last year as the department's most noted professor, in seven of its ratings, matched by the recording of over fifteen-million-page reviews at our website, "Shakespeare's Staging." How much credit is there for such scholarly evaluations? Perhaps, after all, what is needed is to survive to Ninety.

My autobiography seems to involve picturesque elements which lie far outside any meaningful academic context whatsoever. For example, one of my grandfathers was a Gaelic-speaking Highlands crofter from a remote fishing village just south of Scotland's north-west extremity, Cape Wrath, on the border of the United Kingdom's northernmost county, improbably called Sutherland, because the area was settled by Scandinavians voyaging south. Indeed, my ancestral village was called Melvaig, a Danish name (it impinged on Scandinavian-ruled Kingdom of the Isles). In the nineteen-thirties I stayed for long periods with my mother's sister, also married to such a crofter, who built his own house nearby, with no electricity or running water, and with a byre serving as an outhouse. Yet the Highland Scot remains a romantic figure in Western myth. No doubt this sounds barbaric, as my mother was treated to be when she married a Lancastrian and settled in the small Midland town of Burton-upon-Trent; but she reposted that Scotland had universal education while most of England was still illiterate. And the Christianization of Britain was indeed initiated in the Scottish Hebridean islands like Iona. Burton itself was founded by a Celtic saint, Saint Modwen, in the early Middle Ages, and emerged memorably around A.D. 1,000 as the location of a Benedictine monastery, sponsored there by a Mercian warlord named Ulfric, perhaps to expiate his mass-murders of Danes housed at a nearby center at Repton. The abbey was placed by a strategic bridge at the highest navigable point for Scandinavian longships. That bridge was significant, as Shakespeare's Hotspur stressed (Stratford -on-Avon is nearby). The failed Scottish 1745 rebels barely reached it before collapsing. The monastery was powerful but declined by the Reformation, surviving thereafter only in its grammar school, currently renamed after its founder as the Abbot Bayne School. But its religious origins also survived to my time in its daily morning religious service so that education for me implied a necessary religious context no longer fashionable among modern humanists. My books have plausibly been denounced as sermons, but their provocative neo-Christian ethos provokes more explicitly polarized reactions.

Though some of my origins thus displayed notably challenging characteristics from North Britain, and far from supposed metropolitan sophistication, they also made me distinctive and fairly successful in this local grammar school, and I was expected to do well in the School Certificate exams. However, in the term before these I was struck down with rheumatic fever, for which the then cure was prolonged rest until the irritation faded. So, I was expected to do badly. Paradoxically, the break merely refreshed me and I secured seven distinctions. Moreover, it also initially denied me recruitment in one of the earliest school exchanges with France, made by our brilliant French teacher, barely months after the war's end in Europe. But when the Director of Education in Arras decided to participate personally, I was thus the only remaining available recruit, an experience which began my lifetime's commitment to French studies. He became a major civil servant in the Paris government. As a result of regular summers there and in his larger family's home in Rouen I was saturated in French culture to the point that I determined to spend a year in French provincial life as an *assistant d'anglai*s, in one of the major cultural centers outside Paris, at the Lyncée du parc in Lyon. Much of my later scholarship related to tracing the impact of French culture on such major English writers as Shakespeare, Donne, and Milton. Accompanying me and my French-descended wife, born in New Orleans, my whole family explored the riches of provincial France for decades, and my two daughters became experts in French (and other languages) with tenure at major universities in Oxford and Texas.

The pattern of disaster evolving to breakthrough turned out to be the disconcerting rhythm of the rest of my life, which eluded all my plans of attaining professional success, and offers some ominous considerations for ambitious academics. But it attracted popular attention: I was recruited by Sam Wanamaker for his project to rebuild Shakespeare's Globe Playhouse which involved me in working with celebrities from Hollywood (Michael York, Mel Gibson, Mark Rylamce), and several members of the British royal family, such as our enthusiastic patron Prince Philip, thus increasing my popular visibility in Berkeley and elsewhere. Powerful literary figures often experience such drastic reversals of estimation, such as one of my instructors. E.M.W. Tillyard, who was one of the first students to graduate with the new B. A. in English created at Cambridge University after World War I. After decades of celebrity as a literary history authority he became totally derided for his construct of an over-rigid Elizabethan World picture, from which he is still barely recovering.

While I did get an open scholarship in English to puritanical Emmanuel College, Cambridge, I first had to complete my National Service in the army, which included many painful vicissitudes, before my paradoxical promotion to full lieutenant, which was secured by volunteering to stay on, after demobilization, for a major exercise. Unfortunately, this in turn delayed my arrival at Cambridge, resulting in many dislocating complications in accommodation and instruction so that my scholarship was threatened after this first disastrous year. But as an unexpected result I was rescued in my final year by two brilliant scholars, the Bennetts, who ensured that I got a first-class degree in my final exams. However, they also regretfully agreed with the Master of Emmanuel, Edward Welbourne, who was hostile to English graduate studies, that Cambridge had nothing more to offer me, so I had to leave after my first real success there. Fortunately, I received an unexpectedly strong welcome from Sir Maurice Bowra at Wadham College, Oxford, which proved one of my most supportive environments. But then unfortunately again, after a successful two-year D.Phil. there were no academic jobs available in Britain for myself or my American fiancée. I was obliged to accept what has actually proved to be a very favorable offer from the University of California, at Berkeley—even though it was at the other end of the world and cut off from all my previous European connections and with no professional accommodation to my previous academic system, so that my impact there was definitely even more alien than that caused by my Highland derivation, in England.

Moreover, when I arrived in California I found its English Department had hired two identical competitors: we both not only had just completed D.Phil.s from Oxford, even from the same college and faculty, but with identical specialities: seventeenth-century English poetry. My deft rival immediately published a book, but just an anthology and from a commercial press, so that my later Ivy League publication on European amatory verse seemingly outscored him, and he left to be very successful elsewhere. As a supposed Englishman my social status enjoyed a certain cuteness, but retrospectively I fear I never truly belonged in California, which is why my recent recognition in an award as an outstanding professor emeritus at U.C. Berkeley has proved unexpected. Students were impressed by my vocal fluency despite my "strange accent," but outside my interest in the professional theatre my local friendships were flatteringly confined to a French medievalist with a celebrated film director father and an even more famous Impressionist painter as grandfather, and to other international graduates of Cambridge, some of whom came from outside the academic world after savage Pacific war experiences and shared the salutary discipline of military life. Ironically, I now recognize that these testing military experiences gave them also a dimension differentiating us from my other Berkeley contemporaries, more at ease in the prosperity of the American Fifties. I was also fortunately supported by a few older colleagues who had served in World War II (two as captains of ships, one on D Day). However, I was still resented by my peers and successors, who only knew and accepted living in the ivory tower of the academic world. So perhaps my unexpected memorable impact on undergraduates essentially resulted from my lack of their traditional academic conditioning.

That varied background also made me aware of the importance for most undergraduates of skills other than hyper-sophisticated preparations for graduate school—such as broad oral expertise. Increasingly graduate students were warned against my "glibness"—indeed I received notes warning me of pending firings due to favorable references in the student newspaper. Nevertheless, my unconventionality attracted twenty Ph.D. students to my directoral care, while my Shakespeare lecture courses drew up to four hundred students from all levels and faculties. In England I had been relentlessly trained in debate and essay-writing, and I regularly performed in classic drama: Shakespeare, Shaw, Gogol, and medieval drama. I imported this emphasis into my teaching. The resulting use of performances, professional and student, live and recorded, attracted popular interest, despite the fact that at that time the campus had no theatres, so my performances had to be open-air, like most of Shakespeare's. Non-auditors often sat in on my lively classes and productions, though without credit. As a result of this oral conditioning, I was surprised to have to compensate for the fact that the UCB campus had no substantial theatre except the vast open-air Greek one, used primarily for formal events (though I did stage Shakespeare's *Pericles* there, appropriately enough). Nor was such dynamic teaching much stressed, though an award for teaching was initiated just after I arrived, only to be promptly discontinued when several teaching enthusiasts were dismissed for neglecting their research. After my previous professional training as a teacher for the army's educational corps, I was recruited to create a more viable recognition of teaching on campus, and after several years of fraught debate I found myself chairing the committee which succeeded in creating a rigorous award system requiring candidates to meet all other promotion requirements while excelling at teaching, which has proved credible and noteworthy. After some years in this context, I helped the English department to achieve prominence in this field. But I was replaced by a colleague who undermined these efforts and secured my dismissal from any formal role.

Ironically at just this moment the university decided to explore a users' evaluation by questioning a whole graduating class of four thousand on the value of their UCB experiences. The English department did quite well, particularly on the inquiry about any major personal impact of instruction where we received about twenty-five commendations. Half a dozen of our faculty received two or three citations, but I personally received more than the rest of the department combined. This was awkward as many of the others had received teaching awards but I had not, and that year's departmental teaching nomination had already been made. The solution was deliberately awkward. My nomination was made late in a barely acceptable duplication, and I was also told the committee was not able to develop so late any detailed documentation, which I would have to draft myself, and (knowing the process) this I successfully did, leading to my appointment as the chancellor's adviser for educational development, with a budget of several million dollars. For some years I became for once rather more generally popular professionally. And my reputation as a teacher soared, which may explain my terminal high reputation and published praises.

One of these has provided a more comprehensive summary of my experiences made for me by a Berkeley colleague, Muller, winner of the MacArthur "genius award" from which I offer a brief extract:

> My favorite Shakespeare course was taught by Professor Hugh Richmond at Berkeley; I went to all the lectures (as an auditor) and did the readings while I was a graduate student earning my Ph.D. in physics at Berkeley, but this course was very important to me. Whenever I see Prof. Richmond, I thank him yet again for this course. No course gave me more insight into human behavior. Or about writing and persuasion—Shakespeare's methods for convincing us of his insights. Think of Antony's great speech, "Friends, Romans, Countrymen ..." and how he brings a hostile crowd to his own point of view. In what other course would you learn how to do that? Is that a skill that will prove useful in your future life? Let me ask that differently. Is there any more important skill? And it is not just the way that Antony does it. It is the very fact that he does it. Recognize that, and you become aware of an aspect of life that you don't get in a physics or engineering course. About writing...Shakespeare sets the standard, not in flowery language, but in vivid language, language that makes you understand what it is that Shakespeare wanted you to understand. That's why you need to read (or better yet—*watch*) the originals, not the facile study guides designed to give you the plot, and merely help you with a pop quiz. Think of what we learn about life and love from *Much Ado About Nothing*, about how two people who hate each other can change and feel deep and true love towards each other. I can go on and on, and if you had a good Shakespeare course, so can you. Many of the great books are comparably good. (Quora, 02/14/16; https.observer.com /2016/02/1; etc)

This report of my presentations gives a clear impression of the intense impact on students of my course, whether for credit or not, which proves utterly opposed to much then-conventional theoretical literary criticism, explaining its sustained recognition. Muller observes: "No course gave me more insight into human behavior. Or about writing and persuasion."

Richard Muller's report has since been widely reprinted in popular academic media, and it clashes absolutely with the dominant negative perspective current when I was lecturing last century, typified by a quotation from Paul de Man, and still cited recently in the archetypal critical journal, *PMLA* (Kimberly Johnson; "Literary Perspective and the Renaissance Lyric," 134.2, p. 287, March, 2019), which argues that literary perspective offers "incompatible, mutually self-destructive points of view that produce an insurmountable obstacle in the way of any reading or understanding... one that does not invite interpretation." If this allusion seems far-fetched it must be remembered that the cotemporary literary authority to de Man was T.S. Eliot, who similarly wrote: "I would suggest that none of the plays of Shakespeare has a meaning," adding, to deepen the perspective, "I find it impossible to come to the conclusion that Donne believed anything"—he was merely a man who "picked up like a magpie, various shining fragments of ideas as they struck his eye (Johnson, p. 288). While censuring any alert critical intelligence that enjoys such destructive (as well as boring) perspectives, I have earned lasting professional censure.

This extended to the fact that to ensure my unfashionably large lectures' achieved intense vividness and emotional impact, I had introduced recorded scenes and whole performances of classic films with celebrities like Olivier, Gielgud, and dynamic actresses like Peggy Ashcroft and Janet Suzman. To increase personal community in such large groups I sponsored student performance options leading to some fifty productions recorded for class use. The climax to this emphasis resulted from my association with the rebuilding of the Globe Playhouse in London, to which I took my 1996 U.C.B. student production of *Much Ado*. This authentification proved a truly memorable experience for participants. However, to preserve student memories equally well, I also proposed provocative interpretations like the one about Romeo as a mass-murderer. These effects were often considered not fit for regular class-formats, for which I was even formally censured; but I now think they may explain the non-participant interest, reflected in my recent letters. Indeed, I fear that failure to exploit such reinforcements is precisely what explains the decline in modern academic interest in the Humanities.

But the other factor in stirring audience resonance is surely my insistence on the purely personal moral significance of literature, far beyond the sweeping racial and political campaigns now popular. Exactly what this ultimately private impact may be is illustrated by another one of these non-student letters, by Michael Finocchiaro, quoted in Goodreads (08/04/2020).

He writes about versions of my lectures recorded in my book *Shakespeare's Sexual Comedy* (Bobbs-Merrill, 1971):

> Richmond gives a fantastic analysis of Shakespeare in terms of sex and gender. This is a wonderfully written manual for healthy romantic relationships: how to avoid Romeo and Juliet fatality, the pleasure of being with strong women (Beatrice, Rosalind), I really found this to be a perfect balance between literary criticism and a pleasurable interpretation of the Bard's work. Very, very highly recommended.

Unlike de Man's and T. S. Eliot's criticism, I feel this evaluation places my teaching and published works well within the specifications for literature made by Horace, to be both "enjoyable and useful." It seems strange that once fashionable 20th century intellectuals like Foucault and Derrida seem to have fatally avoided this essentially positive stimulus intrinsic to much of their raw material, stressing perspectives that are equally depressing yet still remain citable in influential journals like *PMLA*.

Contributors

Bienvenido Bones Bañez, Jr. holds a Bachelor of Fine Arts from the Ford Academy of the Arts in Davao City. For some time he served as associate professor with the Ford Academy and the Philippine Women's College-Davao. In 2002 he won the Asian Fellowship Painting Competition of the Vermont Studio Center. In 2010, Bañez was included in *Lexikon der phantastischen Künstler* (Gerhard Habarta, 2013). In 2016, he was named a member of the Williamsburg Circle of International Arts and Letters, and has since based himself in the US. He is broadening his horizons in New York City. Website: www.welcomebones666 artworld.trilogistick.com

Marleen S. Barr received the Science Fiction Research Association's award for lifetime achievement in science fiction scholarship. She has published the novels *Oy Pioneer!* and *Oy Feminist Planets: A Fake Memoir.* Her latest book is *This Former President: Science Fiction As Retrospective Retrorocket Jettisons Trumpism.*

Andrew Braunberger is an artist and philosopher living in Florida.

Michael Butterworth is a UK author, publisher and editor who began his career writing for *New Worlds* magazine during the 1960's UK New Wave of Science Fiction. In 1969 he began publishing small press literary magazines, including *Corridor*, and in 1975 co-founded Savoy Books with David Britton. In 2009 he re-launched *Corridor* as contemporary visual art and writing journal, *Corridor8*. He is the author of at least fifteen books, the most recent being *Complete Poems: 1965-2020* (Space Cowboy Books, 2023), and is a regular contributor to *Emanations*. He is at work on *The Sunshine Island*, a memoir of his father who had OCD, and a novel, *Withersoever*.

Ana Cameron writes: 'My work includes visual art based on recycled and found objects, for example scissors and paper, guitar and bass, like my work appearing here, inspired by a word written on a plank of wood washed up by the sea. "Areness" inspired me to write about the self being the observer with the option to choose. My final graduation performance involved facing the audience and one by one inviting them to sit with me and count crumbs. This praxis of sourcing for minimalism in my work colludes a framework and limitation in the vastness of inspiration. As a bass guitarist and performer and producer of my own beats, I derive text-based work through different writing modes and narratives hoping to allow freedom for the spectator.' Diploma, Performance Art/Acting; BA, Theatre with Visual Arts.

Michael E. Casteels' most recent work are the collage Westerns, *ONDO* (nOIR:Z, 2022) and *The Man with the Spider Scar* (Puddles of Sky Press, 2020). He is the editor, publisher, designer, and bookmaker at Puddles of Sky Press.

Kim J. Cowie lives in the UK and has been writing for many years. Kim has written several epic fantasy novels including *The Plain Girl's Earrings* and *The Witch's Box*. He formerly worked in the electronics industry, and as a technical author.

Daniel de Cullá is a writer, poet, and photographer. Member of the Spanish Writers Association. Director of the *Gallo Tricolor Review*, and *Robespierre Review*. He moves between North Hollywood, Madrid and Burgos, Spain.

Andrew Darlington debuted with the poem "Anthem For A Lost Cause" in the arts magazine *Sad Traffic* (1971). Over 3,000 published items have followed, from Music Journalism to Erotica, from closely-researched SF-features to interviews with culture icons—a selection collected into *I Was Elvis Presley's Bastard Lovechild* (2001). Fiction—in the *NEL Stopwatch* anthology (1975)—through multiple magazine and hard/softback appearances around the world to *The Mammoth Book Of Sherlock Holmes Abroad* (2015). Other ventures—*Don't Call Me Nigger: Sly Stone & Black Power* biography (2014). www.andrewdarlington.blogspot.com

Tessa B. Dick grew up in Southern California, and she claims that her efforts to escape have failed miserably. She was already a published author when she met Philip K. Dick, and she has continued writing fiction, nonfiction and poetry. She taught English and Communications at Chapman University for twelve years.

Peter Dizozza and family live in New York's East Village. Since 1999, he is Theater Director for the Williamsburg Art and Historical Center which premiered the musicals Prepare to Meet Your Maker, Paradise Found. The Last Dodo, The Eleventh Hour, The Marriage at the Statue of Liberty (after Cocteau), The Sea Heiress, Float and Bulb, as well as The Woman Artist's Journey and The International Surrealist Film Festival. He is currently scheduling readings for his new Project, "Out of the Idmosphere." Website: www.cinemavii.com

Jeffrey Falla received his PhD from the University of Minnesota. Besides publishing poems, stories, and critical essays he published a book on modifying vacuum tube guitar amplifiers. He divides his time between writing and designing and manufacturing audio amplifiers. www.tonetronamps.com

David Flynn was born in the textile mill company town of Bemis, TN. His jobs have included newspaper reporter, magazine editor and university teacher. He has five degrees and is both a Fulbright Senior Scholar and a Fulbright Senior Specialist with a recent grant in Indonesia. His literary publications total more than 240. He lives in Nashville, Tennessee.

Oz Hardwick is a European poet, photographer, musician, and academic, whose work has been widely published in international journals and anthologies. His published collections include *Learning to Have Lost* (Canberra: IPSI, 2018) which won the 2019 Rubery Book Award for poetry, and, most recently, the prose poetry sequence *Wolf Planet* (Clevedon: Hedgehog, 2020). Oz is Professor of English at Leeds Trinity University. Website: www.ozhardwick.co.uk

Donald M. Hassler has published book-length studies of Erasmus Darwin, Isaac Asimov, Hal Clement, as well as on politics and genre studies. His son who goes by the same name is principal investigator of the radiation experiment landed by NASA early August 2012 on Mars.

Horace Jeffery Hodges was born in the Arkansas Ozarks and obtained a history doctorate at UC Berkeley. He is now a "Gypsy Scholar" who has taught in various places around the globe. He prefers his middle name "Jeffery" and last taught at Ewha Womans University in Seoul, South Korea, where he has retired and settled down with his wife, Sun-Ae, and their two children. He has published articles, stories, poetry, and two novellas as well as various translations from Korean with his wife, e.g., Yi Kwang-Su's novel *The Soil*. His poetry collection *Radiant Snow* was published by International Authors. New books are forthcoming. Blog: www.gypsyscholarship.blogspot.com

Darwin Holmstrom lives, travels, and writes on a sailboat. Prior to escaping from the corporate matrix, he navigated through life as a senior editor at a publishing house, a newspaper photographer and reporter, an adjunct professor, an assistant potato inspector, and a farmer.

Lyle Hopwood is a writer of speculative fiction and fantasy. She has had short stories published in IZ Digital, Aurealis, Interzone and Blood Fiction v2. She lives in Southern California with a holographer, her herptiles and her collection of Kalanchoe.

C. Berton Irwin lives in the Bronx and works in a homeless shelter. He has been writing for thirty years for various publications. He is currently working on a biography of his grandfather, the modernist poet Orrick Johns.

Gareth Jackson is a conceptual artist/experimental film-maker and occasional author operating in the North West of England. He lives with a wife and three cats—none of which are familiars. He edits *Speculative Fictions*. www.speculative fictions.weebly.com

Richard Glyn Jones trained as a psychologist before joining *New Worlds* and working as an illustrator in the 1960s and 70s. After ten years in conventional publishing he started his own firm which published authors ranging from Christine Keeler to Jorge Luis Borges, and he has edited around 40 anthologies, one of which won a World Fantasy Award. Lives in London.

Carter Kaplan has pioneered the application of poetry and fiction to the study of analytic philosophy, as presented in his book *Critical Synoptics: Menippean Satire and the Analysis of Intellectual Mythology*. He is the author of the Aristophanic comedy *Diogenes*, and a novel of intellectual life in trans-Atlantic culture, *Tally-Ho, Cornelius!* His Afterword appears in the International Authors edition of Nathaniel Hawthorne's *The Scarlet Letter*, and he led the committee producing the International Authors translation of Torquato Tasso's *Creation of the World*. His Invisible Tower Trilogy is now available: *Echoes*, *We Regin Secure*, *The Sky-Shaped Sarcophagus*.

Richard Kostelanetz: Individual entries on his work in several fields appear in various editions of *Reader's Guide to Twentieth-Century Writers*, *Merriam-Webster*

Encyclopedia of Literature, *Contemporary Poets*, *Contemporary Novelists*, *Post-modern Fiction*, *Webster's Dictionary of American Writers*, *The HarperCollins Reader's Encyclopedia of American Literature*, *Baker's Biographical Dictionary of Musicians*, *Directory of American Scholars*, *Who's Who in America*, *Who's Who in the World*, *Who's Who in American Art*, NNDB.com, Wikipedia.com, and Britannica.com, among other distinguished directories. Otherwise, he survives in New York, where he was born, unemployed and thus overworked.

Denny E. Marshall has published art, poetry, and fiction. Recent work includes cover art for *Bards and Sages Quarterly* and poetry in *Space And Time*. His flash fiction story "The Window", published by *Sci Phi Journal*, is on the *Tangent Online 2016 Recommended Reading List*. Website: www.dennymarshall.com

C. E. Matthews dreamed of writing and drawing his own sci-fi comics as a boy. He followed this dream by graduating in law, getting a proper job and generally being more grown up than he'd like. He enjoys pretending to understand quantum physics and writing in his vanishingly spare time. He is a Pushcart Prize nominee for fiction appearing in *Emanations: 2 + 2 = 5*.

Laura McPherson's work has appeared in *Night Picnic*, *Cosmic Horror Monthly*, *The Deadlands*, *Paperbark*, and others. Her hybrid chapbook, *inVISIBLE*, is out with Alien Buddha Press. Find her online: www.lauramcphersonwriter.com

Nobuhiro Mido (Nobxhiro Santana) has been enchanted with painting since childhood, but due to family opposition he studied electrical engineering at university. Nevertheless, his interest in panting persisted. He is inspired by art without motifs as characterized by the work of Kandinsky and Mondrian. He creates abstract art using automatic writing and analog/digital collage techniques. Through this activity of conceptualization and production, he sees himself as an investigator into the essence of painting.

Philip Murray-Lawson lives in Paris where he runs Evolution-abc, a language consulting company. His first works were translations of *fin de siècle* author Marcel Schwob. They appeared in *Udolpho*, the Gothic Society periodical, to which Philip also contributed non-fiction. A collection of horror stories, *Heresies* was published in 2000. He has recently written for *Vignettes & Postcards*, an anthology published by Shakespeare & Co.

Poet, musician and art historian, **David Nadeau** has lived in Quebec City (Canada) since 2007. Emperor of the *Holy Faustrollian Empire at the Protectorat de 'Pataphysique québecquoise*, he regularly participates in the activities of the Surrealist Movement. He is particularly interested in the relationships between esotericism and artistic creation, from a clearly anarchist perspective.

Vitasta Raina is an architect and urban planner in Mumbai, India. She is the author of a novella, *Writer's Block,* and a collection of poetry, *Someday Dream*.

L. M. Rainer strongly believes that reading fairy tales is more helpful than eating kale, doing yoga, hiking up mountains or getting up before sunrise. She is the author of *How to Behave* (Pelekinesis) and the website *How To Behave—Etiquette Central* at https://howtobehave.net

Edmond (Dick) Rampen is a professor emeritus of Industrial Design and Sculpture at OCAD University in Toronto. He spends his time painting and sculpting, building and designing musical instruments, designing products for companies, and most importantly surfing.

Born 1928 in Indonesia, **Leo Rampen** lived in Holland from 1930 to 1953, then moved to Canada in 1954. He has worked as a fashion designer, illustrator, artist and documentary filmmaker. He was creator and executive producer of two long-running television series on CBC, *Take Thirty* and *Man Alive*.

Elkie Riches lives in Buckinghamshire, England, and has been writing fiction for many years. Elkie is the author of the novel *Reclamation*, and she has written the Introduction appearing in Carter Kaplan's Aristophanic comedy *Diogenes*.

Hugh Macrae Richmond, emeritus professor of English at U.C. Berkeley, heads its Shakespeare Program, staging Shakespeare, with documentaries like Shakespeare and the Spanish Connection. He has websites: Shakespeare's Staging and Milton Revealed. He publishes about European culture: The School of Love; Renaissance Landscapes; and Puritans and Libertines. His artistry provides book and magazine covers, illustrations for magazines, and posters.

Ebi Robert, a practicing attorney, is an award-winning author. His poems have been published in international anthologies, magazines, and e-zines. His works have appeared in publications such as the *Tuck Magazine*, *The Banner Newspaper, Ovimagazine*, *The Mariner Journal*, etc. He currently serves as the Lead Rep of Poets in Nigeria, Yenagoa Connect Centre; Columnist at New York based Newspaper, *Parkchester Times*. He is the immediate past Secretary-General of the Association of Nigerian Authors (ANA), Bayelsa State Chapter. His first novel is *The Creed of the Oracles*. Website: www.ebirobert.com

Jake Robinson is a West Yorkshire (UK) based writer who recently graduated in English and Creative Writing from Leeds Trinity University. He is interested in the experimental, the speculative, and the absurd.

Alexander Sharov matriculated from Dnipro National University in Ukraine with degrees in English and Psychology. He translates contemporary fiction from Russian and Ukrainian into English.

Spirituality and psychology have fascinated **Victoria Steinsøy** since childhood. With an intuitive understanding of both, she travels the world gathering insights from different cultures and spiritual traditions. In 2021 she published *Truthful Roots*, a dystopian fantasy novel.

Arthur Lee Talley lives in Portsmouth, Virginia. He is focused on digital mediums of creation using his iPhone 6 Plus, and various applications. He has an Associates in Science from Richard Bland College and is a professional software engineer. Website: www.ambientmuse.com

Dmitriy Tarkovsky is a Russian philosopher and man of letters. He matriculated from Moscow State University with a degree in Classical Philosophy.

About International Authors

A consortium of writers, artists, architects, filmmakers and critics, International Authors publishes books exhibiting outstanding literary merit. Dedicated to the advancement of an international culture in literature, primarily in English, the group seeks new members with an enthusiasm for creating unique artistic expressions.

international
IA
authors

www.internationalauthors.info

Printed in Great Britain
by Amazon

28890923R00235